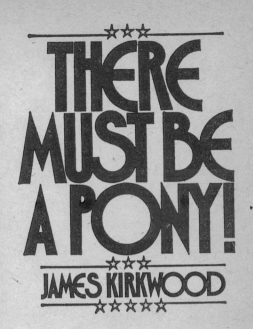

THERE MUST BE A PONY!

JAMES KIRKWOOD

 AVON
PUBLISHERS OF BARD, CAMELOT, DISCUS, EQUINOX AND FLARE BOOKS

AVON BOOKS
A division of
The Hearst Corporation
959 Eighth Avenue
New York, New York 10019

First Avon Printing, December, 1971
Third Printing

AVON TRADEMARK REG. U.S. PAT. OFF. AND
FOREIGN COUNTRIES, REGISTERED TRADEMARK—
MARCA REGISTRADA, HECHO EN CHICAGO, U.S.A.

Printed in the U.S.A.

THERE MUST BE A PONY!

Chapter 1

IF you want to know the truth—it just about kills me to go over the whole thing. Mainly, I suppose, because they haven't let me see my mother since they took her away. And that was over two months ago. They haven't let anyone see her. Not Merwin or Lee or Andy and Midge—nobody. They say it's better that way. Until they start to get things straightened out.

As far as I'm concerned it isn't better at all. I miss her. I miss her right now more than all the other times I've ever missed her. Of course, none of them were like this. They were just routine separations we've always been through. But none of them were anything as terrible as this time....

Well, listen, I better not get started on that. I better dive right in while I've got my steam up.

You probably know a lot about my mother and me from all the stuff that was in the papers and on radio and television—but not everything. So I'll start by explaining about her and how I happened to be living with her this last year and a half.

Actually, she's pretty hard to explain because she's the paradox of the world! First of all, although she's a movie star, she hasn't made a real picture—I mean a good one—in about a century. Some people call her a "has-been," but she's only forty-one years old. What they don't realize is she was practically a kid when she started.

Secondly, she's amazingly intelligent and yet she's stupid. That is, as far as knowing about all kinds of things is concerned she's very bright. She must read about five books a week, mainly because she's got the most fantastic case of insomnia anyone ever had. She can do the *Times* crossword puzzle every time. She's always helping other people and going way out on a limb for them and straightening *their* lives out, yet she can't seem to do a damn thing for herself. Where her own life is concerned she's about as helpless as an infant. And completely impractical! Merwin Saltzman, the author, who's a good friend of ours, says she lets herself be ruled completely by her emotions instead of by her brain.

She's extremely beautiful and kind and gentle. I mean you'll hardly ever hear her say a detrimental word about anyone. But here's the problem: you should see the men she falls in love with! When I tell you what she's gone through with men you'll swear I'm making it up, but I'm not. If you lined them all up—the ones she'd gone steady with and the three she's married—you wouldn't believe it. They might look all right on the outside, but on the inside they're each one more rotten than the next. I start bleeding internally when I think about them! What a crew!

Of course, I'm prejudiced—because if you think I hated *them*, you could reverse it and double it and that's the way they all felt about me. My average with her boy friends is about the most incredible thing you could imagine. All except for one, and that was a fluke. That's mainly what I'll tell you about.

The longest I ever lived with my mother at one stretch, aside from when I was very small, was this last time, a year ago April, when I came out from Ohio to stay with her. It was just about perfect—until the end, that is. We have these friends, Mr. and Mrs. Culp, who have a colossal house at Paraiso Beach, below Los Angeles. He's a writer, and when he got a contract to go to Italy and do two pictures they said my mother could use the house while they were gone. Right away she sent for me. I was living in Elliston, Ohio, with my aunt and uncle. It seems I spend almost every other year with them. That time I was a freshman in high school.

Oh, and *how* I happened to be there that year is typical of the way things always happened with me and my mother. I'm digressing from her boy friends for a minute, but I'm always doing that. I'm the digressor of the world.

When I start telling about one thing, it always reminds me of another and I'm off. You'll just have to bear with me.

You see, when I was in the eighth grade she was renting a beautiful house on Roxbury Drive in Beverly Hills. I wasn't living there; I was going to a Catholic military academy, St. Mark's, in Los Angeles, but I did go home on weekends. She had a cook, a maid, a Ford convertible, and she was making an independent picture and trying for a real comeback.

Along about in March she gave this terrific party one Saturday night. I mean it was a real shindig; there were a lot of fat cats in the business you'd know about if I mentioned them. Well, it turned into a brawl. I couldn't go to sleep for the noise until about four o'clock, but I really didn't mind because I was getting a vicarious thrill out of the proceedings.

I almost minded once, though. I was just about asleep in my bedroom upstairs pretty far away from the revelry when I got the feeling there was somebody in the room with me. I opened my eyes and, although it was dark as hell, I could see this form standing right by my bed, kind of weaving back and forth, hovering over me. I quick switched on the light over my bed, and there was my mother's current boy friend standing there about to relieve himself on me! I yelled "Hey!" and he kind of blinked his eyes and staggered backwards. He was so skunked he was practically unconscious.

"Thought it was the john," he said.

I couldn't think of one single clever remark, so I just sat there in bed like a lump.

He stumbled toward the door, turned, and said, "Sorry, kid, I wouldn't pee on you for the world!"

I allowed as how that was all right.

But as he was going through the door I heard him mumble, "Might be a damn good idea at that!" Then he started to roar with laughter and disappeared down the hall.

Isn't that a charmer for you? Well, that's about par for the course. Oh, he was really clever. I could tell you a few other tricks *that* one pulled, but out of deference to my mother I won't.

The day after the party she wasn't receiving. But she gave the maid twenty bucks to give me to go out and have myself a time. I went to three double features until I had a migraine headache and was almost blind; then I took a cab back to St. Mark's.

The very next weekend I got home Friday evening early, and I could tell something was wrong. The house was like a morgue. The maid, Edna, had been crying, and my mother was nervous and jittery. She'd keep trying to tell me something; then she'd get up and leave the room. I just sat there on the sofa across from the fireplace like an idiot.

Along about six-thirty I found out she wasn't trying to *tell* me anything; she wanted to *ask* me something. Did I have any of my allowance left? Because there wasn't anything in the house to eat.

You see what I mean? One weekend a big party with servants and caterers tearing around and the wine flowing like Niagara Falls, and the next one—did I have any of my allowance left!

Well, of course I did. I'm probably the prime miser of all time. Through bitter experience. I had a lot *more* than my allowance left, but I never owned up to exactly how much I did have, because my mother has absolutely no sense of money.

So I went upstairs, raided one of my secret caches, and gave her twenty-five dollars. She said we'd have a great dinner, then she'd have a long talk with me and explain things. Oh, and not to worry about the twenty-five dollars because she'd sent for some money to tide her over from a friend in New York.

She took off for the store and I took off for my bedroom and started to get my things packed for Elliston. Nobody had said a word, but I always did have an absolutely uncanny sense of "Elliston time."

Honestly, the only thing I resent about my mother is that she never warned me beforehand when the shit was going to hit the fan. You'd be dressing like a king, eating like a Roman, going to a fancy school, any movie you wanted to see—I even had my own horse once but we had to sell it because we couldn't pay the feed bill—then all of a sudden there wasn't anything in the icebox. But you never knew until it happened.

All my life it's been kind of like walking across a beautiful wooden floor in this terrific palace of a house that you knew had one rotten plank in it. But the rotten plank was painted just like every other plank, so you never knew when you'd step on it. You could never be sure *when* you'd step on it, but you could be goddam sure you *would*. And just when you weren't expecting it. I must say there's always been an element of surprise about life.

That's why I learned to hoard money. Even when I'm absolutely broke I've got some money stashed away some place. When it's good times I'm just like a squirrel: I stuff it in my cheeks and then when nobody's looking I bury it in the ground. And I've actually gone that far because my mother knows this about me; she goes on these treasure hunts, so I *have* to be pretty cagey about it.

Sure enough, after dinner we had our talk. Tuesday morning I was on the train headed for Ohio and my aunt and uncle. I swear I know every milk stop from here to Cleveland, which is only about twenty-three miles from Elliston. I'll bet I could even run the train by myself if I had to. Some of those old, weather-beaten geezers you always see leaning up against the station house in little burgs along the way I feel I should almost send Christmas cards to—I've waved at them so often.

Anyhow, during the spring of my freshman year my mother sent for me again. That's when we had the Culps' house at Paraiso Beach. It was a great place: an enormous Spanish-type house about a mile back from the beach, with about three acres running downhill behind it, a barbecue pit, orange and lemon groves, a barn and a hothouse, and just about everything you could imagine. All tall eucalyptus trees and high hedges all around the place so it was completely isolated.

They had a maid, Cecelia, that we inherited. The Culps kept her on while they were gone, but she only came four days during the week and took the weekends off.

They also had a lot of animals we had to take care of, but we didn't mind because they were a three-ring circus.

There was a Scotty named Trouble, a boxer named Penny, and Lord Nelson, a Peke with one eye that he lost when he sneezed too hard once. He was a killer; he wore a black patch over where the eye had been and strutted around like he owned the place. You'd think you'd hate a Pekinese, wouldn't you? Well, I did at first, but when you got to know Lord Nelson you really fell for him. He was the most fearless animal you ever met. He'd tackle a police dog, a pickup truck, anything you could mention. The Culps also had a crazy little Brazilian Weeper monkey named Monkey-Face, a pair of geese that were always in hiding, Eloise and Abelard, and about the meanest son-of-a-bitching parrot you could ever run up against, named Chauncey!

I tried everything to get rid of that bird in an off-hand, accidental way, but Chauncey was indestructible. I even turned him loose on the kitchen floor with all the dogs at eating time one night. That was the one time they'd get nervous and snappy. I didn't have the nerve to watch, so I left the room like a true coward. After about ten minutes of all sorts of barking and squawking I got to feeling like a rat, so I tore back into the kitchen. The three dogs were backed up against the wall making all kinds of noises, but it didn't bother Chauncey. He was waddling back and forth eating out of their dishes like they were his. Even Lord Nelson was cowed.

Well, my mother was trying to nab a steady job in television that year, and I had transferred to public high school in Paraiso Beach. The first month or so that spring she was still going, off and on, with the guy that mistook me for the bathroom at the party. Only he pulled his cutest trick of all time toward the end of June, and that was the last we saw of him. Cecelia told me about it because I was in bed asleep at the time. She used to give me all the news that was unfit to print. It seems this guy, Horton Sprague, wanted my mother to go down to Ensenada for the week-end, but she told him no, she had to stay and take care of me and the animals. He said why didn't she put the animals in the kennel for the weekend, and she asked what about me. He told her she should put me in the kennel, too.

They were having drinks on this deck that led out from her bedroom, and they got into a terrific argument. The house was really three stories high if you counted the game room, which was below the living room. There were great verandas and decks hanging out from each story on the back side of the house, which was kind of built down a hill. Anyway, he kept on drinking, and yapping about me and the animals being a millstone around her neck. He finally got to yelling at her, and when he did that the Scotty, Trouble, started growling at him. He'd really fallen in love with my mother; he'd never leave her side. This jerk got up and went over to where she was sitting and stood over her screaming at her. I guess the dog thought he was going to hit her. He was the type that would, too. So Trouble really started barking at him and then, without any warning, the guy turned around, snatched Trouble up, and threw him right off the deck down three stories onto the tiled veranda that led out from the game room.

Wasn't that a brilliant thing to do to a poor little dog that didn't even know what the hell the score was?

That was the end of Sprague, though. It was the end of Trouble, too, of course. But, you see, that's what I mean about my mother. It would take something like throwing a dog down three stories, or swiping somebody's crutches, or setting fire to a home for the aged to make her realize what complete bastards some people are.

We hunted in pet shops for over a week trying to find a Scotty that looked like Trouble so we could replace him and the Culps would never know. They'd just got him before they left for Italy, and we figured maybe we could pull the hoax off. But he did have these weird markings; you couldn't duplicate them. My mother finally decided to write and say he died, but, of course, she didn't tell how. I tried to get her to say that the parrot had gone completely fruit and killed him, so they'd write back to get rid of Chauncey, but she wouldn't do it.

Chapter 2

ABOUT a week after that madman threw Trouble off the deck it was my fifteenth birthday, and this other guy my mother went out with now and then, Lee Hertzig, took us to dinner at Jack's-at-the-Beach. Afterward we went out on the pier at Pacific Ocean Park where they had a roller coaster and funhouses and about every ride you can think of.

You see, she's always had a stable of guys jockeying for position in case one of them fell out of line. Especially the last few years when her career was on the downgrade. She used to get frantic if she didn't have a lot of men friends paying pretty close attention. The only thing—they'd all be acting like Prince Charming at first, but as soon as she'd give the nod to one guy that they'd be going steady, he'd turn into Simon Legree and start treating her like his own personal slave.

Lee Hertzig and she never really went steady. He'd just kind of show up in between and take her out now and then. He actually treated her all right, but you could tell he'd raffle me off for a door prize any old day. Then, that is—now we're friends. But it took going through all sorts of hell to get there.

Well, after we got out on the pier, Lee, a real big-shot lawyer type, kept on talking about going on this giant roller coaster, which at the time was like suggesting that I be strapped in one of those nose cones with a couple of monkeys and some mice and shot off into space. I have to tell you right off that I used to be the sissy (and there's a word I really loathe) of all times. Until about a year ago. The most reckless thing you could get me to do was to play a game of Chinese checkers. Oh, I was a real sport. I wouldn't go in a swimming pool if there was a dead bee floating around on top. So, naturally, I kept stalling off the roller coaster until we'd played about six games of minia-ture golf. Lee brought it up again, and right away I suggested *another* game of golf to decide the champion-ship. Then he started in on me. "You don't want to be a sissy, do you?"

Isn't that a bright question? Of course nobody *wants* to be a sissy. You aren't a sissy because you decide to be one; it's just the way you turn out. And you turn out that way because the only men you're ever exposed to are such big-mouthed, crude ball-clankers that you automatically don't want to be like them. You don't want to be like a woman, but you don't want to be like them either. So you just sort of remain in a void for a while until you figure out what the hell the score is. I'm pretty sure that's why I was such a sissy in my earlier years.

"Rita, you've spawned a sissy," Lee went on. He was a real nag about it. "Josh is a sissy, Josh is a sissy," he started chanting in a singsong way just like little kids do. People were starting to look, and my face was getting so red it was stinging. If there's one thing I really used to hate it was having attention called to me. My mother, I admit, wasn't much of a help. They'd both had a little to drink at dinner, so she just sort of giggled softly, and he started in louder than ever.

That's another thing! When people keep telling you you're a sissy you start in believing them, and you become *more* of a sissy. If I sound adamant about this business it's because I am. I'm not a sissy any more but, goddam it, I can't stand to hear a grownup call a kid that! If I had a son and I caught him all dressed up in my wife's clothes, lipstick, high heels and all, I still wouldn't call him a sissy. I'd sure in hell sit down and have a good long talk with him, but I wouldn't call him a sissy.

Now I've got *that* off my chest.

No, I haven't. Not quite. One of the things wrong with this country, in my humble opinion, is the "He-Man Myth." A lot of men I've known think that if they break wind (the other word for that is one word I never use and I don't think I ever will)—anyhow, if they break wind loud enough, belch often enough, scratch their balls every two minutes, and tell about every woman they've laid, they're big he-men. The fact is a real man doesn't have to do any of these things.

I heard a psychiatrist say once that all these guys that go around playing pocket pool do it just because they're reassuring themselves they've got a complete three-piece set. It's a reassurance complex. If you have any confidence in yourself you can relax; you don't have to keep checking every other minute to see if all your equipment's accounted for.

And all this talk about laying women. If you really enjoy going to bed with women, then you must really like women and respect them; and if you like them and respect them, you don't go around telling every Tom, Dick and Harry what an easy lay they are.

One of the reasons I've learned about sex is that you run up against a lot of it in the motion picture business. And then I've spent time in New York in the theatrical crowd and tagging along with my mother in summer stock.

I've also been exposed to a lot of weird stuff because of the way I look. I mean if there's a bona fide homosexual within a thousand miles, you can bet he'll find me and make a pass. I don't know why I got stuck with this sensitive face, but I did. All my younger years, when I was a kid, I remember these hordes of women pinching my cheeks and running their hands back over my hair and saying to my mother, "He looks exactly like you, Rita. And those eyes!" I hated it.

I got this gigantic complex people were only talking about the way I looked because they couldn't come up with anything else to say about me. Like how bright I was, or what a smashing sense of humor I had, or about my personality. Mainly, I guess you couldn't tell if I was smart or funny or even *had* a personality—because I couldn't communicate with people I felt because I couldn't do anything brilliant, people could only comment about me like they would about a piece of French pastry or something.

I tried all kinds of gimmicks to change this. For a long time I wouldn't comb my hair unless you tied me down and did it for me. And I have this thick, stubborn hair.

When I'd get up in the morning I'd just brush my teeth, wash, and skip the hair.

I remember one period that was great. I fell down when I was roller skating and knocked my two front teeth out. I looked like Snaggletooth Joe for a while and nobody had much to say *then*, thank God.

It's this sensitive face that makes me talk the way I do sometimes. You know, like swearing and using a lot of cuckoo expressions and sounding off about a lot of controversial subjects. I guess I'm afraid if I don't come on strong I'll really get pushed around. Besides, when you look one way and talk another it has a certain shock value, and people remember you, because it's a dichotomy. At the proper time and place, and around people I like and trust, and women and all, I have a terrific vocabulary. You'd think sometimes I'm a regular Noel Coward, the way I can turn the literary values on. I actually have two ways of talking.

Boy, I'm really rattling on. I swear I'll try to stick to the point. And that reminds me—meanwhile back at the pier . . .

Lee Hertzig was practically screaming "Josh is a sissy" by the time we got to the end of the amusement park. I finally got so upset I did a very unusual thing for me. I ran over and bought a ticket for a ride on a contraption made up of a kind of center tower, like you'd make from an Erector set, with one long pole on either side and a little bucket-type seat at the end of it that you sat in. They strapped you in, and these poles started swinging back and forth getting higher each time, until you finally swung completely upside down. Then you kept doing somersaults like that for the rest of the ride. It was a far cry from miniature golf, but I did it just to show that son-of-a-bitch, Lee Hertzig. I was probably hoping, in the back of my mind, that I'd fall out and get killed so my mother would finally realize what a bastard he was.

As I was getting strapped into my seat, I looked over and there was a man getting into the other seat that I thought was Cary Grant for sure. I was always on the lookout for him, anyway, because my mother, in spite of being a movie star herself, had this Godawful crush on Cary Grant, and she'd never even met him. They'd been to the same premières and functions like that, but she'd never actually been introduced to him, and it was eating away at her. It really became an obsession. She even found out where he lived and drove by his house once just to see what it looked like.

When I got settled I looked again, and it wasn't Cary Grant. But he sure could have been his double. While I was staring at him he glanced over my way. I guess I looked like a frightened rabbit, so he flashed this gigantic smile at me. It didn't reassure me at all. I was beyond anybody's condolences.

Finally the guy that ran the works started the machinery up, and these poles started swinging back and forth; each time they'd swing a little higher up in the air. I thought I'd wet my pants because I was waiting for the time I'd be completely upside down. And they made you wait quite a while; it was like slow torture while these damn poles kept swinging higher and higher. Finally, though, we were really getting up there. It felt like you were a mile up in the air, and for a moment you hesitated completely upside down before you made the somersault. After that you just kept making somersaults like crazy.

I couldn't stand to look, so I closed my eyes; pretty soon I knew I was going to be sick. I started to yell to the guy to shut off the machine, but the louder I yelled the more I could hear my mother and Lee and all the people who were watching laugh. I still didn't open my eyes, though. The next thing I felt this awful warm lump rising in my throat. I turned my head sideways, so's not to throw up in my seat, and let go. And don't you know I hit this guy in the other seat! We must have been just passing, or else he was a little below me, because I got him right on the back of his neck and shoulder.

As soon as the idiot running the ride saw what happened, he stopped the crummy thing and the poles finally swung back and forth, taking their own sweet time, until we got back to the platform and stopped. The poor guy's neck and shoulder were covered with lobster Newburg and peas and God only knows what else.

But, you know, he was so nice about it! I think if I'd been him I would have tossed me right off the end of the pier. Oh, he was upset and all, but he didn't carry on or swear or anything like that. He just let the sadist that ran the machine take him over to a little restuarant across from the ride so he could get cleaned up.

My mother grabbed hold of me and started to mop me up. I could tell she was terribly disappointed in me and probably would have liked to give me a good crack in the face. Lee stood there kind of smirking at me like he was Hitler and I was some poor Jew he was going to make a lampshade out of.

I was feeling extremely fuzzy and like a jerk for throwing up on the guy, so when she finished with me I walked over to lean on the railing at the side of the pier and get some fresh air. She told Lee she wanted to wait around to apologize to the fellow, and they strolled over toward this tacky-looking restaurant. I thought of jumping in the ocean for a while, but I really wasn't feeling well enough.

A few minutes later I could hear my mother and Lee having an argument. They were standing quite a ways from me. Pretty soon I saw him gesture wildly, turn, and stomp away from her. She watched him until he disappeared in the crowd, shook her head, and started walking back over to me.

Lee, at that time, was typical of the kind of charmers she was always getting hooked up with. The kind that would take you way the heck out to Ocean Park for dinner and then just leave you standing out on the end of a rotten pier. He probably said something miserable about me and that started the fight.

Anyway, there we were with no car. It's funny—but somehow my mother and I always seem closest when there's some kind of a crisis brewing. When things are sailing along smoothly she can be fairly distant, but when there's a hitch in the proceedings she gets very warm and gemütlich. Suddenly, without anything being said, we were standing there laughing our heads off, and I was feeling a little more like my old self again.

Then we saw the guy I'd messed up come out of the

21

restaurant and she tore over to apologize. I would have just as soon skipped talking to him, but they got into quite a conversation. Finally she called for me to come over.

"Josh, this is Mr. Nichols," she said.

I shook hands with him.

"How are you feeling, Josh?" Now you know a guy that you've thrown up on has got to be a prince if he inquires how *you're* feeling. Especially lobster Newburg.

You'd never think a man that looked that much like Cary Grant would be alone, but he must have been because the three of us stuck together from then on and had one helluva time on that pier. We played bingo, threw baseballs, rode the Dodgems, went to the funhouse—everything.

His first name was Ben, and he was the kind of a guy you'd go any place with or do anything with because you had the feeling that nothing could go wrong. He really gave you a terrific feeling of confidence. And what a sense of humor! Not a great big yocky one, but more of a small, subtle, twinkling one.

Later on, after we'd exhausted Ocean Park, Ben drove us back to the house at Paraiso Beach, and we sat up until about two o'clock playing blackjack. Finally my eyes just closed on me and I went to bed.

The next morning, Sunday, as I was walking down the hall on the second floor I heard this light snoring. The door to one of the guest rooms was open, so I looked in. There Ben was! God, I was happy! It was like Christmas morning.

That day we all went to the beach, and by dinnertime you just knew he and my mother were madly in love.

Chapter 3

YOU never met a nicer guy in your life than Ben. He was a little older than my mother, a year or so, and he could do anything, was interested in everything, and knew about everything—aside from being one of the most handsome men you'd ever see. He told us he lived in Suffern, New York, and he'd just recently come out to California for one of those advertising agencies that have about twenty names in their title. He was there to straighten out their West Coast office and handle some of their new television accounts.

Ben spent almost every weekend with us. Lost of times he'd come down for dinner during the week, and sometimes my mother would go into Hollywood and meet him there. But he didn't like to hang around Hollywood much. He'd rather come to our house or he'd go almost any place else. During that summer he'd take long weekends from Thursday night until Monday morning and we traveled all over: San Francisco, Tijuana, Carmel, Las Vegas, Coronado, Catalina—we went to all those places with him. But wherever we'd go Ben would always find out-of-the-way places to stay. He hated to go to the "tourist traps," as he called them.

My mother and he really hit it off, but another great part of the deal was that he liked me. He did, too. He was almost the only man she ever went with that ever gave a hoot for me. You see, before Ben, I'd always felt like the missing piece of a jigsaw puzzle that couldn't figure out how to get in with the rest. I knew there must be a place for me somewhere in these relationships she was always having, but nothing ever worked out. So with Ben it was such a new and wonderful feeling to be included. I guess that's the word that describes it. Included!

I don't blame it on her directly because she always

seemed to want me to like her boy friends and for them to like me. In a way, I guess it was my fault because I could never open up enough for anybody to take a real fancy to me unless they made an active effort to help me. And none of them ever did that. Oh, I could think up all kinds of clever things to say, all right, that probably would have struck them as funny or interesting, but I'll be damned if I could actually come out with them. I was too afraid of laying an egg. That was the trouble. Also, when you get the feeling you're not quite acceptable it makes you withdraw all the more.

I remember once when my mother had an apartment in New York. I was about twelve, and it was in the summer. I'd bought her a bottle of perfume because she lost a good play she was up for, and she was very depressed. I was hiding in the living room behind the drapes waiting for her to come home around five o'clock so I could surprise her.

I heard the door open and voices in the foyer. Then she came in with an actor she'd just started going with who was a little younger than she was. I'd only been around him three or four times, so I was embarrassed to come popping out with a bottle of perfume—in spite of the fact that I sort of liked him.

"Josh! Oh, Josh, I'm home!" I heard her calling. Then she told Don, the actor, to make himself comfortable and I heard her walking down the hall toward the bedrooms. When she came back she said, "That's funny. I spoke to him on the phone only a half-hour ago."

By that time it was too late for me to come out; I just stayed where I was.

"Maybe he went out to play," Don said.

I could hear her sigh. "No, he hasn't made any friends around here. And I was so hoping he would this summer. That's why I took this apartment near the Park. But he's ... I don't know—shy and introspective. He's just not a 'regular boy,' Don, and it worries me."

The word "regular" really hit me.

"Oh, Rita, all boys that age are a little ... off by themselves."

"I know, but—Josh is way off!" She almost seemed to

make a joke out of it. "Of course, we haven't really had one home where he could settle down and become completely acclimated to his surroundings." She went on to say how a lot of it was her fault as they talked about me some more. Finally she said, "Don, maybe you could take him around sometime. You know, play a little tennis or go swimming with him."

"Sure," he answered. "I'd enjoy it myself. I like Josh."

"You *do*! Really, Don?" The way she said it you'd have thought he'd just said he liked tarantulas.

"Of course I do," he said. "He's a very bright lad."

"Oh, I'm so glad," she told him. "I know he's bright but . . . Oh, Don, that would be wonderful—if you'd spend a little time with him! I think that's what he needs—a man's company."

"All right, it's a deal," he said. "How's about a little drink on it?"

"I might even let you have two," she replied. "But you have to battle with the ice trays. Come on!" They both went into the kitchen.

As soon as they'd left the living room I tiptoed to the front door and opened and closed it loudly. Then I walked into the kitchen and said hello. It's a spooky feeling overhearing something about yourself that you're not meant to. I was very ill at ease with them until they went out for the evening.

You see, in spite of the fact that I knew she was right about me I was hurt. I never did give her that bottle of perfume. I emptied it down the drain and threw the bottle away later on that night. It wasn't expensive stuff; I got it at the dime store.

When I went to bed later on I started to get excited about the fact that Don had said he liked me and that he was going to spend some time with me. I was sure we'd get to be good friends. I can't tell you how I waited the next few days for him to come by or call. I never saw him again, though. I don't know what happened. I guess they had a fight or something because after about a week I asked her about him and she gave it the old brush-off. "Oh, I don't know, dear. I think he had to go out of town." But you could tell by her tone that she did know. I still had hopes because I figured they'd patch things up. But the following week we went up to a summer theater in Massachusetts where my mother tried out a new play that was so bad the manager made a curtain speech every night practically apologizing for it. So that was that.

For ages I remembered her saying she didn't think I was "regular."

Ben was the one who actually got me over being a sissy. My mother's not too athletically inclined, but Ben was nuts about almost every kind of exercise. So during the day Ben and I were together a lot whenever my mother didn't want to go with us, which was most of the time. We embarked on this terrifically ambitious program to teach me how to do things. We'd go swimming, horseback riding, play tennis—just about everything you could imagine. One thing, Ben never made you feel like a fool when you were first learning how to do something; instead he made you feel like a genius just because you could sit on a horse standing still. He made you want to learn so badly that during the week you'd knock yourself out so you could surprise him by jumping over a flaming six foot wall bareback! It's a wonder I didn't kill myself, some of the things I tried, learning how to ride horseback and how to surfboard.

And Ben touched easily. I've never known many people that have. My Aunt Lilly touches easily but my mother, as much as she might love you, you're very conscious of when she touches you or when you hold her hand or anything like that. But Ben would always be putting his arm around you or touching you and you'd hardly be aware of it until you thought about why you were feeling so secure and warm and all. Some people can handle other people like that and it becomes a plus. Others when they touch you it's definitely a minus. Somebody walks over your grave, and you want to get away from them right away. Or some people, when they put their hand on your shoulder, you feel like they're trying to push you right down into the ground. I'm a nut about touching people I like; I don't mean hanging onto them or mauling them—just touching them freely. I think I'm a good toucher.

I'll give you an example of how really great Ben was.

About the second time we went horseback riding we were going along this beautiful bridal path down in Palos Verdes that winds right along on top of a bluff overlooking the ocean. We were just riding along looking out toward the sea, not saying anything because, like I said, I only spoke when forced to, and *then* I'd usually mumble something that needed an interpreter to figure out. Pretty soon we came to this little promontory that jutted out, the horses stopped, and we just stood still looking out toward Catalina.

Then Ben comes out with this: "Josh, if there's ever anything you're confused about, anything you want to talk over—I want you to let me know."

On top of everything else he could do he must have been psychic. Because about ten minutes before I was thinking of all sorts of things I wanted to ask him about, and wishing the goddam cat would let go of my tongue once in a while. And Ben comes out with that!

Well, that did it all right. I blurted out about a million assorted thoughts on everything you could think of. I told him how I hated being a sissy and shy and never talking, and by the time we started to ride back to the stable he had me feeling like a combination of Einstein, Ed Murrow, and Yul Brynner. If the horse would have done it, I wouldn't have had a qualm about diving off the cliff into the ocean below because I was sure I'd come up singing like a bastard. For the first time in my life I felt like a real person instead of some little, furry, woodland creature that was scared of its own shadow.

Ben explained that I'd had this fantastically abnormal childhood and I never really had a chance to relax and get out of myself. But he said that was all going to be different from now on.

He talked about the way I looked, too, saying that if you had a really sensitive face you always had to prove to people that you weren't the oddball of the world. Also, that some people were always jealous of other people's looks. This had always been a ticklish subject with me, but when Ben talked about it—somehow it didn't bother me. Instead I got to thinking it maybe wasn't so bad after all.

We talked about ball-clankers, too. Ben said that a real

man was masculine, and all that, but he was also gentle and kind and thoughtful.

And he explained how everyone in the world has tons of problems they think only *they* have, but that actually everybody's in the same boat. He told me to start speaking up about anything that came into my mind—that that was the way you learned things and got to know people and how, if you actually talk to people and find out about them, they're usually not the complete monsters you've got them pegged for.

My own personal horizon started to clear up that day like the sky after a terrific storm. We must have talked for hours, and that night at dinner I don't think Ben or my mother got in more than a handful of words. Once, when my mother was clearing the table, she stopped next to my chair and put her hand to my forehead. She thought I was running a fever or something. I talked my head off, and I was even getting laughs. And you know something—I haven't stopped sounding off since, except for periods of shock caused by some catastrophe or other. And we sure in hell were headed for one of those.

Chapter 4

WE got to be a real trio, the three of us. You see, another great thing about Ben was that he didn't seem to know many people out in California to complicate things; my mother and I had him all to ourselves. She was so wrapped up in Ben she didn't care to see her friends, and I never had many in the first place. Consequently we just stuck together having one helluva time.

Of course, we did see some people; you can't live like hermits. But there were very few. One of them was a real character, Merwin Saltzman, who has always been a good friend to my mother and me. Sometimes you wouldn't see him for a year or more, but he'd always show up when you were about ready to kill yourself, things were going so badly. And, by God, he'd cheer you up; he can get a belly laugh from me any day. Well, Merwin appeared on the scene in January and started coming down once a week or so. He and Ben hit it off right away; Merwin tickled the hell out of Ben.

Merwin resembles some kind of a certain tropical bird—a cockatoo or a cockateel, I'm not sure which. He's only five feet eight and very thin and fragile; he has what you call "small bones," and no hips, and a tiny waist, and as far as an ass goes—you wonder what he sits on half the time. What makes him look like a bird is this thin kind of beaklike nose and those tiny, bright blue eyes that blink just like a bird's. He has a high forehead and a widow's peak and then thick black hair that goes straight back and has a lot of gray in it.

And Merwin's a terrific dresser; you know who he dresses like—Fred Astaire. Everything has a kind of English-Italian cut to it—sort of pinched, but on him it looks good. And he wears lots of ascots and kerchiefs and such.

He's really very effeminate, but somehow it doesn't bother people because he's so completely effeminate that what can you do? Actually, he's kind of sexless. I don't think he ever "does it" with anybody. He's more an observer and commentator. And, thank God, he never runs around with a lot of other effeminate people. It's miserable when they travel in packs.

Merwin's a very original writer, too. He'll knock off slick Hollywood movies and then turn around and write something really offbeat like this novel that came out about three years ago. It was about this young guy named Tully, from Montana, who had an affair with his own father. So you can see I use the term "offbeat" advisedly. It really caused a stink when it was published. Merwin said he didn't get why the big fuss. He said if it had been about a guy having an affair with his *grandfather*—then he could understand all the commotion.

You'd love Merwin. Once he was driving Ben, my mother, and me down to Redondo Beach for dinner and we stopped at a gas station. When the attendant came over to the window Merwin said, "Fill it up with Ethyl, please."

"Check your water and oil?" the guy asked.

"Yes," Merwin replied. Then as the attendant was walking over toward the pump, Merwin leaned out the window and yelled, "Sweetie—while you're at it, you might fluff up the tires, too." He's always coming out with something cuckoo like that.

Besides Merwin we used to see Jay Savage, my mother's agent. He'd show up every so often to talk about some deal he had her up for. And that's about as far as it ever went. But you had to give him credit for trying. He was a real huckster. As Ben said, "What he lacks in taste and tactics he makes up for in guts!" And it was true. Jay would really knock himself out trying to figure out some scheme or other. My mother used to be with one of the big agencies that practically owns the industry, but as soon as her career started to fade they dropped her like a hot potato. Then she'd been with a couple of other people until she wound up with Jay. He may not have had entree to the top people at the studios, but he certainly had enthusiasm. He'd knock himself out plugging for you. You had to admire him, even though he was a character.

Jay was a little chubby guy who wore all the wrong clothes. And all different kinds from Ivy League to the horse-blanket-plaid style of sport jacket where the shoulders hung over and dropped almost down to his elbows. Nothing looked right on him except a simple dark suit, but you'd never catch him in one of those. Or if you did, he'd have some kind of a crazy, loud, satin vest that would knock your eyes out. And the funny thing about him was, he thought he was a real fashion plate. He had the largest collection of cruddy-looking suède shoes in the world, too.

It was obvious that his real name wasn't Jay Savage, but he hated it when people questioned him about it. Once a friend of my mother's was at our house when he came by, and when they were introduced she said, "Jay Savage! What a fascinating name!"

"Thank you, *I* like it!" He was all puffed up.

"Yes, it's so basic," she added. "Of course, it's not your *real* name, is it?"

He did a slow burn and said, "No, madam, my real name is Sam Shmuck!"

She wasn't Jewish and obviously had never heard the word and didn't get that he was being sarcastic. "Sam Shmuck," she said. "That *is* an ugly one! I don't blame you for changing it! Not one bit."

Anyway, when Jay would come down to discuss something with my mother he'd always arrive around cocktail time, and it didn't take too much to get him to stay for dinner. Like one word. But Ben and he got along fine because Ben got such a kick out of him.

Then there were the Paganellis, who ran a small Italian restaurant in Paraiso Beach. It was right down near the water, and we used to eat there a couple of times a week. We found out about it like this: Jeanette, the woman who ran Jeanette's Beauty Salon in Paraiso Beach, was married to Roy Clymer, the captain of the local police. It seems Roy had a terrific crush on my mother from when she was first in pictures. So when she first started going to this beauty parlor Jeanette said he'd love to meet her and take her and me to dinner. Mama Paganelli's was where he took us, and we liked it so much we took Ben there the following Sunday. After a while it became almost a standing date that we'd have dinner there with the Clymers on Sunday. Sunday was a great night at Paganelli's—kind of family night. It was more like eating at somebody's home instead of at a restaurant, mainly because the whole family ran it and they were such warm people. The Clymers were wonderful people, too. He didn't seem like a policeman at all, and his wife was an awful lot of fun.

Outside of Merwin, Jay, the Clymers, and the Paganellis, we didn't see many other people on a regular basis. But it didn't make much difference to me who we were with as long as the three of us stuck together.

And if you think *I* was overjoyed with the situation, you should have seen my mother. She was about eighty feet off the ground. It was the first time I'd ever seen her truly relaxed. She didn't worry too much about her career; she started going to sleep at a decent hour and getting up a little earlier; but best of all—she didn't drink so much. Boy, that's one thing Ben couldn't stand: drunk women. There were just a couple of times when she overdid it, and that was enough. Ben really froze up. He didn't make a scene or anything. He just turned into a sheet of steel and didn't utter a word the whole rest of the evening. I don't mean to give the impression that Ben didn't drink himself; he did, and he wasn't any lightweight either. But he knew how to drink.

Actually, my mother never did get sloppy or falling-down drunk like lots of women. She'd just get very slow and thick-speeched and repetitive. And a little ... elegant. That's the word! Kind of like she was a duchess who came to a party for the peasants and didn't like it too much.

She even stopped dressing like she was perpetually going to a cocktail party and started wearing dungarees and old clothes around the house.

Ben was one guy that never got cranky about anything. I mean you never saw him sulking or spoiling for a fight like almost everybody does at one time or another. There was only one thing: every once in a while he'd get very quiet for maybe ten or fifteen minutes. He could be driving a car or riding a horse or just sitting out on the terrace or down at the beach, and all of a sudden he'd kind of lift his face up and look off far away into the distance and not say a word. When he'd do this his eyes would get this terrifically sad look in them. But it wasn't only a sad look; it was a sad, *perplexed* look. Almost like he wasn't quite sure what he was upset about. No matter who was around him when this happened, nobody would talk or hardly move. It was like time froze for a few minutes. Then Ben would be the one to break the silence. He'd sort of shake his head and look around to get his bearings as if he'd been off in a trance or something. Then he'd start in talking like nothing had ever happened.

One other thing: every so often Ben would have terrific nightmares. Several times I woke up because he was crying out in his sleep so loudly. It always upset me when he'd have a nightmare. Actually, it frightened me because somehow you never figured Ben would have them. Just the opposite. He was the exact person you'd want to have around if you had one—to tell you how dumb it was. He never mentioned anything the next morning. I always wished he had because I couldn't possibly imagine what Ben would dream about that would upset him like that. And I wanted to know.

Chapter 5

It must have been a novelty for my mother to go around with a man that didn't give her a black eye, pass out in public, insult waiters, despise her son, wreck her car, bum food and liquor, gamble, and some of the other cunning things that most of them did. Like this one demented son-of-a-bitch she went out with when we were living on Roxbury Drive. And the trick he pulled.

First, I have to explain that she has the overwhelming, abnormal, psychotic fear of mice of all time. If you just say the word "mouse" she starts frothing at the mouth. Anyhow, when she had this house on Roxbury Drive she gave a very important dinner party one night. It was vital to have it come off right because she had a couple of producers there who were considering her for a picture, her agent, and a few intimate friends so it wouldn't seem too businesslike. Her agent—the one she had before Jay—was really trying to set the deal; she was making a terrific pitch for a comeback at that time.

Well, she'd been going out with this one actor that was about forty-five but still thought he was Joe College. He was one of those rah-rah, the gang's all here, anything for a laugh types. He really fixed it up good for her!

When the butler came out with the main course, which was supposed to be roast beef on one of those great silver platters with a great silver dome-like cover on it—guess what happened? He brought it around to my mother so she could give her approval like the hostess sometimes does. She lifts the cover off, and there's no roast beef or anything except one tiny little white mouse tearing around on the great silver platter.

When I tell you all hell broke loose—I mean it *really* broke loose! You'd say how could one woman knock over a whole dinner table. And it was one of those long ones.

34

Well, she did. And within about twenty ferocious minutes, a couple of fist fights ensued, business deals were called off, lawsuits were instituted, and God only knows what didn't happen! The place was a shambles.

I know, because that was on a Thursday evening and I came home from prison, otherwise known as St. Mark's, on Friday. The house looked like a miniature of that railway scene in *Gone With the Wind*, and my mother was still upstairs in her bedroom under sedation. So you can imagine what a mess it must have been.

And you know one sad thing? While I was walking around inspecting the scene of the battle in the dining room, I came across that little white mouse, dead as a doornail, lying there on its back by a broken wine glass, its little feet sticking straight up in the air. I guess *rigor mortis* sets in with mice, too. I gave it a state funeral in a kitchen matchbox out in the back yard.

So what a relief it was for my mother to go around with a guy like Ben; he'd never pull anything like that. Oh, he'd kid her all right, but he knew how to do it. Once we were all sitting out on the terrace off the game room and suddenly Ben starts this two-way conversation with himself.

"Rita Cydney—let's see ... wasn't her first picture something about a robbery? Oh, yes, *The Great Train Robbery!* I wonder what ever happened to her? Last picture I saw her in she played that other young actress's mother ... Oh, what's her name? Little Joan Crawford? Yes, that's it, she played little Joanie's mother. She was very good in it. So believable! I don't know why they changed her name for movies. Her real name's Rita Hinkle, you know!"

It was, too. But when she got into pictures they changed it to Rita Cydney for obvious reasons.

Ben went on and on carrying on this monologue with himself until my mother finally said, "Ben, you're a devil. The way you talk, and at your age! You must have been a frightening little boy!"

"To the contrary," he replied. "I was angelic. I'd just lie there in my bassinet and eavesdrop on my folks. Especially when they'd return from the nickelodeon raving about Rita Cydney!"

She picked up a pillow off one of the outside sofas. "Darling, I'm warning you!"

Ben went right on: "Daddy had quite a crush on you— even planned on leaving Mommy. But they finally talked it over and decided you were too old for him."

With that she threw a pillow at him, and before you knew it we were all engaged in one of the greatest pillow fights you ever saw.

Ben hated phonies, too. One weekend we went up to Lake Arrowhead and bumped into a former actress, Elise Cordon, who used to know my mother. She flew over to our table as we were finishing dinner and made a big fuss about seeing her. Then she went back to her table and hauled back this millionaire husband she'd snagged.

"Henry," she said, tugging him by the arm and plopping him down in a chair, "you rememeber Rita, don't you? She made some of those wonderful old movies, when they really knew how to make them!" She said it like if he could think back to the Dark Ages he might recognize her. He said he did remember her, but he didn't include any kind of comment or compliment, which people usually did. I could tell right off that Ben didn't take to them.

"Well, Rita, I can't tell you what a relief it is to be out of the business. My dear, I didn't know what living was until I married Henry. I take it you've given it up, too?"

"No," my mother said, "I'm still plugging away."

"Oh, dear!" this bitch said, pretending like she'd made an honest *faux pas*. "It's just that I haven't seen you in anything in ages—so I automatically supposed you'd chucked it all."

"I'll wait till it chucks me," my mother said.

"Don't be ridiculous—you look divine, darling! Well, I was going on with my career but Henry didn't want me to. Says it's a shabby life and, of course, he's so right! But then I didn't realize it until I got out of the whole mess. Now I don't have time to think about it. We're on the go every minute, aren't we, Tink?"

Tink grunted.

"That's my nickname for him—Tink! Isn't it silly? Now,

Rita—we have an absolutely gorgeous house in Connecticut which you simply must call headquarters when you come back to see shows and do the town. Then we keep an apartment in New York, and Henry bought me the old house I used to rent in Beverly Hills—for sentimental reasons, didn't you, Tink?"

Tink grunted.

Finally, after she'd talked herself blue in the face, she turned to Ben and said, "You haven't said a word, Mr. Nichols!" Then she turned to my mother. "Of course, he's in the business, Rita. He's got to be with those *divine* looks!"

Before my mother could answer Ben said, "No, you're wrong." You could see a moment of panic fly across her face when she thought of the possibility that maybe my mother had a millionaire, too, and that she'd been making an ass out of herself.

"Oh, really?" she asked. "Well, what *do* you do?" She got very kittenish with Ben. "I'm sure whatever it is it must be fascinating! Come on now—'fess up!"

Without batting an eye Ben says, "I'm a fornicologist!"

She was so ready to flirt with him that before she thought about what he said she automatically answered "Ohhhhh!" like she was saying "How interesting!" But at the end of it you could detect a definite rising inflection.

Thank God the waiter came by with the check during one of your most pregnant pauses ever. We left the two of them sitting there in a stunned condition, to say the least. As we were walking away I looked back, and they practically cracked their heads together diving toward one another, probably asking, "*What* did he say?"

When we got out of the door my mother said, "Ben, you ought to be ashamed of yourself!"

"Not at all," he answered. "The old foofs!" Then we started in laughing, like we always did.

Isn't that great—a fornicologist! I keep waiting for a good chance to pull it on somebody.

Something else. I told you my mother was trying to break into television along about that time, but it wasn't any too regular. She only had about three or four jobs, and they weren't on what you'd call the top shows. I know Ben helped out financially. He was always bringing us presents and buying groceries and taking us every place we went.

Ben was a nut about making your own money. "Beginning with next summer, I think it'd be a good idea if you took a part-time job, Josh." He came out with that one right out of a blue sky one Saturday while we were putting our gear together after about five sets of tennis.

"What about our tennis and horseback riding and swimming and everything?" I asked.

"Oh, there'll be time for that," he said. "I don't mean you should start working full time. But it's important for you to get the feeling of earning your own money."

"That's okay with me. I'm a nut about money anyhow."

Ben started to laugh. He got a big kick out of my mother's stories about what a squirrel I was when it came to storing it away. "I know all about you, all right." He was really chuckling. I could tell it just about killed him to run up against a fifteen-year-old confirmed miser. "But the feeling of earning your own money is different. I don't mean that money's everything, mind you, because it isn't. But it is terribly important. Its main importance ... I suppose ... is the freedom it allows."

We just sat there for a while. I could tell Ben was thinking about whether what he said was the right way to put it. "It's funny," he went on, "but it's not so much having money as the danger that comes from *not* having it. Does that make any sense to you, Josh?"

"I think so," I said. And I wondered if it did.

"You see—" When Ben was trying to explain something to you, lots of times he'd start with "You see—" and then there'd be this long pause while he held up his left hand, kind of half cupped, in front of his chin. It was like he was trying to grasp exactly what he was trying to say himself and almost make it tangible before he'd give it to you.

"You see—when you're grown up, not having money can make you do a lot of things you shouldn't do. That's the real danger. It can make you dependent on people that ... you wouldn't associate with ... otherwise. It can make you ... insecure and ... weak!"

Ben didn't look at me, like he usually did, to get my

reaction to what he'd said. Then I realized he'd gone off into one of those silent periods. He just sat there, staring way off into space as if I wasn't even around.

After a minute or two a ball came bouncing over from one of the other courts. It went right by his shoulder and lodged up in the wire fence. I picked it out and threw it back. Ben was still in the same position; he hadn't moved a muscle. So I sat down again. Then after another couple of minutes he began nodding his head up and down very gently and, without looking at me, reached over and put his hand on my knee.

"That's it. Next summer a part-time job. Anything. It doesn't matter . . . just so you get the feeling of being independent." Then he looked at me. "Okay?" And he flashed that smile that just about knocked you off the bench.

"Okay," I answered.

"All right then. What are we sitting around for? Let's go have a root beer."

We were off and away to the hamburger stand about a block away. We were both nuts about root beer, too.

And, you know—he'd never give me money in front of anyone, not even my mother; he'd always give it to me when we were alone. And after the first few months he didn't actually *give* it to me. We had this secret communication system and he'd *leave* it for me.

How it first happened was like this: We were playing a game of darts one evening after dinner down in the game room. Being as Ben always cooked because my mother was extremely retarded when it came to that department, she was upstairs doing the dishes. Ben had bet me a quarter she'd break something after I'd mentioned that she was really getting pretty good about the breakage problem. She hadn't broken a dish or a glass in a couple of days. When she'd first started doing the dishes it was fantastic: one crash after another. She's very impossible when it comes to doing things with her hands. She's got absolutely beautiful hands. They're very long and thin and artistic-looking, but they're really not very practical. If somebody shakes her hand with any force at all, it hurts her.

I swear to God it wasn't more than thirty seconds after

we made the bet when we heard this terrific crash. It sounded like a whole tray of glasses. I looked up toward the ceiling, bowed, and said bitterly, "Thanks a lot, Mom. You're a real pal." Then Ben and I started in laughing. I don't know about Ben but I almost died. I finally ended up lying on the floor holding my sides. It's murder when you get hysterics right after a big meal.

After a while Ben stopped and stood over me, snapping his fingers. "Okay, pay up, Mac! In fact, I'd say that one was worth fifty cents!"

Boy, that stopped me. "Oh, no! A quarter is what we said!"

"All right, a quarter. But pay up!"

"I'll give it to you later," I said. I was always postponing payments on debts, hoping like hell whoever I owed would forget about it.

"I'm on to you, Buster. Get the money up now!"

Actually, I didn't have any change on me, but at the bottom of the wooden banister leading down to the game room there was this newel post. The top was a piece of ornately carved wood which came off, and inside was a hollow place. One day I kind of swung around it as I came downstairs, and that's how I found out it was loose. Well, since I was always looking for places to stash away loot, I started in keeping some money in it.

I knew Ben would get a kick out of me keeping money in that wooden post, so I said, "Okay, I'll pay up." I was standing right near it at the time. I just reached over, lifted the top off, picked out a quarter and handed it to him.

"Why, you little fox!" Ben yelled.

Ordinarily, I wouldn't have ever shown that hiding place to anyone. But you knew Ben would never rob you or even tell anyone else, like my mother, where it was.

Anyway, when he left for Los Angeles that Sunday night he said, "Check Secret Communications, Josh."

I knew what he was talking about. So I went down to the newel post when my mother was getting ready for bed and, sure enough, he'd left a ten-dollar bill for me.

After that he'd usually always leave something there. Or else under my mattress, or in this pewter mug in the living room that played a German tune when you picked it up.

He always used to kid me and say it's a wonder I got a good night's sleep because of how lumpy my mattress must be with all the money stuffed in it.

Of course, I did stop *keeping* money in those three places—not because I thought Ben would ever take any, but because if he saw I was solvent he might not leave much. Once a fox, always a fox!

Chapter 6

BEN went to New York for a couple of weeks around Christmas. He said he had to see his mother, who was still alive, and to check things with the New York office of this advertising agency. But do you know he wrote a letter to my mother every single day he was away? And you've never seen so many presents as he sent for Christmas, in your life. We were snowed under; everything from an electric can opener to jewelry for my mother, a complete set of snorkel equipment for me, and overcoats for the dogs. Those are just examples; every day a new batch of packages would arrive. Plus long-distance phone calls all the time. And he even wrote *me* once or twice a week.

Ben came back the day before New Year's Eve, and that was the first New Year's Eve I ever spent that turned out the way it was supposed to. Most guys would want to go out to a nightclub and prove what big spenders they were, but the three of us spent New Year's at our house, and Ben made beef Stroganoff, and we had champagne and the works. And baked Alaska for dessert. He could cook like a fancy chef, too. I don't think there was anything he couldn't do. I actually think I would have voted for him for President on a write-in ballot.

He hated the goddam parrot as much as I did, too!

I never wanted anything the way I wanted Ben and my mother to get married. I even started going to church again, because I was trying to be exemplary in every way so that maybe, by an unusual coincidence, something decent would happen. Also, of course, to pray. I'm always going to church like a fiend or else falling away from the church forever. But now I'm going to try to straighten all that out.

But you know—the most demented thing happens to me sometimes when I go to church. I'll go there feeling almost like a saint, ready to confess my sins, take Communion, and all set to ask God to please help me straighten out my life and show me what to do. Then when I actually get in church and kneel down to pray, every dirty word I've ever heard comes sailing through my mind. Isn't that the most warped thing you ever heard of? It doesn't *always* happen, of course, but sometimes it does.

Then is when I'm about the most embarrassed person in the world. Usually I can overcome it, but sometimes, no matter what I tell myself, these words keep flashing by and I just have to get up and march straight out of church. I invariably take a long walk, amounting to almost an overnight hike, kicking myself in the ass every step of the way, telling myself how I'm the rottenest person in the whole universe—let alone the world.

Oddly enough, Ben was a Catholic, too, and I told him about this experience one day. He said it had happened to him on occasions. The way he looked at it, God didn't mind dirty words too much because every word was only made dirty by the mind of the user, that actually most of the words themselves applied to natural bodily functions. He said God, as he saw Him, was not an avenging God but a forgiving God, that He only got upset when you hurt somebody, or committed a real sin like murder, suicide, rape, robbery, and such.

And, you know, that helped me because it kind of took the chip off my shoulder. Somehow I'd always thought God was continually waiting to trap you doing something wrong. Like He was crouching up there behind some cloud with a big club in His hand all ready to pole-ax you if you made a call from a pay phone and your dime was returned by mistake and you *kept* it.

I still go through periods when I lose my temper at God and really tear into Him. Especially this summer I've stormed into church several times with whole tirades I'd practically rehearsed to give Him for continually piling it on us.

As far as being a *good* Catholic, I'm really not; I'm about half and half. My mother's not a Catholic at all. The only reason I am is that my father wanted me to be raised one. Although nobody has seen or heard from him in

43

about a century, my mother has always respected that one wish of his.

Speaking of my father—and nobody hardly ever does—I actually don't know too much about him. He was a Canadian, and it was one of those wartime marriages. My mother divorced him shortly after I appeared on the scene. I have heard from practically unanimous sources that he, too, was one of your less desirable characters in the entire world.

I have one picture of him in a snappy-looking uniform and, as my Aunt Lilly says, "He was a handsome devil!" Apparently she was right on both counts—handsome *and* devil. He looked kind of like a cross between Monty Clift and John Barrymore, and that's not exactly ugly.

Lilly has told me a little about him, but you couldn't get my mother to speak of him if you put her on the rack. I must be honest—she doesn't say anything *against* him; she just doesn't say anything. Period.

Lilly explained that he was a real promoter. When he was in the service and overseas, he and my mother were very much in love. Then he got out early and came to live in Hollywood where the whole thing wore very thin because he wouldn't make an effort to take a job. My mother was doing very well during the war years, but he just kind of plotzed around waiting to fall into some sort of a cushy job in the industry. Finally, he got bored and just disappeared. As Lilly said, "He could charm the birds out of the trees, but when he got tired of it—watch out! He had a mean streak a mile wide!"

But the way I figure it—the hell with him! Not all the time, though. You can't help feeling sad sometimes wondering who and where and why about your own father. At different times, usually on my birthday or holidays, I get to thinking about him, and I make up all kinds of fantasies, excusing him for why he was so rotten and why we haven't heard from him.

The one I use most frequently is that he had this gigantic tumor pressing against his brain—about one hundredth of an inch away from it—that no one knew about. It made him the next thing to a madman and, in reality, he was doing a terrific job not running amuck and slaying about a dozen innocent people before they could catch him. That's why he disappeared: in case it *did* happen, he didn't want to stab my mother and me with a breadknife or something. I know it's not the truth, but what are you going to do in a situation like that?

The three times my mother and I were plastered all over the front pages, I did expect to hear from him. If he cared—no, not even if he *cared*—if he was even a member of the human race, he would have gotten in touch with us. So I guess the best thing to do is to pretend that he's dead. And maybe he is. Anyway, that's why I'm a Roman Catholic.

Oh, I have to tell you something Merwin Saltzman made up about this movie star that's so Catholic she practically gets to vote for the Pope. He said she has Rat-a-Tat Beads made up for herself. And what Rat-a-Tat Beads are, is a rosary that says itself by electricity. Each bead is a tiny electric light bulb, and the whole thing works on a battery. Instead of you fingering the rosary and saying prayers, these little beads light up themselves as they go around telling the rosary. And the electricity causes the thing to make a kind of rat-a-tat sound when it's working. Anyhow, Merwin says this one star has a set and keeps them going all the time, using up several batteries a day and burning out little light bulbs left and right.

Now that idea just about slays me; I don't even think it's sacrilegious it's so funny. Every once in a while I'll say to myself, "I think I'll have a set of Rat-a-Tat Beads made up for myself." Then I go off into hysterics.

I sure could have used a set when I was praying for Ben and my mother to get married. You could almost see smoke pouring out of my ears I prayed so hard. I could have supported a whole candle factory; I was lighting candles every five minutes. I even thought of taking up Christian Science for a while because Christian Scientists always seem to get what they want in life.

When Ben got back after Christmas, he actually started talking about getting married and adopting me, and how my mother wouldn't have to worry about her career any

45

more because he wouldn't want to have her working anyhow. I'd never been so happy in all my life.

Ben could make everything sound like it was in a storybook or something. You know those wild-looking pictures of castles that were always in kids' storybooks, way up at the top of a mountain, kind of half in and half out of the clouds? And there was always this long, winding trail that wound around the mountain and through forests until it led to the door of the castle? Well, Ben always gave you the feeling that if you stuck with him you'd actually *reach* that castle. Not only that—you'd probably find out you owned it!

Like I said, after Christmas Ben would, every once in a while, talk about the time they'd be married and all the different things we'd do together. Well, I started becoming a fiend about *when* they'd actually tie the knot. I think it was because everything was so perfect that I could hardly believe it.

One Friday afternoon in February we were all sitting out on the terrace off the game room having cocktails when Ben said, "You know what I thought we'd do Sunday?"

"Why don't we all drive down to Mexico and get married?" I blurted out.

"Josh!" I thought my mother would spill her drink.

Ben was great about it; he explained that he'd told me to speak up and say anything I felt about anything.

It was a pretty crude thing to come out with, but I was getting an extreme case of anxiety about the situation. Actually, what Ben was about to say we were going to do was rent a sailboat and go over to Catalina on Sunday. He could sail, too.

But, you see, when I brought up the marriage thing he wouldn't dodge it. He explained that he had to wait and see if he was going to stay out on the West Coast and sell his house in Suffern and about his mother and all. Or whether he'd be called back to New York. If he was sent back there he'd get an apartment in the city and we'd all move back and get married; and we could use the Suffern house, where his mother lived, on weekends. Or if he was going to stay in California he'd look for a place to buy out here—and where did we want to live in case that happened? God, we must have sat around for a couple of hours making all these wonderful plans. He said it wouldn't be too long before he'd know what was happening; then they'd set the date.

That night, after I'd gotten into bed and turned off the lights, the door opened and my mother came into the room. I kind of sat up as she walked over and stood right by the side of my bed. I was expecting a real lecture but she just stood there shaking her head slightly for a moment. Then she sat down on the bed very quickly and gave me a terrific bear hug and a kiss. "I love my boy!" she whispered and left the room. I knew she was thanking me for bringing up the subject of marriage.

Chapter 7

THINGS went along perfectly for months. I was learning how to do all kinds of things. I even got on the tennis team at school and started making friends with all kinds of people. My mother could hardly believe the change in me; I couldn't either. All I knew was that I was so happy I had to keep pinching myself to make sure everything was real. She still wasn't getting much work, but that didn't seem to matter any more. She was happy.

Then toward the end of March she got invited to a big director's house up at Santa Barbara. It was going to be one of those enormous weekend shindigs with a lot of people in the industry, so she asked Ben to take her. He didn't seem to want to. In fact, he never wanted to be around a lot of people. But she insisted, saying that these were nice people and, besides, it might do her some good professionally.

Ever since she'd started going with Ben she really looked terrific, and I guess she wanted people to see her. She'd only have a couple of drinks before dinner and her insomnia was practically negligible. It makes all the difference when you get a decent night's sleep. Before, although she was always beautiful, she'd get very thin and nervous and fidgety-looking lots of times. She'd be undereating for fear of gaining weight and worried all the time about her career so that she'd get dark circles under her eyes. She'd practically wear sunglasses from the moment she got up until she went to bed at night. But after all these months with Ben she was definitely in top form and looked like she could pop right back into the movies again.

Another reason for wanting to go for the weekend, I guess, was to show Ben off to some of her old friends. She had a reputation for getting hooked up with bastards; now she had someone she could be proud of without having to defend him all the time. Also, she was feeling extremely peppy that week because Jay had taken her into town several times about a new television series, and there was a definite possibility of her doing the pilot film for it. The producers couldn't get over how marvelous she looked, and from what Jay said they were acting like she could be discovered all over again.

Anyhow, she got very positive about going up to Santa Barbara to this house party and finally talked Ben into it. He didn't seem any too happy, but he did agree to go. I invited Sid Traylor, who was captain of the tennis team, over to spend Friday and Saturday night. He was getting to be a best friend of mine.

That next Monday one of the Los Angeles columnists—I think it was Hedda Hopper—who was also at Santa Barbara for the weekend printed an item about how great my mother was looking, and said the cause of it all was "Ben Nichols, handsome advertising man from New York." That was one of the few times I noticed Ben actually angry about anything. When he came down to dinner on Tuesday he and my mother had definite words. Ben even asked me to leave the room at one point. When I came back after a half hour or so, they were all calmed down. Then a little later he started up again.

My mother hates to be criticized about anything. She'd rather have a man sock her in the jaw (and they have) than to have him criticize her. Actually, in this instance, it wasn't her fault at all. In the first place, as she said, "What's wrong with having your name appear in a newspaper column? They called you handsome, didn't they?" In the second place, she didn't write the column. Finally, things simmered down, but still I could tell Ben was a little upset all evening.

The next day my mother went into town again. When she came home that evening she was doing cartwheels. It had been set; she was going to film the pilot the following Monday, Tuesday, and Wednesday. Then if they sold the series she'd have a guarantee of filming thirty-nine of them at twelve hundred smackers apiece. Boy, we hadn't had such a break in years!

She called up Ben and told him the good news, but he didn't seem to be too tickled about it. I was in the room and heard her say, "What's the matter, dear? You don't sound excited." Then they'd talk some more and she'd ask him again what was the matter.

When she hung up she said, "You know, I don't think Ben wants me to work. Yes, that must be it!" Then she came over and started twirling me around the room. "I've never been so happy, Josh! I'm in love with the most wonderful man in the world, I've already got the most wonderful *son* in the world, and now—a job!" Then she got very serious and took my face in both her hands. "Josh, you've had a horrible childhood—"

"No, I—" I started to interrupt. I got embarrassed when she talked like that. But she didn't give me much of a chance.

"Yes, you have! Oh, yes, you have! You turned out to be an angel anyway. But—it's all going to be different from now on. I promise you! We're going into a new cycle. Oh, Josh, I'm so happy! It doesn't seem right I'm so happy!"

We sure *were* going into a new cycle. Jesus, were we ever!

On Thursday Ben called up to say there was some sort of a crisis over a show his agency was handling and he couldn't make it that weekend. We were both very disappointed, but then my mother was all hopped up about her job and figured she could use the weekend to learn her lines and get all ready for work. That took some of the curse off it.

It was the first weekend, outside of when he went home for Christmas, that Ben hadn't spent with us. "The old house just wasn't the same," as somebody's always saying. But he called up again late Friday evening and about three times on Saturday, so we knew he missed the hell out of us.

I just kind of plotzed around; every once in a while I'd cue my mother. She had a terrific part in this situation comedy series. It was about a sophisticated college professor who'd never been married and finally fell in love and was swept off his feet by this glamorous stage star, played by my mother. They get hitched and she gives up her career to come live in this small college town. The plot was all about her trying to settle down to a different kind of life and about him getting used to being married, let alone to an actress. It was really pretty funny.

Saturday evening one of the authors of the show called up to say they were making some cuts and also putting in some additional lines. He said they'd be ready Sunday afternoon and would my mother like to come over for an early dinner. She told him she couldn't because she had me to take care of, but he invited me, too. I could tell she didn't care to go because she wanted to eat early that night, take a pill, and go to bed so she could get up at six o'clock and be in Hollywood at the studio by seven-thirty. She said she'd just drive over in the afternoon and pick up the script changes. But this writer and his wife only lived in Palos Verdes, which is only a few miles from Paraiso Beach, and they kept insisting they'd have dinner by seven and we could go right home afterward. She finally accepted because, after all, he was one of the authors and she wanted to be in good with the whole group. But when she hung up she said, "Damn-it-all-to-hell!"

About three that next afternoon, Sunday, we were sitting in the living room and I was feeding my mother cue lines when who drives up—Ben! God, we were happy! As soon as they got over hugging and kissing, my mother headed for the phone to cancel the dinner. When Ben found out what she was going to do he told her not to call it off because he had to drive back into town by eight anyhow.

"Oh, Ben, can't you stay here with us?"

"I'd love to, dear, but I've got to get back."

"You can't have a business meeting on Sunday night, can you?"

"You know how these things are, Rita. Lots of this agency business is dealt with over the dinner table."

"Can't it wait until Monday morning, Ben?"

"No, it can't!" he said, almost sharply.

"I'm sorry," my mother said. "It's just that I've got butterflies about tomorrow, dear, and you're so good for me."

51

He smiled then and said, "Oh, fiddle. You'll be sensational and you know it."

"I *don't* know it," she said. "Especially when so much depends on this one episode. If it were just a one-shot I wouldn't worry so."

He jollied her up and told her she'd probably be accepting an Emmy a year from then.

His manner was very strained, though. Usually when he kidded around he was relaxed, but that afternoon he was forcing it like he didn't really believe anything he was saying. And I must say, he looked pooped. Almost like he'd been on a binge or something. Except that he was shaved and clean and well-dressed as usual. But his face and eyes looked pretty haggard and he acted high-strung and jittery. He said it had been one hell of a weekend, filled with all kinds of business crises, and he needed a drink.

"Want to talk about it?" my mother asked, while she was fixing a highball for him.

"Hmn?" he mumbled, like he hadn't heard her. "Oh, looks like we might lose one of our biggest accounts," he added.

"That's a shame, dear! Which one?"

"Christ, does it make any difference?" He'd never spoken that way before. She looked at him like he'd just thrown a chair at her. "I mean do we have to talk about it? I came here to get away from it for a while!" Then he turned to me. "I'm sorry, Josh. Forgive me. It's just that I'm a little overtired and . . ." He got up, walked over to where my mother was standing, took the glass out of her hand, and hugged her, burying his head in her neck. "I love you so much. You know that, don't you?"

She just held him close and nodded slightly.

After a moment he broke away from her, all grins, and said, "I apologize. I'm an ill-tempered, harassed old businessman. Am I forgiven?"

We sat in the living room for about an hour after that, and I never saw him drink so much. I'll bet we fixed his drink about five or six times. But at least he got out of his mood; he almost seemed to be elated after a while.

About five o'clock I went into the kitchen to feed the

dogs and Monkey-Face. After that all three of us took Lord Nelson and Penny for a walk down through the orange and lemon trees to the barbecue area.

We sat around in this large hammock for quite a long time, throwing things for them to chase and talking and laughing.

"Hey, when we get married," I said, "let's see if the Culps won't sell us the dogs and Monkey-Face! Okay?"

"Oh, Josh," my mother said, "they've had them for a long time. They're attached to them. We'll get pets of our own, won't we, Ben?"

"Yes, we will," he answered.

I'd just thrown a rubber ball up against the brick outdoor fireplace; as it bounced back Lord Nelson and Penny both jumped up for it and collided, head-on, in the air. They went ass-over-teakettle. We all laughed.

When the laughter died down Ben had gone off into one of his quiet spells. There he was, gazing off into space with that sad-perplexed look in his eyes. None of us said anything. Even the dogs stopped playing around and settled down by our feet. We must have stayed like that for a full five minutes. It was that time of early evening when most automobile accidents occur. You know, sort of dusky and murky and your eyes play tricks on you. I sat there imagining there were all sorts of cannibals sneaking around in the underbrush, pretending that's why we were being so quiet. Jungle pictures absolutely fracture me. Even the lousy ones.

Finally Ben kind of shivered, and turned to my mother. "It's getting chilly. We better get back up to the house."

As we walked into the living room, Ben said, "I'll have one more drink to toast your job tomorrow!"

My mother hadn't had a thing to drink all weekend, but she joined him on this one.

"If anyone ever deserved a break, it's you, Rita. May this be it!" We all drank to that. I had ginger ale.

It struck me strange the way he said it—like she'd be looking forward to a whole new career. Especially since he'd always said that her new career was going to be marriage. But then I figured that Ben knew she wanted him to be excited for her and was saying what he thought she'd want him to say.

"Oh, dear!" She stood up. "It's ten to six. We'll be late. You sure you can't change your plans and come with us, Ben? I know they wouldn't mind."

"Darling, I've told you—" He started to snap at her again, but he quickly changed his tone, acknowledging it in a look, and said, "I'm sorry, dear. I'd love to but I just can't."

Ben quickly downed his drink and held out the glass to her. I couldn't get over the way he was putting it away. I didn't like to see him drinking like that, but I figured he'd had a rotten time the last couple of days.

I went upstairs to get cleaned up. After I'd been up there a couple of minutes I heard loud voices. I turned off the water which had been running in the bathroom—and they were yelling at one another all right. I went to the door of my bedroom and listened. I couldn't hear what they were saying, but they were having some kind of a fight. That depressed me. It was so unlike the way they always were with each other. Finally, I heard Ben scream out, "Oh, for Christ's sake, Rita, stop it!" Then I didn't hear any more loud voices, so I went about getting ready. About a minute after that, I heard her running up the stairs. As she passed my door I could tell she was sobbing.

When I came downstairs Ben looked up and gave me kind of a half smile, half nod. But he didn't say anything. My mother must have been upstairs about fifteen minutes getting ready, and all that time Ben didn't utter a peep. It wasn't that he'd gone off into one of those special things like he did when we were down at the barbecue pit; he just sat there sort of humming to himself, running his finger around the rim of his glass and staring into the ice cubes. Every so often he'd jiggle them around.

When my mother came downstairs he was fine again. He stood up, threw her a big smile, walked over and took both her hands in his. "You look lovelier than usual—and that's going some!"

"And you're full of the same old stuff," my mother laughed. Then she said to me, "He didn't *kiss* the Blarney Stone, Josh—he *swallowed* it."

"I don't have to be back until around eight," Ben said. "Is permission granted to finish my drink and run up your phone bill before I leave?"

"The place is yours. I still wish you could—" You knew what she was going to say, but then she remembered what kind of a mood he'd been in and cut herself off.

He picked it up, though. "I do, too, dear." There was a pause. "I will walk you to your car, though."

"I suppose I'll have to settle for a good send-off then."

When we got to the car, he gave my mother a long kiss, a real kiss, while I was standing there. They usually didn't do this in front of me. They'd kiss and hold hands, all right, but the kisses would be more or less pecks. This one wasn't a peck. I was holding the door open for my mother. For a moment I thought of leaving it and just walking around and getting in the other side. But that would have been a little obvious, so I just stood there staring at the scuff marks on my shoes.

After she got in the car and I slammed the door, Ben grabbed me and gave me a quick hug, and a pat on the shoulder as I walked away. "Have a good time, Cosmo." Lots of times he'd call me by a different, cuckoo first name. You know, names like Cosmo, Hymie, Bo-Bo, Alphonse, Philias, Throckmorton. Most of the names were ones that you didn't know anyone that actually had them.

My mother started the car up, we all said good-by, and then we began to drive away. We only got about ten or fifteen yards up the driveway when we heard Ben hollering to us. We stopped the car, and he came running up to the driver's side and stuck his head in the window.

"I thought you'd never leave!" he said.

We laughed. She said, "Oh, is that all! We're going to be late, Ben, and I don't know these people that well.'"

"Matter of fact, that's *not* all," Ben said. Then there was a long pause. "You're both very dear to me; you know that, don't you?" He said it more sincerely than I remember anyone saying anything.

She smiled, kissed him quickly on the cheek, and we started to drive off again. Once more we only got a few yards away when we heard him calling "Rita . . . Rita!" She stopped the car again, looked back, and yelled, "What, dear?"

I looked back, too, but Ben just shrugged and let his arms flop down to his sides and stood there staring at her. He looked like a little boy right at the moment. After a few seconds he said, "Nothing. I was going to— Nothing, dear!" Then he clenched both of his fists together and kind of pounded against his legs, "I do love you, Rita. I *really* do!" He said it with such emotion it embarrassed both of us. I could tell. I thought he was almost going to start crying. He lifted one arm, blew her a kiss, turned and walked back down the driveway toward the house.

We drove off. I don't think we said a word all the way to Palos Verdes.

Chapter 8

THIS writer, his wife, and their six kids lived in a crazy stone-type house built right into a hill on about four different levels. His name was Lionel Winden, but it should have been Windbag! I don't know about his writing, but he sure in hell could talk a good game. His wife, too. They were the kind of couple that tell you the same story together. One starts it, then the other chimes in, and it's a contest in rising volume to see who's going to be heard above the other. You could get cross-eyed trying to divide your attention between them. They let all their brats stay in the living room during cocktails, and they were crawling all over each other and you and stepping on any one of the three overbred cocker spaniels that were darting around the furniture growling at one another. The cockers were nervous wrecks.

Mrs. Winden was the type that after each kid, she probably had her toreador pants taken in a little around the waist and seat and her hair dyed another color. It was kind of orange when we met them. She did have a terrific figure and she dressed for it. Every time she bent over to pass us some hors d'oeuvres I expected the seat of those black velvet pants to burst open or one of her breasts to pop out.

We were up to our asses in dips: clam dip, cheese dip, mushroom dip, and the weirdest combination dips you ever heard of. And when you tried each one you had to guess what-all was in it. Then when you didn't guess every ingredient, they'd cackle and honk and Mr. Winden would slap his wife on the ass and she'd say, "Lionel, you *stop* that now!" Then they'd roar some more.

When dinner was served you understood why all the dips. There was *one* casserole dish that had chili beans and pieces of hot dogs in it; you put this on rice. Then a green salad, so sparse that when we'd each taken our first helping there wasn't one lettuce leaf left in the bowl. And chocolate pudding served in an eye-cup for dessert. You understood why Mrs. Winden kept her figure, but you also wondered why the kids didn't have rickets.

When coffee was served, Mr. Winden and my mother went into his study to go over the script changes. Mrs. Winden, having chained the brats in their rooms, came back to the living room where we sat having a contest in clichés.

I was never so happy to leave anyone's house. Not because I was miserable, just so I could have a good laugh. They took us out to the car, where we vowed undying friendship. Then Mr. Winden dropped some *bon mots* about how the show was going to do a lot for all of us. And we drove off, waving and hollering good-bys and carrying on like nuts.

"Mr. and Mrs. Winden," my mother sighed. "Two good reasons for moving into downtown Los Angeles."

We stopped at a hamburger place in Redondo Beach for a cheeseburger and a malted.

While we were driving the rest of the way home I started thinking about Ben. He was really pretty drunk by the time we left, and I wondered if he'd be able to drive all right. As we turned off the highway onto Calle Vista and approached our driveway I almost expected Ben to still be at the house, but his car was gone when we pulled in.

We must have been home by ten-fifteen. My mother kissed me good night and I wished her all kinds of luck—even though I'd be seeing her in the morning. She was going up to study the minor changes she'd been given, take a pill, and get a good night's sleep. I took the dogs out and went to bed myself about eleven-thirty.

I must have gone right off to sleep because the next thing I knew I had a terrific nightmare. I was being buried alive and I was suffocating down in the deep, still earth. They were shoveling dirt on top of me, and at every shovelful the load was getting heavier and heavier. When I felt my chest was finally going to cave in I made a supreme effort to burst out of the ground and found myself sitting bolt upright in bed, sweating like a race horse.

I was surprised to hear noises coming from downstairs. They were very faint, but I could hear people talking quietly. I figured maybe Ben had come back and that he and my mother were in the living room. I looked at the clock. It was ten minutes past one. I was still half asleep, and the sound of people up and about downstairs was so reassuring I forgot about the nightmare and went right off to sleep again.

I got up a little ahead of my mother the next morning at six o'clock and squeezed some orange juice and made coffee for her. When I first woke up I looked in Ben's room, almost expecting to find him there, but the bed hadn't been slept in.

Later, after she came downstairs and we were sitting at the kitchen table, I asked her if Ben had come back after I'd gone to bed.

She was sipping coffee, her eyes glued to the script. "What?" she asked me, without looking up.

"I said did Ben come back last night?"

Then she looked up. "No—what do you mean?" She seemed almost irritated.

"I woke up around one. I thought I heard you talking to someone downstairs."

"Oh, that was the television set," she said. "I took a pill, but I still couldn't get to sleep. So I went downstairs and turned the 'Late Show' on, hoping it would relax me. I turned the volume way down. I'm sorry if it bothered you. Why didn't you yell down to me?"

"Oh, it didn't bother me. I only woke up for a minute."

She started to study her script again. She looked tired and seemed very nervous.

"Didn't you get much sleep?" I asked.

"*Hmn?*" she mumbled.

"Did you get any sleep?"

"Not more than a couple of hours."

I started to ask her if she wanted me to cue her, but before she could even hear what I was going to say she snapped at me, "Josh, can't you see I'm trying to study? Please!"

"I'm sorry," I said, and kept my mouth shut until it was

59

time to see her off. She was still very distracted. She made about three different trips upstairs for odds and ends before she finally got as far as the car. I opened the door for her and said, "Kill 'em stone-cold dead, Mom!"

She turned and gave me a quick hug. "I'll do my best, dear. Oh, and don't pay any attention to me this morning. You know how I get!"

I waved good-by to her as she pulled away. Then I just fooled around until it was time to walk out and catch the school bus.

I really wasn't "with" school too much that day. Because my mother had been so nervous I got nervous for her. I kept thinking about her and wondering if everything was going all right.

There was supposed to be a tennis match with Hermosa High after school, but it started to rain about two o'clock in the afternoon and it was postponed. I went home and de-flea'd the monkey and talked to the maid, Cecelia.

She was all excited about an old boy friend of hers. He was a steward on one of those freighters that takes on a few passengers, and his ship was going to be docked in San Pedro for two days. She asked me if I thought my mother would mind if she took Tuesday and Wednesday off and then came back and worked the weekend instead, so she could see him before he went off to the Orient. I said I didn't think she'd mind a bit. After all, Cecelia really worked for the Culps and we were lucky to have her. They were still paying her.

My mother got home about eight o'clock, happy but dead-tired. She said the filming went great but it was nerve-racking work and asked if Ben had called. Since he hadn't, she put in a call to him at his hotel. But he wasn't in. I told her about Cecelia, and she said of course she could take off.

She didn't even have a cocktail; we had dinner about eight-thirty and she was in bed asleep by ten. I helped Cecelia with the dishes; then she got all ready to drive back into town in this old beat-up car she had. She was all gussied up. I must say she looked very attractive. As she was going out the door I yelled, "Don't do anything I wouldn't do!" at her. I hate expressions as tired as that, but sometimes, with some people, you just know it'll tickle the hell out of them, so you say them anyhow.

"Why, Mr. Josh, shame on you!" She stood in the doorway, cackling like an old hen. I thought I'd have to carry her out to the car. She finally pulled herself together and took off. I let the dogs out after she left. Then I finished my homework, watched a little "terriblevision," as Ben used to call it, and went to bed about midnight.

God, it's amazing how I can tell you now, months later, every minute of that next day. You'd think you'd only remember what happened *after* a catastrophe struck, because then you're actually aware that something world-shaking in your life has occurred that's going to affect you for years. But I can remember every single tiny thing— from when I first woke up—like I have it on home movies.

I can tell you what my mother and I had for breakfast, and the position we sat in, and what we said, and how we said it. My mother beat me downstairs at six that morning and fixed the coffee. I remember her saying, after tasting it and puckering her face all up, "Making good coffee can't be that difficult! It's only water and coffee!" Then she threw it out and made a cup of instant tea. She could drink instant tea, but she hated instant coffee. I don't believe she ever did learn how to make regular coffee that was any good. I had orange juice, a piece of raisin toast with grape jelly, Ralston Wheat-Chex, and a glass of milk.

"Darling, if we shoot overtime tonight, you can rustle yourself up some dinner, can't you?" she said as she went out the door.

On the school bus I sat next to Ralph Brunner who had just transferred from Helena, Montana. I don't think I'd hardly ever spoken to him before. He was about two years younger than I was.

"Can you swim?" he asked me out of a clear blue sky.

"Sure, can't you?"

"Nope, not in the ocean, I can't."

"What do you mean—not in the ocean?"

"I can swim in a pool but not in the ocean."

"Well, if you can swim in a pool you can swim in the

ocean. It's even easier in the ocean, because the salt keeps you up."

"What salt?" he asked me.

"The salt in the water in the ocean."

"Oh ..." He said it like it was news to him that the ocean was made up of salt water.

We just sat there riding along for a while, but it was beginning to gnaw on me that he was under the delusion he could swim in a pool but couldn't swim in the ocean. I decided to set him straight.

"Can you really swim in a pool?" I thought I'd check the essentials before I went off in a cocked hat.

"Sure, I can."

"Then you can swim in the ocean," I said.

"No, I can't. I never even saw the ocean until January."

"Yeah, but that has nothing to do with it."

"Maybe. But I can't swim in it."

"How do you know?" I asked him.

"I've never been *in* it," was his answer.

"Then how do you *know* you can't *swim* in it?"

"I just told you. I've never even been *in* the ocean."

Christ, it was turning into one of your more befuddled conversations and I was getting so mad I could have knocked him off his seat. "Oh, nuts," I mumbled and started looking out the window.

"Do they have sharks?"

"Does who have sharks?" I knew damn well what he meant, but I decided to be specific and drive him crazy.

"Do they have sharks in the ocean?"

"Of course in the ocean. You don't think *they* have sharks in swimming pools." I hit "they" very hard.

"Who's *they*?" he asked.

"How the hell do I know? You were the one that asked if *they* had sharks in the ocean."

He looked at me as if I were the one that was nuts.

Sweet Jesus, what can you do with a dummy like that? By that time we pulled up to the schoolyard and I certainly never talked to him again.

You see! I can remember everything about that day. I had a hamburger with pickles and onion and a chocolate

62

malted for lunch, and a Hershey almond bar. I had that for lunch almost every day—but I usually had a hamburger with pickles and onion and *mustard*. Somehow on a soggy, wet day mustard doesn't appeal to me, so I didn't have any.

It was really grim-looking out. Those California spring fogs by the beach can be pretty miserable. One day you're playing tennis and swimming and your nose is peeling, and the next you'd think you were in London. This was definitely a London day. The tennis match was called off again, so I got home from school about three-thirty. I lit the kindling wood that was still in the fireplace just to cheer the living room up a bit. It was one of those enormous Spanish-type living rooms with beamed ceilings and white walls and a lot of tiled floors and scatter rugs. But on a chilly day the tiles made the room about as cold as a public toilet.

As soon as the fire caught on, the telephone rang.

Chapter 9

"HOUSE of Wax," I answered. I thought it might be Ben. Sometimes I answer the phone with all kinds of repartee anyhow.

"Hello . . . ?" It was a woman; I had succeeded in confusing her. "Hello . . . is this Paraiso Beach 4162?" she asked. She had a husky voice.

"Yes, it is."

"I wonder if you could tell me—is Mr. Nichols there?"

Something intuitive told me to play it extremely cool. I can be an intuitive character at times.

"Mr. Nichols?" I inquired.

"Yes ... Mr. Benjamin Nichols." Funny! I'd never thought of Ben being a Benjamin.

"No, he isn't," I answered, like somebody's top butler.

"Oh, I see . . ." She hung up without as much as a thank-you. Not that I'd actually given her much information, but people usually say thank you.

She sounded like a Ritzy-type secretary, but it was strange because Ben had only received about two phone calls in all the times he'd been down to our place. He made a lot but he never got any.

I went and got Monkey-Face and brought him into the living room by the fire because monkeys catch cold for no reason at all and get pneumonia and die before you know it. The dogs were conked out in this trophy room Mr. Culp kept next to the living room. He had all kinds of antique guns and pistols and swords and keys to a lot of castles and palaces in Europe. He's a collector.

I remember sitting on the hearth, scratching Monkey-Face's belly, when I looked up into the fire and thought, "We're moving toward something today. I don't know what, but I know it's something."

Just about that time the phone rang again. It was the same woman.

"I'm sorry to bother you, but you do *know* Mr. Nichols, don't you?"

"Yes, I've met him," I answered. Met him! That was an understatement. But something kept telling me to be as formal as possible.

"Would you have any idea where to reach Mr. Nichols?"

"No, I wouldn't. Unless you try the Château Marmont. That's where he stays."

"I'm calling from there now." Her voice was about as chilly as the day was. "This *is* Miss Cydney's residence, isn't it?"

"Yes, it is."

"Thank you!" She hung up again.

All of a sudden I was dying for something sweet, so I went into the kitchen with Monkey-Face on my shoulder in search of food. There wasn't anything faintly connected with being sweet in the whole house. There was some bitter chocolate for cooking, but I passed that by.

Then I found a package of Sally Lonsdale's Quick Cake way in the back of a cabinet. It's a kind of a do-it-yourself kit. They've got the cake mix, the instant frosting, and the pan you bake it in, all inside the one box. It's supposed to be so simple there's even a picture on the package of a little girl about six years old whipping the whole thing together. She's so small she's standing on a kitchen chair so she can reach the mixing bowl.

Well, good luck to that little monster on the package. I swear I followed those directions like a paper trail. It looked great when I put it in the oven, but when I took it out it looked like a goddam volcano. All around the edges and sides were completely scorched. In the center the cake had just blown up and cracked down the middle, and there were two lips of uncooked batter curling back on either side. All I can say is it's a good thing Sally Lonsdale wasn't in the immediate vicinity at that moment. The little girl on the package either. As Sid Traylor and I used to say, "Nobody loves a smart-ass, little girl! Pow!"

Of course, my flop with the cake just about drove me

wild for sweets. I got on my bike and rode down to Sepulveda Boulevard to this gas station where they had a vending machine. It must have been close to five when I got back; it was so foggy by this time I almost turned off into our driveway too soon and crashed into a eucalyptus tree. It would be just sort of misty for stretches, but you could see; then all of a sudden you'd come right into a pocket of fog that was so thick it was like gray whipped cream. The phone was ringing when I pulled the bike up to the front door. I just about broke my neck trying to get in the house, down the hall, and across the living room before it stopped. That's one thing: if I get to the phone after it's stopped ringing I can spend hours trying to figure out who the hell was calling.

"Hello, Darling." It was my mother. "How did you make out in the tennis matches?"

"Canceled again. It's so foggy down here you can't see your nose." There's a brilliant cliché. Sometimes I spend hours trying to think up variations on what people say so I can come up with something different. Like, "It's so foggy that—any foggy joke!" But then people look at me like I've lost my mind and say, "Whaaat?" And I have to say, "Skip it." And I hate skipping things before people understand what the heck I'm trying to get at.

"It looks like we're going to be working overtime. I might not get home until eight, dear. So if you're hungry, so ahead and eat."

"No, I'll wait for you."

"All right, dear. Oh, has Ben called?"

I said no, and was just about to tell her about the other phone calls when I heard some guy in the background screaming, "Miss Cydney! Miss Cydney—on the set!" She said good-by in a hurry and hung up. It sounded good to hear them calling, "Miss Cydney—on the set!"

About that time I decided to bleach out a new pair of dungarees Ben had bought me. I went up to the bedroom and brought them back down to the utility room, which was right off the kitchen. It was one of those days where you think of all kinds of things to do that you don't ever want to take time to do on a good day. Or a reading day—it was good for that; but I felt too restless to plop down in a chair and just sit there and read.

These new dungarees were so stiff they could have marched around by themselves. I ran a lot of hot water and put about three quarters of a bottle of bleach in with them. I was up to my elbows, stirring the dungarees around so they wouldn't come out all splotched, when the phone rang again. I answered it in the kitchen, dripping wet, hoping I wouldn't be electrocuted.

"I'd like to speak with Miss Cydney, please!"

"She's not home. She's working today."

"How nice for her!" It was the same woman but her voice had a different tone about it. Not so cold and efficient as it had sounded before, but sort of cocky and belligerent. The way she said "How nice for her!" meant anything but that; I didn't know what to say next, so I didn't say anything.

"Would you tell Mr. Nichols I'd like to speak with him, please?"

I felt like saying, "I told you, Mr. Nichols isn't here." But there was something about her that made me simply say, "Mr. Nichols isn't here."

"Oh, that's right. Mr. Nichols isn't there, is he? And Miss Cydney isn't there either?"

"No, she's working. She'll be home around eight if you want to leave a message." There was definitely something cuckoo about this woman.

"In due time, in due time. She'll get a message in due time!" And she hung up.

I figured it was some woman who had a crush on Ben and was a little bit crazy at the same time. Probably somebody living at the Château Marmont that he'd opened the elevator door for once and she thought she had it made. Boy, when we'd go out someplace every woman watched him like a hawk. It was really head-turning time when he came into a restaurant. With some men, women *sneak* looks; but with Ben they just *looked*; I think they were always trying to figure out which movie star he was.

I went back to stirring the dungarees, but I couldn't help wondering how she got a hold of our number. We weren't listed in the book or in information because it was the Culps' number.

About that time the dogs woke up and joined me in the utility room. Monkey-Face had been perched on the ironing board buffing his fingernails with an old piece of brick that we kept around for that purpose. He was always giving himself a manicure and then holding his hands out in front of him, just like a woman would, as if to say, "Um-hum, not a bad job. Not a bad job at all." Well, Penny and Lord Nelson and Monkey-Face decided to have their regular afternoon game of grab-ass. God, they were a crew when they got started. I mean they loved each other. Those two dogs would let the monkey do anything to them. Sometimes Monkey-Face would get on Penny's back and ride him just like a jockey does a horse. Then he'd get on the Peke's back, and Lord Nelson would sag down in the middle from the weight, but he didn't mind. Then they'd wrestle and Monkey-Face would grab a hold of some pretty delicate spots and pull for dear life, but they'd never bite him or snap at him. They'd kind of chew on him gently. Then they'd start racing around for dear life like they'd all taken fits. They'd just go tearing back and forth from one room to the next, jumping up on top of, and over, chairs and hassocks and sofas.

I got tired of the dungarees and left them to soak so I could lie down on the floor and roll around with the three of them. It always drove the rotten parrot crazy when we'd all play together. And it didn't make sense because if you tried to play with old Chauncey he'd take your finger off. He'd just sit in his cage, which was in a little alcove off the kitchen, lurching back and forth on his perch, screaming his head off. The only thing he could say was, "Are you a Communist?" And he sure in hell said it enough. He'd make anyone confess.

Monkey-Face, Penny, Lord Nelson, and I just lay on the floor rolling around for about a half hour or more and Chauncey was screaming his usual when the phone rang again.

"Hello."

"Put Ben on the phone!" It was her again.

"I told you—"

"I don't want any of that crap! You tell that son-of-a-bitch I want to talk to him and I mean now—this instant, or he'll be goddam sorry!"

"Mr. Nichols isn't—"

"None of that *crap*, I said!" She was really screaming at me by this time. "You tell that bastard to get out from under the bed and get on this phone!"

I didn't know what to say, so I came out with about the dumbest thing in the world. "I think you must have the wrong number." That—after all the times she'd called!

Somehow it struck her very funny; she started roaring with laughter. Then she started coughing and pretty soon she was choking to death, which if she only would, seemed to be a pretty good way to get out of the conversation. I just hung on waiting to hear this "thawump" in case she dropped to the floor, but after several minutes she pulled herself together. And you know what she said?

"You're cute! Who are you, darling?" Well, then it struck me that, of course, she must be pretty drunk. Drunks are always switching from beating the hell out of someone to hugging them to death. She wasn't drunk when she first called, but she must have taken the bottle out pretty soon afterward.

"I'm Miss Cydney's son," I said, like a little gentleman.

"Oh, you poor darling! And what's your name?"

I didn't like the inference one bit, but I gave her a civil answer: "Josh."

"Josh? What a sweet name." All of a sudden she loved me. Then she started in with this very intimate voice. "Listen, Josh, you be a lamb and tell Mr. Nichols to come to the phone. Now will you do that, like a good boy?"

"Honest, I told you ... He isn't here."

"You goddam little pimp! I *know* he's there. And for his information I just got a report that his car was picked up in Paraiso Beach along the highway. So you tell Ben *and* that mother of yours ... All right, look—it's ten past six now! I'll give Ben until seven to call me, and then there's going to be trouble. Trouble for Ben and that slut!" She was screaming again. "If he's off on one of those sneaky toots of his, throw cold water on him. Ten past six. I want a call by seven, and I mean seven! Have you got that?"

"I can't tell him to call because—"

"Seven o'clock!" She hung up. Boy, she was a killer. She was what you call one of your more colorful characters.

The afternoon certainly wasn't lacking for phone calls.

Chapter 10

I WAS really getting curious as to what the hell was going on. I couldn't figure out Ben's car being picked up down at the beach and him not being with us or at his hotel. The more I thought about it the more nervous and worried I became. Not so much for Ben but for my mother. Somehow you always figured Ben could take care of himself.

Right about then Penny started whining and pawing at the kitchen door to go out. So I opened it up and he and Lord Nelson took off down the hill in the fog.

Running along in back of the house was this enormous tiled veranda that led out from the game room. You could also get to it from steps that led down from the kitchen. Beyond that were about three levels of terraced ground planted with flowers, and after that a lawn. The lawn sloped downhill and led to this large grove of citrus trees which had a path down through it that took you to another lawn where there was a big brick fireplace, barbecue pit, a hammock, and lots of outdoor-type furniture. There was also a croquet course down there with flower beds around the sides. Beyond the barbecue area was about another half acre of trees that kind of went downhill to a barn and a little cottage where a gardener used to live. But now the Culps only had a Japanese fellow come around a couple of times a week instead of keeping one full-time. There were either fences or walls around the whole place. It was great for the animals because they had the run of the grounds.

After I let the dogs out I started stirring the dungarees again. I was determined to break those Levis down to where they'd be comfortable to wear.

The next thing I knew Penny was back pawing to get in the kitchen door. I let him in; he had his tail between his legs and was shivering like he'd just come in out of the snow. It wasn't really freezing out, but it was as foggy as I'd ever seen it and kind of raw and certainly damp as hell. I asked Penny where Lord Nelson was—as if he'd tell me.

Pretty soon I could hear the Peke start in to yap. It seemed like he must be down by the far lawn because he had one of those piercing little barks and it sounded distant. Since it was over a hundred and fifty yards from the veranda down through the trees to the barbecue pit, I didn't walk down right then. I stepped outside the kitchen door and called to him. He stopped yapping for a minute, but then he started right in again and I figured why get laryngitis. He thought he was a big game hunter, and I figured he was probably stalking a lizard.

I'd forgotten about Monkey-Face being out of his cage until I heard a tremendous crash that almost made me jump out of my skin. I let out a war whoop, Penny shot out from under the table, and Chauncey started in asking all of us if we were Communists. I looked around and saw this gigantic punch bowl in more pieces than you could count. And there was Monkey-Face jumping up and down way up on top of the highest cabinet in the kitchen where they stored it. He was laughing like a demon. The little son-of-a-bitch had climbed up there and pushed it off.

I couldn't reach him, and he wasn't about to come down. So you know what I did? This daffy streak came over me and I got out a big pot, filled it with water, and put it on the stove with a little salt in it. Then I lit the fire and told Monkey-Face we were going to have boiled monkey for dinner. Isn't it stupid to go to all that trouble when you know an animal doesn't understand a word of what you say? But, you see, I always pretended Monkey-Face was a human being who'd been cursed. He *knew* what I was saying; he just couldn't do anything about it.

So there I was stirring the water in this big pot, telling Monkey-Face he better turn out to be a tender monkey, when the knocker on the front door started banging.

I was sure it was the cuckoo lady I'd been talking to on the phone. I thought of not answering it at all, except that Penny ran up and down the front hall and kept barking so loud I had to shut him up.

Standing outside was about the most gnarled old guy you could ever hope to see. He had a one-piece coverall suit on, a goatee like a billy goat, and a felt hat sprinkled with Willkie buttons. I'm too young to ever remember Willkie, but he must have put out a lot of buttons because every so often you crash up against a batch of them.

"You look like a bright lad," he said. "Any trash, salvage, old furniture, books, papers, magazines, old clothes you'd care to dispense with? No charge for taking them off your hands. No, sir. I cart anything away free. Yes, sir, that I do!"

What a line! Parked behind him was an old wreck of a truck filled with everything, *including* a kitchen sink. On top of all the stuff was a big brass bird cage. I thought of giving him something to put in it—like Chauncey, for instance. A character like that ought to have a crazy old parrot to go along with him.

"Well ... my mother's not home right now," I told him. "Anyway there isn't much around in the way of trash."

"Oh, it doesn't necessarily have to be trash. I'm not particular. May I come in and have a looksee?"

I was dying to let him in because it was such a crazy day. Besides, I liked him automatically. You knew he could probably tell you some wild tales, but you also knew he could con you out of anything once he got in just because you did take to him. I'd probably be helping him dismantle the Culps' grand piano after about a half hour of talking to him.

"It's okay with me," I said, "but my brother's got the measles and the doctor's on his way over for his evening visit." Boy, I could really snatch them out of the air sometimes.

"My, my ... that's a pity. And so we come to the termination of a brief but nonetheless delightful friendship. I bid you good day!" He tipped his felt cap with the Willkie buttons and started to walk toward his truck.

I had the lousy feeling come over me that I'd let him down. I knew I didn't owe him anything, but still I felt like I'd foreclosed his mortgage or something.

"Hey, mister—is any of that stuff in your truck for sale?"

He stopped, turned around, doffed his cap again, and said, "Most definitely. But don't feel obligated to make a purchase, young man. That would distress me." He was a mindreader, that guy.

"I don't feel obligated. I just might find what I've been looking for."

"And what might that be?"

I was hanging myself up; I didn't know what the hell I was looking for. "Well . . . I tell you—something that might bring good luck," I ad-libbed.

"Aha!" He flourished his right arm around in a circle and ended pointing upwards with one finger like Mandrake the Magician. "I think I have exactly what you're looking for!" He went to the back of his truck and let down the gate with me following him. He dug around on the floor among all kinds of boxes and tin cans and jars until he produced a little white box like you'd put a bracelet in, with a rubber band around it. He snapped the rubber band off, flipped the lid open, and thrust it out in front of my face. There were five sets of rattles off rattlesnakes lying in a bed of cotton. They were graduated in size from the biggest down to the smallest, and they were beauties.

"That's it," I said. "Just what I've been looking for— something like that. How much?"

"Ordinarily, I'd be asking two-fifty for the set, but when I spy somebody living in a beautiful house such as this I automatically raise the price to five dollars. I charge according to what the traffic will bear." He stopped and watched carefully for my reaction. I was smiling for all I was worth because all of a sudden it occurred to me how great it was standing there in the fog, dickering over rattlesnake rattles with a real character like him. When he saw me smiling he said, "But then, on the other hand, you're a very special young man, so that brings it back down to two-fifty. Do we have a deal?"

"We have a deal," I answered. I tore up to my bedroom and raided a secret cache I had there, for the proper amount. When I handed him the money he turned over the little white box to me. Then he dug around in the back of the truck for a moment and came up with an old quill pen. "Business is business, but friendship is another thing.

74

Allow me to present you with a small token for the latter's sake." He handed me the pen; the writing end was crushed into a little knob but the long feather was in good shape—blue and green.

I thanked him and he got into his truck. "Once more we come to a parting of the ways." He tipped his cap, and started the thing up.

"Hey, wait a minute. I'll be right back!" I raced into the kitchen, got two cans of beer from the refrigerator, and ran back to the truck.

"Allow me to do likewise," I said. He got a big kick out of this and chuckled his head off. Then he thanked me for my patronage and I watched him drive off into the fog. His old truck clanked and clattered away like it was going to fall apart right in the driveway.

I just stood there for a while making up this story about how that guy was my real father, and he knew damn well who I was when he showed up. He thought of telling me, but when he saw the elegant house I was living in he decided things were okay with me, and he, being a peddler and all, decided to leave things the way they were. That was the only time we'd ever met. I'd never know until he died and willed his truck to me; then I'd find out. When they'd drive the truck up to my house I'd look at it, then up toward the sky, and say, "Gee, Dad, why didn't you tell me? I'd rather know you were a trash peddler and a character than to think you were a madman with a brain tumor." No, the *real* line is, after looking at the truck, "Funny! Now that I look back, I thought there was something 'strange' about the man!"

When I went back into the kitchen to clean up the punch bowl and see if I could catch Monkey-Face, I realized Lord Nelson was still barking. He'd been yapping forever. I looked at the clock. It was six-forty on the nose. Penny was back lying under the kitchen table and Monkey-Face was still up on top of the cabinet, staring off across the room like he had this fantastic decision to arrive at. Chauncey had shut up finally.

The house seemed extraordinarily quiet. Except for the distant sound of Lord Nelson's barking. It seemed to almost have a whimper to it.

I walked out the kitchen door, crossed the veranda, down the steps onto the lawn, and started toward the citrus grove. It was getting pretty dark by this time. The fog was crawling around the bushes and flowers and the trees—yet you couldn't feel the breeze that was making it move. It moved like it had its own secret power. I remember wondering, just as I got to the path that led down through the trees, why they hadn't turned on the foghorn down at the beach.

As I walked down through the citrus grove I tried to stay in the exact middle of the path. Because of the recent rain and the fog every leaf was covered with shimmering drops of water just waiting to be jiggled so they could shower down on you. But it was impossible to avoid brushing up against the branches. Every few steps I'd feel the moisture hit my face and neck. The sound of the drops falling down through the leaves and twigs seemed to be magnified as if I were hearing it through a stethoscope. It was hushed in there among the trees. Hushed and heavy and close and muffled.

Halfway down through the grove I stopped. I can't forget the sensation right then. I had the most terrific impulse to turn around and run back—not to the house—but right on by it to the driveway, out to Calle Vista, then up to Sepulveda Boulevard and away! I actually turned and looked back toward the house, but I couldn't even see to where the trees ended because of the fog.

Somehow there was no choice but to walk on down to where Lord Nelson was. I can't understand to this day how I felt—I didn't know, of course, but I had this unmistakable feeling—that there was something down there. I almost ran the last few yards along the path that led out from the trees onto the lawn and the barbecue area. Lord Nelson's barking was sharp and clear now. But in between the barking I could make out these little whimpers.

When I emerged from the trees the change in light made me squint and look upwards. The fog wasn't quite as thick as it had been in the grove. It was more dusky-like. You could tell it wasn't actually night yet up above the mist. There was almost a nimbus hanging over the open lawn.

Then I looked and saw the Peke about twenty yards away, sitting on the grass, barking toward this old-fashioned swinging hammock that was covered with a dark green awning kind of material with faded yellow stripes. It was covered at the back, top, and the two ends, and was by far the largest piece of garden furniture down there. It was placed facing the brick fireplace with all the other chairs and things centered around it.

It was perpendicular to me as I came out of the trees, and, although I couldn't see in it, I did see an arm hanging down from the end nearest me and the toes of a pair of black shoes pointing out from the far end toward where the dog sat.

I could feel my stomach constrict; in fact, everything inside me tightened.

I called to Lord Nelson, and the sound of my voice didn't belong down there. He stopped barking as soon as I said his name and almost crawled over to where I stood. He paused for only a second, looked up at me, and then slunk right on past me to the path and disappeared into the grove, his tail between his legs.

I looked back toward the hammock, staring at the arm and those black toes for any sign of movement. There was none. In my mind I thought to call out, "Who's there?" but something stopped me. Either my voice refused to come out or I wouldn't let it. I'm not sure which.

I don't know how long I stood there. I felt compelled to walk over to where I could look in that hammock. I felt I was being pulled toward it by some force—almost magnetized. Yet I tried to resist it. Standing there, everything around me seemed to shimmer. And inside my head there was a quivering sensation. Like the chills when you've got a fever. Except they weren't really physical; they were more back behind my nose and eyes and up in my forehead. I don't think I was actually shaking.

Finally, I *made* my legs move me forward. It took a conscious effort on my part to get them to work. If I'd been wearing metal braces my legs couldn't have felt any heavier, any stiffer. I began to walk toward where Lord Nelson had been sitting. For some reason I avoided looking into the hammock until I got to almost the exact same spot.

Then I turned and saw Ben lying there.

He was dressed in the same dark gray suit he'd worn Sunday afternoon, except that his tie was off and his white shirt was open at the neck. His face was straight up, and there was a gaping crimson hole to the right side of his forehead, about at the hairline. A coagulated line of blood stretched from there across his cheek to his mouth and on down to his chin, ending up in a cluster in the crook of his neck.

I was perhaps five yards from the hammock. I stepped closer to within a few feet of where he lay. His eyes were open, staring straight up toward the top of the hammock. He was badly in need of a shave; his chin and the sides of his face were covered with a blue stubble. And then I saw the ants. Lots of tiny little ants were crawling around the hole in his temple and around his nose and mouth.

Christ, they made me see red! I hated those ants at that moment worse than I can remember hating anybody or anything in my whole life. My eyes started to well up, not from shock or sadness, because I guess I was beyond that, but from the reaction to those goddam ants.

I knelt quickly by Ben's shoulder, took the handkerchief from his breast pocket, and brushed the ants away. Instead of getting up, I found myself kneeling there. I was so close to him. I felt the warmth of my breath as it left my mouth. I also sensed that mine was the only warmth; I was getting none back from Ben. I just knelt there and stared at him, taking it all in. I think I knew to take a good look, as if I were photographing it exactly as it was for all time so that my memory in days and weeks and months to come wouldn't distort the way it *actually* was. If I try to recall my emotions or sensations looking back to that exact moment, it's mainly a feeling of having been hypnotized.

Ben's left arm was bent at the elbow and his forearm crossed his chest, the hand resting palm down. His right arm hung down from the hammock; the fingers of his right hand rested, palm up, on the grass. I took hold of his right arm in order to bring it up and place his right hand on his chest, too, but his arm was stiff. The minute I felt it I let go.

I kept watching his face. Although I knew there wouldn't be any reaction, nevertheless I kept waiting for one. After a while it struck me that the look in Ben's eyes was the same as he'd get when he'd go off into one of those quiet spells of his. When I looked at his eyes I could have sworn he was thinking of something. But when I looked at his mouth, it was too set, the lips too thin and cold and expressionless.

I was aware of so much. My senses seemed to be more alert than ever before. It was quiet; it was so quiet that the stillness had a sound and I could *hear* the fog moving slowly. I didn't just *smell* the grass and flowers and trees; their scents penetrated my nostrils so that it almost hurt. I didn't just *feel* the dampness; the wet seemed to touch and hold me all over. And although it was getting darker all the time, everything stood out in sharp, clear focus to my eyes. I get shaky thinking about it now.

When I looked at Ben's eyes, his mouth, the line of blood, even the wound itself, somehow there was no feeling of revulsion, but only a tightening knot of sadness right in the middle of my chest that someone like Ben should be seen like that, in such a state of disarray. God, even like he was he was still one of the most handsome men you'd ever see. To me he looked like Caesar must have looked after he'd been assassinated. There was something noble about him.

I don't know how long I'd been kneeling there when I heard myself saying, "Oh, Ben! Oh, Jesus, Ben!" over and over, softly, like I was almost bawling him out for being dead.

That's the way with Ben—even lying there with a bullet in his head on a goddam, spooky, foggy day like that he wouldn't frighten you. The whole thing would just about *kill* you, but Ben himself, lying there, wouldn't *frighten* you. I mean the reason I let go of his arm wasn't because it was so horrible to touch Ben, but because I had the feeling I'd be forcing him or hurting him.

When something like that happens it's so completely different from the way you'd imagine it being if you thought about it. I was terrified when I stopped halfway down through the trees and felt like running back. And I was scared when I saw his arm and the toes of those black shoes, and when I was walking to where the dog had sat before I really took a good look. But once I looked and found what it was and saw clearly with my eyes—I wasn't scared any more.

And you'd think when you stumbled upon something like that you'd start bumping into yourself coming and going, racing around trying to figure out what the hell to do and who to call and about the police and all—but you didn't. You didn't because you knew that the minute it happened time stopped counting for anything. There was all the time in the world now.

Chapter 11

I FINALLY stood up, but only because my knees were aching and I was feeling cold and shaky. I kept on looking at Ben because I wanted him to blink his eyes and look over at me and tell me it was a joke. I remember thinking then that I'd have to notify someone. I knew at the same time I would call Merwin Saltzman.

Standing there, I saw the gun for the first time; it was on the grass a little under the hammock, right near where Ben's right hand had been touching the ground. It looked familiar; it looked like one of the guns in Mr. Culp's collection. I bent over and did a dumb thing—I picked it up. It was one of Mr. Culp's, a funny-looking, European-type gun, so old I was surprised it had fired at all. I just held it a while; then I put it down on the swing next to Ben's leg.

Those lousy ants were beginning to crawl over Ben's face again, so I decided to go back to the house. I must have been down there twenty minutes by that time. I reached over and touched Ben's shoulder with my hand. "So long, Ben!" I said. I felt that I'd had my own private farewell with him, I guess.

As I started walking up toward the house a screwy thing happened. The minute my back was turned to Ben I got so scared I thought my heart would stop, and after about three steps I broke into a gallop like God-only-knows-what wasn't chasing me. I mean I really crashed into the kitchen, and scared the hell out of the animals. I didn't even realize the phone was ringing until I'd been hanging onto the sink for a while trying to catch my breath.

It was that crazy lady again; the second I heard her voice I hung up.

Lord Nelson was barking outside the kitchen; I'd

slammed the door before he could come along with me, so I opened it up and let him in.

The phone started ringing again but I went upstairs, turning lights on left and right, to my mother's bedroom and got her phone book so I could look up Merwin's number. I waited for the phone to stop ringing—which took about forever—and then I dialed.

"Hello?" Thank God he was in.

"Merwin, this is Josh. Listen—this is kind of an emergency. Can you come right down?"

"What's the matter, sweetie?" He was always calling everybody sweetie.

"You know Ben? Well, I just found him down by the barebecue pit. He shot himself!"

"What?"

I repeated what I'd just said.

"Josh, you're not kidding, are you!" He didn't say it like a question, it was more a fact. I guess he could tell from my voice. I was still out of breath from tearing around.

"No, Merwin. I've just been down there with him."

"Oh, my God! Is he dead?"

"Yes. Can you come right down?"

"Of course. Oh, you poor baby! Where's Mother?"

"She's working on that TV thing. I guess I could find out where to reach her from Jay but I don't think I should call her, do you?"

"No. I'm practically in the car now. Don't call anybody or do anything! Just wait for me!"

"Oh, and Merwin—there are ants all over his face!"

"What?" he asked.

I don't know why I threw that in. "Nothing," I said. "But hurry, will you?"

"I'll be there within forty-five minutes!" He hung up.

The minute I got off the phone I raced around that entire house like a wild man, locking doors—and there were a lot of doors to be locked—and turning on lights. I don't know what or who I was afraid of but I think it must have been everything. I got Penny, Lord Nelson, Monkey-Face, who jumped right into my arms, and I even dragged Chauncey, cage and all, and locked us all in the little bathroom right off the main hallway as you come in the

82

front door. It was a tiny little room that only had a john and a washbowl in it; it didn't even have a tub or shower, so you can imagine how small it was.

The poor animals! They didn't know what the hell was up; it took them about fifteen minutes to calm down in there. Penny kept barking and what with that and Chauncey screaming "Are you a Communist?" in a place that acted like an echo chamber, Monkey-Face got excited and nipped me on the neck. I swatted the monkey; he got hysterical and that made Lord Nelson start yapping. What a crew we must have been! Now that I look back I can see the humor in it, but at the time it was nothing but grim. I finally got a glass from the cabinet, filled it with cold water, and kept dousing the goddam bird until he shut up. And when Chauncey quieted down Penny stopped barking; then I made up with Monkey-Face and finally got the Peke to shut up.

I finally settled down on the floor, one dog on either side of me, the monkey on my shoulder, and the parrot right next to me in his cage. And there the five of us sat, staring at each other like a tree full of owls. In retrospect I can wonder how the hell I ever got the brilliant idea to lock us all in that dumb bathroom, but at the time it seemed like the most logical thing in the world.

After they all quieted down was when I really started getting terrified. I imagined I heard heavy footsteps getting closer and closer; then I heard individual voices like two people were calling to each other across a lake high up in the mountains; then the individual voices turned into crowd noises like a lynch mob.

But worst of all—I got this awful idea that Ben was walking up through the citrus grove with that hole in his head and those ants crawling over his face, and that he'd be going all around the house trying to get in the locked doors. All of a sudden I was afraid of Ben; not when I was down there kneeling right next to him and looking at him and even touching him—but when I was locked in the bathroom with the lights on and all the animals around me and Merwin on his way. It's crazy the way things affect you.

Then I got this impulse to run down and see if Ben was

really there; I got to thinking maybe I'd just had a fit or something and my mind had snapped. I tell you, if those guys in the little white jackets had shown up about that time they wouldn't have had an argument from me. I'd have hollered, "In here, fellas! Here I am!"

After about a half hour you'd have thought Chauncey had been throwing water at *me*; I was wringing wet. I couldn't have been any wetter if I'd swum all the way to Catalina. Every so often I could hear the phone ringing out in the hallway. Once I even imagined someone had picked it up and was talking.

By the time I heard a car driving up outside I was almost out of my mind. The suspense from the time I heard the motor cut off until I heard the door knocker just about finished me. Of course, the dogs started barking like fiends. I almost strangled them shutting them up; but I wasn't going to come out of that bathroom until I knew it was Merwin. I finally beat them into submission, lay down on the floor, and shouted out the crack at the bottom of the door, "Merwin?" I was never so glad to hear anything in my whole life as I was, "Yes, Sweetie." I almost didn't *open* the bathroom door, I almost went *through* it. It was only about ten steps from there down the hall to the front door, and there was Merwin.

After an awful lot of clasping and holding onto one another we went into the living room and sat down. I told him everything that had happened: Ben's visit on Sunday, the last two days, the phone calls from that woman, and how I happened to find Ben. He just sat there taking it all in and shaking his head. When I finished he said, "I better walk down there and have a look." I told him I'd go with him but he said no, I'd been through enough. Actually, I wanted to go down there again, and with Merwin around I wasn't so frightened any more. I guess I still couldn't believe Ben was lying down there the way I'd told it to Merwin.

We walked into the kitchen so I could put Monkey-Face back in his cage. The phone rang.

"I'll get it," Merwin said. "Hello . . . Oh, Rita baby!" He shot me one of your most helpless looks in the world. I wondered what he'd say to her. It turned out he hardly said anything. I couldn't hear what she was saying but I could tell she was almost hysterical. Merwin kept trying to tell her to calm down, but he could hardly get a word in. Finally, he said, "Rita, now promise one thing, sweetie. You won't take a drink. Not one! And you'll get in your car and drive right down here, this minute!"

It seemed like she knew about Ben from the way he was talking, and yet I couldn't figure out how she could because I was the only one that knew outside of Merwin, and Merwin hadn't said a word. She apparently didn't want to come home. She was all set to go someplace else because he was having a helluva time getting her to promise to show up. After a while he said, "Listen, Rita, I have something to tell you about Ben.... No, I can't talk about it over the phone." She was hysterical again. "Yes, I know where he is but I won't tell you until you get here," Merwin said. God, I was confused. I couldn't figure out what she was so wild about. Then he said, "Don't be an ass, sweetie! Get into your car and get back here. Josh and I will be waiting for you!" She kept wanting to know about Ben and he kept saying he wouldn't tell her until she showed up. He really gave her hell; I mean he was talking to her like John Wayne on a mad day instead of Merwin Saltzman. When he hung up he said she was on her way.

Then he told me what she was so upset about. She'd been trying to call Ben because we hadn't heard from him. Finally at the Château Marmont they said that Mr. Nichols wasn't in but that Mrs. Nichols was there. Boy, it seemed like the shit was just never going to stop hitting the fan that day. It was Tuesday, April 4, but it should have been Tuesday, April 1. That crazy lady was his wife! I couldn't believe it.

I got to thinking, if my mother was that upset at finding out about a wife, what would happen when she learned Ben was dead? Merwin said she kept insisting she was going over to the Château Marmont and find out what the hell was up, but he'd convinced her to come home.

"Well, Josh, I'd better go down there. I'd rather you stayed."

"No, I'll come with you."

He looked at me like he was seeing me for the first time. "All right, baby."

It was night by this time, so when we got out on the veranda I switched the lights on there and also turned the floodlights on down by the barbecue pit. It was still foggy but it wasn't nearly as thick as it had been. It was kind of wispy now. I noticed the foghorn was going.

When we got to the citrus grove, I walked ahead of Merwin a couple of steps. It was dark in there. Within a few seconds he reached out and took my hand. "I'm all right," I said, and pulled it away. He reached right out and took it again. "It's for *me*, if you don't mind, sweetie!" That tickled the hell out of me.

But about halfway down the suspense started in. You see, I was sure I'd either taken a nap in the afternoon and had a nightmare, or I'd been hit by a fever, or else I inherited that brain tumor from my father—but I was pretty damn sure Ben wasn't actually lying in that swing. Finally I couldn't stand it any more; I had to get down there and find out. I jerked my hand away from Merwin and ran like a fiend down through the trees, with Merwin yelling "Josh ... Josh, wait for me!"

But as I came out of the grove I could see that arm hanging down, and I knew it hadn't been my imagination. I ran right in front of the hammock and somehow with Ben lying there exactly as I had remembered him I felt safe.

I heard Merwin gasp. I turned and saw him standing right at the end of the path leading out from the trees. He could only see Ben's arm and the shoes sticking out, but that was enough.

"Oh, my God!" Merwin's face was white. Even under the yellow flood-lamps, which made the whole area seem like a movie set, his face was deadly white.

He walked slowly over to where I was standing, looking toward the hammock all the time, like he was in a trance. When he reached my side we stood for what must have been minutes.

After a while my eyes focused on those goddam ants again. I quickly went to Ben, took the handkerchief, which I had left up by his shoulder, and brushed them off as best I could. I really couldn't swat at them the way I wanted to because I couldn't get over the crazy idea that Ben could feel it if I were rough.

"Come on, baby. Let's get out of here!" I looked at Merwin; if anyone ever looked like they were going to take a nose dive, it was him. Merwin sure wanted to make a speedy getaway, and I couldn't blame him.

Except a funny thing happened. When I noticed how scared *he* was, I got calm as a snail. I took a long last look at Ben because I figured this would be the last time I'd see him. Then we started back. Halfway up through the trees I stopped.

"What's the matter?" Merwin asked.

"I don't know," I told him. "Suddenly I got a feeling like we shouldn't leave Ben down there all alone." We just looked at one another. I was sure Merwin felt the same way once I'd mentioned it, but actually there wasn't anything to do unless one of us stayed down there with him. That prospect wasn't too appealing. "What do you think?" I asked him.

He nodded his head. "I know how you feel, baby ... but— Come on, let's go up."

When we got to the house Merwin fixed himself a drink right off the bat. Then we sat in the kitchen and started talking. It wasn't until then that all sorts of questions popped up: Why did he do it? And when? How come he had a wife? What would she do when she found out? What would my *mother* do? Who would we notify? And what the hell had been going on all this time with Ben? Especially the last question. Ben was like such a perfect guy in every way that to have him kill himself and to find out he'd been lying all along and that he had a wife was just about too much to take in one day. In one century even!

It seemed like a bad joke that somebody was bound to make right. But when you tried to figure out *who* could make it right there was only one person—Ben! And you knew that Ben wasn't going to help you any more.

"Do you think we should call the police before Rita gets here?" Merwin's face was still chalk-white.

"I guess so—except I don't think it would be a good idea for her to drive up with a lot of police cars and a hearse piled up in the driveway."

Merwin sat there and thought for a while. "No, she shouldn't have a lot of people around when she finds out. Poor baby! God, I don't know what she'll do!" Boy, he was right. She'd be home in a little while. I was really wondering what was going to happen and how we were going to tell her.

Chapter 12

I WAS anticipating my mother coming home so much I got up about three times to go to the door because I kept thinking I heard a car turning off the main road.

Merwin finally said, "Relax, Josh. You're a bundle of nerves!"

And I was, too. Since coming back up to the house I was really getting ticky. And as soon as you felt yourself getting that way and tried not to be jittery—the worse it got.

"You want to play a game of Chinese checkers?" Now would you ever think I could ask a question like that in the middle of the most unequaled crisis in any of our lives? Merwin looked at me like he couldn't believe what I'd said. Then he started in laughing. I couldn't believe it either, so pretty soon I was laughing. It was nervous laughter but at least it was better than screaming—which is what you felt like doing.

After we settled down, Merwin said, "All right, sweetie, why not?" I got the board out. While we were setting it up the phone rang. I could tell by Merwin's face about the last thing he wanted to do was to answer it, so I picked it up.

It was Ben's wife. I wouldn't even begin to repeat the things she was screaming over the phone. I kept trying to get her attention by saying, "Listen, lady . . . Wait a minute, Mrs. Nichols . . . Hey, wait a minute!"

It was so strange: her calling Ben and my mother and me every name in the book and me knowing her husband was lying down there with a bullet in his head—and not being able to tell her.

Finally I was screaming "Wait a minute!" as loud as she was cursing at me and Merwin was yelling for me to hang up. I did. Then I picked the receiver up, listened for the dial tone, and just let it sit there on the table so she couldn't call us again. Because that whole relationship was getting us absolutely nowhere.

It didn't seem much like Chinese checkers time after that. While we were setting the board up the phone began that awful buzzing sound like it does when you've got the receiver off the hook. I put it under the cushion of one of the chairs, but you could still hear it. Also, the foghorn was sounding off mournfully every few seconds. We just kind of sat there staring at the board until Merwin sighed and said, "It's no good, Josh. I'm not up to it."

"I'm not either," I told him. I packed all the stuff away. Then we started giving vent again to all the questions we each had thought up, none of which were answerable because the whole thing was unbelievable. The more we talked and wondered, the more stunned we got.

Finally, we heard a car pulling up in the driveway. I glanced at the clock. It was twenty-five minutes to nine. Merwin and I looked at each other like a couple of guys that were about to walk the last mile. He gave me a kind of twisted half-smile and patted me on the arm; then the two of us, along with the dogs, walked down the hall and out in the driveway to meet my mother.

She looked beautiful; she still had her make-up on and a very smart tailored suit with a frilly white blouse. She has about the most gorgeous pair of legs you could ask for. They're very thin but they're also very shapely. And this beautiful blue-black hair was all piled up on top of her head some way they'd fixed it at the studio.

We all hugged each other as if she'd been away on a trip around the world or something. Then she asked if "that woman" had been calling up our house. After I said she had, she got very upset and started in hugging me all over again.

Mainly, she wanted to know what Merwin was going to tell her about Ben. He told her to come in and sit down. We all went in the living room.

"Sweetie, why don't you let me fix you a drink first?" Merwin was headed for the service cart. His voice was very unsteady.

"I don't want one! I want to know about Ben! Where is he?"

You wonder about it, when you have to tell someone something as world-shaking as we had to tell her, and you

90

think it's going to be impossible. But somehow, when you get to it ... it comes out very naturally and simply. Later on when you tell it over and over it gets all emotionalized, but when you first give it to someone out of pure necessity—it's almost like a factual newscast. When, where, how! You couldn't get into the why of it yet. Just the fact of its happening was enough to comprehend at first.

And you'd think my mother would start in screaming and crying and go off into shock when you actually told her about Ben being dead. But nothing happened the way you preconceived it in your mind.

I told about the phone calls and letting the dogs out and Lord Nelson's barking and me going down there to get him. Then Merwin took over. All this time she was sitting there stone-still; she hadn't made a sound. When Merwin actually said the words that Ben was lying there, dead—my mother took a deep intake of breath and closed her eyes for what seemed an eternity. I thought she'd never open them again. When she did, she nodded ever so slightly for Merwin to go on. Then he told her the rest.

You see, in a way, I guess the fact of her finding out about Ben's wife earlier was almost good—to cushion the real shock. I can't imagine what she would have done if things were sailing along smoothly with no sign of a hitch and you had to meet her when she came home from work and say, "I've got some bad news. Ben's dead!"

When Merwin finished she came over to me and took me in her arms and held me very tightly for a long time. She wasn't shaking or sobbing or anything—just holding on for dear life.

After a long while, she pushed me away at arms' length, but kept holding onto my arms, and looked kind of searchingly into my face. "How terrible for my poor baby!" she said.

For months after that everyone was looking at me, shaking their heads and either saying "Poor baby ... Poor kid ..." or something like that.

But my mother wasn't crying or anything—not yet.

It's a good thing we hadn't notified anyone yet because there was something for her to take part in. Merwin and she talked about what to do, and as soon as he mentioned

Roy Clymer she got right on the telephone and called the police station. He wasn't there, so she called him at home and told him what had happened. While she was telling it, especially the part about how she'd talked to his wife at the Château Marmont, she started to get very emotional. She was really gasping for breath. I thought for sure she was going to start in crying, but she didn't.

Boy, Captain Clymer was there within fifteen minutes with a couple of cops and the local coroner.

In the meantime Merwin really talked to my mother like a Dutch uncle. He explained that the only way to get through something like this was to look at it as another one of Life's colossal bad jokes and go along with it. That if you started in taking it seriously and wondering what it was really all about, you probably couldn't stand it. She listened to him very calmly and kept on nodding. He said if she wanted him to come and stay with us for a while he would. She said she thought that would be fine. My heart was breaking for her. And she was looking so beautiful I couldn't get over it.

I think that's what kept us from going completely to pieces. I felt sorry for her because I knew how much she loved him and what tough breaks she'd had before; she felt sorry for me because she knew how much I worshiped him and for the experience I went through finding him and everything. Everyone felt so sorry for everyone else that it kind of evened our emotions out and kept us from turning them inward on ourselves.

"Of course," Captain Clymer said, "we don't know the background or any of the details, but it's pretty obvious Ben got himself too involved and couldn't take it any more." Roy Clymer had listened to the whole story. He sat in the living room shaking his head back and forth. "I just never figured Ben to be that kind. Never in a million years," he sighed. "Well, we'll go down, have a look, and get him out of here. I'll notify his wife when I get back to the station."

When I offered to take them down there I thought my mother would have a fit.

"I've been down there twice already," I explained.

"Let him come along if he wants to," Roy said.

She looked at Merwin and then at me. "I don't under-stand you, Josh." As we were walking out on the veranda, I heard her say to Merwin, "A few months ago he was frightened of those blackbirds that swoop around the back yard. Now he says, 'I've been down there twice already!'"

I led the way down through the trees. There was Captain Clymer, who really looked like he'd be some high school basketball coach, definitely a good guy; a movie cop, dumb-looking and even dumber-talking; a for-real cop, crew-cut and college diploma probably; and the coroner, a little round, chubby guy with pink cheeks and a shiny, bald dome except for a little fringe on the sides.

When we got down there, the dumb cop looked at Ben, said, "Stupid bastard!" and started taking flash pictures like some retarded kid who'd been given a Brownie set on Christmas morning. I felt like kicking him in the ass when he said that! He was really a klutz with the camera, too; he practically twisted himself into a pretzel holding the thing at the right angle to take a picture. You had to feel sorry for him though, because you knew he was going absolutely nowhere on the force.

The for-real cop only took one quick look, said "Oh, my God!" and then I don't think he actually looked again. He got very busy walking all over the place, always looking away from the hammock. Finally he took out a little notebook and began writing in it. He tripped about three times on the wire wickets for the croquet course; the last time he took a real header.

But the little coroner was the one. He kept clucking over Ben and going "Tch-tch" and mumbling little phrases like "Right in his prime" or "Fine-looking specimen" or "Pity. It's a pity and a waste and a crime!" Then he'd give out little bits of information like "The beard keeps growing for a while, you know." He was busy as a bird dog. It was like he'd caught a rare giant moth for his collection and, having caught him, was sorry about it one minute and delighted the next.

"Is this where you found the gun?" Roy asked me.

"No, it was on the grass, kind of under the hammock a ways."

"How did it get up there?"

"I picked it up to see if it was one of Mr. Culp's—"

"Never pick up a gun at the scene of a crime, kid!" The dumb cop had to get his two-bits in.

Roy Clymer kind of sighed, "Well, it's okay, really. This kind of weather isn't conducive to lifting fingerprints! *Is* it one of Mr. Culp's guns?"

"Yes," I said, "it's one of the ones he kept in a glass case."

"It's a wonder the thing fired at all."

Then Roy asked me for my story of the afternoon and how I found Ben. Merwin and my mother had told him all the details up at the house. So I told him myself this time. He seemed satisfied that that's the way it was.

With the cops and Roy and the coroner around, Ben didn't seem like Ben any more. It was almost like he was a stranger and someone had said, "Hey, you want to come along with us? We have to go look at a dead guy." I didn't like it. I was glad when they started talking about how to get him out of there.

I pointed out the dirt road that ran along the property right on the other side of the barbecue pit. It would be much quicker to drive down there than to have to carry him all the way up to the house. Also, I figured it would be better for my mother not to be around any of that kind of activity.

The little coroner stayed down there with Ben, and the rest of us walked back to the house. On the way I heard Roy and the dumb cop talking about how this was his first official job as coroner. That's why he was so excited.

We could hear my mother crying almost as soon as we got out of the trees. The lights were on upstairs in her bedroom and I guess the dam had really busted. You sure couldn't blame her; she could say things to Merwin that she wouldn't want to say in front of me. That probably started in getting her hysterical.

Roy winced when he heard her, and the other two kind of hung their heads. It's a good thing the dumb one didn't make a crack. I really would have let him have it. I don't know with what or how, but I would have done *something* drastic.

Roy didn't even come back in the house. He thanked me for my help, said they'd take care of everything, and he'd call us in the morning if there were any details that had to be straightened out. I walked around to the driveway in front of the house with them and stood in the doorway as they drove down around the side road. Then I went into the living room and sat down.

My poor mother was really letting go. I couldn't help hearing little bits and pieces in between crying that she would sort of scream out. It made my blood turn cold. I couldn't stand it after a while; it was like listening in on somebody's confession in church. So I went downstairs to the game room where I couldn't hear anything.

The Culps had the game room fixed up terrifically, but I don't think there's anything as miserable as a terrific game room when there aren't a lot of people in it playing games. After a while I got the impression the slot machines were staring at me, so I went upstairs and got Penny and Lord Nelson and brought them down to keep me company.

I must have sat there for almost forty-five minutes thinking all kinds of gruesome thoughts about what had happened when I heard footsteps upstairs. I was dying for company. I raced up. Merwin was looking for me. He said my mother was better now and she'd be down in a minute. I told him about the police and that Ben was probably gone by now. He was definitely relieved to hear that.

Pretty soon my mother came down. I don't have to tell you what her eyes looked like. She'd changed into a slack suit and she looked about fifty years older than when she'd come home. She was all right coming down the stairs, but as soon as I *asked* her if she was all right she started in crying again. She came over and started hugging and kissing me. Merwin finally had to kind of drag her away because I was starting to go to pieces myself.

Thank God the phone rang! Merwin got it, and you know who it was? Mama Paganelli! It sure shows you the way news gets around. Anyhow, she'd heard about Ben from Roy's wife and said they were getting ready to close up for the night, but if we hadn't eaten anything did we want to come down there and have a bite, that they wouldn't let anyone else in.

It was an offbeat idea to go to a restaurant at a time like that, but if you knew the Paganellis you'd understand why we accepted. Also, you got the feeling that if you stayed in that house for about five more minutes you'd find out you were in purgatory. Because what was there to do but sit around and stare at each other while the world crashed down around our heads?

Mama Paganelli, Mario, her husband, Dolores, their daughter, Joey, the son, and Elena, his wife, were all waiting at the door to greet us. The way they took us in you'd have thought we'd been trapped down one of those mine shafts for at least a year. You never saw such hand shaking, hugging, and carrying on in your life; and, before we even sat down Mama Paganelli was weeping buckets. She had these enormous breasts heaving up and down. I thought they'd come sailing right out through her dress if things got any more violent inside there. She kept hanging onto my mother until I thought she'd smother her.

Well, I don't know how it happened—I guess because she was crying so much and by that time we were numb— but all of a sudden we were laughing at Mama Paganelli. Then pretty soon she was laughing and crying at the same time, and the next thing you knew we were all sitting around and everything was all right. Relatively speaking, that is.

As soon as we settled down, Papa Paganelli turned to Mama Paganelli and asked her what time Ben had been at their place Sunday night. She said she thought it must have been around seven-thirty because he'd left by the time they turned the television set on at eight. We all chimed in asking questions about what he'd been like, what he'd said, and so on. Papa Paganelli said Ben was pretty drunk when he arrived and sat at the bar. He'd had about four or five drinks in a row, made a phone call, and left soon after. Mama Paganelli had asked him about us, and Ben told her we had to go to dinner someplace. Joey, the son, said he was worried about him driving and had tried starting up a conversation with Ben, but he seemed preoccupied and didn't enter into the spirit of kidding around as usual.

We all supposed he'd started to drive back to our house and for some reason left the car on the highway and walked the rest of the way. Then he must have got the gun out, gone down to the lower lawn, and shot himself.

Drinks were being served one after the other. My mother was pouring them down. After a while they brought out all kinds of antipasto, spaghetti with clam sauce, garlic bread and red wine. Before you knew it we were all wolfing it down—even my mother. The last thing you'd think you'd be doing on a night like that would be gorging yourself.

After we'd been there about a half hour Captain Clymer came by with the for-real cop, whose name turned out to be Jerry. Right away we told him Ben had been at the restaurant Sunday, and the Paganellis told their story again. That seemed to clinch it as far as Roy was concerned about his death being suicide. Roy told us Ben's wife had been notified and he was going to meet her in forty-five minutes over at the coroner's. That kind of put a pall on things for a while. But then Merwin started in being very caustic about Ben, and pretty soon he was getting a few laughs. The next thing you knew it had turned into what you'd almost call a party.

You see, the whole situation was so rotten there didn't seem to be any other way to cope with it when you were with a group of people.

I remember Merwin saying at one point, "Inconsiderate son-of-a-bitch!"

"Who?" Roy asked.

"Who? Ben Nichols! If he had to kill himself, at least he could have gone back to his wife. I mean those are the rules of the game—it would seem to me."

Then everyone started giving Ben hell. And yet everyone there who knew Ben had loved him. Of course, everyone but me was drinking, and that loosened them up; but even to me it didn't seem in bad taste, like it does when I tell it now.

There was a lot of serious talk also. Roy told us Ben's car had been picked up Tuesday around noon on Sepulveda Boulevard, and they'd traced the registration to the Château Marmont. That's how his wife knew he was in our vicinity. And the coroner said he'd been dead about forty-eight hours; so he must have come back Sunday night and done it either before we got home or after we'd gone to bed. Roy asked my mother and me if we'd heard anything that sounded like a gunshot or if the dogs had been barking or anything like that.

"No," she answered, "I didn't hear a thing. Did you, Josh?"

"No," I said.

Then I remembered waking up, hearing her downstairs, thinking Ben had come back, and later finding out it was the television set. I didn't mention it because it didn't seem important.

Besides, by that time Roy was telling her that Ben's wife sounded very drunk on the phone and really didn't seem to comprehend what had happened. He'd talked to the management of the hotel and asked them to make sure she got somebody to drive her down to the coroner's. They said they'd arrange it so that she wouldn't drive herself.

Right after Roy and Jerry left, my mother suddenly remembered she was supposed to work the next day. Nobody had thought of that! The Paganellis said to forget it, that nobody would expect her to show up, but Merwin made a big pitch for her to go to work. He said it was lucky she had something to do and for God's sake to go ahead and do it.

She just sat there in kind of a daze while everyone was talking pro and con. Then we realized she was really blind drunk. But very quietly drunk—about ready to pass out. It wasn't only being drunk; it was the combination of being up since early in the morning, the strain connected with filming the show, plus the emotional shock, *and* the drinking that knocked her out. Finally, she kind of mumbled that she *would* go to work. We all but carried her out to the car.

She slept on my shoulder all the way back to the house. It was one o'clock when we got there. Merwin and I put her to bed and set the alarm for seven instead of six-thirty. Then I went to my room; Merwin took a guest room across the hall.

Chapter 13

THE minute my head touched the pillow my brain started whizzing around like one of those UNIVAC machines, trying to sort out all the answers to just what the hell the day had been about. I couldn't begin to tell you what-all I was thinking about; it would be much easier to tell you what I didn't think about. I was thinking so hard I could hear grinding noises inside my head. I started getting dizzy; for a while there I was expecting to fall off the damn bed frothing at the mouth. I just couldn't figure out Ben and my mother, and his wife, and killing yourself, or anything.

Finally, I was just going off into one of those fitful sleeps when the next thing I was aware of was this terrific crash of glass.

"You murdering bitch! Come out here—you murdering bitch!" I recognized the husky voice immediately. It was Ben's wife.

My bedroom overlooked the driveway, so I tore to the window and peeked out between the curtains. God, it was an eerie sight! She was standing in the driveway yelling up toward the second floor where I was—not right at my window, but toward the windows of Merwin's bedroom across the hall from mine. There was a carriage lamp on a post in the driveway down by the front door that we usually left on; that was the only light, and she was standing right near it.

She was quite a bit older than Ben, but you could tell she must have been a very attractive woman in her time. She was a little plump and not too tall, but she had these gorgeous legs just like my mother's. All she had on was a mink coat that was hanging open and a slip and very high-heel shoes. Her face was oval with these great big eyes and arched eyebrows like semicircles above them. Her hair was light brown and quite long, and by this time, disheveled as hell. The light made her look like she didn't have any make-up on at all except she did have more dark red lipstick than anyone you ever saw. She had this very large sensuous mouth. I guess everybody had always told her that was her strong point, so she really slapped the lipstick on. I must say it fitted, though. It didn't look messy or ugly but it sure attracted your attention.

"You destroyed my Ben . . . My poor weak baby . . . You killed my baby . . . !" She was shouting that. Then she put her hands up to her face and held her head and started sort of moaning. Thank God my mother's bedroom was on the other side of the house, facing out over the veranda and citrus grove and the barbecue pit. I decided to go into Merwin's bedroom and see what he was doing.

He was just hanging up the phone when I opened the door. He'd called Captain Clymer, who was coming right over. We both went to his window and knelt down to peek out through the curtains.

She was still holding her head and moaning. "Oh, my God, I saw my poor baby lying there! And he wouldn't talk to me. I tried to talk to him but he wouldn't answer me . . . and I knew he was dead!"

When she said "dead" this tripped something off. She dropped her hands down from her face, snapped her head up, and screamed "Dead?" like she was asking a question. Then she started in screaming again.

"You murdering bitch! You took him away from me and then you *killed* him! My poor, sweet, weak little baby!" She shook her fist up at the window.

Then she staggered right up toward the house so we couldn't see her for a minute or two; but we could hear her trying the door. Thank God the doorbell was out of order. After a while she lurched back into view.

She was extremely drunk; there was no doubt about that. There was something heartbreaking about seeing a well-bred woman faltering around a driveway in a mink coat and slip and her hair all mussed up. You knew she was well-bred, not because she had an expensive mink coat but because, drunk as she was, she had terrific posture. Her back was straight, her shoulders were back, and the way she held her head mostly let you know. She might wobble a lot when she walked, but whenever she'd stand still she'd really take a stance. She'd plant her feet way apart and throw her head back and shake her hair. There was an unmistakable elegance about her.

After a while she started looking toward the flower beds that bordered the driveway, then toward the circular flower bed lined with bricks that was in the center of it.

Pretty soon she went over, bent down, and tried to pry a brick loose, but most of them were cemented together. She was going to start throwing things again! She couldn't get one, though; so she straightened up, looked toward the far side of the drive, which was also planted and lined with bricks, and weaved over there. She bent down and pretty soon came up with a chunk of brick about half the size of her hand.

She was quite a ways from the house. So she staggered back to the little circular flower garden and took one of her stances when she got about even with it. Instead of heaving the brick right away, she raised it up in front of her face and kind of spoke to it.

"He preferred a whore to a drunk . . . my baby did . . ." Then she started asking the brick if a whore wasn't worse than a drunk any day. She started to sob, and we couldn't make out just what the hell she was saying until she suddenly looked up toward right where we were and screamed, "I'll kill you, you filthy whore! You has-been! You whore!"

Boy, she swung her right arm back and threw that brick like she was trying for an Olympic record. It only clonked up against the house. She tossed it so hard, though, she lost her balance and started to stagger forward. She took a couple of quick steps as if to catch up with herself, but this just propelled her even faster and she flew right up in the air and almost dove onto the gravel driveway face down. It was a brutal fall!

Merwin and I both looked away. He clutched my arm so hard I thought he'd draw blood with his fingernails.

When we looked back down, she was lying there completely still with her coat hiked way up on her back and her slip pulled up above her knees. It was enough to turn your stomach.

"Do you think we ought to go down?" I asked Merwin.

"Oh, no, baby! They'll be here in a minute. And she's probably passed out."

I felt like we should go down and help her, but you knew you better not get involved if you could avoid it. And, most of all, you didn't want my mother to have to get in on this.

After a while she began to stir a little. Finally she rolled over on her back; then a little later she pulled herself up into a sitting position. Her knees were all scratched and bloody. There was a raw spot on her chin that must have really stung. She wasn't crying though; she just kind of sat there in a daze rubbing her legs, and every so often she'd put one hand up to her chin. You could hear her whimpering very faintly.

And that's what she was doing when Captain Clymer drove up. He got out of a police car with another cop I hadn't seen before. The cop was in uniform but Roy was just in regular clothes. She didn't pay much attention to them, even when Roy put his arms around her waist and started lifting her; but when he got her on her feet after a lot of hauling and tugging, she threw her arms around his neck. As he picked her up and started to carry her toward the car, she began talking.

"I'm sorry ... Oh, God, I'm so sorry!" she kept saying to him. That was the thing that made me so goddam sad the tears just streamed down my face. She had her head right against his chest. All of a sudden she seemed like some little baby girl that had broken all her toys. It's strange, but even with her calling my mother a whore and a has-been, I felt sorry for her.

And you had to love the Captain, he was so gentle with her. He eased her into the back seat and got in beside her. Then the other cop got in the front seat and they drove around the driveway and out.

I wondered where her car was, but we found out later she'd left it in Hollywood, that she'd been taking cabs all over the place.

Merwin and I kept kneeling there at the window for minutes because the whole experience chilled you so you

102

couldn't move. That's almost the saddest I felt during the whole lousy predicament.

Finally Merwin got up and said, "Not a word about this to your mother!"

"No. But what about that first crash? She must have broken a window downstairs someplace."

"If she doesn't notice it, don't mention it. I'll have it fixed while she's working. Well, baby, better try to get a few winks!"

As we said good night Merwin hugged me. The tears were still coming out but I wasn't sobbing or making any noise until I got into my bed. Then I really let loose. I don't know how long I cried until I finally fell asleep.

Chapter 14

THE next morning we worked at getting up, having breakfast, and facing the day like one of those submarine crews in the old war movies you see on television that have to sneak into a Japanese harbor and blow up a warship. In other words, we were pretty grim.

When my mother came down she was dressed in the suit she was wearing for the television show. On the outside she looked very beautiful and smart; but on the inside you knew she was a mess. Everything she did—it was like she was walking a tightrope. Even just pouring coffee. I mean I had the feeling she might drop the whole pot on the floor or else miss her cup completely and pour it all over the kitchen table. She didn't, actually, but I had the impression that at any minute she might do something extremely erratic.

We didn't talk about any of the big things; we stuck to the essentials of getting through the day: Cecelia would be back in the afternoon, and my mother would leave a note that we'd all be eating in; Merwin would drop me off at school, then go into Hollywood and pick up some clothes and his typewriter; my mother thought they'd finish shooting that day—things like that.

When she was going out the door, she turned around, ran back, and gave me a hug that almost cracked my ribs. And she starting in shaking and trembling, but she wasn't crying or anything.

"Rita, do you want me to drive you in?" Merwin asked her. "I can take care of all my business and pick you up at the studio when you're through."

"No," she said, "I'll be all right. And I'm not sure when I'll be finished. It would just complicate things."

"You sure?"

"Yes, I'm fine. I'm all right!" Then she stopped hugging

me and said, "Josh, you don't have to go to school if you don't want to."

"I'll go. I don't mind." The reason I didn't mind was that I didn't want to be left alone in the house.

"You're positive?"

"Sure," I said.

"You'll be all right, dear?"

"Yep."

"I'm very proud of you!" She hugged me again, then held me away from her and looked right into my eyes. "Very proud of you!" Then she hurried out the door.

That was the first time she'd ever said that, I think. I knew she loved me and all because a mother has to. But she'd never said anything like "I'm very proud of you!" Or, at least if she had, never with that kind of deep down conviction. It carried me through the whole day.

And it was a day that needed carrying through, I can tell you.

When Merwin was driving me to school he said he hadn't mentioned anything to my mother but there would probably be an awful lot of talk going around and all sorts of items in the paper. Boy, that was one of the greater understatements.

When I got to school, a few minutes before classes began, there were all sorts of kids waiting out in front for me. As they say in jungle movies, "The tom-toms must have been going all night!" I don't know how news gets around so fast but it sure does. Especially in a small beach community like that. One freckle-faced guy, Bert Jonas, a freshman, was the first to come up to me. "Hey, Josh, I heard somebody got knocked off at your house. That true?" Isn't that a subtle way of putting it?

Then another guy chimed in, "Yeah, my father said your father killed himself!" I tell you there was more misinformation floating around that school than you could shake a stick at.

Between classes that morning a little cross-eyed girl with pigtails grabbed hold of my sweater and tugged. "Did your mother really shoot her boy friend?"

Ed Mapes, a guy in my English class, said, "Hey, Josh, I

heard you found a dead body!" That was about the most accurate statement I heard all day.

At lunchtime practically every kid in school wanted to eat with me; a lot of them asked if they could *take* me to lunch. And by afternoon I was really getting the feeling that I was the biggest celebrity to hit Paraiso Beach in years. Kids that had never even spoken to me were angling for one position of buddy-buddy.

One day you were nothing at all; the next all of a sudden you were a big hero. And it wasn't because of anything you did—that was the crazy thing. You just happened to walk down in the back yard to get the dog and you found Ben lying there dead. But from the way everyone was acting you'd have thought you'd prevented the next world war or hit the moon or solved the integration problem.

The weather had cleared up that day. At lunchtime it was announced that the tennis match with Hermosa Beach would be held on our courts right after school. Our athletic coach, Ron Duerr, came up to me and said not to worry about playing, that he understood prefectly well. When I told him I thought I *would* play, he couldn't get over it. He kept looking at me and shaking his head and asking me, "Are you sure, Josh?"

The whole school practically stayed to watch me, and I never played so well in my life. I was fourth on the team, but I was the only player that day that won his singles. Then I went on with my partner, Sid Traylor, and we won our doubles match.

But I have to explain. All day long I'd been thinking of my mother and wondering how she was getting along. After all the crap she'd been through in her life—now this! Now Ben and his wife and all his lies and God only knows what else. Consequently, I kept getting madder and madder at Ben, and thinking that he was probably as rotten as all the other guys my mother had gone with. Only he was a genius at hiding it, until he finally pulled the lousy trick of killing himself in our back yard. In a way, I struck back at him by riding on the crest of all the attention I got through his death.

So I guess I was saying to myself, or rather to Ben—that afternoon when I was playing tennis—something like "I'll show you, you son-of-a-bitch in Cary Grant's clothing. If you think I'm going to sit around and cry after the way you let us down—you're nuts! You taught me how to play tennis; well, take a look at this!" Then I'd serve an ace like I was possessed or something. And, Christ, kids that had never even thought about tennis were applauding. The more they'd applaud, the better I'd play. Then I'd get to thinking how crazy it was to be playing tennis at a time like that and I'd get all confused. And the more confused I'd become, the madder I'd get at Ben. By the end of the match I was playing like a demon.

You see, you had to get Ben down off that goddam pedestal or you'd go nuts! You had to believe he was a louse of some kind or a paranoid case or something screwy—or you couldn't stand it. So you played it up big, as if to say "Sure, we knew he was a psychopath but he was kind of fun to watch—for kicks."

It's funny! When Ben was alive he helped me get over being a "sissy"; then his death actually started me on the road toward being the extrovert of all times.

By the time I started playing doubles with Sid Traylor I was hot as a pistol. I was whamming that ball over and taking chances I never would have thought about before. I kept hearing Sid murmuring, "Jeez!" behind me when I was playing up at the net.

Toward about the middle of the second set a couple of cars pulled up next to the tennis courts and several reporters and photographers got out. I could tell they were asking different kids which one was me, but I pretended not to pay any attention. Boy, they started in taking pictures like I was in the finals at Forest Hills.

The minute we won the match they came tearing out on the court and introduced themselves and started in firing questions and taking close-up shots of me. It was right then that Merwin drove his car up next to the fence and came racing over.

"Come on, sweetie, let's get out of here!" He grabbed my arm and we started toward the car.

"Let us talk to the kid for a *minute*," one of the reporters said, grabbing my other arm.

"Let go of him!" Merwin snapped.

They started a tug-of-war with me in the middle. I felt like a wishbone at Thanksgiving. The reporter wasn't about to give up until Merwin let go, ran around me, and gave him one of the smartest kicks in the shin you ever saw. The guy yelped, grabbed his ankle and we raced toward the car with the rest of them in hot pursuit. It was like a scene in a movie with us trying to make a getaway. The reporters and photographers were shouting after us and snapping pictures and the kids around the tennis courts started yelling and whooping and going crazy.

When we drove up to the house there were all kinds of cars parked around the driveway and men and even a few women reporters hanging around. They all started calling to us and converging on us. Just then Jerry, the cop from the night before, came out of the house. With his help we managed to fight our way in and slam the door.

Cecelia was back. As soon as she saw me she started in hugging me and crying and saying, "Poor baby!" After we got her simmered down she said that all hell had been breaking loose. The phone had been ringing, people were trying to get in the house, telegrams had been arriving.

By the time my mother got home from work it was a madhouse, and the evening papers were out featuring all sorts of cute headlines:

STAR'S SON FINDS BODY

PARAISO BEACH TRYST ENDS IN SUICIDE

HARD LUCK GIRL'S LOVER SLAYS SELF

You see, because my mother had had such an on-again, off-again career, and because of this terrific concussion she got from being thrown from a horse when she was making a Western; because of her three ill-starred marriages, her rotten luck with boy friends, and having gotten mixed up in several colossal brawls of theirs in public places—with all of this, plus Ben's death, they started calling her "Rita Cydney, Hard Luck Girl of the Movies."

I don't think I've told you about her other two marriages. The first one was before I was born, when she was very young. I don't know too much about it, but it was right after my mother made her first big splash in pictures. She'd been sent to New York for a big publicity campaign and she met this very attractive guy there. They had a whirlwind courtship and eloped to some place in Maryland. Naturally, the press found out about it and their pictures were plastered all over the papers. They went on a honeymoon to Florida for a week, but the studio insisted my mother get back to New York for the opening of her picture. Well, she and her husband had been at the Plaza Hotel about four days when a knock comes at the door, my mother answers it, and there's a woman standing there with three kids. Yep, the son-of-a-bitch was already married with three kids. He'd upped and left them in Chicago about two years before and never bothered to get a divorce. So that marriage went down the drain in record time. It was annulled. How about that luck? God, my poor mother! She was only about eighteen then. Talk about getting off on the wrong foot!

Then there was my father. At least that lasted a couple of years, mainly because he was away in the service most of the time.

The third marriage took place when I was four, so I don't remember too much about it. Anyhow, she married a director, Sanford Sheldon. He's still around, not a particularly famous director, just a regular run-of-the-mill kind. He'd been going with his script girl for a couple of years but they had a terrific falling out. During that time my mother was working in a picture he was directing. They struck up a romance in record time and eloped one weekend. It lasted about ten months until the old torch started burning. He and the script girl got back together again, and he took off for Mexico and a quickie divorce. That was that. As my mother used to say, "It was short but painful."

I could tell you about a few engagements that blew up in her face, but instead I might as well let you in on what-all we discovered about Ben—not right after I found him, that is, but in the weeks that followed.

First of all, he'd been married to this woman, Ethel

Heisler, for about seventeen years. She'd inherited more money from her father than you could possibly count no matter how much time you had. They used to call him "Midas" Heisler because he couldn't stop making one fortune after another. Apparently no matter what he touched he'd become another millionaire. But never in the way that causes a lot of publicity like a Teaxas oilman or the Fords or Rockefellers. He'd just kind of buy out companies or buy into companies and dabble in real estate and the stock market and so on. But very quietly. By the time he died he really had a potful stashed away. Most of it went to his only child, Ethel.

She was so much in love with Ben that she kept them on a honeymoon for about the first five years, traveling all the hell over the world. She was an alcoholic and very high strung, so Ben never did work at anything because he had his job cut out for him just attempting to keep her straightened out. And she didn't want him to work either; she wanted him available at all times.

And talk about jealousy! From the stories that got around, she practically invented it. We heard they never even had maids or women cooks; they always had houseboys and chefs. So you can imagine how she'd just about hemorrhage at the idea of him working in some office chockful of secretaries and things.

It must have been murder to have been married to Ben and have this big jealousy problem. As far as women were concerned, Ben was a six-foot hunk of catnip.

Another one of her big problems was she couldn't have kids. He'd wanted to adopt some, but if she couldn't have her own I guess she didn't want any. Also, she probably wanted all of his attention; she didn't even want to share him with children.

She'd been in several institutions because she'd go and have these nervous breakdowns every so often. The last time she'd had one it was a blockbuster; she'd been away for over a year. That was when we met Ben.

We found out that Ben had never worked before in his life (except right after he got out of college—soon after that he met up with her). And he wasn't a big shot with that advertising agency either. Her father's brother practically owned it. He was just kind of learning the business because with her away for a while he had time to work at something.

Ben's mother wasn't alive either. When he went back East at Christmastime, he really went back to visit his wife in the sanitarium.

It also came out that Ben had been gambling heavily; he was in debt for about sixty thousand dollars! And, you see, he didn't have a penny of his own money. I mean he came from a good family, but they'd lost it all by the time he grew up.

Some sob sister in one of the papers advanced the theory that he was gambling so he could make money to leave his wife and marry my mother. That was one of the things you couldn't possibly even begin to believe or you'd go right out of your mind. If you thought about Ben lying there with that hole in his head, all damp and soggy, and the ants, and you thought he'd really been *trying* for you—then you'd never get over being sad. You'd probably be sad the rest of your life. You had to tell yourself that gambling was just another one of his crummy vices. You had to hate Ben ... as much as you could.

Chapter 15

MERWIN had to go out and help my mother get past all the reporters when she got home from work. I'm sure they didn't worry about him beating any of them up, but he gave you the feeling he could really cause *some* kind of trouble if he set his mind to it.

She was a nervous wreck, not only because of all the hard work shooting this pilot film but because a lot of reporters tried to get to her at the studio. They had to sneak her out the back way; even so, some of them got on her trail and followed her all the way to Paraiso Beach. When she stopped at a red light one of them hopped out of his car and tried to get in with her, but she pressed that little button down and locked the door. It's a good thing she didn't have the top down.

Captain Clymer came over right after she got home and kind of dispersed the crowd. He didn't look any too happy when he walked into the living room. Pretty soon I was asked to go upstairs for a while so they could talk.

That evening our house was like Grand Central. You never saw so many people coming and going. It's amazing the different types of people that are drawn to a tragedy. Lots of people phoned or came over that you'd never expect to hear from in a time like that; then again, lots of people you expected to be right there you never even got a postcard from. Then there were some that just wanted to get on the band wagon, and a few with this terrific morbid curiosity (I'm a fine one to talk—I'm really an ambulance chaser at heart). There were all kinds, that's for sure.

This one couple, Stella and Ef Hayes, showed up after having been on radio silence for months. Of course, my mother would never call Stella when she was going with anyone that was anywhere near a whole man because Stella was practically a registered nymphomaniac. She talked the strongest game of sex in the business. She'd never met Ben, and it's a damn good thing because she'd have eaten him up like one of those deadly piranhas from Brazil. I've even see her make passes at *Merwin*, who once said about her, "She's the most completely functional female in captivity. There might be some of the species to equal her in the heretofore unexplored regions of the world—remote jungles, swamps, and deserts, but I somehow doubt it." He used to call her "the Vestal Virgin" just for the hell of it.

She even came right into the bathroom once when we lived on Roxbury Drive while I was taking a bath. "Don't mind me, lambchop," she said. With that she pulled down her panties or whatever she was wearing, pulled up her skirt, and sat down on the john. She kind of did it all in one motion so you didn't actually see anything. Anyhow, I was so nervous and I got so busy splashing around, it's a wonder I didn't drown myself right there in the goddam tub. Then, when she got through, she insisted on scrubbing my back. She kept on dropping the soap; then she'd play "submarine" under the water, looking for it. She finally realized I was getting so squirmy I was about ready to break out in shingles, and she left, saying, "I'll give you five more years and then it's open season. Only don't get any more gorgeous or I might not be able to stand it. *Grrr!*" She was always growling at men. But I was only thirteen years old then.

Stella looked like the kind of gal that's always playing the "other woman" in plays. Not really beautiful, you know, but very chic, and well-groomed, and snappy. And, most of all, a very sharp tongue; to say her speech was risqué was putting it mildly. But Ef, her husband, didn't seem to mind her talk. He was a little, wizened-up guy with very thin hair. And she was what you call "a real hunk of woman." Sometimes, when they'd be introduced, people would look a little surprised at them being man and wife, because they were one of your more incongruous couples. But Stella'd say, "Don't judge a book . . ." Then he'd grin this sly little grin and she'd elbow him and laugh this whisky laugh of hers. I mean they obviously have something going there.

Anyway, by the time I came downstairs, after they'd all

had a conference, you could tell there was a definite pall over the group. Stella and Ef were slugging it down by that time. Pretty soon other people began arriving. There must have been about twelve for dinner that night: Jay Savage; Roy Clymer and Jeanette; Stella and Ef; Thor Tanner, who'd directed the pilot film my mother had just finished, and his wife, Effie; and Lee Hertzig, the smart-ass lawyer that left us on the pier the night we met Ben. Only his attitude toward me was really changing; he was treating me like a prince all of a sudden.

Honest to God, I think the best way to win friends and influence people is to find a dead body in your back yard.

The phone was going all the time, but about the only call my mother took was when my Aunt Lilly and Uncle Al called up from Elliston. My aunt was hysterical, because they'd heard one radio broadcast where they got the whole story mixed up and said my mother had shot her lover. My mother got on the phone and talked to them forever, telling them what really happened. Then Merwin took over and calmed them down some more. After that my aunt asked to speak to me.

"Hello, darling! They said you found the body!"

"Yes, I did."

"Oh, my poor little Josh!" My aunt's a sweetheart. She went on for minutes about was I all right and how was I feeling and so on. Then she really killed me.

"Listen, Josh . . . now just answer this yes or no. I know Rita doesn't want to upset me but what is a family for anyhow? Isn't that right?"

"Yes, Aunt Lilly."

"Now I *know* Rita and I *love* her . . . You know that, don't you, Josh?"

"Yes, Aunt Lilly."

"Of course, I do. Your Uncle Al pretends he feels differently at times but his bark is worse than his bite. Isn't that right, Josh?"

"Yes, Aunt Lilly." I was beginning to sound like a broken record.

"I mean actually he's very fond of her even if he doesn't show it all the time. And he'd certainly want to stand by and help at a time like this! Wouldn't you, Al?" I heard her ask him on the other end. And I heard his reply, "Oh, for Chrissake, Lilly, stop all that crap and get to the point!"

I knew what the point would probably be, and it was tickling the hell out of me.

"Did you hear that, Josh? See what I mean? Al's worse than ever!" He started in to say something but she cut right in with "All right, all right—if you'll be quiet for a minute, I'll ask him!"

"What is it, Aunt Lilly?"

"Well, dear, as I said ... I know Rita doesn't want to worry us. And if I weren't prepared to stick by her through thick and thin I wouldn't ask, but ..."

"Yes?"

"Well ... all right, then! I'm not saying she would have done it on *purpose*, you understand ... but— Well, it could have been an accident. Maybe he hit her or something. So did she— And you can tell me because your uncle and I think we should know the truth. But we won't say a word to anyone back here in Elliston. You know we wouldn't do that. But—*did* she shoot him? Just answer yes or no! Because if she did, I'll come right out there and stand by her."

"No, Aunt Lilly!" I said.

"Josh, you can tell me the truth."

"I swear."

"On your word of honor now. Remember, I'm her sister!"

"Scout's honor!" I wasn't even a Scout but "Scout's honor" was always good to throw at grownups.

"Well . . . all right. But, listen, if you change your mind—call us back when you can talk. You know the number?"

"I won't have to call, Aunt Lilly. Honestly!"

"If you say so. But I mean it. I'd come right out there on the next plane. The business is still going downhill because your uncle won't ever go to the plant, but that wouldn't—"

"Oh, Lilly, stop all the shit and—" Uncle Al can be a very basic guy when he wants to.

"I'll bet Josh could hear that! Can you hear your Uncle Al and all his refined talk?"

"Kind of."

"See?" she said to him. "He can hear you all the way out in California with all that dirty—" Then he must have started to come toward her because I heard her say, "All right, all right—take it!" Then she quickly said, "Good-by dear. Love to Mother. Here's Al. He wants to say hello!"

"Good-by Josh," he said. "If there's anything we can do let us know!"

"I will. Thanks, Uncle Al!"

"Okay. Good-by."

As soon as I hung up the phone, my mother turned to me and said, "I'll bet a dollar Lilly thinks I did it!" I didn't say yes or no, but she could tell by the expression on my face because I couldn't help smiling. The next thing you know we were all laughing our heads off.

Dinner was buffet style. And right after everyone had settled down in the living room with their plates and all, we heard this terrific commotion in the kitchen and this batty woman rushed in followed by Cecelia.

"Rita Cydney, come to the Temple of Dynamic Repentance and redeem your soul! Drown your sins in the baptismal font! Give up your life of seduction and join God in everlasting life! Cast down liquor, cigarettes, and fornication!" Boy, she was a powerhouse—a little, scrawny, old birdlike woman in a dusty black dress that had no shape at all and long gray hair that hung down to the middle of her back. And beady eyes, like a vulture. But she had a voice that was a combination of Andy Devine and Paul Robeson. You wondered where it came from.

"Miss Cydney, she just bust in the pantry door and right through the kitchen!" Cecelia reached out and grabbed her by the arm. "Now you come on out of here and quit botherin' folks!"

The woman snapped her arm away from Cecelia, wheeled around and shouted, "Unhand me, savage!"

That did it. Cecelia flew at this mass of gray hair shrieking, "Why you psalm-singin' bitch!" And they were off and away. You never saw such a hair-pulling contest. It took Roy Clymer, Merwin, and Lee Hertzig to pull them apart.

They finally threw the woman out while she kept on screaming that the end of the world was right around the corner and how we were all going to fry in hell.

My mother laughed it off, said to forget about it, and went up to her bedroom and got Cecelia a Miltown. Then she took her out in the kitchen to calm her down.

Captain Clymer called up and ordered a couple of cops to stay out by the entrance to the driveway and keep all the nuts away so we could eat in peace.

We finally settled down to dinner. About halfway through Merwin got up and went out to the kitchen; about ten minutes later he came tearing back in the living room and gave a great imitation of this religious fanatic. He'd put on this old flowered wrapper that Cecelia used to work around the house in, a big straw hat with a lot of wax cherries hanging off it on one side, and he carried one of those big bags that women keep their knitting stuff in. He raved and shouted and made up all kinds of things like going to hell on the American or European plan. With one you got orange juice, coffee, and toast every morning. But Merwin said there was no guarantee that the juice wouldn't be boiling and the toast would undoubtedly be burned to a crisp. "The only saving grace is the coffee, which is always piping hot and really quite tasty!"

Then he picked up a tray from the sideboard and started marching around the room banging on it and singing, "Throw a nickel on the drum, save another drunken bum!" And before you knew it, everyone in the room was up and marching around snake-fashion, singing and shouting hallelujah and laughing and scratching.

That's what we were doing when the Assistant District Attorney from Los Angeles walked in. We were just starting to cross the hall and troop into the dining room so we could circle the big table in there. Merwin had gone into something he made up on the spot called the "Hallelujah Cha-cha-cha," but it was really more like a conga line. I was about in the middle of crossing the hall when I saw two local cops standing right inside the front door with this middle-aged guy in civilian clothes between them. They had about the most agonized looks on their faces I've ever

117

seen. And the civilian guy was just planted there with his arms crossed and one of your more hatchetlike faces.

The director's wife yelled, "Come on, kids, get saved!" Someone else shouted, "Don't be party poops!" But leave it to Stella! She looked right at the guy in the middle and said, "Come on, honey. Hop on the line and work off some of that potbelly!"

Unfortunately, Captain Clymer was on the end of the line; he was the only one that knew that the guy *was* the Assistant D.A. I don't have to add that the party came to a screaming halt when Roy reached the hallway. He started clapping his hands together, coughing, and trying to get everyone else to stop. Right away he started introducing the D.A. around so everyone would realize who the hell he was and knock off. Roy's face was crimson. When he got around to introducing Merwin, standing there in Cecelia's wrapper with that cuckoo hat on, he just gave up and said, "Oh, well . . . Hell!"

The Assistant D.A., whose name was Elton Rutger, gave us all what is called a "scorching look" and said: "Maybe I've got the wrong information but I was under the impression somebody died around here yesterday. This is 308 Calle Vista, isn't it?" He was a charmer. Then he turned to Captain Clymer. "Captain, you do a mean conga . . . if that's what that was!"

You never heard so much hollow laughter in your life.

"I hate to break up the festivities, but I'd like to have a little talk with Miss Cydney and you, Captain, if you don't mind."

You never saw such an exodus into thin air. You heard this great starting-up of motors in the driveway and they were off. It sounded like the Indianapolis Speedway. The only ones who stayed were my mother, Roy, and Lee Hertzig.

I was sent up to bed along with Merwin, who exiled himself for the rest of the evening and wouldn't leave the upstairs part of the house. It's about the only time I ever saw him really embarrassed.

It seemed like a good idea to get to sleep early, but it wasn't that easy. The phone kept ringing, and every so often a car would pull up in the driveway. My curiosity was killing me. I mean I couldn't help wondering about the Assistant D.A., and Lee Hertzig, who, in spite of being an old friend of my mother's, was a well-known criminal lawyer, too.

There's another thing that kept me from falling asleep. Every time I'd close my eyes I'd see Ben lying there in that hammock. So naturally I'd open them again. I've always been a heavy reader, but the next month or so after I found Ben I'd read every night until my eyes were aching and I was practically knocked out from lack of sleep. Then I'd just about pass out with the lights on. I'm glad I wasn't any younger and also that I'm practically six feet tall. It probably would have stunted my growth. Even to this day that picture of Ben will sometimes flash in front of me just as I'm about to drop off to sleep.

Chapter 16

WHEN I came downstairs Thursday morning Cecelia was the only other person stirring. "Folks up and around until almost three-thirty in the mornin'," she said.

I figured my mother wouldn't be up until much later and the same with Merwin because he probably waited until the D.A. left to find out what was going on. After breakfast I walked out to get the school bus. There was a police car parked right near the entrance to our driveway.

As I passed the car one of the cops leaned out the window and said, "You Miss Cydney's son?"

"Yes."

"Where are you going so early?"

"To school."

"Oh . . . Oh, yeah. . . ." He said it like it was a big discovery that kids went to school. "Okay, go ahead." They were acting like they owned the place. I wanted to ask them what *they* were up to, but you hardly ever get any satisfaction asking cops questions.

If I was a celebrity at school the day before, I was really President Eisenhower on Thursday. Everybody and their uncle was crowding around me. And the ones that didn't crowd around stared.

I'd really got my tongue back from the cat, as far as talking to my mother and Ben and Merwin and people I knew fairly well were concerned. But as for communicating with kids my own age—I hadn't quite mastered that. Until around this time.

For once in my life I had something that everybody wanted to hear about. It's a great feeling to experience. You didn't have that awful nervousness way down inside of you about saying the right things because you knew that, at last, whatever you said—people were interested. When people *care* about listening to you and what you've got to say— Well, you can't beat that feeling. And finding Ben was my own private experience. Gruesome as it was it belonged completely to me. I wasn't just tagging along or reporting it secondhand. And whether people liked me or disliked me or didn't have any opinion, they all wanted to hear about it. If I pretended I didn't enjoy that, I'd be a liar.

During recess, around ten o'clock, this girl, Josianne Tucker, came up to me. "Josh, I've been meaning to ask you—could you come to my birthday party? My parents and I would love it if you could."

Meaning to ask me! She'd never spoken to me in her life before. I don't think she'd even said "Hi" in the hallways like most kids do. She had her nose so far up in the air it's a wonder she wasn't always hobbling around with her leg in a cast from falling down steps and things.

But she was pretty. Not pretty, beautiful! She had this white, white skin and this black, black hair that she wore in a pony tail. And I'm such a sucker for pony tails it's almost pitiful. Her eyes were almost purple.

But do you know what I said to her? I pulled myself up to my full height and said, "I'd be delighted to attend, but I don't believe we've been introduced!"

You see what I mean? I never would have come out and said anything like that until around this time. But you see what a little confidence will do for you? I would have *thought* it but I never would have come out with it.

She looked at me like I was nuts. Then she started laughing and said, "Oh, Josh! Don't be silly! It's Saturday night at six o'clock for dinner and madness!" She started to walk away, kind of swivel-hipped; then she turned and said, "Oh, by the way, we're in the book." Boy, she was way ahead of her years, that one.

I had this one miserable teacher, Hannah Erber, for English. We hated one another. I hated her because she hated me; but I don't know what *her* problem was. She was always snapping "Speak up, speak up!" at me when I'd have to read aloud or answer a question. Of course, I was the prize mumbler of the world. But all of a sudden after I found Ben she was treating me with a little more respect. Then again, I was starting to speak up. So I don't know which came first. But that day, at one point, she said, "I didn't quite catch that, Josh," in a very mild voice.

The funniest thing that happened that day was when I went to the john at noontime and this guy, Ed Sargent, who'd been a sophomore for two years and was seventeen, came up and stood next to me at the next urinal. I'd never spoken to him much because he had a regular job at a garage after school and drove his own jalopy and treated all the other kids like—well, like kids. In spite of the fact that he had a brain the size of a pea.

He had a great opening remark. He turned to me after a few seconds and said, "Hey, Josh—you ever kill a cat?"

"What?" I asked him.

"Did you ever kill a cat with your bare hands?"

"No, I don't like to get them dirty. I've got a special little gas chamber for killing cats." Of course, I was kidding, but Ed Sargent went right along with it.

"No kidding? Where'd you get it?" he asked.

"I made it myself."

"How many cats have you killed?"

"Oh, God, I don't know. Probably a couple of dozen."

"Hey, that's great! I killed two with my bare hands once."

"Terrific!" I said.

"Yeah, I hate cats. I sure would like to see your gas chamber sometime."

"Okay, I'll even let you try it out."

"What do you mean?" he asked me, like he was catching on.

"I mean I'll let you drop the pellets on some cats," I added.

"No kidding?" He got a great kick out of that and started laughing this simple-tit laugh of his. When he calmed down he started in frowning because I'd aced him on the cat deal. His next remark really killed me. "Hey, can you come?"

"Come where?" I asked him.

"*Come*! You know."

"Oh, *that*! Yes, of course," I said. Then it dawned on me that the poor dope figured if he couldn't find a dead body he'd at least outdo me at something. That's why this line of questioning.

"Four times in one afternoon?" he asked me.

"I thought for a minute. I felt like saying, "No wonder you're retarded. It's probably affecting your brain—such as it is." But you couldn't say anything like that. Besides, he was a mammoth guy. I decided to let him win or God knows what he'd ask me next. So I said, "Nope, only three times."

By that time he was finished; he just gave me what he imagined to be this terrifically superior look, which actually came across as moronic, zipped up his fly, and walked away. Now what's going to happen to a guy like that? He'll probably hang out his shingle after a while—"Ed Sargent, Cat Killer!"

About an hour before school was to let out a note arrived saying for me to go to the principal's office. When I got there Merwin was waiting for me, and it was all arranged for me to leave with him.

"How come I'm going home early?" I asked him as we left.

"Captain Mansan, from the District Attorney's Office, is coming down later. They want to go over the details before he arrives." Merwin didn't seem any too happy.

"Who's *they*?" I asked him.

"Roy Clymer, Lee Hertzig, and your mother."

When I got in the car I saw the afternoon papers stacked on the front seat. By this time the headlines and sub-headlines had changed for the worse. Things like:

WIFE DENIES HUSBAND'S SUICIDE

PROBE MYSTERY DEATH IN STAR'S YARD

NO SUICIDE, SAYS MATE

They were really playing it up big.

"Looks kind of spooky," I said to Merwin.

"Hmn?" Merwin was way off somewhere.

"I said it looks kind of spooky, doesn't it?"

123

"Oh . . . No, not really They're just filling up space with a hot story. It'll blow over in a few days."

I looked at Merwin. He was driving like we were going to a funeral. "What do you look so worried about then?" I asked him.

"I'm not worried, Josh. It's just a royal pain in the ass, that's all!" If that's what it was, it turned out to be the biggest pain in the ass I've ever heard of.

There was a different set of cops outside the driveway when we turned into it, and a few other cars. Merwin had to slow up to get the cops' okay to drive up to the house. While he did that, a couple of photographers popped out from nowhere and started snapping pictures of us. They looked like nice guys, so I waved to them. That seemed to break Merwin's mood and he began laughing.

"You're getting to be a regular ham," he said.

We were both laughing as we walked into the living room, but it didn't last long. My mother, Lee, and Roy Clymer were looking like they'd just found Ben all over again. We sat right down and got to the business of the day. But not until she'd hugged and kissed me about a dozen times. For weeks afterward, every time I'd come home from school or even in from the back yard, she'd hug me like I'd been up to the North Pole for about six months. When you lose someone I guess you hold onto whoever's left like a fiend.

Lee Hertzig did most of the talking. "Now, Josh, there's nothing to worry about. This afternoon some men from the District Attorney's office will be coming down here. All you have to do is tell them about how you found Ben and answer any questions they ask."

It's funny, but I was getting to like Lee. When you just knew him personally you didn't much care for him, but when you saw him involved in the business of being a lawyer he was a different person. I guess before I was always exposed to him after a hot day in court or in his office when he was trying to let off steam, and he probably didn't want to kid around. Then again, he wasn't treating me so much like a kid any more; he was treating me like an important witness.

We went over the whole thing about the last time we saw Ben and how funny he acted. My mother told it, mainly, and then she'd look at me for confirmation. She never said they had an argument, though. She said that he was nervous and irritable and worried. She did tell about how he snapped at her when she asked if he wanted to talk about why he was so upset.

But she didn't mention the fight they had when I was upstairs in my room getting dressed. I figured it might have been very personal, so I never brought it up either.

After she got through talking Lee stressed the fact that Ben had never told us he was married and how my mother didn't find out until *after* he was dead that he did have a wife. That seemed to be the most important point. We also went over the whole business of the two days before Ben was discovered and then, last of all, the day I found him.

"If that son-of-a-bitch had only left a note!" Lee smacked his fist into the palm of his hand. "That's the least he could have done!" Lee was terribly upset about there being no note. They all spoke about why Ben hadn't, or if he had, where he would have left it. From the way they talked they'd torn the place apart that day searching for one.

After a while they said they had some other things to talk over and I could go up to my room or down to the game room or wherever I wanted. What I wanted to do was stay and listen, but I realized that was out of the question. What I didn't want to do was go down to the game room. It was the one place in the house I associated most with Ben. We'd all spent so many evenings in that room together. And the way I was feeling about Ben now I didn't want to be put in the position of sitting down there alone with my thoughts making it some kind of a shrine to him.

I decided to go out in the kitchen and talk to Cecelia. As I left the room I heard Lee say to my mother, "Josh is holding up surprisingly well. He's turning out to be quite a boy!" That made me feel good. He was bragging about me now; a couple of months before he'd have sold me to the gypsies any old day.

Cecelia was peeling potatoes when I walked into the

125

kitchen, but you'd have thought she was peeling onions. The minute she saw me she started in crying.

"Mr. Nichols was the nicest man I ever did meet and he and your mother were so much in love . . . everything seemed perfect."

I walked over and put my arm on her shoulder. She looked up at me, her eyes all full of tears. "And you—poor little angel, have to go down there and find him like that! If you and Miss Rita weren't such fine folks I wouldn't set foot in this house again. I swear it! I don't know what the Lord's thinkin' about when he allows goin's on like this."

I stayed with Cecelia in the kitchen until the men from the District Attorney's office arrived.

Chapter 17

AFTER the law had talked to my mother for over an hour and a half they asked to see me. One thing—when you talked to them there was never anyone else around. They never talked to my mother when I was there, and they never talked to me when she was in the same room. I guess they were always trying to cross somebody up.

For some reason it was decided that my session would be held down in the game room. Somehow the idea of going down there with them didn't bother me. They were all kind of nondescript-looking. I mean you wouldn't recognize them if you saw them on the street the next day. Until you got through *talking* to them. Then you sure-in-the-hell would.

"Now, son, we're going to ask you some simple questions, and we want you to tell us the truth." Captain Mansan motioned for me to sit down.

"What do you want to know?" I asked.

"Tell us about the last time you saw Ben Nichols and the two days following, up until and including the time you found him."

I began telling them about when Ben arrived on Sunday and how upset and nervous he was and about all the drinking he was doing.

Your mother and he were fighting that afternoon, weren't they?"

"No," I said.

The Captain got this sly look on his face. "Come now, son! Your mother just told us he swore at her several times and raised his voice. How do you account for that?"

"Well, yes . . . he was irritable but only because he'd had a bad weekend in town, he said. But they didn't *fight*, and he apologized right after he swore."

Then, all of a sudden, I wondered if my mother had told

them about the argument they'd had, whatever it was about, when I was upstairs getting dressed. I sure wasn't going to tell them I went to the door when I heard Ben shouting and tried to listen. You see, even when a person's innocent you find yourself avoiding telling every little detail, especially under pressure.

But the Captain didn't mention anything about it. He did ask if they were ever alone that afternoon and I answered, "Only when I tore upstairs to change my shirt before we went out to dinner." I made it seem like a much quicker trip than it actually was. He just nodded when I said that; he didn't question me further on that point.

I went on to stress how Ben wouldn't let us get out of the driveway because he kept telling us how much he loved us. Then I got mad at having to tell things like that to those three guys. Nothing seemed personal any more. After talking to them for a while you wouldn't be surprised if they asked to see your b.m. chart.

I told them about going to dinner and coming home early. They were very interested in about who went to bed, at what time, and in what order.

"My mother went right upstairs. She'd been given some changes in her script. She wanted to look them over and get to sleep early so she'd be on her toes when she went to work the next morning."

Captain Mansan asked, "And there were no phone calls that night? No late night visitors?"

"No."

"Nothing unusual? No commotions? The dogs didn't bark? You didn't hear anything that sounded like a shot?"

"No. I took the dogs out for a while and then went upstairs to bed myself."

"About what time was that?"

"Between eleven and eleven-thirty."

"And by that time your mother was in bed?"

"Yes." Then I thought about waking up later and hearing her downstairs. "Yes, I guess so," I added.

"What do you mean—you *guess* so?"

I wanted to leave an opening in case she told them about coming downstairs and turning the television set on when she couldn't get to sleep. "I mean ... I don't know whether she was actually asleep then or still studying her script. Her room's on the other side of the house from mine."

"Oh," Captain Mansan said. He didn't go on any further about that evening, so I supposed she hadn't told him about going downstairs.

I started wondering why we were keeping things from them. But you didn't get to wonder too long about anything because they kept prodding you to go on.

We went over Monday without too many hitches except they kept wanting to know how my mother was acting. I even found myself skipping over Monday morning when she was a little sharp with me.

Finally we got to Tuesday, the day I found Ben. They didn't interrupt me until I got to the first telephone call Tuesday afternoon from Ben's wife.

"Then you knew at the time he had a wife, didn't you? And your mother knew it, too, didn't she?" Captain Mansan thrust out his arm and pointed his finger right in my face.

"No, I didn't."

"But you just said you got home from school, lit the fire in the living room, the phone rang, and it was Ben's wife asking to speak to him!"

"Well, it was."

"Then you and your mother knew he was married!" Boy, all of a sudden he was whipping into action.

"No, we didn't," I said.

"Then why did you say it was his wife?"

"Because I know now that that's who it was. But I didn't know then."

"You're positive of that?"

Suddenly I was beginning to dislike this Captain.

"Yes, sir." I figured I'd better call him sir.

"Well, from now on tell us what happened as it happened, without jumping to knowledge you've learned since."

I said all right. From then on I referred to Ben's wife as "that lady" or "her."

Things went along until I got to the part about calling

up Merwin and saying, "I just found Ben down by the barbecue pit. He shot himself!"

The Captain really pounced on me then. "Why did you say he shot himself?"

"Well, I—" That's as far as I got.

"You didn't see him shoot himself, did you?" He had his big paw in my face again.

"No, but I—"

"Merwin Saltzman didn't *ask* you if he'd shot himself, did he?"

"No."

"He didn't *suggest* that he had?"

The guy who was taking our conversation down in shorthand hunched forward, and the other guy, Hodges, stood up from his chair like they were really hot on the trail. The three of them started looking like a pack of bloodhounds to me.

"No." I was feeling pretty dumb at this point.

He threw what he thought was a real curve at me next. "Maybe your mother was the one that told you to say suicide. Of course, that must have been it. You wouldn't make something like that up yourself."

I looked at him for a moment. "She didn't even know Ben was dead yet!"

"Oh, yes, that's right.... She was working, wasn't she?" How about that for devious tactics! He mustered up some more steam and went right on. "All right, Josh, then why did you say he shot himself? Come on, you can tell us."

I had to admit he had me there. Now that I look back on it, I don't know why I did come to that conclusion outside of the fact that I didn't do it, my mother didn't do it, and Cecelia was away. So that left only Ben.

"I figured that he had," was my answer.

"You just *figured* he had!" Hodges said, practically mimicking me. "That's pretty queer figuring." Mansan kind of gave him a look to shut up.

Then the Captain really launched into me. "Isn't it true your mother and Ben Nichols had an argument Sunday evening? Isn't it true that your mother found out he had a wife and she confronted him with this and they had a fight?" I just took a breath to answer and he was in there

130

again. "It's perfectly natural, if your mother did learn he was married, that she'd be upset. You know that, don't you, son?" Boy, he was an oily rat!

"But she didn't know he was married!" I said.

"How old are you?"

"Fifteen."

"Your mother—would she have discussed this matter with you if she had known it?" I was beginning to feel like I was in a courtroom instead of a game room.

"Yes, I think she would have," I said.

"You mean your mother is in the habit of discussing things of an 'intimate' nature with you?" He took out one of those little after-dinner cigars that look like overgrown cigarettes and started to light it.

"Well, yes . . . I gues so." The way he said the word "intimate" was kind of sneaky.

"Tell me this, son." I hate being called "son." "Did Ben Nichols ever threaten to commit suicide?"

"No."

"Did he ever talk about suicide in any way at all?"

"No, not that I remember," I told him. I did recall that Ben had listed suicide in with the major sins that God didn't like, but I sure wasn't going to bring that up.

"Then it strikes me as strange for you to get on the phone right after finding his body and say that he shot himself."

The old saying "Crime doesn't pay" was beginning to look like the truth all right—even if you *didn't* do it. Even if you just found the body, it didn't pay.

The Captain just puffed on his cigar and stared at me. Nobody said anything for quite a while. I know *I* didn't, because I couldn't think of anything to say.

Finally he spoke up after practically blowing smoke right in my face. "Well, son, doesn't it strike you funny? I mean jumping to a conclusion like that?" Then his voice changed to a kind of patronizing tone. "Now, Josh, you're a bright lad—that's plain enough to see. And you can tell me the truth. The only way anybody's going to get hurt in this case is by *not* telling the truth. You understand that, don't you?"

"Yes, sir." That was the first time I'd heard anybody refer to Ben's death as a "case."

"Then have you any other explanation for saying that Ben Nichols shot himself?" He wasn't going to give up no matter what.

"Well, he acted kind of funny Sunday night."

"Oh, come now, son. Lots of people *act kind of funny* without shooting themselves." He had a way of repeating what you said that made you wish you'd never said it. "Isn't that true?"

"Yes, sir." I was sure getting tired of this routine, and I wished to hell Lee had been with me.

"All right, son, go on. We'll get back to this later."

I finished telling the whole story the way it happened, except when I got to the part about Ben's wife showing up in our driveway I didn't repeat exactly what she'd yelled up toward the windows. All I said was that she was throwing bricks and that she was so drunk I couldn't tell what she was saying.

When I finished, Captain Mansan and Hodges really started in with a barrage of questions. They were going so fast and furious that I'd no sooner start to answer one when one of them would shoot another at me. Did my mother and Ben fight a lot? Weren't we great friends of Captain Clymer's? And a lot about precisely how my mother acted when she came home and was told Ben was dead.

Then Captain Mansan asked me if Lee Hertzig, Roy, and my mother rehearsed me in what I should say before he got there. "They went over every detail and told you exactly what to say, didn't they?"

"No, sir." Things were not looking too bright.

"Surely they told you I was coming down, and that you'd be talking to me?"

"Yes, they told me that," I said.

"And what else did they tell you?" The Captain's eyes were narrowing; he was an insinuating bastard if ever there was one.

"They just told me to tell it the way it happened."

"And that's all?"

"Yes, sir."

132

Then Hodges spoke up. "You planning to follow your mother's footsteps and go into movies, Josh?"

"I don't know." I didn't see what that had to do with anything until his next crack.

"Because you're a damn good little actor already!"

"Okay, Hodges, that's enough!" The Captain really snapped at him. "Well, son, that's all for now, but we'll be talking to you again."

Christ, I could hardly wait!

When I told Lee Hertzig about the questioning after they'd left, he didn't seem any too happy. And when he thought about it a little more, he started to get mad as hell. My mother was upset, too.

"Why weren't you with him?" she asked Lee. And there was a real edge to her voice.

"Rita, when a fifteen-year-old has to have a lawyer with him to answer a few questions—it really begins to look suspicious. Can't you see that?"

"Not when they treat him like that, no!" She was getting tears in her eyes.

"I had no idea they were going to bear down on him as hard as they apparently did. Those bastards!"

I was sorry I'd told them about the questioning, but then Lee had wanted to know in detail everything they'd asked. He said it was important that he know.

Chapter 18

THAT evening there was the usual collection of curiosity seekers and reporters hanging around the driveway. If it hadn't been for Captain Clymer they'd have been running all over the grounds and through the house; he had a whole battalion of men guarding the place, keeping people at a safe distance.

The director and one of the producers of the proposed television series showed up for a visit; so did Stella and Ef, and Jay Savage. Jay was just about jumping with joy because one of his clients was getting so much publicity. It didn't matter what kind it was as long as they spelled her name right. Merwin was busy as a bird dog making drinks for everybody because Cecelia had taken off for town.

Our house vacillated between one big cocktail party and one big funeral parlor for weeks. When there were people around it was like a cocktail party; when there was just the family left—Mother, Merwin, myself, and Cecelia—it was more like a funeral parlor, in spite of Merwin's valiant efforts to buoy things up.

By about nine o'clock that night my mother was really blind. You see, it really wasn't her fault, but people kept plying her with liquor in the hopes she'd be able to get over the crisis without going completely to pieces. Sometimes it would work, and they'd cart her up to bed in a numbed condition, more or less oblivious of what was going on. But then again it would backfire. Like this night.

People kept dropping in and out, and she'd have a drink or two with each one of them, so naturally she didn't have much of an appetite. After a while Merwin drove me down to Mama Paganelli's to get a bite of dinner. When we got back, as we were coming in the door, I heard her call out in this drugged voice, "Is that my baby?"

Stella looked out into the hall from the living room and

said, "That's your gorgeous baby, sure enough! *Grrr!*" I told you what a growler she was.

"Don't bring him in here ... don't want him to see his mother like this!" I could tell by her voice that she was terribly drunk. I got shivers up and down my spine. Merwin held my hand tightly as we walked down the hall to the stairway, but you had to pass the open living room door to get to it. When she saw me going by, she made a lunge from her chair to close the door. It was a futile attempt because I was already there, but I guess a person's perspective is way off at a time like that. Anyhow, she fell almost as soon as she got up from her chair.

"That's my baby! Come kiss your no-good mother good night ... my sweet baby!" By that time Stella and Ef were at her side to help her up. "Let me alone!" she screamed at them. "I want my Josh! Josh, baby!" She really yelled at me. Naturally I started going to her. But when I came in the room and she focused on me, she put her arms over her head and said, "Oh, God! It's bad enough finding Ben—he has to see his own mother make a spectacle—" I couldn't stand it any longer. I just tore to her side, knelt down, and put my arms around her.

That isn't what I wanted to do; I wanted to run upstairs to my room. But it practically made me sick to hear her talk like that and it seemed the only way to stop her.

Well, I started in bawling and she started in crying, and then Stella fell apart, too. If Merwin hadn't gone to the linen closet and come back in and handed each of us a big bath towel—God only knows how long we'd have been wailing. When he did that, Ef broke up, and so did Jay, and finally, one by one, we did, too. Then I went up to my room. But you know, as soon as I got undressed and in bed I started crying again.

The next day, Friday, was Ben's funeral, but Lee refused to let us attend because Ben's wife would be there, and there'd be lots of photographers and morbid nuts hanging around the place waiting for some kind of incident. Not that we would have gone anyhow. Ben was about as popular as a lousy mattress with all of us.

Even so, at two o'clock in the afternoon, the time of the

funeral, a terrible pall fell over our house. In the first place, all the reporters and people that had been hanging around had disappeared; you knew where they'd gone. Although you didn't want to be there, still there was a strange feeling of being left out. Almost of being quarantined. In a way, too, you felt that by being alone in the house you were being punished. I can't really explain it but it was a lousy, lonely, eerie feeling.

Merwin had to go into Hollywood on business about noon, so there was just my mother and me. The phone didn't ring once and we didn't speak for hours. She stayed up in her bedroom and I just sort of wandered around the house. I'd sit in a chair for a while and then I'd get up and just stare out the windows. After a couple of hours I went upstairs because I thought maybe we could keep each other company or something, but when I got to the door of her room I could hear her sobbing very quietly. I figured I'd better not knock. So I went back downstairs and cleaned out Monkey-Face's cage. After that I cleaned Chauncey's cage. Then I took the dogs into the utility room and gave them both baths.

Merwin got back about four o'clock. He sure was a welcome sight. Shortly after he returned, the phone rang several times; then Jeanette Clymer came by. Pretty soon it was like we were back in the world again. That evening the papers were really frightening.

OFFICIAL INQUEST LIKELY

SUICIDE THEORY FADING FAST

WIFE CRIES FOUL PLAY!

Plus the headlines and feature stories were pictures of Ben, his wife, my mother, and me all over the place. All kinds of pictures. You wonder where they get ahold of some of the weird snapshots they dig up. A couple of the papers had complete coverage of the funeral, too. There were the usual gruesome shots of Ben's wife being supported by a couple of men. The papers were careful to point out that one of them was her lawyer who had come on

136

from New York. There was one blood-curdling picture of her trying to jump into his grave at the cemetery. I couldn't help wondering why she hadn't taken him home for burial. I wished she had. I didn't even want him buried in the same state we were in.

One of the papers carried a pretty nasty story based on an interview with Ben's wife. It had this slant: she'd gotten wind that Ben was having some kind of an affair, so she came out to California and had a long talk with him. He admitted it, and agreed to end it by telling my mother it was all off. He drove down to Paraiso Beach to confront my mother; that was the last she ever saw of him. There was your motive—a spurned woman. This article practically said that my mother got out a gun and shot him. Also Ben's wife kept yapping about how he'd never shoot himself because he was brought up a strict Catholic. That was in every paper.

That evening we really had a top-level conference: Lee Hertzig, Roy Clymer, Merwin, Jay Savage, a press agent named Sally Knapp, who had worked with Jay many times, my mother, and me.

As soon as we all gathered in the living room my mother said, "Lee, can't we leave Josh out of this? Please!"

"Rita, I think it's best if he stays. There's nothing going to be said that would be wrong for him to hear. And I think we all ought to be aware of exactly what the situation is."

Lee said things didn't look too good at this point and went on to explain why. First, it looked like Captain Clymer was going to be in serious trouble because of the way he'd handled the whole thing. Also the coroner. It was his first official assignment, and he was so delighted and eager to please that once somebody had said the magic word "suicide" he'd concentrated on fixing Ben up. He'd cleaned Ben, shaved him, fixed the wound and waxed it—thereby getting rid of all clues such as fingerprints, powder burns, etc. That was the first mistake. That and Roy Clymer accepting the fact that Ben had shot himself without any investigation. And, worst of all, Roy being a friend of my mother's pointed to collusion, Lee said.

Then, of course, Ben's wife having claimed that he was

going to tell my mother it was all off and that he was coming back to her. Also, that he was a Catholic and wouldn't think of killing himself; but mainly, that there was no suicide note. And the fact that he'd been lying in our back yard for a couple of days before anyone found him looked a little fishy. Also the gun was one of Mr. Culp's and came from our house. Jesus, by the time Lee got through telling why things didn't look "too good" you could just about imagine Roy, my mother, and me all strapped in matching electric chairs.

Lee went on to mention a few things that were on our side. He explained that any man that could carry out a full-scale deception the way Ben did must be a little off his rocker. He said he'd assigned a couple of private investigators to dig up anything and everything about Ben's life that tended to prove he was erratic. Also the fact that his wife had been in a couple of mental institutions would weaken her accusations.

What's more, there were a couple of people who were around my mother the last day of shooting the television pilot, when she tried to phone Ben and got his wife instead. They were willing to describe her condition as almost hysterical. And Ben had been dead almost two days by then, so that pointed toward my mother not knowing he was married. Lee said one of the main points in our favor was Ben's heavy gambling debts. This proved he was unstable and had good reason to be upset because maybe pressure had been put on him.

Lee told us there'd be some more men coming down from the District Attorney's office the next day to kind of re-enact the scene of the crime. They'd have an official court photographer, etc. If they weren't satisfied with all the details they'd probably call for an official investigation and inquest into Ben's death. And if foul play was indicated, there could possibly be a jury trial.

When he said "foul play" you knew he meant my mother. Although nobody said anything, it got quiet as a tomb. Everybody stared holes through the floor.

Roy Clymer was looking more miserable than anyone. If there was such a thing as an invisible pill, he'd have hocked his soul for it.

"Christ-on-a-buckboard," Sally Knapp says, and she leaps up from her chair. "Jay asked me in on this thing. If I'm going to help out I've got to have a say. Okay?" She looked around at everybody in the room, including me. She had a way of looking at you that made you give her some reaction, so I kind of tossed her a nervous smile and nodded ever so slightly. This knocked her out. "The kid says okay!" And she started in roaring. She had a laugh like a muffled cannon that began way down in her stomach somewhere; then it traveled up to her throat, and when she opened her mouth there was one enormous bellow, kind of like a wounded water buffalo; then it turned into a cigarette cough.

After she finished hacking, Lee said, "Shoot!" And she did.

"If you'll excuse the expression, the way you've handled the press on this thing is crap, plain crap! No interviews, except a few sterilized statements from 'her lawyer and her agent': *Miss Cydney is terribly upset and unavailable for comment at this time.* Well, that's what I call crap!"

Then she turned quickly to my mother. "I don't mean you, baby. Of course you're upset. You've got every right to be. Dirty bastard like that! I'd like to bring him back for half a dozen quick rounds. I'd show the s.o.b.!" And she would, too.

"First of all," she went on, "you've got to make friends with the boys and girls of the press. I know it's a drag, but I suggest you call it open season tomorrow and have them all down here. Let's face it, kids—we've hit the front pages. We're not going to get off them by ignoring the reporters. You know damn well they're going to print somebody's version. So far the stories have been coming from the Widow Nichols and the D.A.'s office. I'd say it's high time you presented your case. So you get chummy with the press, win their sympathy, and two to one they'll clear up this whole mess for you. What do you think?"

"The only thing to do," Lee said. "They've been put off long enough. Of course, we had no idea it was going to mushroom like this, but it has, and we need all the help we can get."

"You're damn right!" Sally boomed. "And we've got a

great angle: *Mother and son taken in by a psychopathic—*"

With that my mother was up out of her chair. "Ben was not a psychopath!" She almost screamed it.

Merwin went to her and put his hand on her shoulder.

"Honey," Sally said, "I'm not saying *what* he was. A psychopath, a chronic deceiver, or just a crazy, mixed-up, middle-aged kid. But I do know this: he must have been some kind of a crackpot; and if we can make him out to be Jack the Ripper it won't be going too far. He's got to be the villain in this case. It's him or you! Take your pick."

"She's right, Rita." Lee walked over to my mother. "Ben's reputation is unimportant compared to the position you're in."

She was really upset, though; she started to say something, but Merwin cut in with this thick British accent.

"After all, Rita, even you have to admit—he did end up a bit of a shit!"

Merwin could really alleviate tension at the right moment. I mean my mother didn't laugh or anything, but she did smile this kind of nervous smile, and you knew she realized the truth of the situation.

"Okay, I'll contact the press," Sally said, "and try to get a top reporter and photographer from each of the dailies."

Jay suddenly had a brainstorm. "Listen, what about if I get a few more of my other top clients to mill around? Like—here's the angle: *Stars of show business flock to Rita Cydney's side.*" Boy, talk about promoters!

"For Chrissake, Jay!" Lee said. "This isn't a sideshow. It's damn serious business." He pointed to my mother. "Your client here is in serious trouble, believe it or not!"

"Aw, come on. Everybody knows she didn't do it," Jay said. "The papers like to make a big deal whenever a celebrity's mixed up in a magilla like this. So why not cash in on it? I'm telling you, this thing's going to help sell the TV series. I talked to the packaging boys yesterday. They're all excited. They look on this as a big break. You wait and see!"

"And I'm telling you something!" Lee yelled. "*You* wait and see if you don't have to get permission to film it inside San Quentin!"

Everybody looked at Lee with their mouths open.

140

Finally Merwin spoke up. "You don't think there's a chance this would actually come to trial, do you?"

"There's a possibility anything might happen. A case like this is like a brush fire. It can die down in no time, but it can also be fanned at the right moment and develop into a forest fire."

"But it's obvious Rita's had nothing to do with—"

"Obvious to us, yes! But not to the District Attorney's office, the papers, and the public," Lee snapped. "And here's something to remember: Mrs. Nichols is loaded; she's got money and therefore influence. If she wants to cause a stink she's perfectly able to do so. And from the way things are going, that's what she's got on her mind."

He turned to my mother. "I'm not trying to frighten you, Rita, but rather to get everybody here to comprehend some of the problems we're up against. I have no doubt we'll surmount them, but it's not going to be like bobbing for apples."

Jay Savage left a few minutes after this with his tail between his legs, shaking his ferretlike head, kind of murmuring, "Jesus, I had no idea . . . I mean . . ."

After he'd gone Lee said, "I didn't want to say anything in front of Jay—but I think it would be a good idea, Roy, if you and your wife didn't see too much of Rita and Josh for a while. It's a lousy thing to have to bring up, but I think you understand."

"Sure, I do," Roy said. Then he turned to my mother. "Rita, a lot of this is my fault—in fact, most of it. But, believe me, I had no idea— Look, I know it's going to come out all right, but I hate to see you have to go through this."

"Forget it, Roy. You were only trying to make things easy for us," she said.

"Of course, you'll be here tomorrow, Roy, when the D.A.'s men come down, but I think it would be better if you weren't here for the press." Lee was trying to be as tactful as possible.

"Right. See you tomorrow, Rita. By, Josh ... Miss Knapp."

After Roy left, Sally said, "It's a shame! If he hadn't

tried to help, this whole mess probably wouldn't have come up."

"You're so right," Lee agreed. "It doesn't look too good for him, either. They've taken the local police off the case entirely. From here on in, the L.A. cops are handling it." And he told us the little coroner was already on his way out of a job.

You see, in a way, if my mother hadn't been a celebrity of sorts, the whole thing wouldn't have got to be so sticky. But everybody's always a little impressed and anxious to help somebody that's famous, no matter how much they deny it. It's like when stars go into restaurants or night clubs or to a theater—they always get the best seats and service. Well, that idea carries over even to something like finding a body in my mother's back yard. Roy had a crush on her, the coroner was impressed, and the rest of the Paraiso Beach cops were, too. So everybody was trying to clear it up in a hurry and make it as painless as possible for her. That's what made the whole thing look suspicious.

Then Lee, Sally Knapp, my mother, Merwin and I had a short briefing on the activities of the next day: the way to dress, how to act, and what to say.

"The angle to keep in mind," Sally, said, "is *Mother and son taken in—Mother and son deceived—Mother and son hoaxed!*"

My mother spoke up. "I hate to have Josh dragged through all this unpleasantness. It's not normal for a young—"

"I don't mind, Mom! Honest!"

She had to smile a little. "I know you don't!" She shook her head. "Josh, I don't know what's come over you. But that's not the point." She turned to Lee. "I was wondering. . . . Maybe I could send Josh back to Ohio with Lilly and Al for a while until this is all over with."

"I understand your feelings, Rita, but I've got to go along with Sally. It's important for us to stress the angle of a mother and her son trapped in an unfortunate predicament over which they had no control. Not just a picture actress at the unhappy end of a messy affair. Besides, Josh has been through the worst of it, finding him like that."

142

"The way you talked today," my mother said, "makes me wonder if we *have* been through the worst of it!"

"Let's hope so," Lee said. "But it's vital to have Josh here. After all, he's not only your son—he's your alibi. He was with you Sunday night."

I was glad I wasn't going to be shipped off. Also, in a crazy way, it was exciting to be needed, to be important to my mother. I'd never felt that way before. It had always been the opposite; I'd always had the idea I was excess baggage.

Sally suggested we feed the press people kind of a buffet lunch and have them at the house before the D.A. guys arrived.

"Good idea, Sally," Lee said. "That way they'll be simmered down by the time the police get here."

He asked Sally to make the necessary arrangements. They both had a lot of work to do, so they took off for town, saying they'd be down first thing in the morning.

We turned in early, but I don't think any of us slept too well around that time. You'd wake up in the middle of the night and just lie there grinding gears. My mother was back on the pills, too.

Chapter 19

EARLY the next morning Merwin and I drove down to Paraiso Beach and picked up a ham, a turkey, and all kinds of cheeses and salads to feed the newspaper people with. By the time we got back to the house, Sally and Lee were there; and my mother was downstairs dressed in a long-sleeved, high-necked, brown wool dress. She looked extremely beautiful, but not flashy.

When we finished unloading all the stuff we'd bought, we gathered in the living room for a last minute talk-through. It was like getting ready for an opening night on Broadway; you sure wanted to put your best foot forward.

Pretty soon the first of the newspaper people began to arrive in trickles. Lee and Sally suggested my mother and I go upstairs until everybody was there. Then we could meet them all at once and handle the thing with some degree of order. So we went to my mother's bedroom, Merwin took off for the dining room to help Cecelia set up this buffet, and Lee and Sally acted as the welcoming committee.

Captain Mansan and the rest of the men from the District Attorney's office weren't due until three in the afternoon; Sally had asked the press to be there between eleven-thirty and twelve so that by the time the cops got there all the initial excitement would have died down and the cops wouldn't be sore about it.

My mother and I were in the middle of a Scrabble game when the phone rang. It was a long-distance call from Andy and Midge Lansing. They'd called several times before because they were very worried about everything they'd been reading in the papers and hearing on the radio. They'd been spending the last six months or so at this new ranch he'd bought in Wyoming. They were phoning to say they'd be back in California within a couple of weeks and not to worry about money or anything. My mother was relieved that they'd be around soon, because they were two of her friends who really had their feet on the ground.

Right after she got off the phone Lee came up and said that practically everybody had arrived, that some of them were helping themselves to food and coffee, and as soon as they got settled down in the living room he'd call us and we could come down. "Don't be nervous about a thing. They all seem delighted at being asked. The mood feels just right. Oh, by the way," he added, "after introducing you two, I've got a little speech I'll toss at them, a more or less chronological account of what happened. Following this, I think it'd be wise to have an open question period and then let them get their pictures. Rita, this is going to help a lot, you'll see." Then Lee turned to me. "And, Josh, don't let them get you down. Act natural, speak up. You can be a great help to us. There are quite a few gals down there, and we're counting on you to win them over. Okay?"

"I'll do my best," I said.

"Fine!" Lee started to leave.

"Oh, Lee!" My mother stopped him. "Would it be all right if I had . . . just one tiny Scotch on the rocks?" He kind of frowned at her. "I really need it. One won't do any harm—to relax me!"

"All right, if you stick to one. I'll send Merwin up." He went downstairs.

Suddenly I felt embarrassed in front of my mother because I felt she was embarrassed. We sat there, not saying a word, avoiding looking at one another. Frankly, I wished I could have had a drink, too. Finally, I suggested we go on with our Scrabble game. I don't know why, but in times of stress it always seems better to me to have an independent activity, instead of sitting around staring at the walls or at each other.

As she reached over for a tile she knocked the whole thing off the coffee table we were playing on. She was nervous as a cat. We were picking the letters up when, thank God, there was a knock at the door and we heard Merwin's voice, "Fifteen minutes, Christians!"

As he came in the room my mother said, "And don't think I wouldn't *rather* be thrown to the lions!"

"Pish-tush! They're a grand group," Merwin said. She gave him a wry look as he handed her a glass. I'm telling you she went for that drink like she'd been in the middle of the desert for weeks.

About that time Sally Knapp came in, all smiles, and whacked me on the back.

"Hiya, kid! Well, here we go! Rita, you never looked lovelier! Go out there and slay 'em! But don't wait for the laughs!" She started roaring and then coughing. She really knocked herself out sometimes. While Sally was pulling herself together, my mother brushed her hair, freshened up her lipstick, and away we went.

As we walked down the stairs I felt like we were part of some big movie set, and they were all ready to start the production when we got there. Sure enough, when we entered the living room the flash cameras began popping left and right. They were going at such a rate we were temporarily blinded.

"Okay, gang, let's take it easy. They'll pose for pictures later on!" Sally was snapping at them. I couldn't see for a few seconds, but I could feel my mother squeezing my hand. I thought she was going to break my fingers.

Lee told them to knock off, too. When I opened my eyes, I saw about seven or eight women and about twelve men standing or seated around. I must say they looked like a nice bunch of people; they sure looked interested, that's one thing. Lots of them had plates of food they'd put aside when we came in, and the ones that didn't have cameras either had notebooks out or were scrambling for them.

As we walked over to a sofa that had been left vacant for us, Lee introduced my mother, Merwin, and me. Right off the bat one of the ladies said, "Hello, Rita. I'm terribly sorry about all this!" Then others chimed in. Some of them knew her and a few knew Merwin. A couple said, "Hi, Josh!" as I passed. And, of course, I heard one woman say, "Isn't he adorable!" There's a word I could do without.

After they quieted down, Lee started in with his speech. In a very factual way he told about the whole Ben period from when we first met him up until his death. He didn't tell about me throwing up on him or any of the little personal details like that. Just the essentials.

You couldn't have asked for more attention. They sat there like a band of bird-watchers tracking down some fantastically rare specimen. Most of them were taking notes and you could hear the sound of pencil on paper and pages being turned every so often. But the thing that impressed you was the fact that not one of them interrupted. Of course, Lee kept up a pretty good pace, being a lawyer and all, and being used to addressing juries and such. He was really a pretty good actor; he even had me fascinated, and I knew what the hell it was all about. He'd just gotten to the part where my mother called Roy Clymer to tell him about me having found Ben when the phone rang. Lee had arranged for Cecelia to take all the calls in the kitchen so we wouldn't be stopping and starting through the whole interview.

Within a few seconds she came in to the living room and said, "I'm sorry to interrupt, Mr. Hertzig, but they say it's urgent. There's a call for a Mr. Hannah from the *Telegraph*."

With that a guy stood up. "Right here," he said.

"You can take it over there," Lee pointed to the phone in the living room over in one corner by this antique desk of the Culps'.

Everyone sort of relaxed as he went to answer the phone. One lady turned to my mother and said, "You really shouldn't have gone to all this trouble, Miss Cydney." She was indicating her plate and the food and all. Then a couple of others agreed with her and said how good it was. There was a lot of small talk going on until we heard this Mr. Hannah say over the phone, "Jesus Christ—you're kidding!" Everyone shut up like clams.

My mother took that opportunity to ask me to go up to her bedroom and get her cigarettes. She was going through a period of smoking one special brand of English cigarettes, and she wouldn't look at any other kind; but she'd forgotten to bring a pack down. She's one of the worst chain smokers you ever met. I hated to leave, because this Hannah guy was obviously getting some hot news. Everybody's ears were about falling off. But what could I do? I mean it wouldn't have looked right for me to get into an argument with my mother in front of the press.

I went upstairs cursing whoever the hell invented smoking. As I turned the corner at the top of the stairs I stepped right on one of Lord Nelson's paws. He let out such a yipe I thought for a minute I'd broken his leg. I carried him into my mother's bedroom, rubbed his paw, told him how sorry I was, and went through the whole "I didn't mean it, puppy!" bit.

By the time I found the cigarettes and got to the head of the stairs people were tearing down the hall and going out the front door screaming "Good-by" and "Thanks" and "Sorry" and "We'll get together later on this!" I stood there dumbfounded. The ones that had brought hats and coats were mauling each other, trying to get them out of the hall closet. It was mayhem. By the time I got to the living room the only people left in there were Lee, Sally, Merwin, and my mother, all looking absolutely stunned.

"Hey, what happened?" I asked.

Sally just stood there, shaking her head. "Well, I'll be a—! If this isn't a *Stella Dallas* party I never saw one!"

"Closed before we got to New Haven," Merwin said.

"I wouldn't say we bombed, but we've sure had the wind taken out of our sails!" Lee said.

My mother just stood there like she was in a trance. Finally she said, "I haven't flopped like this since *Outlaw Lady*!" That was a big budget picture she made when she was very hot in the business that turned out to be so lousy they never even released it. It's been on television, though.

Cecelia came in from the kitchen just then. "Where'd they go?" she asked. "Somebody yell fire or what?"

I asked what happened again, but nobody paid any attention to me. They all started looking around at the plates of half-eaten food, coffee cups, cigarettes still burning in ash trays, and suddenly they began howling with laughter. They laughed so loud and long that I started in and so did Cecelia, even though we didn't know what the heck we were laughing at. It wasn't until the phone rang that we found out. It was the District Attorney's office calling Lee to explain what had happened: Some big-time gangster, Irving Beiber, who lived in a beautiful mansion in Bel Air, had his house bombed. You probably remember when it happened. Not only that, he got killed. But here

148

was the big scoop: he was having a giant conclave at his place of about seventeen other big-time gangsters from the East. It was like they were having a convention, only instead of Shriners they were gangsters. Anyhow, I guess some other local mobster didn't want them muscling in out there and thought this bomb would knock the whole bunch of them off. Beiber had the drapes drawn in the living room, so whoever tossed the bomb naturally figured they'd all be in there plotting how to take over the whole state of California and probably part of Mexico. But here was the twist. The entire mob was down in his private projection room watching a stag movie that featured this famous movie star. She made it before she was famous, of course. Well, Beiber had just gone upstairs to answer a phone call when—boom! In sails this bomb through the window. So he was the only one that got it. A couple of other guys were injured downstairs from falling plaster and debris, and another guy had a heart attack and dropped dead on the spot.

What a story that was! And that's what caused the press to vanish into thin air. The phone call for Lee was to explain that the D.A. guys weren't coming down either.

"This could be a terrific break for us," Lee said.

"You're damn right," Sally pitched in. "This thing'll knock Los Angeles on its ass. I'm happy to say, Rita, it will make your case look like pretty small peanuts!"

"I still feel like a spurned Elsa Maxwell," Merwin said, looking around at the scene of the festivities. It was true; this was supposed to be a big day for us, and it fizzled down to nothing.

But Lee kept saying it was a lucky coincidence, that the cops and the newspapers would be so busy with the gangsters and all the ramifications that our situation might be forgotten about.

It worked out that way for about the next ten days, too. For a few days there were a couple of articles about us, saying the case was still being looked into, or investigated, or probed—stuff like that. Then for about a week we dropped out of sight completely.

Chapter 20

EVEN though we were off the front pages for a while I was still a big local celebrity around the beach and at school. Remember I told you about this girl, Josianne Tucker, that invited me to her party? Well, I went, and if I do say so myself I was garnering lots of attention. The guys at the party were always inviting me out in the yard to sneak a smoke; and the girls were always sidling up to me asking me if I liked to go to the movies, who was my favorite singer, what did I want to be when I grew up, etc. And they all wanted to know "what it felt like" to find a body! Kids really are morbid characters. Much more so than most grownups.

One guy, Mickey Emerson, in my grade at school, came up to me while I was eating—while I was *eating*, mind you—and said, "Hey, Josh, can I ask you a question?"

"Sure," I answered. I didn't know what kind of a warped mind he was carrying around with him.

"I heard a guy tell my dad once that when you die you shit in your pants!"

"What?" I asked.

"Yeah. The muscles relax and you can't help it. It just automatically happens. How about that?"

"Yeah, crazy!" I said.

"No, I'm asking you—what about it?"

"What do you mean—what about it?"

"Is it true?"

"How the hell would I know? I haven't died yet!"

"You found a dead guy, didn't you?"

"Yes, but—Christ, I only *found* him. I didn't do an *autopsy*!"

"Yeah, I know, but—"

"Mickey, will you get away from me! I'm trying to eat!" See what I mean about kids?

In a way though, I'm being a big hypocrite when I say they're morbid and warped if I intimate I'm not. Because from the time Mickey Emerson brought that up it started gnawing away at me until I finally asked our doctor. When I found out it does happen sometimes, I got to thinking about all those beautiful, romantic death scenes you see in the movies. I especially thought about Greta Garbo dying in Robert Taylor's arms in *Camille*. It was so disillusioning it was frightening. They showed it on television about a month ago; I had to turn off the set just as he came into her bedroom.

At the party that night I got my first kiss. And I mean *real* kiss! Along about nine o'clock Josianne asked me if I'd go out to the garage and bring in another case of Cokes. I said sure, and she said she'd come along with me and show me the way. She showed me the way all right. Did she ever!

We went into the garage, which was quite a ways from the house, through a side door. Josianne flicked on a switch and a small yellow globe lit up.

"Where do you keep the Cokes?" I asked her.

"Oh, skip the Cokes for a minute," she said.

"I thought you were running out of them." I turned around and she was leaning up against the closed door, staring at me, cool as a cucumber. She didn't even bother to answer; she just kept right on staring. Finally she kind of sighed and said, "Tell me something, Josh?"

"Sure."

"Have you ever gone steady?"

Gone steady! I hadn't even gone with a girl at all, steady or unsteady. But kids never want to admit to other kids anything they haven't done. I mean if she'd asked me if I had any illegitimate children running around I probably would have hemmed and hawed and said I really couldn't tell, I hadn't checked lately.

"Yeah, I guess so—I suppose you'd call it steady!"

"Oh, tell me about it, Josh!"

"I'd rather not talk about it," I said. I had to say that because there wasn't anything to talk about.

"Were you terribly hurt?" she asked.

I figured I was into the scene and I might as well play it

out. I didn't say anything; I just lowered my head and nodded.

Boy, that did it. She was all over me like a plate of hot soup. "Oh, Josh, how awful!" She was hugging me and pressing my head up against her shoulder and petting me.

She felt wonderful, very soft and warm, without being moist. Lots of girls around that age tend to get very damp and sticky when they get involved in any close contact with you.

I was loving it until she started running her hand through my hair. I don't know why but I hate it when someone fiddles with my hair. I've really got an aversion to that. It's not that I don't want to get my hair mussed up either. I suppose it's some mental block that goes back to when I was very young.

When she started giving the old head a real workout, I pulled away from her. "I'm okay," I said. "I'm really practically over it!"

"I'm glad! Because I wouldn't want to catch you on the rebound!"

I was beginning to wonder what she had planned when she up and told me.

"Josh, let's go steady!"

Out of a blue sky! I didn't know what to say.

"Gee, Josianne, we hardly—"

"I know what you're going to say but it doesn't make any difference! Don't you see—it's something chemical. All the great love affairs are chemical! Don't you feel that?"

"Well, maybe. I guess . . . I never really thought—"

"Don't think, Josh. Just kiss me!"

"Right now?"

"Yes, right now . . . unless you don't want to." She really knew her way around.

"Oh, I want to all right. . . ." And I did. It was just that I wasn't quite sure how to go about it.

"Well . . . then?" She reached up with her right hand, put it behind my head, and brought me down toward her.

So I did kiss her. I swear I'd never kissed a girl before in my life, but it turned out to be one of those lucky things. She'd obviously been doing a lot of research by going out into the field because she was an expert. And I just kind of fell into the right thing to do out of willingness, intuition, or whatever. Anyhow, we must have stood there in that one spot by the garage door, glued to each other, for a full five minutes, only coming up now and then for air. It was a whole new world!

After a while we were both getting a little shaky and flushed. I was getting this terrific erection and I kept trying to lean back away from her, but the more I leaned back, the more she'd push her body up against me. Finally, there was no keeping the secret any longer, so I just pressed right back and let nature take its course.

I started to feel like my knees were melting right down into my calves, and Josianne was breathing so heavily I thought she was going to have an attack of some sort. Just when I was wondering how it was all going to end she pulled away and kind of panted, "We'd better get back to the house. They'll be wondering."

We were almost out the door when I remembered what we'd come out there for in the first place.

"Hey, what about the Cokes?"

"Oh, we've got two more cases in the kitchen," she said.

Boy, what a character! A *femme fatale* at fifteen. She's probably pregnant by now.

The party lasted until after midnight. About every half-hour or less she'd come up to me and say, "Josh, let me show you the hothouse," or "You haven't seen my father's study, Josh. Follow me." I saw the basement, her bedroom, the sun deck, the rock garden, and I don't what else. Every time we'd get off by ourselves we'd lock in this terrific embrace and stand there for minutes. By the last couple of sessions I was getting to feel like a regular Casanova, smooth as all get out.

A couple of times we were interrupted but only by other kids, so it was all right. Thank God, her parents never caught us or I'd probably have been taken out and shot. I was lucky it was such a mammoth party and her folks were kept hopping all the time supervising things.

Toward the end of the evening I was getting this fantastic ache around my groin and associated regions. I was really getting worried. I thought I'd popped a gasket or blown a tube or something—I didn't know what!

I felt like a rat when I was thanking her parents for "such a great time." If they'd only known what went into making it so great, the jig would have been up.

When Merwin came by for me about twelve-thirty I could hardly make it out to the car. I was hobbling along like some old man who'd just gotten off a horse after about eighty consecutive years of riding.

Josianne started to walk me out to the car, but she took hold of my arm and stopped me as we were walking under this enormous umbrella tree. "I'll bet I had a better time at my party than anyone else," she said.

"Me, too." That was a pretty dull way to express my satisfaction, but I was in such pain I could hardly talk.

"Josh, think about going steady and let me know." She gave me a quick peck on the cheek and started to pull away.

Then I did a cuckoo thing. I had a terrific desire, suddenly, to grab hold of her pony tail, yank her head back, and bite her on the neck. And that's exactly what I did. She squealed a little too loud for comfort, so I released her. I really didn't bite her too hard; it was more of a nip. She took a step back away from me and said, "Oh, Josh! *Ummm.*"

"I don't know why I did that," I told her.

"I loved it!" she said. Then she shook her head back and forth, sighed, said, "Oh, Josh, we'd make a gorgeous couple," and started to run back toward the house. About halfway to the door she stopped, turned, and yelled, "Call and let me know! I'll be waiting!"

She was an operator all right. You had to give her credit for knowing what she wanted and setting out to get it. I didn't care for her tactics, but the end product was great. She was beautiful, too, and that pony tail fractured me. Sex was finally rearing its ugly head. And about time, too. I'd been getting to feel definitely retarded in that department.

"Did you have a good time, sweetie?" Merwin asked.

"A swell time, except I've got this miserable stomachache," I said. Somehow I didn't feel like telling Merwin what was really bothering me. Mainly, I guess because I figured he wouldn't know about it. I remember thinking, while we were driving back to our house, that if only Ben had been around, he would have explained it to me.

When I woke up the next morning, Sunday, the ache was gone and I was feeling fine. Monday was when the *Look* photographer came down, so I didn't go to school that day. On Tuesday Sally had arranged an interview with a woman writer who was going to do a story on my mother and me for one of the wire services.

Ever since Saturday night I'd been thinking about Josianne Tucker and whether I wanted to form an alliance with her. I was weighing the pros and cons like crazy, and they were coming out about even. She was certainly beautiful and smart and everything, but I figured maybe she was too smart. I'd seen her on the courts several times and she played a great game of tennis. It certainly struck me that she'd wear the pants in any relationship when it came to making plans and running the whole works.

By the time I went to school on Wednesday, though, I'd decided to have a go at it. I mean I was only fifteen. I figured you couldn't get too hopelessly entangled at that age. Also one plus factor in the decision was that I definitely would learn the facts of life with Josianne.

I didn't have any subjects with her because she was in the other section of the sophomore class. During recess I was looking for her but I couldn't find her anywhere. At noon I decided to take her to lunch when I caught up with her. I was just bending over in the hall putting my books in my locker when someone tapped me on the shoulder.

I turned around and there she was. "Oh, hi, Josianne. I've been looking for you!" She gave me such a crack in the face that I saw double there for a few seconds.

"Hey, what's the big idea?" I asked her.

"I told you to call me! How long did you think I'd wait?"

"Yeah, but—"

"Well, you can just skip it as far as I'm concerned. I'm going steady with someone else!" And she flounced off.

Boy, that was the shortest chemical romance in history! I can't deny that I felt a little relieved. Especially after *that* little scene. She'd have undoubtedly made my life hell on wheels. I hate predatory women. . . . Not really. I get a kick out of them as long as I don't get hooked up with them myself.

Chapter 21

DURING the period we were off the front pages my mother seemed to relax a little. Of course, friends and acquaintances were still rallying around like crazy. There wasn't an afternoon or evening that somebody or other didn't drop by. She's always had loads of friends, anyhow.

Lee and Sally were around almost every day. If one wasn't there the other was. Sally was getting items planted in all the columns about what a crime it was that Ben pulled this trick on my mother. Lee said things looked better for us every day the gangster thing dragged on. And it *was* dragging on, too. It started to die down after a few days, but then one of the local California gangsters was found stuffed in the trunk of his car on Mulholland Drive. I guess it was in retaliation for the bombing. Anyhow, that stirred up a hornet's nest again, and the papers were wild with stories about how California was going to be like Chicago in the twenties and thirties if the cops didn't take action pretty soon and stop all these massacres.

Jay came down one day and said the chances were great for the television series to be sold to a sponsor within a couple of weeks. He also got my mother the lead in one of those hour Westerns. Mainly, I think, because she'd gotten all the publicity about Ben. She worked five days on it, and it did her a lot of good. She stopped drinking and took up the early-to-bed, early-to-rise routine.

Also we could use the money. We actually didn't have to worry, though, because Merwin was always wonderful about taking care of bills and things that we couldn't handle. But you didn't like to bleed him dry. He'd always take the curse off making you feel like a leech by bragging about whatever terrific salary he was making at the time. I think he overquoted just to make us feel all right.

During that time *I* even got an offer to be in a movie. It was right after my mother had finished working on the Western. Jay came down one day, all excited, and handed me a script. "Rita, your son's got a picture offer!"

"What?" she said. "Why, that's ridiculous! He's never acted in his life!"

"Recently he's been displaying definite tendencies," Merwin cut in.

" 'Never acted before in his life'!" Jay said. "The kid's only fifteen. What do you want—a long list of credits? He's got to start somewhere."

I was so excited I didn't know what to do. I had the script in my hand. *Hell Bent Teen-agers* was the title.

"How about it, Josh?" Jay asked me.

"I think it's great, Jay. How come they want me?"

"The producer, Sam Gutman, is a friend of mine. He saw your picture in the papers last week and thinks you're perfect for the part."

"Now wait a minute! What's this all about?" My mother reached for the script, took one look at the title page, handed it back to Jay and said, "Oh, no! Not for a minute!"

"But, Mom, you haven't even read it," I pleaded.

"I don't have to. I know Sam Gutman. It's one of those trashy teen-age quickies. I wouldn't want you to see it, let alone act in it. Besides, you know how I feel about that anyway!"

She's always been dead set against me being an actor. You see, in spite of all the crummy times we've been through, she's always tried to bring me up like a scion of some wealthy, old, established, Boston Back Bay family. In theory, at least. It sure in hell hasn't worked out that way. But she's always had that conception in the back of her mind. That's why all the forays into military academies, boarding schools, and tutors.

Every time some woman would start drooling to my mother about what a ladykiller I was going to grow up to be and how, if I decided to be an actor, I'd probably be a great hit in the movies—she'd throw cold water on it.

"I don't care if he turns out to be a cross between Apollo and Adonis" (once she said Apollo and Louis

158

Jourdan—he's the other actor besides Cary Grant that really slays her), "he's going to have no part of this rotten life. He's going to college and become a doctor or a lawyer or—"

"An Indian chief!" one woman cut in.

"Yes, by God, an Indian chief rather than an actor! At least that has a little dignity. An actor's life is for the birds, all other reports to the contrary."

But Jay was a tenacious character. He kept pounding away at my mother. "Just because the kid's got a small part in a picture—"

"Only a small part?" I asked.

"Listen to him!" Jay got a kick out of that. "Well, it's not the star part but it's a good one. You play the kid brother of the leader of this teen-age gang. He worships you because you're the only decent thing in his life. You see, your parents are bums. Your mother's an alky, your father's a junkie. You get killed about halfway through the picture but—"

"I get killed—really! How?" That fascinated the hell out of me. From that moment I knew I'd put up a pitched battle to be in it.

Jay went on with the plot. "Your brother takes you out drag strip-racing with his gang—against his better judgment. But you insist. You say, 'Gee, I don't want to stay home. Mom's blind drunk again.' Anyhow, you all pile into these hopped-up cars and drive out to the desert looking for kicks. There's a wreck. You get tossed out of your brother's car, but you're still alive. Then one of the cars behind him runs over you. By the time your brother gets out of the wreckage of his car and over to you—you die in his arms saying, 'Try to keep Pop off the stuff!' "

"Jesus, that sounds terrific!" I was picturing my big death scene already.

"Josh, will you stop that swearing! You're getting worse every day!" In spite of the fact that practically every one of my mother's friends swore in front of me, she hated it when I talked that way. And, oddly enough, she hardly ever swore. Unless she absolutely lost control of her temper—then maybe she would, but not in everyday conversa-

·tion. She looked at Jay as sarcastic as all hell. "Sounds like a perfectly delightful picture!"

"They use doubles and stunt men for the tricky stuff. There's no danger—"

"I'm not talking about that and you know it!" she said. "I don't want Josh to be an actor, in the first place. In the second place, the only reason Gutman's made the offer is to cash in on all the cheap publicity we've been getting."

"Look, Rita—so the kid has a part in a picture. That doesn't mean he's going to grow up to be an actor, does it?"

"Don't try to wheedle me into it, Jay! And he's not 'the kid.' His name is Josh, if you don't mind."

Boy, once she gets on her high horse about a major issue, she'll start picking on every tiny, insignificant, minor thing you say.

"*Josh*"—and he hit my name like a hammer—"Josh can earn five hundred per week, with a two-week guarantee!"

"Mom, please—I want to!"

"No."

"But why not?"

"Sure. Why not?" Jay asked. "You want the ki—Josh to go to college. Okay, you bank what he makes for him and use it toward—"

"Yeah," I chimed in, "that's a great idea. I can put myself through college. Then I'll be a lawyer or something."

"I said no!"

Jay turned to Merwin. "You talk to her. It's a great chance for the— It's a great chance for Josh!"

"I don't see the harm in it, Rita," Merwin said. "Might even be a good idea, after what's happened, just to keep him busy. Keep him from brooding—"

"Brooding!" she said. "He's been having the time of his life from what I can see! Having his picture taken down by that hammock, giving out interviews . . . ." She was really getting touchy.

"Oh, Rita, come now! I don't—"

"*Merwin!*" She has a way of saying your name when she gets in one of those moods that makes you feel if you utter

160

one more sound the whole Swiss Alps will come sliding down on your head.

All of a sudden the discussion was over. Jay left shortly afterwards. As he got to the door he kind of threw over his shoulder "About Josh—I won't tell Sam it's off yet. Think it over for a day or two." She didn't even answer him.

You get to a point with my mother where you know it's no use pursuing the subject any further. You might as well save your voice. You just have to lay low and bring it up at a later date. Or better yet, get a third party to bring it up for you. That point had definitely been reached, so I went upstairs to sulk for the rest of the day.

That's another thing: she hates it when I sulk. But I wanted to be in that picture so bad I could taste it, and I felt she was being unreasonable. I sat up in my room planning all kinds of tactics to get her to agree to let me do it. I'm the plotter of the world. I was rehearsing all kinds of speeches and rebuttals like— "You'd think, after getting me all involved in another one of your messy love affairs, and letting me find him with that hole in his head and all those goddam ants crawling over his face, you'd at least let me do something pleasant for a change!" Once I start cooking these things up in my mind I go way out. Like— "All right, Mom, if that's your attitude I'll be forced to tell the District Attorney that I heard you downstairs talking to Ben early that morning. That I peeked out of the window and saw you both walking down back of the house to the barbecue area. You were arguing. You sounded angry. Shortly after you disappeared down through the trees I heard you screaming at him. Then a shot rang out. You came back up to the house and went to bed!"

"Why, Josh, you know that's a lie!"

"Ah, yes! *I* know, Mother, and *you* know—but will *they* know? I think not! I believe you realize now how very important this movie job is to me. I refuse to let anything stand in the way of my career. Not even you, Mother!"

Anyhow, you can be damn sure I'd never go through with it. Not with *my* mother. Because when she turns on the cooling system she gets to be just like an iceberg. It destroys me.

After an hour or so I heard her walking down the hall toward my door. She stood there a while, listening. Then she knocked.

"Josh?" she said. I didn't answer at first. "Josh?"

I thought I'd make her wonder. She tried the door several times but I'd locked it.

"Josh, are you in there?"

"Yes."

"What are you doing?"

"Nothing."

"Then why is the door locked?"

"I don't know." She always cows me into giving these vague answers when what I really wanted to say was "It's my room, isn't it? Well, that's why the door's locked!"

"What do you mean—you don't know?"

"I just locked it, that's all!"

"I want to know *why* you locked it?"

"I'm resting."

"Can't you rest with the door unlocked?"

"No."

"Don't give me short answers, young man!" Boy, there's the danger signal—*young man*! That means there's trouble in the boiler room, all right.

"What do you want me to say?" I asked.

"And don't get fresh!"

Christ, you can't win at a time like that. So I just didn't say anything.

"Josh, did you hear me!"

"Yes."

"Well?"

"Well, what?"

"I'm telling you—don't get fresh!" She jiggled the doorknob again. "All right, Josh, open the door! You and I are going to have a little talk!"

"I'll come downstairs later on. I don't feel like it now." Boy, I was really getting nervy.

"Now listen—I'm just about fed up with you. And don't think you're fooling me. You're sulking—that's what you're doing in there. Sulking! Like a little girl!"

It was the last that did it. I loathe it when grownups get mean like that. I wasn't feeling at all like a sissy any more, but I guess my resentment to that kind of talk was still very strong.

"I know that's what your doing!" Her voice was getting more shrill by the second. "Well, isn't it?"

"Okay then, why do we have to go through the Spanish Inquisition—if you're so sure?"

"Josh, I'm telling you—I'm not enjoying standing out here one single bit. You'd better unlock that door and do it this minute."

"Nobody's asking you to stand out there, you know!" I think I was being possessed by the devil at this point.

"You're going to get such a slap in the face it'll make your head spin!"

"That kind of talk isn't going to get me to open the door," I said. Suddenly I felt this silly streak coming over me. Mainly, I guess, because we were both acting like kids, screaming at one another through the door. Also the nervous tension of having an argument with her made me kind of giggle.

"I'm not being funny," she snapped. "I meant what I just said!"

"If you keep telling me you're going to beat me up I'll never open the door."

"Do you want me to call Merwin and have him hear the ridiculous way you're acting? I thought you were beginning to grow up, but apparently I was mistaken."

I didn't want Merwin to get involved, so I didn't answer for a second while I was figuring out how to get out of this.

"All right, Josh, that's what I'm going to do."

I heard her start to walk down the hall and something perverse as hell made me yell after her: "While you're at it—why don't you get Ben? He could always handle me!"

Now what I said that for I'll never know. I suppose having this stupid fight was a way of letting off steam for both my mother and me. It was a pretty poor excuse; but you had to get rid of it somehow, so you picked the most trivial thing in the world and let go.

When I said it I heard her footsteps stop. She stood out in the hall for quite a while. Then I heard her walking away very softly.

I felt like a real monster.

About a half hour later Merwin knocked on my door. "Sweetie, may I come in?" I went to the door and opened it. "Your mother's very upset," he said.

"I know. I'm sorry about bringing up Ben," I told him, "but I'm upset, too. I don't understand why she won't let me take that part. It's only a couple of weeks, and we could use the money. What's so awful about it?"

"Sweetie, you've got to understand about your mother. God forbid, I don't want to sound like a Pollyanna, but she's only thinking of your own good. She doesn't want you to grow up and live the kind of life she's had."

"Why would I do that? At least I wouldn't have all the rotten boy friends she's had. Or a lot of the cuckoo friends."

"Don't you see, Josh—it's because of the instability of her professional life that she's gotten so mixed up in her personal life."

I asked Merwin what had *really* happened with her career. I never quite understood why she hadn't stayed at the top. He tried to explain it to me.

"You've got to keep in mind that Rita came into the motion picture business when she was only a couple of years older than you are now. She'd had no experience, no training, no indoctrination of any sort. A beauty contest and, suddenly, by a fluke, the lead in a movie and a star at eighteen! She wasn't equipped for it. It was all too quick, too unprepared for. Oh, sure, five or six wonderful years, playing beautiful young things, requiring very little acting talent, but—"

"She's a good actress now," I said.

"Of course, sweetie, but it took a long time and she learned the hard way. The first success came so easily I'm sure she felt everything else would follow just as naturally. But it takes serious work, hard work. Becoming a good actor or actress—a really good one—is no snap. Rita neglected her career those first few years. She got caught up in the glamour, the social life, the peripheral fluff of Hollywood—as was only natural for a beautiful, exciting *and* excitable young girl.

"Then, eventually, she got thrown into a couple of roles

that were beyond her. She began to slip. And, Josh, remember this: for every one person around to help boost your buns up the ladder, there's an even dozen ready to step on your shoulders on the way back down.

"Acting—probably the coldest, cruelest profession there is. Certainly the most unstable *and* the most personal, thus compounding the felony."

I certainly couldn't argue with him about the dangers of it.

"I think I know how it went with your mother, Josh. You see, once she began getting rejected in her professional life, she started looking for acceptance doubly hard in her personal life. She began running around with the sophisticated set, the so-called sophisticates. Actually, on the inside, they're a fairly hollow bunch. They take what they can from a person: youth, beauty, fun. And the returns are meager indeed: a pat on the back at first; then a kick in the ass when you're no longer a novelty.

"So your mother started looking for an exciting love-life. The minute you start that frantic search, you're in trouble. When it happens, it happens—but you can't do the Golden Fleece bit, baby. And when you can't find the one real person for you—and unfortunately, in your mother's case, whoever he is, he's managed to keep himself hidden—then you start settling for the attractive ones, the wealthy ones, the influential ones. Even worse—the fun ones! Pretty soon you're just looking for company, for someone to spend time with. That's what happened to Rita.

"If she weren't a good person, if she hadn't all the right instincts, this would be a condemnation. But your mother, Josh, has some remarkable qualities. She's loyal, she's kind, she's gentle. She has one failing: she falls in love with charming no-goods, thinking she can change them, no doubt. She needs to be needed. Most of all, she's a thoroughly nice human being. But I think you know that."

"Yes, I do," I told him.

"Actually, if she ever finds the right man, she'll make a wonderful wife. God only knows, she gives herself completely, heart and soul." He kind of chuckled. "Why, Sugar-on-a-stick, I *am* sounding off. Old Granny Saltzman! Do I sound like an old poop?"

"No." I laughed. "It helps me straighten things out in my mind."

"I'm not saying Rita's perfect, but then who the hell is? The worst you can say about Rita is that she's soft and weak, and not the wisest of mortals. Oddly enough, those very qualities are redeeming in a way. If she were a little colder, harder, a shrewder woman, she might—on the outside at least—be more successful and therefore seem to be a happier woman. But she's a tried and true softie. Yet, conversely, she's got a marvelous strength. She's had to be strong to be able to keep her head above water after all she's been through. Thank God, she's an incurable optimist. Mainly, I think, because of you, Josh!"

"Because of me?" I asked.

"Yes. There's not a doubt in my mind that if it weren't for you she'd have given up long ago. She wants for you, baby! Do you understand what I mean?"

"Yes, I think so."

"When I say *wants*, I mean not only things, but happiness, normalcy, a way of life. That's actually why she's against this movie thing."

"Yes, but just because I'd be in a movie doesn't mean my career would turn out the same way hers did."

"True, but she's indoctrinated by her own life and experiences. She wants to guard you against the same tough times, the struggles, and the heartbreaks."

"I understand all that, but even so—"

"And remember, baby, this is a frightening period and we're not sure the worst is over—not by a long shot. So above all, make every effort to be kind and understanding to her."

"I'm trying to," I told him. I had been, and I felt like the lowest snake there is for the things I'd said when she was outside my door.

"At any rate, sweetie, she loves you dearly! Mind you, I still don't say there's anything wrong in your taking a flyer for two weeks to act in a movie." He stood up from his chair. "I'll still have a talk with her when she calms down and do my best to convince her."

"You will? Honestly, Merwin?"

"But, of course! I can probably bore her into it. However, if she doesn't come around, try to understand and let it go." He put his hands on my shoulders. "You're so very young, Josh. You've got many chances ahead of you. This is a drop in the bucket."

"Okay. I promise I won't make a Federal Case out of it," I told him. "I guess I'll go down and make up with her. Don't you think?"

"I'll cut you out of my will if you don't." Merwin walked toward the door. As he was going out into the hall, he stopped, turned around and said, "You know, Josh, at times I almost wish I had a son like you. But, of course, the whole idea is absurd. I'm really not built for child-bearing. Too tiny around the pelvic region!" he slapped his hands against his hips, looked up, and, as soon as he saw me smiling, went to his room.

What a character! Merwin always knew how to say something wild to snap you out of a mood when you had to do something you didn't relish. And I wasn't looking forward too much to making up. I didn't mind it once it was done. It was *how* to make up that always seemed tricky. I hate to get involved in a lot of hashing-over talk. The best way is to do it emotionally.

That's what I did that time. I took a deep breath, ran out of my room, clomped down the stairs, and when I got to the bottom I yelled out, "Mom!"

"Yes?" She was in the kitchen.

I tore in. She was sitting at the breakfast table over a cup of coffee. I ran right over to her and threw my arms around her. "I'm sorry, Mom. I was a jerk!"

She hugged me back. Then she said, "You're not such a jerk. You're pretty clever, Josh." I guess she meant the way I just came in and grabbed her to avoid any long-drawn-out scene.

It was Saturday and Cecila was gone. The next thing you knew we were talking about what to fix for dinner and everything was relatively all right.

Chapter 22

ABOUT the middle of the following week our situation started getting hot again. The gangster thing was petering out. They'd taken them all into custody, but they really couldn't pin much on them; all they could do was to kick them out of the state. Honest to God, I don't understand gangsters! They've each got a record a mile long filled with every crime in the books. But unless they have newsreel pictures of them machine-gunning a whole family and dumping them in the river personally, they can't get anything on them. They're always released on account of a stupid technicality. Then you take a good guy that's a little broke. He gets caught shoplifting a tube of tooth paste. They haul him to the police station; slap him in jail; he can't make a phone call; he loses his job, and his wife leaves him. There's something screwy somewhere.

It was on a Wednesday evening that Ben's wife had an interview in one of the papers in which she accused the District Attorney's office of suppressing the facts surrounding her husband's death. There was a big picture of her in her hotel room surrounded by two of her lawyers from the East. She was looking very elegant and sophisticated and, most of all, determined. A far cry from the way she was that night in our driveway. The implications she made about my mother were pretty scary. There was no doubt about the fact that she was out for blood. She even blamed my mother for Ben's getting involved in gambling debts—which we didn't even know about until after his death.

Lee came down on Thursday afternoon along with Sally. They seemed far from happy. This time my mother insisted on me being left out of the meeting. I was sent upstairs. After I'd been in my room about forty-five minutes I heard a car drive up. I looked out the window. It was Roy, the little coroner, the dumb cop, and the other cop, Jerry. It looked like the whole cast was there. It was about four-fifteen then. At six-thirty I was still sitting up in my room wondering what the hell was going on and wishing I could be in on it.

I decided to call up Sid Traylor to see if we were playing tennis the next afternoon. I went into my mother's room and picked up the phone to dial, but Lee was on it. The only thing I heard was, "Right. Then we'll bring the boy in." The guy on the other end said, "Hold it while I check the time," and went away from the phone. I was dying to listen, because I wondered if the "boy" was me; but when the other man walked away from the phone I was afraid Lee might hear me breathing or notice the echo, so I hung up.

After I'd been back in my room about fifteen minutes Merwin came in and asked me to come downstairs. They were all sitting in the living room. The combined word for the way they looked was—*grim*. My mother's face was pale and rigid like she had wax poured over it and it had cooled off. After exchanging half-hearted greetings, Lee said, "Josh, tomorrow morning at eleven your mother and Merwin will drive you into town. You'll go to Captain Mansan's office and they'll take a deposition from you. That's simply an official statement concerning the circumstances of Ben's death."

"I've already told them about that," I said.

"I know, but this should clear it up for once and for all. Then you won't have to be involved any more. Okay? It's nothing to be nervous about. Tell them the same things you did when they were down here before. Only I can promise that this time they'll treat you with a little more respect."

"Josh," my mother said, "go in and tell Cecelia we'll be eating a little late tonight. About eight."

By the time I came back in the living room everybody was getting ready to leave. They were so solemn you wondered where they were leaving for—Siberia? When my mother, Merwin, and I were left alone in the living room I asked what was going on.

She didn't say anything, but Merwin spoke up. "Sweetie, it's ... Lee wants to get this whole thing cleared up before

169

it drags on any longer, that's all!" I could tell there was a lot more to it, but I could also tell this was no time to be asking a lot of questions.

The three of us had dinner in almost total silence until around dessert and coffee time. Then they started talking about Lee having found out that Ben had sired an illegitimate child by some woman in England years ago and that his wife had been paying for the support of the child. They also learned that Ben had tried to get her to agree to a divorce several times in the past, and that after one of these unsuccessful attempts to get his freedom he'd smashed up a racing car in Italy. That happened in 1953, and there was talk at the time that maybe he was trying to kill himself. My mother and Merwin spoke about all these things like I wasn't even present, so I never entered into the conversation.

After dinner we went into the living room. We'd only been in there a few minutes when the phone rang. Merwin answered it. He turned to my mother after a while and said, "Jay says it looks like they've found a sponsor for the series. He wants to talk to you."

"Good," she said, and she walked to the phone. But there wasn't much enthusiasm in her voice.

When she got on the phone all you heard was, "Yes . . . uh-huh . . . I see . . ." for a long time. Then she said, "Well, of course I'm excited about it, but—" She looked around at me and said, "Josh, will you go out in the kitchen and help Cecelia? I've got to talk to Jay for a while."

I knew damn well something was up, but it was fairly obvious that it wasn't for my ears to hear. I was pretty sure I'd find out sooner or later, though, because everyone was so used to talking in front of me someone was bound to make a slip.

Out in the kitchen with Cecelia I remembered something. "Hey, Cecelia, haven't you seen the evening paper?"

"Why, no, I haven't! And Miss Rita usually brings it in here for me to read right before you folks have dinner."

When I went back in the living room I asked my mother about it. She said she guessed they just didn't deliver it that night. Merwin excused himself after he'd had another cup of coffee because he had some writing to do. He'd been so tied up with us he'd been neglecting his work.

Just about that time Stella and Ef popped by for a surprise visit. As we met them at the door, Stella said, "We saw the papers tonight and thought we'd better drive on down."

My mother gave them the "Cheese it, the kid!" sign, and they clammed up.

I decided to make it easy on them. I excused myself and went upstairs. My motives weren't really that pure, though. As soon as I hit the second floor I tore for my mother's bedroom and got on the phone to Sid Traylor.

"Hello, Sid. This is Josh."

"Hey, Josh, how about us tonight!"

"What do you mean?" I asked him.

"In the papers," he said.

"That's why I'm calling. We didn't get our paper tonight."

"You didn't see the *Examiner*?"

"No," I said. "But I had a hunch there was something in it. Everyone around here's being evasive as hell."

"You and your mother and this Mrs. Nichols are plastered all over it. And remember those pictures they took the day we played tennis against Hermosa Beach?"

"Yeah."

"Well, they've got a big picture of you and me on the courts. You're serving and I'm just kind of standing there like a dodo bird. My dad went down to the store to buy a whole slew of them. I'll bring one to school for you tomorrow."

"Great," I said. Then I remembered. "Damn it all! I won't be in school tomorrow. I've got to go into the District Attorney's office in the morning."

"Yeah? Hey, things are getting pretty hot for your mother, aren't they?"

"What do you mean? You got the paper handy?"

"It's downstairs. Wait—I'll go get it!" He left the phone and came back in a minute or so. As soon as he picked it up again I told him that if anybody got on the phone from downstairs to automatically hang up. I'd hardly got the last word out of my mouth when somebody started dialing. We both hung up in a jiffy.

I sat there being eaten alive by curiosity. I was waiting a good long time so whoever was on the phone downstairs would be off by the time I tried to call again. But while I was sitting there the phone rang and before I thought about it I picked it up. By the time I found out it was Jay, my mother was on the other end from downstairs. "What are you doing up there, Josh?"

"Just thought I'd better call Sid Traylor and tell him to get the assignments for me over the weekend," I said.

"He'll get them anyhow, won't he? Isn't he in most of the same classes you're in?"

"Well, yes . . . . but—"

"Then please stay off the phone. Lee's going to be calling later, and I have some calls to make, too. You go to bed early now. I'll see you in the morning. I'll be up early." I said good night and hung up.

I had to practically hypnotize myself into going to sleep after reading for a couple of hours. One thing: I knew I'd get the morning paper because they delivered it around seven-thirty, and when my mother said she'd be up early I knew she wouldn't be up that early.

That's where I was mistaken. She was having coffee when I got downstairs at a quarter to eight, and there was no sign of a paper. I looked out the front door: nothing.

She hardly said a word more than good morning to me; so I felt I'd better keep my mouth buttoned up and not start asking a lot of questions. We had a somber breakfast with Merwin, who went right upstairs afterwards to do some writing. I just kind of knocked around the house. The phone was ringing, off and on, but it was always for my mother, so we hardly spoke at all.

About ten o'clock Merwin stopped work and we took off for downtown Los Angeles. It's one of the ugliest cities in the world, and it sure doesn't help any when you drive through it in total silence. You just get to concentrate on how Godawful depressing it is. Even the people on the streets look beat by it. Merwin wrote a novel about Hollywood once. In it he described Los Angeles as a place where a lot of old people go to die and then don't. I think they ought to blow Los Angeles up and build it over again so it looks like Beverly Hills.

On the way we passed a couple of newsstands. Several times I could make out part of my mother's name in the headlines but I couldn't tell what they said. I was beginning to feel there was a plot afoot to keep me in the dark.

We ended up at Lee's office. I'd never been there before; I didn't realize he had such a terrific setup. He had a couple of assistants and secretaries, a switchboard operator, and the works. And enough plants in his reception room to make it look like a tropical rain forest. We sat outside for only a few minutes when we were ushered into his private office. He must have spent a fortune having it decorated. Lee was seated behind this desk about the size of an airplane wing. We were introduced to a Mr. Craig, one of his assistants, a little thin swarthy guy with glasses and a very intense face.

"Josh," Lee said, "Mr. Craig will go along with you so I can get a full report. I don't believe there'll be any problems at all. When you're finished he'll bring you back here. You're a little late, so you better be on your way."

My mother came over and kissed me good-by; her eyes were starting to well up, so we made a speedy exit. As we drove over to the District Attorney's office I said to this Mr. Craig, "What's up?" He mumbled something about routine questioning and didn't say another word until he spoke to the guy who was sitting at the desk in the D.A.'s outer office.

"Captain Mansan's around but the D.A.'s held up. You'll have to wait awhile," the fellow at the desk said.

Wait *awhile*! That was at eleven-thirty. About one-thirty, the District Attorney himself came in with three other guys and breezed into his office. I knew who it was because everyone snapped-to. A few minutes later Captain Mansan came down the hall with his crew, and about five minutes after that we were ushered in. I was introduced around and shook hands with everybody. The D.A. didn't throw his arms around me or anything but he at least seemed friendly. "I'm an old admirer of your mother's, young man," he said.

173

I felt like saying, "Then why don't you get off her back?"

Some giant of a guy made me take an oath that what I was going to say was the truth. After that the District Attorney told me not to be nervous, that this was customary procedure, and that after they got all this information from me they wouldn't have to call me again. I told them I didn't mind and away we went.

I won't bore you with all the questions and answers that followed, except to say that the District Attorney only spoke a couple of times and then very mildly. He let Captain Mansan do practically all the questioning. And nobody ever raised his voice or stuck his finger in my face. It was all very controlled, and somehow that made it all the more frightening.

You see, the first time it was almost like a satire the way they went at me. This time, because of the calmness and the methodical way they were operating, it seemed all the more real and consequently all the more serious. If Captain Mansan asked me a question and was dissatisfied with my answer or appeared to doubt it, instead of jumping down my throat he'd rephrase it a couple of different ways and ask it again. If I kept on giving the same answer, which I usually did, he'd let it drop and go on to something else. Several times he'd come back later on and ask a question he'd asked previously like he'd just thought it up freshly in his mind. You definitely got the feeling they were looking for any kind of slip.

They went over the last time we saw Ben, on Sunday, in minute detail. When we got to that part, Captain Mansan took out a sheet of paper and started working off it. Mansan kept trying to get me to say that Ben and my mother were fighting. Finally, after about ten minutes spent on that, I spoke up and said, "It takes two to make a fight, and my mother never even raised her voice to him!" When I said that the D.A. smiled and told the Captain to go on with the questioning.

I again skipped over the part about hearing Ben yelling at her when I was upstairs getting dressed. Also, I didn't tell them about my mother going downstairs and turning on the TV set after I'd gone to bed. I'd been meaning to ask her if she'd told them about it but she'd been so touchy lately that a good chance never came up. It worried me about why we were hiding something that probably wasn't important. It wasn't that I doubted her. I just couldn't understand it. But since the police never questioned me about it, I figured my mother hadn't mentioned those two things. Then I couldn't help wondering if she'd spoken to Lee about them. If she had, I couldn't understand why he wouldn't have checked with me to see if I was telling everything. And if she hadn't, I couldn't figure why she'd keep something from Lee, who was her lawyer. Also, if she *wasn't* mentioning certain things, I couldn't help wondering why she hadn't checked with me to see if I was skipping them, too.

After about forty-five minutes, a young kid came in with all kinds of delicatessen sandwiches, potato salad, Cokes, coffee, and Danish pastries. We all took a break while we picked out what we wanted to eat. Then we started in again, and I was talking with my mouth full for quite a while. My mother would have had a fit.

The whole session took about an hour and a half—because of all the questions that kept interrupting me. When I did finish, the District Attorney picked up a piece of paper he'd been making notes on and asked me about eight or ten questions himself. They were mostly the same as Captain Mansan had asked, and had mainly to do with whether my mother had ever fought with Ben or threatened him or accused him in any way and whether there was a possibility she could have known he was already married. Finally, the D.A. came over, thanked me for my time and for being so cooperative, and Mr. Craig and I left.

As we were going down in the elevator Mr. Craig turned to me and said, "Good job, Josh." That made me feel pretty good. I thought we'd become buddies on the way back to Lee's office, but he never opened his mouth again. Except to swear at a fat lady who waddled out in front of his car right in the middle of a block without a crosswalk or anything. He stuck his head out the window and yelled "That's a good way to get some of the blubber knocked off—you silly bitch!"

My mother was all over me when I walked into the office. She, Merwin, and Lee seemed to be in fairly good moods by then. Mr. Craig gave a very good report of my meeting with the D.A. "The kid handled himself like a real pro!" he said. Everybody congratulated me.

Lee checked over the list of all the people that were going to be questioned the next day. Boy, they had everybody that had ever been connected with us on call for questioning—from Cecelia to the Paganellis to the writer and his wife where we had dinner that Sunday night. It was shaping up like a spectacular.

We had a much more pleasant drive on the way back to Paraiso Beach. We weren't having community singing or anything like that, but some of the tension had disappeared from both Merwin and my mother.

As we pulled up to the house we saw about six or seven cars around the driveway; when we went inside, Sally was there with some reporters and a couple of photographers. They were all people that had been down the day of the gangster bombing. My mother was definitely put out at finding them there, and showed it. Sally took her in the dining room and had a chat with her, though. When she came back she was doing her best to smile and be gracious. You could tell she didn't mean it, but she was making an effort.

She asked Merwin to fix them drinks if they wanted them. Then she said, "You don't mind if my son excuses himself and takes his nap, do you?"

"Mom, let me stay! Besides, who ever takes a nap any more?"

That got a laugh from the gang but it didn't even get a smile from my mother. So I started heading out of the living room.

Sally said, "Rita, he can come down for a few pictures with you later on, can't he?"

"I don't know. We'll see!" She was acting very curt.

"I'll call you in a little while, Tiger!" Sally patted me on the ass as I walked by her.

I was getting upset about all of a sudden being excluded from meetings with the press and everything. The damage had been done by this time, I figured, so why the change of policy? I decided to call Sid Traylor to find out what the hell the papers were saying, but he was out playing tennis. About an hour later Sally knocked on my door and told me to come down for some pictures.

I could tell that my mother was in a foul mood when I walked in the living room. Her face had a very sharp look about it and her movements were jerky and abrupt. They started taking pictures of her sitting in an overstuffed chair with me perched on one of the arms. I lit cigarettes for her at first. Then they took some with her holding a glass and me pouring water into it from a silver pitcher. Her hand had been a little shaky when I lit the cigarettes, but by the time we got to the ones where I was pouring the water she was actually trembling. And her breathing was unsteady. I think they could tell she was losing her patience because they were snapping pictures like crazy, a mile a minute. Finally, one of the women reporters asked Sally if she could have a couple of pictures of me taken down by the hammock. My mother turned on her in a flash.

"Do you have any children of your own?" she asked her. The woman was a little surprised. "Why, yes. A little girl, thirteen."

"How would you like it if she'd gone through an experience like my son's and people were constantly dragging her down there, making their point to that hammock?"

The woman looked stumped for words and hesitated a moment. My mother leaped right in. "I thought not!" Then she walked right to the center of the living room and started wringing her hands. She kind of looked from one to the other of them, jerking her head around in little tight movements. Finally she just blurted out, "I'm telling you— I want the goddam hammock taken out of here!" She hardly ever swore like that. Sally headed for her immediately. As she went to take her arm my mother shook her off. "Sally, do you hear me?" She was shouting at her like she was deaf although Sally was standing right smack in front of her. "I want that hammock out of there this afternoon. Do you hear me?"

"Yes, honey." Sally was almost whispering. "I'll take care of it!"

But she wouldn't let Sally off the hook. "I mean it! I'm not kidding!"

"Yes, dear," Sally said. "I'll arrange it."

"Do you know somebody that can do the job?"

Sally kind of looked around at the press people as if to hint they ought to take a powder. Most of them were getting their things together; none of them were looking directly at my mother. "Well . . . I . . . I'm sure I can find someone, Rita."

"Don't lie to me now! *Can you have it taken care of?* Because if you can't, I'll do it myself!" She wheeled around to the reporters. "You can take pictures of me dragging it away! Would you like that?" She really started to go to pieces then. She was sobbing and kind of choking at the same time. Sally put her arms around her and began leading her out of the room. When they got to the door, she screamed, "I don't care what you do—burn it or blow it up—but get rid of that hammock!" As they were going up the stairs I heard her cry out, "I don't want him going down there again!" Then she called back to me, "Josh, don't you go down there!"

"All right, Mom!" I mumbled. I don't think she even heard it, because I could hardly speak. I was getting all choked up myself. It was frightening because it came over her so quickly.

"Do you understand me, Josh?" she called out. I said as loudly as I could that I did, and I could hear Sally assuring her on the stairs that I wouldn't go near the hammock ever again.

The newspaper people were standing there in complete silence. I was doing my best not to fall apart in front of them. After a moment or so one woman came over and put her arm around me. "I'm sorry, Josh. Tell your mother we didn't mean to upset her." Then, as each one filed out, they said something to me like "It'll be all right, son," or "Thanks for the pictures." They were very nice.

Merwin, who'd been upstairs writing, must have heard my mother when she was yelling to me. I could hear him talking as Sally and he were taking her to her bedroom.

I sat there alone in the living room wondering when this mess would be over with. For the first time since finding

Ben I began to feel very tired and weary of it and also terribly worried about my mother. It began to dawn on me that the whole thing wasn't as much fun as I'd tried to make it out to be.

They were still upstairs when I heard the evening paper clomp against the door. You'd think I'd tear down the hall, out the door, and practically attack it, from the way I'd been so curious before, but I didn't. I walked very quietly out there and picked it up. It was folded over, but when I opened it up the headlines hit me smack in the face. *NICHOLS CASE MAY GO BEFORE GRAND JURY ...* All of our pictures were on the front page again: Ben, his wife, my mother, and me. There was a gigantic article that took up three full columns saying that because of all the fishy incidents involved in the case, and the fact that Ben's wife was really putting the pressure on, it looked like the case would go to the Grand Jury to see if an indictment would be brought against my mother.

When you saw it in black and white on the front page it began to look spooky as hell! The newspaper also printed this one still picture of my mother taken from a movie called *Conquest of Africa.* In the picture she was looking down the barrel of a huge elephant rifle, aiming right at the camera. What a dirty trick to play! It made it look like she was aiming at Ben! They had two pictures of him on the front page. One in a bathing suit taken on the Riviera and a wedding picture with his wife. I just stared at those pictures. "You rotten son-of-a-bitch!" I said. I hated Ben that moment more than I ever had since his death.

Chapter 23

As I was standing there by the front door I heard a car turn off Calle Vista into our driveway. It was these terrific friends of my mother's, Andy and Midge Lansing. They couldn't have showed up at a more appropriate time. Just seeing them made me forget our troubles for a while. Andy screeched to a halt in front of the house, popped out of the car, lifted me way above his head, and swung me around. He's about six-four you know. When he put me down, Midge started hugging and kissing me to death. They're a wonderful couple. They look terrific together because he's so huge and she's so tiny. They must be very much in love. I hardly ever remember seeing them argue, let alone fight. I guess they don't dare fight. He'd crush her to death if they even played grab-ass.

"We just got back today," Midge said, "and we came right down."

They were both full of sympathy about the Ben thing. They'd met him once before they went to take over this ranch in Wyoming, and they liked him. After consoling me Andy said, "Where's your old lady?"

"Upstairs. She's not feeling too well," I told them.

"Of course she's not," Midge said. "Poor angel! But we'll take care of that. Everything's going to be all right, Josh. We'll get this whole bit cleaned up in no time." Then the two of them went whooping and hollering through the house and up to my mother's bedroom.

Oh, God, I was glad they were back!

I walked into the living room to finish reading the gruesome paper. About fifteen minutes later they all came down. Everything seemed fine. Even my mother had perked up; she was talking like there hadn't been a scene or anything. I forgot about the paper and had it in my lap when she walked into the room. Oddly enough, she just looked at it and said, "Oh, Josh, don't read all that trash!" Then she went right on talking to Andy and Midge. I guess seeing them and knowing they were going to be around for a while cheered her up more than anything.

Merwin fixed drinks, and there we all were having a cocktail party like old times. I tell you, it was screwy the moods you sailed in and out of!

Suddenly my mother came out with "Oh, Josh, I forgot to tell you—tomorrow afternoon we're driving up to Andy and Midge's for the weekend." They own several ranches; one's only a couple hours from Los Angeles.

"Gee, that's great!"

"Josh, I hear you're quite a rider these days," Andy said. He turned to Merwin and Sally. "I remember when he wouldn't even pet a horse."

Right away I looked forward to getting up there and riding all the hell over the whole place. I was also looking forward to getting away from the house at Paraiso Beach. It was starting to get me down.

They all stayed for dinner, including Sally. Merwin was very funny that night. He was going to be questioned the next day, too, and he was making up all sorts of answers.

"What did you do immediately after seeing the deceased?"

"I retched a total of seventeen times."

"Had the deceased ever spoken about suicide or threatened to take his own life?"

"Not in so many words! However, when he'd come down for the weekend he'd go to sleep in his bed, all right. But in the morning we'd invariably find him curled up in the oven!"

You see, it was all a big joke again. Everyone was beginning to hate Ben with a vengeance at this point. Nothing was sacred.

Later on, when it was time for Andy and Midge to start driving up to the ranch, they suggested that I go with them right then. My mother jumped at the idea.

"Josh, go upstairs and start packing. I'll be up in a minute to help you."

I tore upstairs, put on my dungarees, and started laying out the stuff I thought would come in handy at the ranch.

She followed me in about ten minutes. She took a much larger bag from the closet than the one I'd picked out and began filling it with an awful lot of extra shirts, shorts, socks, and pants. She was really throwing stuff in that suitcase. All of a sudden I became a little panicky.

"Mom, you *are* coming up tomorrow afternoon, aren't you?"

She stopped packing, looked up at me, and flashed this nervous kind of smile at me. "Of course, Josh. What did you think?" Then she saw I was looking at all the things she was packing. "Oh, darling—you know how I over-pack!"

For a minute there I had the uneasy notion I was being shipped off—like to Elliston again. Then I got to wondering—if the questioning didn't go well the next day, maybe they wouldn't let her go. I didn't want to bring up anything morbid like that, so I stood there not saying anything.

She came out with "I can't wait to get away for a day or two. And I'll bet you can't either!" she said. Then she gave me a kiss on the cheek and said very softly, "It's not so much fun any more, is it, Josh?"

"No," I said.

"When it's all over we'll go away on a trip! Just the two of us! How's that?"

"I'd like it," I told her.

"Good. It's a promise!"

I wanted to ask her about what exactly she was going to tell the District Attorney, but she'd been in such a good mood ever since Andy and Midge arrived I didn't want to chance smashing it. Besides, she didn't kill Ben; so nothing could really go wrong, I told myself. It might look bumpy for a while until everyone, including his neurotic wife, was satisfied that the bastard had killed himself. Then we could sue for defamation of my mother's character or something.

By the time we were ready to leave for the ranch, at about ten-thirty, I didn't feel there was anything fishy any more. Merwin was going to stay home and look after the animals, and also get a lot of work done on his screenplay.

My mother kissed me good-by out in the driveway. I wanted to wish her and Merwin good luck in the morning,

182

but they'd been avoiding all direct talk during the evening, so I thought I'd better not bring it up and cast a pall on the group just as we were pulling out.

I sat in the front seat between Andy and Midge all the way to the ranch. I'd always liked them because they were very affectionate and warm toward me, even before, when I was such a dolt. They'd always made an effort to understand me and make me feel comfortable. They didn't have any children of their own; that's probably why. Sitting there with the two of them and the radio playing and Midge hugging me every so often and talking about everything you could think of and then Andy squeezing my leg if I said something he got a kick out of—something like that has always been a very special experience for me.

It's hard to explain, but, as much as I love my mother, I find myself, many times, wishing I were part of somebody else's family. It's lonely to have only a mother. Sometimes it's more than wishing, it's almost an aching. When I'm with a couple or a whole family, and enjoying their company, talking and laughing and sharing some experience, I get a terrific sensation of well-being and warmth and belonging. It reaches a peak where I'm enjoying myself so much I consciously stop and acknowledge it. As soon as I do that, I start going downhill. Because I realize I don't really belong with them—that the car ride, dinner, picnic, or whatever will be over, and that's the end of the one particular experience. I start getting depressed then.

Boy, I'm really spilling the beans, aren't I? Well, I've gone this far, so I might as well tell you about this recurrent dream I'm always having. It'll really make you gag. I've had it almost as far back as I can remember.

I'm in an adoption home with a lot of other kids. I'm always about seven or eight years old, and I have on short pants. I never get any older. I had the dream a couple of months ago and I was still in short pants. Anyhow, I'm sitting in a room with dozens of other boys and girls all about the same age. We're waiting for all these couples to be brought in to look at us. The room is a big, gray institutional-type one with benches to sit on and straw mats on the floor. One side is all windows like a schoolroom.

They look out into a playground which never has anyone playing in it because we're always inside waiting to be adopted. Every other blind on the windows is pulled down. The reason for this is that some of the kids have pimples or crooked teeth or warts; and the matrons—there are two of them—don't want to have it too light in there because some of the parents might pass up the kids that have these little imperfections. Also, maybe some of them didn't clean their fingernails or their ears.

The mats are on the floor because we usually have to wait a long time for the parents to arrive, and the matrons make us take naps so we won't be tired and cranky when they do show up. None of us go to sleep, though. We lie down on the mats and pretend to be asleep for a while; but we don't let ourselves actually go off. You see we don't want to be all rumpled and kind of messed-up like you are after you've taken a nap. So we lie very still, flat on our backs, our eyes shut. After a while the suspense is killing us as to when the parents will arrive, and we just lie there with our eyes open, staring up at the gray ceiling. Some of the kids start to whimper and cry a little, and the matrons shush them.

I never cry, though; I don't want my eyes to get all red and swollen or my face to break out. I guess I have the idea, also, that people won't pick a kid if they think he's a crybaby. I get very rigid instead and start to shake a little. And I start feeling chilly. Right then is when I usually hear the footsteps, lots of them, coming down the hall from far away.

The matrons turn on the lights. Not bright lights but enough to make it seem decently lit. We all scramble to our feet, brush ourselves off, and sit down on the benches.

The footsteps take forever to reach the door. I begin to perspire. I never have a handkerchief with me, and every time I have the dream I kick myself in the ass for not having one.

The parents finally come in. There are usually about fifteen or more couples. They kind of drift in, walking sideways, back and forth, and around our benches. It's almost like they're choreographed except there's not so much a pattern to their movement as there is a rhythm.

I always spot the couple I want to adopt me right off the bat. My conception is extremely corny. They're attractive, well-dressed, and solvent-looking. They're not what are usually called "young marrieds." They're more youthful-looking, middle-aged people. You just know the man is sort of distinguished and wise and kind. And the woman is very lovely in a motherly sort of way, not like a movie star or anything like that. The quality they have above all is a terrific warmth. They look like couples you see in commercial ads in the magazines. You know—the couple that retires to Florida while they're still able to enjoy it on a hundred and sixty dollars a month. They seem safe.

The other couples are not too bad. Some of them are a little young. They're always very happy with themselves. They have a look on their faces like they're picking out a pet instead of a child.

There are some that are a little too old. They usually search much harder than anyone else. You get the idea that once they make their choice the woman will burst into tears, and the man will start comforting her and leave the child they picked ... just standing there alone.

Then there's usually one couple that's searching frantically. You get the idea that they haven't come to adopt a child but rather to find their own baby who got mixed up or lost and sent to the orphanage by mistake. They're very nervous and seem to break the rhythm of the other couples.

I get so nervous after a while, so apprehensive about my couple not picking me, that I finally shut my eyes and start saying Our Fathers and Hail Marys like crazy. I alternate them. I say them so fast I'm sure they don't get a word of it in heaven.

Finally, after what seems like ages, I feel a hand on my shoulder. I open my eyes quickly, and practically every time it's my couple standing there smiling at me—the man with his hand on my shoulder, the woman with her arms outstretched to me. I point at myself as if to say, "You mean—me?" The woman smiles and nods; the man kind of chuckles. I rush to the woman's arms and she presses me very close to her so that my face is snug up against her side, right below her breasts. I almost get lost in the folds

185

of her dress. It's very dark and warm when I'm pressed up against her. That's when I usually wake up.

I've had variations on this dream. A couple of times I've felt the hand on my shoulder, looked up, and there aren't any parents there. Not only that, but all the kids have disappeared. The matrons, too. Everybody has taken a powder on me, and I sit there alone in that lousy gray room.

Once the dream got cut way short because when the parents first came in the door there was an awful commotion. Somebody was obviously shoving their way past the others into the room. It was my mother! She came crashing through the mob at the door, this awful frowning expression on her face. She started looking around the room, snapping her head from one kid to the next. I slumped down on the bench, looking toward the floor, so she wouldn't notice me because I had the feeling it was wrong of me to be there. I had the idea she'd beat the hell out of me if she found me. She found me all right and slapped me silly. She yanked me right off the bench and started cuffing me in the ears and dragging me out of the room, down this long hallway. When we got to a very long, steep stairway at the end of the hall, she gave me one gigantic shove and sent me flying off the top step. That's when I woke up. I'd fallen right off the goddam bed onto the floor!

I suppose these dreams are fairly obvious; almost anyone could figure them out.

Well, it took about two hours for Andy and Midge and me to drive up to the ranch. For about an hour and a half I was having a great time. We were playing word games and laughing and scratching, and I told them all about being questioned by the D.A. For a while we had the radio going and Andy would talk back to the commercials.

But, you see, toward the end of the trip, I started wishing that Andy and Midge were *mine,* that I was going home for good. I got very blue and sat there like a lump.

"What's the matter, Josh?" Andy asked, after a while.

"Nothing," Midge cut in before I had a chance to. "He's just tired. Aren't you, cowboy?"

I said yes, that was it—and we played it that way until we got to the ranch. They knew I was in some kind of a mood but they were nice enough not to press the point. There are some times when you don't want to be jollied up, and it's great when people realize it.

It was almost one o'clock when we got to the ranch. I was pooped. They gave me a little cabin all to myself about a hundred yards from the main ranch house. It had double decker bunks, Indian rugs on the floor, and a fireplace. I hardly remember getting into bed. The more depressed I get, the quicker I go to sleep. It's really sick the way I start in yawning when I get myself in a funk. Still, I guess it's better than staying awake and smoking tons of cigarettes or drinking. It's probably the healthiest sickness. "Back to the womb!" Merwin says.

Chapter 24

THE next morning I was awake at six and feeling great. God, it was a beautiful day, one of those crisp, clear, pungent mornings. The kind that smacks you right in the face and almost makes you dizzy.

Their ranch is up in the mountains along the Ridge Route between Los Angeles and Bakersfield, nestled in a valley with rolling hills on both sides and one big flat table mountain rising up in front of you. There's a stream, practically a river, that runs right down from the mountain through the valley and past the ranch buildings and corrals and all. The buildings are very crude-looking on the outside. They're either made out of adobe or old-looking wood. But on the inside they're very comfortably furnished and warm and livable.

First, you come to the cluster of buildings where Midge, Andy, their cook, Sinsiona, and their foreman, Perce, live. Beyond this group of buildings—which includes my cabin, another cabin Andy uses as an office, a smokehouse, and a garage that holds four cars—there are corrals, barns, shelters, stables, and such. Then past all of these is the bunkhouse where the cowboys live and eat. It's a whole community by itself. A real ranch, too—not one of those dude ones. They raise Hereford cattle and horses.

It's only about two and a half miles from the main highway, the Ridge Route, and a little country store and gas station. But it seems like you're hundreds of miles from civilization once you turn off onto their private road, which runs alongside the stream, and start driving up into their valley.

Sinsiona, the cook, is an Indian woman who weighs about two hundred pounds. Once you've eaten one of her meals, you understand why. She has to live with it. She cooks up a storm. And isn't that a funny name for the foreman of a ranch—Perce? Short for Percy, of course. He's a tall, wiry, grim-looking character who never says more than he has to. I think he's seen too many Gary Cooper movies.

That morning Sinsiona served orange juice, eggs, sausages, hotcakes, biscuits, all kinds of jam, coffee, milk—everything you could think of. By the time I got through eating I was so full I felt like going back to bed for a while.

"Josh, how'd you like to ride with us this morning?" Andy asked me.

"I sure would!" I was dying to show off how I'd learned to ride.

When we got out to the corral they gave me a great little bay horse named Tuffy. He had the most terrific personality of any horse I ever rode. He was quick as lightning, almost like a polo pony the way he moved. But he did have a stubborn streak in him. I mean if he decided he wanted to go one way and you wanted to go another you had a tussle on your hands.

"Don't let him get away with a thing," Andy said, "or he'll walk all over you. Show him right off you're boss and you'll get along fine."

I did show him, too. It took a little while, but by the time we were a mile or so up the trail he wasn't pulling many of his tricks.

"You've got a good seat, Josh," Andy said. "Hasn't he, Perce?"

"Yup," Perce said.

Boy, did that make me feel good.

It was a fine ride. Because Andy had been away for so long he really wanted to check the place over. We rode way up Coon Trail to the top of Table Mountain where we checked a whole herd of cattle for new-born calves. Then we went down the other side until we found a gang of wild horses that were hiding out in a gorge. We checked fences, salt blocks for the cows, water troughs—the works.

Sinsiona had packed lunches for us, so we stopped and ate under some trees by the stream on the far side of the mountain. In the afternoon Perce pointed out, from a distance, a whole mess of rattlesnakes sunning themselves

189

on some rocks in the middle of a field. We couldn't get too near them because horses are scared stiff of snakes.

If I hadn't had to worry about my mother it would have been a perfect day. I couldn't help wondering whether the questioning with the District Attorney would clear the whole thing up for once and for all or whether it would be the beginning of some real trouble. So, naturally, several times during the day I gave Ben a good cursing out. I was getting to be an expert at that.

We left the ranch about eight-thirty and didn't ride back to the stable until after four. Andy and I raced for about the last mile and, in spite of Tuffy's being a small horse, I didn't end up too far behind. A couple of lengths was all. I don't think Perce liked the idea of us racing but, after all, they were Andy's horses.

As we walked into the main ranch house I was expecting Midge to tell me all kinds of complications had set in and my mother couldn't make it. But I was wrong. Midge said she'd phoned and would be at the ranch by six o'clock. Boy, that was a relief!

We were all cleaned up and sitting in the living room by the time we heard her car drive up. She seemed to be in a fairly good mood. We were asking her every question in the books as we helped her in with her things, but all she'd say was "I simply have to have a drink first! Then I'll talk."

It was like that with almost all of her friends. Whenever they arrived some place or were leaving for another or made any move whatsoever—they always had to have a drink. It was like plasma. You'd have thought they were diabetics and actually had to have a drink or they'd keel over. I always wondered what would happen if kids were that way:

"Johnny, it's time to go to school. You'll be late."

"Mother, I simply *have* to have a milk shake before I can stand the ordeal of that school bus."

Or: "Johnny, will you get in this house! And get upstairs and take off those soggy clothes. You'll catch pneumonia!"

"Mother, I can't possibly make it upstairs until I've had a hot fudge sundae—with crushed almonds!"

That would make about as much sense as parents always

saying they can't possibly do something until they've had a drink.

After my mother had snatched her highball out of Andy's hand, Midge started in firing questions away at her; so did I.

Finally she said, "Wait a minute! Wait a minute! You two are worse than the District Attorney. Let me catch my breath."

"You had time to catch your breath all the way up in the car!" Midge said. "Come on, quit stalling! I mean—is the whole thing over with?"

"Midge, what a stupid question!" she snapped at her. "How do I know? I hope to God it is, but that's up to them. Lee's in touch with the District Attorney. He'll let us know as soon as they've come to a decision. As for me, I'm sick of it! *Do you mind very much if we drop it for the time being?*"

"No, of course not, dear. I'm sorry," Midge said.

"I came up here to relax and get away from it!" When you apologized to my mother about something she'd never let it drop right away. "As far as I'm concerned I'm forgetting about it for the weekend. I hope you'll help me!"

There was an uneasy silence during which it seemed to be mutually agreed to knock off about the case.

Midge was the one to speak up. "All right, it's going to be a fun couple of days. And that's that! How about another drink?"

"I know it'll come as a shock to you—but I'd love one!" my mother said. See, a drink always solved everything. It was like Indians passing the Peace Pipe.

That night Midge and Andy had another couple, Hank and Ginny Brace who owned a ranch nearby, over for dinner. We had a great evening. Midge is a real organizer. We played all kinds of games including charades and Michigan. I won six dollars. So you know what a good mood I was in.

About eleven o'clock Merwin called up. He'd been on the phone to his agent in New York; they decided he better fly back East for a few days to see about his latest novel which was in the galley stages. He was going to take a plane early the next morning. My mother talked to him about what to do with the animals. Merwin had called Cecelia, but she said much as she loved us she wouldn't stay in the house alone, even for one night. I was glad when she told him to call the vet's at Hermosa Beach and arrange to have the menagerie boarded for a day or two.

I got on the phone to wish him a good trip, and when we were saying good-by he said, "Remember the *Monitor* and the *Merrimac,* Josh boy. And all the other *frigates!*"

He could always break me up. The way he said "*frigates*" made it sound really dirty, but actually it wasn't. I was howling as my mother took the phone from me.

"I'm sure whatever you were saying to my son was absolutely filthy," she laughed. Then she told Merwin that as long as the animals were going to be boarded out we might stay at the ranch through Monday.

After she hung up we played some more games. I must have stayed up until about two o'clock.

The next day, Sunday, the Braces had invited us over to their ranch for a big barbecue they were throwing. It turned out to be a wild time. We got there about three, and by four-thirty there were about thirty people having drinks, pitching horseshoes, and sitting around in groups telling jokes. After a while everybody went over to the corral, where some of the men started in roping calves. A couple of the guys were a little potted and started clowning it up. One of them, Manny somebody, got a saddle blanket and picked out a yearling steer for a bullfight. He was strutting around, screaming "Ah-hah!" and stamping his feet. He put on a real show. The poor steer didn't know what was going on. He'd paw the ground and start to rush at Manny; then we'd all begin shouting and he'd stop and look at us and get all confused. It ended up with Manny pretending he was the bull and chasing the steer all over the place.

All during the proceedings everyone was deferring to my mother and me. We were the real celebrities of the party because of all the stuff in the newspapers. Nobody asked questions or spoke directly to us about the case, but you could tell everybody was very much aware of who we were and what we were involved in. There was one little girl a couple of years younger than me who kept staring at me all afternoon. Every time I'd look up she'd be peeking at me from some place or other. Of course, my mother was used to being the center of attention, but it was still new to me. I can't say I didn't like it; I really think I'm a ham.

Around six o'clock the actual eating began—and not a minute too soon. Everybody was staggering around by this time. They had wooden tables, a little better than picnic ones, set up all around their patio, which was enormous. We had steaks, roast corn, and about the best salad you ever tasted, plus all kinds of other things to pick at in bowls at every table.

My mother, myself, Andy, Midge, and about four other people sat at one table having a great time. Toward the end of dinner one of the guests came out from the main house and said there was a phone call for my mother. She got up and followed him back into the living room. I wondered how she could ever get a phone call there, but then I guessed whoever was phoning her had tried Andy and Midge's and been told where we all were.

Right after she left a young Mexican fellow, not more than twenty years old, appeared with a guitar and started walking among the tables singing Spanish and Mexican songs. He was terrific. The whole place quieted down. People kept on eating, but they were very careful not to bang their silverware or set their glasses down too hard. He must have sung for almost a half hour.

When he finished, Ginny Brace, the hostess, came over to see how we were making out. She looked around and asked where my mother was. I didn't realize she hadn't come back. That's how great the singer was.

"I don't know," Midge said. "She went to answer a phone call. I'll go find her."

Midge took off toward the house. By that time everyone was finished eating except me. I started woofing down an extra helping of strawberry shortcake that had been left at my mother's place. All of the rest of the people at our table kind of dispersed, including Andy. Pretty soon they had the Hi-Fi playing, and some of the couples were dancing. I couldn't see any of my group, so I supposed they were all inside drinking or playing games. I started to walk toward the main door leading into the living room when Midge came out.

"Hi, fella! How about a dance?" She had a big smile on her face, but anyone could tell it was a front.

"Okay," I said. As we were heading toward the other couples I asked her where my mother was.

"Oh, she wasn't feeling too well, honey. Andy's driving her back to the ranch. He'll come back for us later. Nothing serious—just an upset tummy."

"Who was the phone call from?" I asked her.

"Huh?" You can always tell someone's going to lie when they pretend not to hear a simple question like that, especially when you're right next to them. They're stalling for time. Also, you never have to repeat the question. They answer it when they figure out what they're going to say.

"Gee, I don't know. She didn't mention it. Probably from her agent. That series is getting pretty hot, isn't it?"

I wanted to say, "Yes, and so is the District Attorney." But what can you do? We were dancing by this time and I started to ask more about my mother, but Midge got very enthusiastic about teaching me the finer points of the cha-cha-cha, which I wasn't too hot at.

Pretty soon I was catching on to it well enough so I could stop staring at my feet. Midge was bubbling over about my proficiency. "You're moving like a Latin now, Josh!" I guess it went to my head, because after a while I was turning all over the place. We were spinning around like tops. That's when I swung around and clomped this little girl in the jaw with my elbow.

It was the little girl who'd been gawking at me. She was sort of stunned there for a moment. I apologized to her and her father like crazy. They were both very sporty about it. As soon as we all settled down and I was introduced around by Midge, her father said, "Why don't we let the young folks have a go at it?" They didn't even wait to find out if we wanted to. He and Midge started laughing and scratching and danced away from us.

This little girl, Kim, must have done all her previous dancing with other girls because it was a toss-up as to who was going to lead. We were practically straight-arming one another. I could dance fairly well then if my partner was good, but if I was thrown together with a novice it was havoc. Thank God, the cha-cha-cha music ended after a while and some regular dance music began or we both would have had to have our feet bandaged.

We hadn't spoken much because we'd both been concentrating too hard on just keeping our balance. But then she started asking all kinds of dumb questions. "What grade are you in?" "How old are you?" "Where do you go to school?" Blah, blah, blah. After a while I began wishing I'd knocked her out when I bumped into her. But finally she said, "I've been reading all about you and your mother in the papers." I guess that was inevitable.

"Gee, that's swell!" I answered, with tons of false energy.

"Everybody's been trying to figure out what *really* happened!" There was a long pause during which I was supposed to give her the low-down. I just let her dangle while we continued stepping all over each other. I could tell it was killing her. When she couldn't stand it any longer she took a deep breath and said, "What *did* happen?" Then she added quickly, "Oh, I won't tell anyone. I promise!"

Anything to break it up, I thought. "Do you really promise?" I asked her.

"Oh, yes, I do!" She practically leaped at me. She'd stopped dancing completely, which was just as well.

"Come here," I said, "over by the tables!" I turned to walk over to one of them, and she stepped on my heels she was so anxious. She sat down right next to me, and when I leaned way forward on the table she did the same thing. She was breaking out in a sweat.

"You really promise now?"

"Oh, I do, I do!" I raised my eyebrows like I doubted her. "Cross my heart and hope to die!" she added.

"What else?" I asked her. I wasn't going to let her off the hook that easily.

"What do you mean?"

"What else do you promise on?"

"Well ..." Her eyes were rolling up into her head she

was thinking so hard. "Ah ... May both my parents be run over by a train if I breathe a word."

"Passenger or freight?" I tossed at her. I like to see how far I can go with some people.

Didn't bother her a bit. "Which do you want?" she asked me.

"Freight," I told her. "They're longer and heavier."

"Okay, may both my parents—*and* my grandparents—be run over by the longest, heaviest freight train in existence if I divulge one syllable!"

By this time I was beginning to enjoy myself. "Well, you see, it was this way . . ." I didn't know exactly what I was going to say. I was just going to ad-lib some wild story, mostly for my own amusement. But I didn't get any further.

"Your mother shot him, didn't she?"

Even though she was a little girl and I figured what the hell did she know—still I'd never actually heard anyone say those exact words before. It shook me up.

"Do you mind if we drop it? It kind of depresses me!" I wasn't kidding either. That was the first time I said what I meant.

When I did that, her whole expression changed and she became a real person, too. She looked at me very seriously and just said, "Oh ... I see." We sat there in silence for a minute or so. I was trying to figure out a way to end it when I saw Andy walk into the patio. As I started to get up from the table she reached over and touched my arm.

"Josh, if anything should happen—you can come and live with us. I'd have to ask my parents, but I know they'd say yes."

I couldn't help liking her then. She said it like she really meant it. "Thanks," I told her.

I delivered her back to her father and joined Andy and Midge, who broke up a huddle when I arrived. They both put on a big display of general hilarity. But as far as I was concerned the barbecue had turned out to be a bomb.

About a half hour later we said our good nights and thank-yous. As we were getting in Andy's station wagon, Ginny Brace, who by that time was saying good-by to some other people, called over to our car, "Midge, tell Rita we'll be praying—" She stopped short when she realized I was there. "Tell her we all hope she feels better tomorrow!"

I knew damn well people don't say they're going to be praying for you if you just have a "tummy-ache."

On the way back to the ranch Andy turned the radio to a station where there was a disk jockey interviewing lots of people—so we wouldn't have to talk, I suppose. I vowed then and there to ask my mother to tell me exactly what was going on as soon as I got back.

When we got there the lights were on in the main building where my mother was staying, so I knew she was up. But Andy said, "Your mother's probably asleep by now, Josh. She went right to bed. See you in the morning!" Midge quickly kissed me good night. It was obvious I was to go up to my cabin without coming in. I decided that maybe I'd better wait until morning so I wouldn't upset her any more than she already was.

Once I got undressed and ready for bed, sleep was the last thing I felt like. I was feeling worried and depressed and every other unpleasant feeling. I started to read a paperback copy of *On the Beach*. As soon as I got onto what that was about, I really got depressed. I figured it would be my lousy luck to have the world come to an end while I was alive. Probably just as I was undressing to go to bed with a girl for the first time. I remember having seen a copy of the *New Yorker* on a shelf in the bathroom, so I went after it. It was about five months old but I must have read every word from cover to cover, including the ads. It was probably three-thirty before I went to sleep.

Consequently, I didn't get up the next morning until around ten. After I'd washed up and pulled myself together and planned just how I was going to approach my mother, I started walking down the hill from my cabin. The first thing I noticed was that our car was gone. It had been parked under a trellis the evening before. Just to make sure I tore around the corner and looked in their big four-car garage. It wasn't there. I knew my mother had flown the coop.

Chapter 25

MIDGE was in the kitchen with Sinsiona when I walked in. She was quick to leap to some sort of explanation.

"Honey, that call your mother got was about the television show. She has several appointments today and didn't want to wake you. She'll phone tonight." She went on and on about how wonderful it was going to be for my mother to be working steadily.

By this time I was pretty sure the case was going to the Grand Jury. If only for one reason that everybody had forgotten about completely—school. I should have been back in school that day. My mother had mentioned only the Friday before that I was going to start attending regularly, and there were going to be no more days off for any reason. Unless something unusual had come up, and my mother had a reason to definitely not want me around, I would have been there.

Also, the morning paper was missing from the table.

I decided to saddle up Tuffy right after breakfast, to ride to the country store, about two and a half miles away, get a paper, and see for myself. I liked Midge so much I didn't want to put her in the position of having to tell me. I was pretty sure my mother had made her and Andy sign a blood oath to keep me in the dark.

Sure enough, while I was eating breakfast Midge came out with the excuse I'd been waiting for. "Oh—Rita said not to worry about school. She thought it over, and decided a little vacation would do you good. Especially since you like it here and we like you." She gave me a big hug. "Andy said to tell you he'll be back in time for lunch. He's got some place to take you this afternoon."

"Good," I said. They probably had a schedule of activities planned to keep me absolutely dizzy. After I'd eaten I told Midge I thought I'd saddle Tuffy and ride around the ranch a bit. I practically heard her gasp a sigh of relief as I went out the door. She was probably patting herself on the back for handling it with such aplomb.

It didn't take me long to saddle up Tuffy and get on my way. I didn't want to ride past the ranch house on the road leading to the main highway, so I went by the stream and followed it on the other side of the trees until I got well past the buildings and around the first bend. Then I hit the road and cantered for a while. Tuffy was always very peppy in the morning.

When I got to the store I tied up outside and walked into the rack where they kept the magazines and newspapers. The first thing I saw was a batch of papers from Bakersfield with a big picture of my mother on the front pages and the heading, *STAR FACES GRAND JURY*. It was what I'd anticipated; but no matter how much I expected it, it was still a shock to see it in print.

There were a couple of people being waited on, so I just stood there reading the accompanying story. It said that probably the following Monday the Grand Jury would decide whether Ben's death had been suicide or murder and if formal charges were to be brought against my mother.

Instead of feeling more depressed I kind of relaxed after the initial shock wore off. At least I knew what was what. As I took the paper over to the counter to pay for it, a woman who was standing there with a list a mile long glanced at the headlines and said to the man that ran the place, "Hear she's staying up at the Lansings'. Well, if you ask me—"

The man gave her such a look! I swear his eyes practically crossed.

She caught on, too. She looked over at me quickly. Her mouth formed the shape of "Ohhhh!" but I don't think she actually uttered a sound. Then she went right into giving him hell because the price of the coffee she used had gone up two cents.

I took the paper and left. Now that upset me! People who didn't know, had no way of knowing, what actually happened—they were the ones that decided your fate.

Suddenly, I began to wonder how many innocent people

199

had been tossed in jail or even electrocuted by mistake. Always before I'd thought no, it doesn't happen, it couldn't. I started in thinking that Barbara Graham was probably innocent.

It was getting warm by the time I rode back, so I didn't canter any of the way; I didn't want Tuffy to get over-heated. As I rode past the first building I saw Andy and Midge sitting on the screened-in porch off the living room having a drink of iced tea.

"Hi'ya cowboy," Andy said. "Where you been?"

"I rode to the store and got the paper," I told him.

Midge started in having a fit right away but Andy cut her off. "I told you and Rita last night you couldn't pull it off. The boy's not deaf, dumb, and blind. He's got a right to know."

I told them I felt I had to talk to my mother about it; it was agreed that when she phoned that evening I could. Then they both tried to reassure me the Grand Jury would be a break and really clear things up for once and for all.

Andy and Midge were wonderful. They obviously had plans for the afternoon but they just let them drop. They could tell I wasn't in the mood for making believe everything was copasetic.

After lunch I took a walk by myself up the hill from where my cabin was to an old, abandoned pomesite mine. It was dark and cold in there. I must have sat there for a couple of hours thinking all sorts of things. I got to wishing I could just stay up there in the mine and go to sleep like Rip Van Winkle and wake up to find out it had been a nightmare and everything was all right.

Later on, I went back to my cabin, gave it a thorough cleaning, and took a nap. It was around five-thirty, and I was half waking up when I heard Andy yelling up the hill to me that my mother was on the phone.

I tore down to the living room. Midge was talking and Andy was standing next to her. They put me right on and then left the room.

"Hello, Josh ..."

"Hi, Mom."

"Midge told me you found out."

"Yes, I did."

"I wish you hadn't. I wanted you to have a nice vacation without worrying, don't you see?"

"I'd rather come down and be with you."

"Well, that's ridiculous!" She started to sound very impersonal and efficient. "Everything's fine. Matter of fact, I'm not staying at the beach. I'm in town with Stella and Ef."

"How come?"

"I've got so much to do, dear. They're going ahead with the television series, and there are all sorts of conferences. Actually, I didn't feel like staying at the house alone. As soon as Merwin gets back I'll go down."

"What about Penny and Lord Nelson and Monkey-Face? Is Cecelia there?"

My mother tried to make a joke of it. "No, dear, Cecelia didn't relish staying there either, so they're still being boarded. I called up today and asked for them. They're fine. Oh, and I also spoke to your school. Your principal, Mr. What's-his-name, said it's perfectly all right, he understands. Besides, you're getting good grades, so he's not worried a bit."

I started to ask her specifically about the Grand Jury but she got very annoyed, as I might have guessed she would. "Darling, I don't want you to *worry* about it! Lee says it's merely a formality, that everything will be fine. Will you do me a favor and stop talking about it!"

Stop talking about it! I'd only mentioned it once.

"When will I be coming home?" I asked her.

That brought on a whole tirade about how most young men would jump at the chance to be on a ranch for a vacation like I was having. Of course, what I wanted to say was "Yes, but most young men's mothers aren't going up before the Grand Jury on a murder charge!" That would have gone over like a lead balloon. Yipe!

She tried to make it seem like everything was coming along just fine and that, if I doubted her, I could always call Lee and he'd tell me the same thing. Everything was peachy. I was getting goddam sick and tired of hearing how wonderful everything was and then the next day reading those catastrophic headlines in the newspapers.

I wanted to ask if I'd be called to testify, but I knew

this particular phone call had had it as far as any more questions about the case were concerned.

"Now, dear, I want you to relax and have a good time. I'll talk to you every day on the phone. Promise me you'll forget about this whole idiotic mess and have some fun."

"Who—me? Oh, sure. I won't give it a thought!" I said, with as much sarcasm as I dared.

There was a long pause during which she was probably figuring whether or not to pick me up on it. She didn't, though. She got very jaunty, told me to have a ball, and hung up. It's like having a doctor tell you that you've got cancer but not to worry about it or your time will be cut in half.

That was on a Monday evening. The next few days were miserable even though Andy and Midge couldn't have been more thoughtful or more diplomatic. If they figured something really interesting was happening they'd rope me in on it, but they didn't force me into any activities. If I wanted to talk, they'd discuss the situation with me; if I didn't, they kept mum. They must have promised my mother they'd keep the papers from me. I never once saw one around the ranch. But at one point during the day I'd manage to ride Tuffy down to the country store and get my news that way. I'm sure they knew it, but they never said anything.

The newspapers, although they always had some story about us, weren't giving us headlines. I suppose they were waiting for the big day at the Grand Jury hearing. There were lots of articles about Ben's past that I guess Sally Knapp was planting through information Lee's investigators dug up. There was one saying that Ben had asked his wife for a divorce several times and intimating he was hung up by the fact that she was supporting his illegitimate child in England. There was more about him trying to kill himself in that racing car accident, a lot more about his gambling tendencies, and several articles mapping out his wife's past and her many times in rest homes and sanitariums. The whole campaign was designed to discredit Ben and his wife. That was sure all right with me.

On Tuesday night when my mother called up I spoke to

Jay, who was with her at the time. He went babbling on about the television deal. After I talked to him for a while my mother got back on and, because she seemed to be in a fairly good mood, I took the plunge and asked if I'd be coming down to testify on the following Monday. That did it! She upbraided me for not letting her forget for a minute what was going on and for being morbid. The conversation ended up on an extremely chilly note. I was miserable. I had the awful feeling things were going wrong and there must be some way I could help if they'd only let me stick around.

On Wednesday Andy and Midge drove me about thirty-five miles to this terrific wild animal farm. They knew I was nuts about animals of all kinds and jungle pictures, and they figured this was a legitimate excuse to capture my interest and "get me away from it all." They knew the owner, who used to be a lion and tiger tamer and was scarred from stem to stern, so we got the royal tour. It fascinated the hell out of me. I had my picture taken with lions, alligators, boa constrictors, and I even got to ride an elephant. We spent hours there and had dinner on the way back at this fabulous Chinese restaurant that you'd never expect to find way up in the middle of nowhere.

On the way home I was actually feeling pretty good—and dead tired, to boot. As we started to turn off the main highway onto their road by the country store I said, "Hey, Andy, do you want to stop now and let me get the papers or do you want me to sneak back later? It's your horse!" They both got a big bang out of that and stopped.

The papers had the usual stuff about Ben and his wife, but they also had an article about me and a picture, too. It was all about how I was noticeably missing from the scene and that I was being kept out of things as much as possible at my mother's request. It made it seem like I was in hiding. It was kind of fun to read.

Back at the ranch there was a message my mother had phoned and to call operator so-and-so, which Midge did. She talked to my mother and to Lee (they were at his place), and then I got on the phone. My mother only wanted to hear about the wild animals and did I have a good time; then Lee took over. I was dying to ask him to level with me and give me the lowdown on just how things stood, but I had to be careful because my mother was obviously right next to him. We talked about things in general. Finally I said, "Lee, answer yes or no—is there a possibility I might be coming down for the Grand Jury?"

"Could happen, Josh. I'll know more in a day or so and I'll be talking to you." That's all he got to say because my mother whipped the phone away from him and started asking me if I was sleeping well, and dumb things like that.

"When's Merwin coming home?" I asked her.

"He's got his ticket for tomorrow. He might have to stay over until Friday. I'll be talking to him later on this evening."

"Then will you be moving back to the beach?"

"Yes, of course, dear." She knew I was getting around to when I would be coming back, so she started in telling me to relax and have a good time and all of that. It made me so goddam mad. I mean—after all that had happened she was practically becoming a fanatic about my welfare. So I did a crazy thing. While she was rattling on about how I'd begun to look thin and peaked and something about me putting on weight, I just hung up the phone.

"Josh, did you hang up?" Midge walked quickly over to the telephone.

"Yes," I said. "Honest to God, I'm getting tired of her attitude."

"I know, dear, but you've got to realize the strain she's under. That's why she's acting this way." We hardly got beyond that when the phone rang again.

"I'll get it," Midge said. She picked it up. It was my mother wanting to know if I'd hung up.

"No, of course not, Rita. We've been having trouble with the phone all day." My mother obviously reminded her we'd been *gone* all day. "Well, you know what I mean, Rita! Sinsiona told us there'd been trouble with the phone. She even had the repairman out." My mother wanted to talk to me again, so I got back on.

"Josh?" she asked, in a funny kind of way.

"Yes."

"Are you all right?"

"Of course I am. Why wouldn't I be?"

"I only asked," she said. "No need to get fresh with me."

It was obvious we weren't hitting it off. We both realized it, so we ended the conversation quickly without further bickering. I could tell that in one minute she'd be calling me "young man," and we'd be off and running.

That evening Andy asked me if I wanted to go on the roundup with him the next day. Ordinarily I would have jumped at the chance, but somehow I kept thinking I'd be called to come down at any moment, that something would happen and I'd be needed.

Chapter 26

THE next morning Andy was gone by the time I got up. Over breakfast Midge reminded me they were going to a formal dinner-dance at the local country club that evening. She said she hoped I wouldn't mind being alone, that Sinsiona would cook dinner for me and Perce. She asked if I wanted to drive into this small town with her while she got her hair done, but I decided to stay at the ranch. I had a weird feeling something was coming to a head.

Midge left about eleven. As soon as she was gone I put a call in to Lee at his office. His secretary said he was in court. She'd have him phone me about four-thirty or five.

The rest of the day was a nervous waste of time. After lunch I walked down by the stream, sat on a boulder, and tossed pebbles in the water. I was trying to think things out, but I couldn't concentrate worth a damn. I saw Midge drive up about three and went to meet her. She'd had a permanent, a facial, manicure, the works. She looked great. I carried some packages into her bedroom for her, and then she kicked me out because it was going to be a big night for them, and she wanted to take a nap. "Poor Stretch!" she said. "Up at five, out on a roundup all day, and *I* take a nap. Oh, well, I'll take an extra half hour for him."

Around four o'clock I went into the kitchen and sat there waiting for the phone to ring. At ten minutes to five, when nothing had happened, I put in a call myself.

"Mr. Hertzig just came in the office," his secretary said. "Wait a minute, I'll see if I can get him." After hanging on for about five minutes I heard Lee pick up the phone.

"Hello, Josh. I'm pretty busy right now. Let's make it quick." He sounded very businesslike and not in too good a mood. "You *will* be coming down to testify. I've known that all along. Actually, your mother's been so upset by everything else I didn't want her to worry about that, too. I'll tell her later on today or tomorrow. We'll probably be seeing you Saturday sometime. Okay?"

"Okay," I said.

"Don't say anything to Rita when you talk to her tonight. Let me handle it, Josh."

"All right, Lee." He started to say good-by but his whole tone made me apprehensive. "Lee . . ."

"Yes?"

"How does it look?"

He kind of sighed before he spoke. "Frankly, I don't know, Josh. We're doing our best but the goddam press has given it such a play, all out of proportion, that it—" I guess he remembered who he was talking to and what my mother would do to him if she found out he'd laid the cards on the table. "Don't worry—we'll straighten it out. I've got to dash now. See you over the weekend!" And he was gone.

To say he didn't sound too optimistic would be the understatement of the world. Yet it wasn't what he said, but his distracted manner that had me worried. My conversation with Lee made me even more restless than I'd been before.

There was no sign of the gang coming back from the roundup, Midge was still napping, so I decided to saddle up Tuffy and ride down after the paper. We cantered all the way to the store. There was an enormous picture of my mother on the front page and the heading read, *FORMER GUN THREAT DIVULGED*. I couldn't imagine what the hell it meant. I just about went blind I read it so fast. Jesus, what a lousy break! I guess Ben's wife had some investigators working for her, too.

Anyhow, there was a whole story about a weekend my mother and a man she was going with spent at an estate out on Long Island a good ten years before. I'd never even heard anything about it. Their hosts, a Mr. and Mrs. Henning, threw a big party for my mother, and later on in the evening my mother and this man the papers said she was engaged to, Cedric Morris, whom I don't remember, had a fight. He was apparently flirting with some other woman, and my mother called him on it. They got into this fracas which kind of dampened the festivities. He said he was packing and taking off. He went upstairs and was in the midst of getting his stuff together when my mother followed him to his bedroom. They had another argument and he swore he was leaving. He was a big sportsman with tennis rackets, a .22 rifle, a pistol, and all that sort of equipment. According to the paper, she suddenly grabbed this pistol and said she'd shoot him if he tried to leave. He ran into the bathroom and locked himself in. She stood outside the door yelling at him. He climbed out the little bathroom window to the balcony, went downstairs, and called the local police over the objections of Mr. and Mrs. Henning, who went right upstairs and told my mother what was going on. Of course, by the time the police arrived she'd put down the gun. But this guy, Cedric Morris, insisted she'd threatened to shoot him and asked the police to stay until he cleared out.

That was the story. Whether it was true or not I never found out, but it sure made my mother seem like an unstable person. It also added that the local police report of the incident stated they were both intoxicated.

Somehow I didn't want to take the paper to the ranch with me. I just read it over several times, got back on Tuffy, and started riding back. It seemed like circumstances were just ganging up on us. God, I was getting depressed!

For a moment I thought about Merwin. It was good to know he was on his way home. If you thought about the end of the world, which I'm always doing, it was kind of reassuring to think maybe Merwin would be with you. At least you'd get one last belly laugh out of it.

As I got near the ranch I could see the dust and hear the sounds of the roundup coming in on the far side. I'd already finished unsaddling Tuffy when Andy rode up. Boy, he was filthy.

"Great day, Josh! Wish you could have been with us."

"Me, too," I said.

I told him I'd take care of his horse so he wouldn't be too pressed for time. He thanked me and walked over to the main building. I unsaddled his horse, dried him off, and gave him a good brushing. By the time I got to the living room Midge was all decked out in a fire engine red dress. Andy was in getting cleaned up.

"Hi, Sweetie. Where have you been?"

"Plotzing around."

"Plotzing around getting the papers, you mean. I saw you ride by. Well, what junk did they print today?"

"I didn't get them," I said. "I just took a short ride."

I don't know why I lied about it except I didn't really want to talk about the incident with my mother and the gun. I seemed to have reached a point where I had to think the whole thing out myself.

They both looked great as they tore out to get in their station wagon.

Perce and I sat down to one of your quieter dinners around seven. I made a few feeble attempts at conversation, but all I got for my trouble were a few "Yups." I gave up about halfway through and spent the rest of the meal trying to figure out whether he was ill at ease and wishing he could think up something to say or whether he just didn't give a damn. I decided on the latter.

After dinner Perce went into the living room and started reading this gigantic pamphlet about the different diseases cattle can be afflicted by. It was complete with all kinds of gruesome illustrations of emaciated cows. I sat there for a while until the silence became oppressive. Then I went back to the dining room to wait for the nightly phone call from my mother. Sinsiona was banging around out in the kitchen, and I was just sitting there looking out the window.

It was then I noticed how light it was outside. There was a full moon so brilliant it made it seem like daylight and you had on dark glasses. The whole countryside was bathed in an eerie light. You could see individual trees standing out on the side of a mountain a mile away. It was so bright you couldn't see any stars, only this gigantic yellow-white moon and a few planets. Everything threw a shadow: the ranch buildings, trees, the horses that were grazing nearby.

It was the kind of night that made you want to run out and roam around in it. I decided to take a walk, but first I thought I'd better make a phone call to my mother. Then I figured the heck with it. Lee said he'd tell her tomorrow about me having to come back to town, so there really wasn't too much to talk about tonight. I went in and told Perce that if my mother or Merwin called to tell them I'd gone for a walk and would talk to them later, if they wanted, or the next day.

I went along the stream past all the other ranch buildings and corrals. When I walked by the bunkhouse I could hear some of the cowboys playing poker. They sounded like a bunch of high school kids. The radio was on and Okie music was blaring out. In the large pasture to the right of the stream I could see hundreds of cows and calves they'd brought in on the roundup. They were standing there like plaster of Paris statues, very quietly. Every so often one or two of them would let out a kind of mournful "moo." They were probably knocked out from the trip. They seemed to be aware of the moonlight, too—like they were taking moonbaths.

After about a mile and a half I saw a little hill jutting up all by itself in the middle of a flat meadow on the left side of the creek. It looked funny sitting there, like it was put there or built by somebody. On top of the hill was one scrawny evergreen tree. It seemed like a good place to go sit and think about things. I crossed over the creek, hopping from rock to rock until I came to the last one from the far side. I knew the distance from it to the bank was too far to jump without getting wet, and I was right. I got soaked halfway up to my knees. There was a warm breeze blowing, though, and the moon was so strong I was sure it would dry me off. My feet didn't feel cold, just sort of tingly; so I ran across the meadow until I got to the bottom of the hill. I even started running up the hill but that didn't last long. By the time I got to the top I realized it was a much bigger hill than it looked from the distance. I was huffing like a steam engine. I flopped down in the grass under the one lone tree.

There are certain times in my life when I reach a point and gain . . . like a great perspective on everything that's going on. It doesn't last long, maybe only an hour or so. Then I get all bogged down again until I reach another peak when I seem to be able to straighten the whole ugly mess out again, at least in my mind. Usually it happens during a trip, on a train, or up in a plane. I can look back and see things very clearly. I don't mean the view; I mean the way I'm living and my environment and the people I'm currently tangled up with. Most of all, the way I'm handling myself. In a way, it's like New Year's Eve and I make all kinds of resolutions.

Sitting up on top of the hill that night was one of those times.

At first I just lay there looking off at the view. The whole mile and a half I'd come from the ranch was sloping gently up toward Table Mountain. That, plus being on top of the hill, let me look down on the stream, the cattle, the ranch buildings—everything. It was beautiful.

After a while, I stood up and walked around the top of the hill looking out in all directions and, as I did, I suddenly felt all this strength and energy welling up inside me. Like when Popeye grabs that can of spinach and gulps it down. Next thing I knew I was climbing the tree. It wasn't very tall. There was only one branch about halfway up that was big enough to hold me and be comfortable on, but I found a crosspiece where another branch grew out from the main one and sat there swinging in the breeze.

It sounds squirrely and I guess it was. I started to think back over the whole Ben period. And for the first time in ages I wasn't depressed by it. Confused, maybe, but not depressed or sad. I was recreating in my mind everything from the first night we met him on the pier, and going along from there like I was watching a movie that I'd seen before but had forgotten the ending to. You see, I wasn't anticipating the lousy end.

I was remembering specific incidents down to the very last detail. Like the time we got roped into a small dinner party given by some snob friends of the Culps. The host and hostess were elegant and formal and phony. All they talked about was family background, good breeding, and crap like that. I could tell Ben was dying to shake them up. Sure enough, when the butler came around with dessert Ben leaned way back in his chair and said with a Shanty Irish accent, "No, thanks. Me belly's as tight as a drum. You could crack a louse on it with your thumbnail!" I laughed so loud the water I was drinking came right back out through my nose. My mother bawled the hell out of both of us when we left.

Suddenly I was standing up there on that hill smiling for all I was worth. I was missing Ben; I wasn't hating him any more. I was actually deriving some kind of pleasure out of remembering the trips we all took together, the tennis games, horseback riding, swimming, and, most of all—the long talks.

By God, you could blame Ben for a lot of lousy things that were happening to you—but you had to give him credit for the best times you ever spent, too. I found myself saying, "Thanks, Ben!" And I realized I was thanking him for something much greater than good times.

Finally, the thought struck me that Ben couldn't have been as rotten as we'd all been saying he was. He just couldn't have been. I guess the reason I hadn't figured that out earlier is because it takes time for things to sink in and take their proper perspective. Especially after you've practically been in shock.

You couldn't know somebody for almost a year and be with them constantly if they were a bona fide stinker. But, then again, if Ben wasn't a rat how could he have left us in the mess he had? It didn't jibe. There was something missing someplace. When you thought back, he was such a good influence on both my mother and me that he had to be basically good. And if he were basically good he couldn't have killed himself in our backyard without letting us know. He would have gone away and done it, or he would have left a note. Or he wouldn't have killed himself in the first place. We could have worked something out. There had to be some way he could get away from his wife, if he wanted to. What's more—there had to be some explanation for what happened. It couldn't go on being a mystery for the rest of our lives.

Before I knew it I was playing "What If," a game I'm great at. It's like daydreaming. Actually, it amounted to "What if Ben weren't dead?" In my mind I went over a typical day: getting up in the morning, the three of us having breakfast, Ben going off to work, me to school. I'd come home in the afternoon with a tennis trophy I'd won, and my mother and I would be so excited we'd hardly be able to wait until Ben came home so he could see it. When he did arrive he'd break out a bottle of champagne, and my mother would serve a terrific dinner. She'd be a great cook after she got married. Then Ben and I would be playing all sorts of games until she finished the dishes. Like the time down in the game room when we'd made the bet and right afterward my mother broke all those dishes—and how hard we laughed. And when Ben demanded payment for the bet I took the quarter out of the newel post. Boy, what a kick he got out of—

Christ—the newel post! Why hadn't I thought about looking there for a note? It hit me in a flash. I almost fell out of the bloody tree. I didn't, but I did climb down right away because I was getting so excited it was hard to keep my balance up there.

As soon as I got my feet on the ground I came down to earth the other way, too. No, I thought; if Ben were in a suicidal mood he wouldn't leave a note in a coy place like the newel post down in the game room. Besides, I'd have found it before this. But no—I wouldn't have, because I hardly ever went down there after Ben's death. Come to think of it, I'd never fiddled around with the newel post after that. I would have *thought* about it, though; Ben had left money for me there. But money was different from a suicide note. Anyway, Ben would leave a note for my mother. Not for me. So he definitely wouldn't leave it in the newel post.

The more logical I got about why it was a crazy idea for me to come up with, the more this hunch kept growing that somebody should look there.

I hardly remember getting back to the ranch except I must have run most of the way because when I flew in the kitchen door I was winded. My mind was racing as fast as my body, working overtime going over all the pros and cons of the idea. It didn't make sense at all. Yet, in a way, maybe if you had the idea you were going to kill yourself and you weren't sure you could pull it off, maybe you'd leave a note hidden—to cover yourself in case you did.

I decided to at least call Merwin at home and ask him to go down and look. I wouldn't ask my mother because she'd blow her top and accuse me of being morbid and having a one-track mind. I figured if Merwin didn't answer, if he wasn't back from New York yet, I'd skip it until I got back to town, and look, myself, over the weekend.

I put in a call to our house at Paraiso Beach. There was no answer. Maybe my mother had gone to the airport to pick Merwin up or else they were out to dinner. Still, I had the feeling somebody should investigate this idea right away, so I put a call in to Stella and Ef's place. I only let it ring twice. I hung up before anybody could answer. I realized I was getting carried away with myself. I'd really be in Dutch if I got everybody excited and then there was nothing but air inside the post.

Sinsiona must have heard me pacing around because she came in the back door and wanted to know if I'd like a piece of cake and a glass of milk. I said no, and asked her if there'd been a call for me. She said the phone hadn't rung once.

I went up to my cabin and decided I'd better cool off. I tried to read, but that damn newel post kept popping up in my mind. I'd find myself staring at one page for twenty minutes at a time without having read a single word. I'd borrowed some saddle soap from Andy before he left to give my boots a good once-over, so I started on them. No use. I wasn't good for anything but thinking about the fact that there was something in that post.

After a while I decided I'd better go to bed and sleep it off. Things are always much saner in the morning. Like every time I write a letter late at night I always tear it up the next morning when I read it over. I've always gone way off on a tangent of some sort. At night when I'm writing it I think how clever I am; then in the morning I think how nuts I was.

As soon as I got in bed and turned the lights out, all I could see were newel posts. Talk about counting sheep! I tried hypnotizing the different parts of my body and putting them to sleep, but no such luck. Then I remembered something somebody said to me once, "If you ever get a strong emotional impulse, don't stifle it—act on it!" Who the hell said it to me? God, it was Ben—the first time I'd ever been to the races at Caliente. I'd picked a horse just by its name and by watching it walk around the paddock. Ben had given me two dollars to bet that first race. I had my mind made up, but then I figured what did I know about races! I switched and bet on the horse Ben was on. My horse came in and paid sixty to one. And that's when Ben said to follow your first hunch—if it's a strong one— and to go along with emotional impulses, if they're honest ones. That did it! Remembering Ben was the one who said it made the connection. Almost like a retroactive message from the grave, I told myself. I also told myself I was—in Jay's language—"Mishoogena!"

Nevertheless, I was on my way to the kitchen in my bathrobe and slippers in no time at all. The moon was even brighter than before, and I suddenly started wondering if there was really a thing called moon madness. Because if there wasn't already, I was certainly experiencing a first. I tried phoning home again but still no answer. It was about a quarter to eleven. I guessed maybe my mother was still staying with Stella and Ef, and thought of phoning there again, but I didn't want to get my mother any more nervous than she already was. I got Information and Lee's home phone number, but before I could call, a cuckoo thought occurred to me. I got this notion that unless I, myself, looked in that newel post there wouldn't be anything there.

It was right then that I decided to go down to Paraiso Beach and find out. I was going into town probably the next day anyhow, according to Lee. At least the day afterward. I'd just get dressed, walk to the main highway, and hitch a ride to Hollywood. I had over twenty dollars in case I got stuck and had to flag a bus or something.

Andy and Midge wouldn't even know I was gone until morning because they'd be getting home late and would never have any reason to come up and look in my cabin. And by morning I could phone them if there was a note; if there wasn't, I'd just hitch back so my mother would never find out about the whole stupid idea. Unless, of course, Merwin and my mother were at the house by the time I got down there. But if Merwin was there he'd smooth it all over. At least I was pretty sure she wouldn't be there alone.

Having figured out all these angles, I tore up to the cabin, dressed, took my money out from under the mattress, and started walking on the dirt road toward the highway. It never seemed too far on horseback, but walking was a different thing entirely. I was nervous as a cat for fear Andy and Midge might start home early by some fluke, and there I'd be in the bright moonlight walking along the road like some kind of a nut.

It was about midnight when I got to the highway. The store was closed and so was the gas station, but there were cars and trucks going by regularly. It's the main inland route from Los Angeles to Bakersfield, Fresno, and San Francisco, so there's always a certain amount of traffic no matter what time it is.

Chapter 27

I'D never hitchhiked before and that added to the excitement. I took my place out in front of the phone booth right next to the gas station. I closed the door of the booth so the light would go on and people would notice me standing there. Badly as I wanted to get to Paraiso Beach, I was hoping like hell a truck wouldn't offer me a ride. I've got an aversion to big trailer trucks with all the noise that goes with them and the way they creep up hills and screw up traffic.

I'd only been standing there about ten minutes when a dark green Buick sedan came careening along. It almost hit me as it swerved to a stop pulling over to my side of the road. There was a very well-dressed couple in their late thirties or early forties sitting in the front seat.

I could tell the woman was drunk because she was trying so hard not to show it. She sat up very proper and straight and mouthed each word with great care. She'd never heard of Paraiso Beach, but she asked me if Hollywood would be any help to me. I said yes and piled in the back seat.

When the man started the car up we really lurched forward. I decided he was a little drunk, too. For a long time nobody said a word. I was wishing they'd turn on the radio or talk among themselves. I kept feeling like I should start a conversation, but I didn't have anything to say to them. So I just sat there looking out the window, pretending I wasn't there.

After a while I got to thinking what a fool I was taking off on a wild goose chase. Once I was in a car heading south, I didn't have such a strong hunch about there being a note at all. I started worrying about how I'd hitch a ride back. I actually got to laughing at myself sitting there in the car. At one point I was just about to ask them to stop and let me out. But just then—after we'd been riding about twenty minutes without a word spoken—the man suddenly looked around at me and said, "My wife's a son-of-a-bitch!" Then he went right back to watching the road.

His wife looked over at him with great indignation. "Well, that's a nice thing to say in front of a perfect stranger!" I was just about to break in and say it was okay when she looked back at me and snapped, "Besides, *he's* the son-of-a-bitch!"

She turned around and that was the end of that little repartee. I suppose all I had to say was "Why?" and we'd have really been off. But I kept my mouth shut.

From that point on he started driving like a demon. He was passing every car on the highway. And there were a few he almost didn't pass. He was swerving around curves and racing up and down hills like a madman. I was leaning every which way in the back seat trying to help him drive the car. In a way, I guess it was a good ride to have because what with trying to figure them out, and his driving, I was certainly diverted from my own problems.

After a bloodcurdling hour or so we were coming down from the mountains into San Fernando Valley. I was wringing wet by this time. We followed Ventura Boulevard in to Highland Avenue. When we got about even with the Hollywood Bowl I leaned up and told them I'd get off at Hollywood Boulevard. I was a nervous wreck by the time I got out of the car, thanked them, and slammed the door.

It was still a beautiful moonlight night, but it was getting a little misty out and there was a chill in the air. The clock on the Bank of America said ten minutes after two. The bars here in California close at two, so there were whole armies of displaced people cruising around the streets. They all looked hungry, and I don't mean for food.

While I was standing there getting my bearings, two guys in kind of jazzy outfits came along from opposite directions. As they passed each other one guy said, "Hey, man—how's the stem end of your bladder?"

"Hanging!" the other one said.

"Crazy!" the first one called out, going right on by.

Boy, the conversations you hear if you just sort of listen.

218

I wondered if they knew one another. I guess they must have.

I decided I'd better walk two blocks down to Sunset and hitch a ride to La Cienega and out La Cienega until I got to the airport. From there I could get a ride on Sepulveda right on down to Paraiso Beach.

As I walked down Highland to Sunset there was one big, black convertible that kept going around the block and coming back. The guy in it was about fifty, very well-preserved-looking, tanned to within an inch of his life, and sleek gray hair. He must have had the car on automatic pilot because he looked every place but where he was going. He kept giving me the eye and grinning, but I kept looking down at the sidewalk. About the third time around he slowed down to about two miles an hour and said in a husky voice, "How about a cup of coffee?" I continued walking and didn't look over. The next time he came by he said, "There's something in it for you!" I kept on staring at the sidewalk like I hadn't even heard him. I must have looked like a push-over the way he kept at me. Finally, he spotted some other guy on the opposite side of the street. The next thing I knew he made a U-turn and was over heckling him. As I got about to Sunset I looked back and he'd had much better luck. Just to show what a morbid curiosity I have, I got to kicking myself for not asking "How much?" when he said he'd make it worth my time.

I reached the corner of Sunset and Highland and was just about to step down off the curb when a lavender sedan, souped up so it sounded like a speedboat, and covered with all kinds of chrome and a toy skeleton dangling in the front window, roared up to me and stopped. It was filled with coloured people. I couldn't count them, but it was packed like one of those circus cars that keeps unloading clowns in the center ring until about thirty of them have piled out. All I could see was a tangle of arms and legs, rows of gleaming white teeth, and pairs of wild, clouded eyes. They must have been hopped up on something because I don't think they were drunk. A skinny girl sitting next to the window in the front seat flailed her arms toward me.

"Hey, chicken, wanna have a ball?" She turned around to the back seat. "Who-wee, Billy Jo, ain't he cute?"

"Cutest lil' ole jail bait I ever did see," Billy Jo squealed.

The first one turned back to me. "Hey, chicken, you ever hear of Jelly Roll?" This knocked them all out. They were laughing and slapping each other fit to kill.

Then one of the guys in the front seat said to the one that had been talking to me, "Pearl, you ain't givin' Jelly Roll to nobody 'til I get me my slice!"

Pearl giggled and turned to me. "Come on, chicken, we'll have us a gang bang. You can be anchor man!"

I didn't know what to say so I came out with "I can't. I'm waiting for my folks."

"Bring 'em along," Pearl squealed. "The more the merrier!" They all got a kick out of that, too. Just then a police car pulled up on the other side of the street and the cops looked over toward us. Billy Jo spotted them and said, "Hey, Georgie, let's cut out!"

"What for?" asked Georgie. "Don't you want the chicken?"

"Not with Lilly Law lookin' on!" she said, indicating the cops. They all looked over, straightened up, and drove away very soberly and properly like they were in a parade.

I stood there for about fifteen minutes. The only cars that even slowed down were either driven by drunks or degenerates of one sort or another. Nobody stopped, though. The normal people tore right on by like they didn't see me, and even the nuts didn't actually come to a halt. They'd cruise on by slowly and glare at me. Several of them went around the block a couple of times, but I was giving out with no encouragement. I could just picture me being picked up by some ghoul and found days later, in little pieces, all dismembered and wrapped up in newspapers, scattered over several counties, and deposited in trash cans and rain sewers.

When it was obvious I'd have to go through a whole marathon of crackpots if I was going to hitch the rest of the way home, I decided to splurge and take a taxi. It killed me, but standing around with my bare face hanging out, watching all the nuts go by, was getting me no place.

220

A yellow cab finally pulled up in front of the drugstore on the other side of Sunset. I tore over and jumped in.

"Hey, how much to go to Paraiso Beach?" I asked him.

"Paraiso Beach! Why don't you hitch?" Boy, there was a cabbie that was really out for business.

"I don't feel like it," I said. "How much?"

"It's up to the meter."

"I thought cabs gave flat rates for trips like that," I told him.

"Not this cab. Strictly meter."

"Well, could you do me a favor and tell be *about* how much it might cost?"

"I told you, kid. Depends on the meter."

"Yeah, but you must know *approximately*!"

"You wanna know the truth?" He turned to me. "I don't wanna go to Paraiso Beach."

"I never would have guessed it!" I told him. "You know, it's funny! I never realized passengers had to go where cab drivers wanted to go. I was actually laboring under the stupid impression it was the other way around."

"Huh?" the cabbie said in a dopy sort of way. You can't waste sarcasm on some people.

"Oh, nuts!" I said, getting out and trying to slam the door right off its hinges.

It didn't look like my night at all. I began to feel that all these preliminary skirmishes were signs that there was absolutely no possibility of there being a note.

Another cab pulled up and the driver started talking to the cabbie I'd tangled with. I went over. As I approached, the first cabbie said, "He wants to go to Paraiso Beach!"

"Okay," the new one said. "Hop in, kid." Everyone's *always* calling me "kid." We started up. "You really going to Paraiso Beach?"

"Yes, if someone'll take me there."

"Sure, I'll take you, but it's gonna cost. Why don't I drive you out Wilshire or Pico past West L.A., Beverly Hills, and on out to Sepulveda? From there you can hitch straight down easy enough."

"Okay," I said. At last a decent guy.

On the way out he told me what he thought about television, radio-active fall-out, the cops, artificial insemination, smog, his wife, his mother-in-law, whom he liked *better* than his wife at the present time, and Simone Signoret, the French actress, whom he liked better than his mother-in-law. He was one of those philosophical cabbies that you run into in New York all the time. I'd never hit one in California before. I liked him. I was glad he didn't make me talk too much. All I had to say was "Yes ... Uh, huh ... Sure ... You're right ... That's the way I feel ..."

When we got out by Sepulveda it was starting to get foggy because we were getting near the ocean. I'd been watching the meter like a hawk. When he pulled over to the far side of Sepulveda Boulevard it clicked $7.35. I gave him a dollar and a quarter tip. He thanked me and wished me all the best. As tight as I am I always overtip. I feel if I don't a waitress or cab driver or someone's going to call me a crumbum and make a scene. Besides, I feel sorry for people that have to deal with the public every moment of their working day. I don't know how they do it with all the cranky people you come in contact with.

Standing on Sepulveda, I lokoed west toward where the fog was rolling in and hoped it wouldn't get too thick too fast. It wasn't too bad; you could see the moon shining through it. There wasn't much traffic. In fact, only about five cars passed me before one stopped. A very nicely dressed lady in her late thirties with a great lantern jaw, driving all by herself. "I'm going as far as Laguna," she said. "Will that help you?"

"Fine," I said, opening the door. "I'm only going to Paraiso Beach."

I got in the front seat next to her. It was warm in the car, she had on some terrific kind of perfume, and the radio was tuned to an all-night music program. I felt very safe and secure. She did, too, and she wanted me to know why. I'd hardly been in the car five minutes when she reached over, pressed the button of the glove compartment, and flipped it open. A light went on inside. It was smack in front of my face; I couldn't help but see in. There was an opened carton of cigarettes and, right in front of it, one of the prettiest pearl-handled revolvers you ever saw. She reached her hand in very calmly, picked up the gun, and put it to one side. Then she took a pack of cigarettes from the carton, put the gun back where it had originally been, and shut the glove compartment. She opened the pack and lit a cigarette, offering one to me. I told her I didn't smoke because I figured that would make me seem like a nice clean harmless youth and she wouldn't worry. And besides, I *didn't* smoke. When she put the cigarettes down next to her purse I saw that there was already a pack half opened lying there with her cigarette lighter.

I got such a kick out of that. I guess this was a routine of hers. She probably didn't like to travel alone, so she had this little scene planned to show me that she had a gun in there. The only thing that didn't make sense was that I could reach the gun easier than she could. All I'd have to do would be press the little button, the door would pop open, and I'd reach in and take it. Or anyone else that was riding with her could. That tickled the hell out of me. I wanted to tip her off that she should keep it in her lap or somewhere she could get to it first.

We'd been riding about ten minutes when she said, "Paraiso Beach? Isn't that where they had the murder?"

Boy, that cheered me up. "I thought it was suicide," I told her. I wanted to see what-all she'd say.

"The way the papers talk, I gathered this Rita Cydney shot him. Maybe not, though. I haven't been following it too closely. The papers out here are so full of sensationalism one doesn't know what to believe!" She didn't seem to have an ax to grind one way or the other. Because of that I was anxious to hear her talk about us some more. Also she seemed to be fairly intelligent.

"I go to school with her son," I told her.

"He found the body, didn't he?" she asked.

"Yes, he told me all about it."

"The poor boy!" She kind of clucked sympathetically.

"I've met his mother several times and I don't think she'd kill anyone," I said.

"Oh, that's one thing you can never tell, not really. You'd be surprised at the people who are capable of murder!" she said. "It's frightening!"

The more she skipped over my mother, the more I

wanted to pump her. But she left me with that last delightful thought about who-all was capable of murder.

I was thinking of how I'd get her talking again, but soon she was driving with her head practically touching the windshield. She made a few remarks about the fog and then didn't seem to want to talk any more. I couldn't blame her. It was really thick by then; she was giving all her attention to the rotten visibility.

I just sat there thinking of all the possibilities. When I first started off on my little jaunt I felt so dumb about making the trip I was hoping for some reason Merwin had been delayed and therefore my mother wouldn't be home. Now, with the fog and all, I didn't care how furious she'd get—I wanted her and Merwin to be there.

Then a strange thing happened. For the first time, riding along the highway, practically on instruments, I got to wondering if my mother could possibly have done it. Maybe the thought had skittered wildly across my mind before for a fleeting moment, but I'd shoved it away immediately. But now—I guess partly because of what the woman had said and partly because the police and the newspapers were being so tenacious about the case, and the fact it had dragged on for so long—I let my mind dwell on whether my mother could actually have taken a gun and shot Ben through the head.

Also, I kept thinking about waking up and hearing voices and then my mother snapping at me the next morning, saying she couldn't sleep and had gone downstairs and turned the television set on. More than that—I still couldn't understand why she hadn't told the police that. Or if she had, why they hadn't verified it with me.

Actually, when I went over all those details in my mind, each one specifically, they all had plausible explanations. She did have trouble sleeping. And especially when she hadn't worked in so long and was starting a job that could mean so much to her. And she always got a little irritable when I asked a lot of questions. So that explained her snapping at me the next morning. As far as not telling the police about waking up and walking downstairs—well, at first we didn't think things were serious enough or that Ben's death was really that much their business. By the time they'd made it their business they'd already stacked so many circumstances against you, it was natural to protect yourself by not giving them an opportunity to hold up more phony evidence in front of your face. I knew damn well she didn't do it! Mainly, because she's so high-strung she surely would have cracked up by this time.

But here's a cuckoo thing: in spite of rationalizing all these factors, I got a wild mental picture of finding my mother prowling around the house, all alone, with a wild look in her eyes, covering up her tracks.

Suddenly the fog thinned for an instant, and right ahead of us was the intersection where the main street from Paraiso Beach crossed the highway.

"I'm about a mile and a quarter past here," I told her.

Sure enough, after we passed the intersection it got thick as whipped cream again. There was a street light right by our road, Calle Vista, but it was on the other side of the highway and not too bright. I figured that wouldn't be much help at all. We crept along for a while until I thought I saw this sort of faint glow on the opposite side of the highway, and I knew I couldn't be too far off. I asked her to stop.

"I hate leaving you off in the middle of all this," she said.

"Oh, I'll be all right," I told her, as my stomach started tying itself up in knots. I wanted to suggest that she better not continue driving in all that fog, that she could stay at our house. But she probably would have thought I was some kind of a junior sex fiend.

I thanked her for the ride, told her to drive carefully, and got out. I stood there with the fog swooshing up against my face and watched the car ease away from me.

Chapter 28

I TOOK about three steps and fell ass-over-tea-kettle when I tripped myself up on one of those short guide-posts they have along the highway to keep cars from going off into a ditch. Boy, things were going just grand! I was pretty damn sure all I was going to get for my brilliant brain wave was the shit scared out of me.

I picked myself up and brushed myself off as best I could. I was covered with gravel and dirt which clung to me because it was so damp and sticky out. I didn't see the light patch I thought I'd seen from the car. There was an old post right opposite from where our road hit the high-way, so I walked along the dirt shoulder of the road with my arm out hoping to hit it, and I did. I yelled at the same time because it surprised me. My voice sounded very muffled and thick in all that fog. It didn't seem to leave me; it just hung right around my face. I knew I was across the highway from our road, so I started to walk over. In a second I could see the glow from the street light.

From there on I knew my way well enough. Our drive-way veered off to the right about a hundred or so yards down Calle Vista. I walked right down the middle, staying on the white line which had just been repainted, luckily enough.

I hoped the dogs were still in the kennel because they'd start up an awful ruckus and probably terrify everyone, including me. When I finally got to the driveway the fog seemed to get a little bit thinner. I walked down the drive thinking more about the scene I might come up against with my mother than my idea about any note. Even though it wasn't as foggy as it had been out on the highway, it was awfully dark and close walking in between the eucalyptus trees that lined the drive, so I had to take it easy.

Once the trees ended and I came out into where the

drive became circular, I could see the outline of the house ahead of me in the mist. There wasn't any sign of light. The carriage lamp out in the drive wasn't even on, nor was there a light in the hall or any of the windows as far as I could see. I quickly looked to the far side of the driveway where there was a little extension to park your car if you didn't want to leave it right in front of the house. There weren't any cars parked there.

The moment I realized nobody was home this Godawful fear grabbed hold of me. Fear of what—I don't know. Just plain unadulterated fear. Christ, why did I always get myself into situations like this when I was alone? It was foggy exactly like the evening I found Ben. And quiet as a tomb. I stood there in the open space, just beyond the trees, unable to move for a moment.

I started hating Ben worse than ever for getting us into this mess and hating myself for being such a dumb bastard as to come all the way down there by myself on a foggy night, with nobody home, and at three in the morning, to boot! I started damning my mother and Merwin for not being home. I even cursed Lee out. You see, I thought if he hadn't teased me that night on the pier I wouldn't have gone on the ride and got sick and we never would have met Ben. I'm a great one for blaming everyone once I get started.

When you let yourself get terrified like that you're not only afraid of dead people and ghosts and things; you're afraid of doors, windows, bushes, trees, fences—everything! When you look back on it, it seems ridiculous to be afraid of a tree, but at the time you wouldn't be a bit suprised if a couple of branches closed in on you and shook you until your teeth rattled! At least I wouldn't be.

I started trembling while I was standing there. I mean really trembling. It got so bad I knew I'd have to move in some direction or I'd shatter and fall into little pieces right where I was. I made my legs propel me forward and started to walk across the circular driveway toward the front door. I hated the sound my shoes made as they crackled across the gravel. I tended to almost bend back as I got near the house for fear it would fall down and envelope me.

I looked up at it and got an awful start. Now that I was close, I could detect a small yellow glow around the edges of Merwin's bedroom window—coming from behind the closed drapes. I thought maybe my eyes were playing tricks, but the closer I got the more I could tell there was a lamp on up there. His window was open and the breeze moved the drapes ever so slightly allowing a tiny bit of the light to flicker out at the bottom of the window.

I stopped right by the lamp-post, looked up, and called out, "Merwin!" I froze, waiting for an answer. If only I could hear that funny thin voice call back, "Yes, Sweetie?" There was no reply.

Suddenly I thought of the wild idea that maybe my mother was there alone; but why would she be in Merwin's room? I called out, "Mom! Oh, Mom!" No answer.

Then I thought maybe it was a burglar. And don't think I would have minded if there had been one! Anybody for company. "Anybody home?" I called up. Total silence.

The idea struck me that Merwin had been the last one at the house before he went to New York. Maybe he'd left a light on when he took off that afternoon without realizing it. I made a definite statement to myself that that's what it was and tried to pull myself together. I made myself think how ashamed I'd be the next day at high noon with the sun shining down and all kinds of normal activity going on. It didn't help a bit.

There's only a certain amount of time you can go on terrifying yourself, and then I suppose you just drop dead from a heart attack. I was expecting that to happen at any moment, so I made myself continue. I don't remember taking the key to the front door out of my pocket, but I do remember having one helluva time getting it to fit in the keyhole.

Once I'd unlocked the door and flung it back open I yelled "Anybody home?" once more. I don't think I waited too long because a case of the black horrors came over me. I started tearing around like a rabid fox. I'll bet I had every single light on in the downstairs part of the house within fifteen seconds. Not only that, but I had Lena Horne singing away like crazy on the phonograph, and the TV set making a hollow whooshing sound because there wasn't any program on that late, just a test pattern, but it looked great to me. I even remember wishing the rotten parrot was there.

There were two alternatives left to me after I'd raced around the downstairs part of the house. Either I could go down to the game room or I could go upstairs and check on Merwin's bedroom and the light. Both were about as appealing as facing a firing squad. Somehow going upstairs won out because I'd always had the idea that if Ben's ghost was any one place in the house it would be in that lousy game room.

I tore up the stairs practically with my eyes closed, switched on the hall lights, and about five steps further was looking in Merwin's bedroom. It was empty, and a little lamp on a round table next to his easy chair was on. The room was tidy, the bed was made, and I felt like a fool for letting the light, which looked so innocent now, scare me when I was outside the house. I didn't look in my room, my mother's room, and especially Ben's room. I felt what I didn't know wouldn't hurt me. I went back downstairs and just stood in the hallway.

I guess what I was trying to do was to think up some excuse not to go down to the game room. Finally I told myself, "Come on, Inspector Philo Jerk, get it over with and get the hell out!" I remember making up my mind that I'd race down there, look in the newel post, and then tear out of the house up to the highway and get a ride back to Hollywood with an escaped convict if he'd only stop and pick me up. Anything but stick around that miserable house.

The only way to get down to the game room from inside the house was through a door and down the stairway leading from the pantry in between the dining room and the kitchen. I ran through the dining room, turned left at the pantry, and opened the door. A musty, damp blanket of air hit me in the face. I reached down the side of the wall and switched on the game room lights. There at the bottom of the stairway was the wooden newel post, standing there like it was making fun of me, almost saying, "You came all the way down to Paraiso Beach for this? Ass-hole!"

Suddenly I couldn't just run down, take a quick look,

and run back. Again I got a case of the anxieties. "Anybody down there?" I called out. Then I heard myself kind of laughing. "Ha, ha—I know you're down there!" I said. I actually think I've experienced the feeling a person gets before he's about to snap.

I kind of crept down the stairs keeping my eyes peeled for the ever-widening view of the room as I walked down lower and lower. The game room was dank and clammy— but it was empty. You see, nobody had used it in such a long time that the dampness had really set in. You could see streaks of perspiration running down the wood panel- ing. I was standing right by the post. I looked around the room thoroughly to make sure nothing was down there. There was a john at the far end of the room. The door was open but the lights from the room didn't hit inside, and I wished they had. I thought of going in there and turning the lights on but I told myself, "Oh, come now, buster— you're cracking up." I turned to look back up the stairs just to make sure Fu Manchu or somebody like that wasn't following me.

As I did, my eye caught a picture of Patsy Kelly on the wall a few feet up from the bottom of the stairs. It was one of those great smiling pictures where she was winking out at you. I'd met her a couple of times when we'd been down to the house before we moved in. She was a good friend of the Culps, and I'd seen lots of her old pictures on television. I liked her; she was always so kind of happy and wacky and yet with this great big heart and tons of warmth. Somehow her smiling out from the frame at me gave me the courage to turn around and put my hand on top of the post. But I couldn't lift it off right away. That moment meant too much to me.

I had to consciously tell myself to take it off. When I did, I lifted it very gently and leaned over slowly and kind of peeked in, like maybe a jack-in-the-box would jump out at me.

The first thing I saw was money. Green bills all crumpled up in there with a few quarters and some more coins mixed in with them. Christ, Ben had been there! I thought my heart would pop right out through my chest. Then, in an instant, my hopes sank. I figured he'd put it there maybe a week before his death and I just hadn't looked.

I quickly started clawing in the post. When I grabbed at the bills and yanked them out a lot of the change clattered to the floor. I almost wanted to go "Shhh!"

As I was pulling the last of the bills out I saw something white down in there and also something yellow. An envelope! I recognized it right away as one of my mother's little fancy envelopes with pale blue flowers around the edges. It was for thank-you notes and things like that. Below it was a sheet of yellow typing paper like Mr. Culp and Merwin used for first drafts of their writing. I almost ripped them apart getting them out. They were sort of jammed in down there.

On the outside of the envelope, in pencil, was written "Rita." The yellow sheet of paper had been folded over several times. I opened it up. Both sides had been scrawled on, and at the top of one side I saw "Dear Cosmo!" I told you about Ben always calling me different names just for the fun of it. Well, Cosmo was one he'd used before. I started to read it but I was so excited my eyes kept skipping to the middle, the bottom, and back to the beginning. The writing was very erratic—but more than that, I just couldn't concentrate. My whole nervous system was doing nip-ups.

The envelope was tiny; there couldn't have been much writing inside there so, in spite of the fact it was addressed to my mother and sealed—I tore it open!

Dear Rita!

I love you. But as I failed my entire life—I failed you. I do love you! I won't ask forgiveness, only that you know—I love you!

BEN

Oh, God, that sobered me up. My eyesight was blurred by the time I'd read it over maybe a dozen times. Then again I'm not sure I did read it over. Maybe I just stared at it.

The mystery we'd lived with for so many weeks was walking out one door, and sadness was pouring in to replace it.

Sadness! There must be a more meaningful word some place!

I walked to a red leather chair near the pool table and sat down. I felt like I'd had Novocain injected into my blood stream—that's how heavy and weighted down I was feeling. I turned on the stand-up lamp, smoothed out the sheet of yellow paper, and began reading it very slowly.

Dear Cosmo!

You always liked to hear stories so I'll tell you one more. Shall I start out once-upon-a-time? Yes. Because you represent all the once-upon-a-times I might have had.

Sooo, once-upon-a-time a psychiatrist had twin sons age eight. One was an incurable pessimist—the other an incurable optimist. Their father became alarmed and decided to try an experiment. Christmas Eve he filled the pessimist's room with everything a boy could wish for; and he filled the optimist's room with horse manure. Early the next morning he went to observe their reactions.

The pessimist sat among the toys, books, clothes, sporting goods—just sat there—eyeing the presents suspiciously, trying to figure out what the catch was. His father sighed and walked toward the other boy's room.

When he peeked in the door he saw him standing waist high in the middle of all the manure, shoveling it up in the air over his shoulder and laughing—as you would say, Cosmo—like a fiend! "Son," the father said, "what's the matter with you? What are you so happy about?" The boy turned, still laughing, and replied, "Gee, Dad, I figure with all this horse shit—there must be a pony!"

So, Josh, don't do as I did—do as I say. Hunt for the pony I couldn't quite locate. And even if you never find him—you'll live Life looking. It's more fun that way.

Love,
BEN

Chapter 29

I CAN'T tell you how many times I read that note. But I do know it was quite a while before it began to dawn on me that we were saved. I mean my mother was free. Our troubles were over! I wasn't afraid any more, I remember that. But I don't actually recall the stages of excitement welling up that finally exploded within me and made me tear to the phone and call up my mother at Stella and Ef's. I somehow got myself in this elated state, forgetting the sadness that knowing the truth about Ben would eventually bring.

I was shaking again, only this time with anticipation of spreading the news. I don't actually recall the conversation, but I know I spoke to Stella and Ef before they could waken my mother. It was hysterical. They couldn't believe it, and I kept having to repeat it over and over. "I found the notes!" I kept saying. "The notes from Ben!" I heard them screaming and yelling to my mother.

When she got to the phone she couldn't comprehend what was going on, where I was, how I'd gotten there or anything. I just kept telling her everything was all right, that I had the notes in my hand, that I was at the house at Paraiso Beach, and to come down right away. After a while there was a lot of shouting in the background and then everyone seemed to be on the phone at once. I didn't actually tell them what the notes said or anything because it was all too frantic to go into details. My mother couldn't get over being groggy. She said something about for God's sake she hoped this wasn't any sort of a joke.

Finally, Stella got on and told me to stay put, they'd be right down. I remember telling them to call Lee, and before I knew it we'd hung up.

Right away, without thinking what time it was, I phoned Andy and Midge. Another jangled-up call but, of course, they were delirious about the notes. Midge started to bawl me out when I told her I hitchhiked down, but Andy shut her up because, after all, finding the notes was about the most important thing in the world. He said they were on their way.

After I hung up with them, the phone rang. It was Lee. He was calling because he couldn't believe it. When I assured him I had them right in my hand he shouted it was a miracle. He was practically in his car, he said.

I looked at the clock in the game room; it was twelve minutes after four in the morning. The next thing I did was count the money. There was thirty-seven dollars and sixty cents. I pocketed it. How I could be so money-conscious at a time like that I don't know. Or devious. Because, you see, I never told anyone about the money part of it until weeks afterward. It's just one of those crazy inbred things I'll have to live with, I guess.

Then I did a nutty thing. There was a bar down in the game room; so I got myself some ice out of the little refrigerator and made myself a Scotch and water. That's the first drink, outside of wine or tasting somebody's cocktail, that I'd ever had.

I was starting to feel my oats. I even began looking around for cigarettes, but there weren't any down there. So I took my drink upstairs with me—along with the notes, of course. I got a cigarette out of one of the boxes in the living room and lit up. Then I turned the TV set off so they wouldn't think I was potty when they came down. I also turned about a dozen superfluous lights off here and there. Lena Horne had quit singing, so I turned the record over and started playing the other side. Then I sat down in an easy chair with my drink and cigarette, not actually enjoying the effects of either, but enjoying the hell out of the experience of having them.

I have to admit that I started thinking about what a genius I must be to get the brain wave to come down and look in the newel post. I was sure, that night, I had some mystic powers which had been denied all others and that these powers would some day be enlarged so I could stop wars, find out what happened after death, cure cancer, and God only knows what not!

234

I kept on drinking my Scotch and water until I began to feel kind of warm and fuzzy. It was a good feeling until I started, later on, to get a little dizzy, too. I must have poured myself a hooker. I hoped I wouldn't get sick. I think the reason I didn't was because you're always hearing about everyone getting deathly ill the first time they take a good stiff drink, and I refused to follow the rule. When I finished it I decided to go upstairs and get cleaned up. I'd really gotten pretty dirty from that fall. Also I figured a shower, on the cold side, would pick me up and offset the effects of the drink.

When I got to my bedroom I undressed, went into the bathroom, and hopped in the shower. Now, it's funny, but I told you I wasn't scared after finding the notes. Well, I wasn't—until I was standing under the shower. The water was making so much noise that I started imagining all kinds of sounds coming from downstairs. I got panicky, so much so that I got out of the shower dripping wet and locked the bathroom door. Then I turned the water off, put my head right next to the door, and listened like crazy. I couldn't hear anything. I had a lot of soap all over me, so I turned the shower back on and got back in. The minute I was standing under the water I thought I heard noises again. Isn't that nutty? I actually imagined I heard doors opening and closing and people creeping around and voices. That was the quickest shower I've ever taken. Of course, as soon as I turned the water off I couldn't hear anything but my own breathing.

Then I remembered I'd left the notes in the living room. I imagined that someone was sneaking in to destroy them. Someone! Maybe Ben himself was wandering around down there with that awful hole in his head and those ants still crawling around his face. I also got the idea that Ben had communed to me from beyond the grave while I was sitting up in the tree in the moonlight. Before I knew it I was perspiring so much I couldn't possibly dry myself off. I'd get my back dry and then start wiping off my legs but by the time I'd finished with them my back would be sopping wet again.

You'd think I'd laugh at myself being locked in a bathroom scared silly for the *second* time in a couple of months, but I didn't. I was just as frightened as I'd been when I holed up in the downstairs bathroom with the animals the night I found Ben. I was turning into some kind of a bathroom nut! I kept telling myself what a dope I was, that I'd better get dressed, go downstairs, and get the notes; but I'll be damned if I didn't stay in the bathroom, imagining all sorts of weird things, until I heard a car pull up outside. As soon as I heard Stella, Ef, and my mother shouting my name I tore out of the bathroom, put on a robe, and flew down the stairs. We all crashed into one another in the hall.

"The notes—where are the notes?" Stella kept screaming. Ef, too. My mother was smothering me and, of course, crying. We all kind of rolled into the living room, clutching one another, and Ef was thumping me on the back. I handed my mother the notes, which were right on the coffee table where I'd left them. She read hers first and then she started to read mine but, she, too, was so excited and emotional she couldn't wade through it all. It's funny! Nobody ever finished my note the first time through. Everybody always started it, and then way later when they'd heard the whole story of how I happened to come down there—then they read it. Sometimes not for hours.

I have to tell you now that the impact of the notes—I mean the fact that they proved Ben had really cared for us—didn't hit right away. It was like the night we found Ben: going off to Mama Paganelli's, and almost having a party. The excitement of there just *being* notes detracted from what they said and what they meant.

When my mother first read hers she was crying, but then she'd been crying from the moment she met me at the bottom of the stairs.

Of immediate interest to her, Stella, and Ef was how in hell the whole thing had come about. So while Ef started making them drinks I began telling the story from when I took the walk up at the ranch. I hadn't even finished it when Lee arrived and we went through another burst of excitement.

It's no use telling about each individual person that arrived, because they all followed the same pattern. First, they'd come tearing in and everyone would be hugging and handshaking with everyone else. Then came the fascination of actually seeing the notes and holding them, followed by the reading of my mother's, the kind of scanning of mine, and then wanting to know how I'd got the idea and about getting down to Paraiso Beach from the ranch.

I can honestly say that from early that morning to about a week later it was like the Fourth of July, Christmas, Easter, and Mardi Gras time all rolled into one.

By ten in the morning you couldn't get another car in the driveway. Everyone and his brother was down there: Andy, Midge, Stella, Ef, Lee, Roy, Jeanette, Jay, Sally, and several Paganellis, including Mama Paganelli, who was rustling up breakfast for everyone. By noon some of the local police had joined us along with a few advance scouts from the District Attorney's office. All sorts of reporters and photographers were beginning to trickle down, too.

Merwin had been delayed and was arriving at twelve-thirty, which was why nobody had been home. Andy drove in to pick him up at the airport and also to get Cecelia whose car was on the fritz. They arrived back around two-thirty; at about the same time Captain Mansan and his group of inquisitors descended on us. They were the only ones who didn't act delirious; they actually seemed to be a little disappointed.

They headed right for the notes, and one man was assigned to whisk them off to a handwriting expert. This caused a big stink with the reporters and photographers who kept wanting to take pictures of me lifting them out of the newel post. Someone said "The hell with 'em! Fake it!" Sally Knapp got one of those small envelopes of my mother's and wrote "Rita" on it herself. Then she scribbled all over a piece of yellow paper to kind of duplicate my note, and we went on with the picture taking.

Later on, the little coroner even showed up. I hoped all this would help him get his job back. I don't think he was too used to drinking because Cecelia found him passed out in her room about an hour after he got there.

The writer and his wife, Mr. and Mrs. Winden—whose house we had dinner at, the Sunday night Ben must have killed himself—came by with one of the producers of the

237

series and the director. They tried to grab a little attention by announcing the television series would go into production within two weeks, but nobody gave them much time except Jay, who kept trying to corner the reporters about it.

If you think they treated me like a hero for *finding* Ben, you should have seen the hullabaloo *this* time. I bet if I'd said I wanted to marry Princess Anne they would have sent a matchmaker over. Lee slipped me a fifty-dollar bill at one point. He was overjoyed.

There was no end to the excitement. Along about six o'clock I was actually getting a sore throat from telling the story so many times. And it's a wonder I didn't have my shoulder dislocated from having so many people banging on me.

Incidentally, my mother never did give me hell for hitchhiking down in the middle of the night. Every time she'd hear me tell about it she'd just shake her head in amazement.

Chapter 30

BECAUSE of all the press people being around, and also the people connected with the televison series, Lee, Merwin, and Sally were making a concerted effort to keep my mother from drinking too much so she'd look okay in all the pictures that were being snapped. Also, so nobody would be able to circulate rumors that she was hitting the bottle.

But when she couldn't ease her nerves at a time of crisis you knew something was going to happen. After hours of all this excitement she began to get jumpy and irritable toward all the people that were hanging around. I didn't see the actual incident that started clearing people out, but I heard this great hubbub coming from the dining room while I was talking to a lady reporter in the living room. Naturally we went in to see what had happened. My mother was in tears, with Lee hovering over her, and some guy was standing a few paces away rubbing his cheek with his hand. She'd obviously slapped his face over something he'd said or done. I never did find out which. She kept saying to Lee, "Get him out of here!"

"I didn't mean anything by it," the guy kept repeating. "It was all in fun!"

"Lee, I want him out of here!" My mother was almost getting hysterical.

The fellow she slapped saw she wasn't kidding and started to leave. Lee and Merwin began going around very nicely, suggesting that everybody wind it up and take a powder. One thing nobody thought about was the fact that none of us had gotten much sleep. I hadn't had any. I'd been up since the night before, and I'd called everybody else about four in the morning to tell about finding the notes.

Roy Clymer and Jeanette had a good buzz on. It must

239

have been a terrific relief for them to know he was vindicated in accepting Ben's death as suicide. As they left she really gave me the old hugging treatment. Her eyes were getting all moist. I think he got her out in the nick of time, before the dam busted.

After a while the only ones left were Stella, Ef, Andy, Midge, Jay, Merwin, Lee, Sally and me. What you'd call the family group. By then somebody had fixed my mother a good stiff drink, and things were calming down considerably. My eyelids were beginning to feel like aluminum shutters. They were starting to close automatically as if someone had pushed a button. I wanted to stay up in the worst kind of way because this was a red-letter day for my mother and me, but I couldn't make it. Besides, I was starting to get a headache.

There didn't seem to be any organized plans for eating, so my mother asked Cecelia to find me some dinner in the kitchen. Cecelia said I could have anything I wanted. I suggested hot cakes and sausages with every kind of jam we had. I'm nuts about hot cakes. If I ever get sent to the electric chair the newspapers will carry a big story about how I requested hot cakes for my last meal. We all sat around the living room chattering like magpies until Cecelia came in and announced, "Mr. Perry Mason's supper is served!" That got a laugh from the gathering. They wouldn't let me go until they'd passed me around the living room like a volleyball and showered me with rounds of verbal applause. My mother, of course, got very emotional. I had to be pried loose from her by Sally.

While I was stuffing the last hot cake down my throat I heard somebody cry out from the living room. The kitchen's quite a distance away, so I couldn't tell exactly what it was. I walked in through the dining room toward the living room to try to make out what was going on. As I got to the hall I heard my mother's voice, very excitable, almost frenzied.

"Don't you see? Don't you understand? I lied to you, Lee. I came downstairs that night and watched television. But I never told anyone—not a soul!"

"Now, now—Rita," Lee said. "It doesn't make any difference, it's all over with!" Everyone else chimed in, too, reassuring her it didn't matter.

"But it *does*! Why *didn't* I tell you? That's wrong . . . ! but I was so frightened!" She raced on, blurting out all the fears she had. As I walked a few steps down the hall so I could see in the room, I heard her say: "Josh knew. Even Josh knew! My baby knew, but even he didn't say anything! Don't you see . . . Oh, my God!" I looked in the door. My mother was pacing around the room gesturing wildly with her arms. Lee got up and was going toward where she was at the far end of the room.

Suddenly she turned and rushed at him. "Lee, it's finished now, isn't it? Tell me, it's all done with!"

"Of course it is, Rita! The only thing left to do is— forget!" He put his arms around her. She started to cry and Midge and Stella went to her.

I decided maybe it would be best for me to go right upstairs to bed. Nobody had spotted me, so I started to walk away when my mother called out, "There he is! My baby!" She ran across the room and threw her arms around me. "Josh knew—didn't you?" I didn't answer. She pulled herself away from me, looking me straight in the eye. "Didn't you, dear? You knew and yet you didn't say anything. And I was embarrassed to say anything to you— my own son!" She turned and faced the group. "Isn't that frightening?" They all tried to laugh it off, but she was getting insistent. She looked back at me. "You knew, didn't you, Josh?"

"Knew what?" I asked. I didn't want her to realize I'd been listening.

"That I hardly slept all night Sunday evening, that I was downstairs with the television set on—"

"Oh, that," I said, trying to pass it off.

"What you must have thought! Oh, Josh—you didn't think your mother . . ."

"Mom, forget it! I just figured the bloodhounds were on our trail, and what they didn't know wouldn't bother them."

"Oh, Josh, I would have spoken to you about it . . . I wanted to, but I felt that if you decided to say anything . . . It was Providence . . . don't you see? I was leaving it up to Fate!" She turned to the others. "I wouldn't have asked my son to lie, but—oh, what a horrible thing I *was* asking of him! I let him carry a burden like that!" She took a few quick steps back into the living room. "I'm no good. No good for myself or anyone else!"

"Rita, don't be silly!" Stella said.

"Stop talking that way, honey," Midge cut in.

"It's true. It's true." She pounded the back of a chair with her fists. "If I hadn't gone to dinner, that night . . . Why . . . oh, *why* did I go?"

"Rita, you had no way of knowing," Lee said.

"No way of knowing!" she screamed at him. "But that's just it—I *did*! He was drinking, almost in tears several times. He was—" She turned to me. "We'd never seen Ben like that, had we? He was entirely different from the way we'd ever seen him. He acted so strange! Oh, God, if I hadn't gone . . . If only Ben had told me about . . . We could have worked it out! I know we could!"

Everyone was cutting in, trying to get her to stop going on that way.

See, when you learn the truth about something—like finding the notes and knowing how Ben must have felt— then suddenly you start picking your brain apart trying to figure out ways it would have worked. But it's too late.

I kept standing where I was, in the doorway leading into the living room. I wanted to leave, but my mother kept asking me questions. She never waited for an answer; a nod of affirmation would do. But she did keep almost leaning on me mentally.

Suddenly she said to Lee: "Tell me the truth. If I had gone before the Grand Jury—what would have happened?"

He shrugged and said, "Rita, will you please stop all this talk! It's over. Finished. Try to forget it."

"I only want to know, Lee. I must know!"

"There's no way for any of us to be sure, Rita. My own personal opinion is that it never would have come to trial. The Los Angeles police were pressured into the whole business. Once they'd gone through the formalities of a Grand Jury hearing, I'm sure it would have been dropped."

"But you were worried, Lee. Why were you so worried?"

"Rita, do we have to go on about it?" Lee asked her.

She got almost angry. "Yes, we do! I have a right to know. Don't you realize, I haven't had a decent night's sleep for weeks and weeks without being so drunk or drugged I could hardly get up the next morning! It's true, I haven't. And I say I have a right to know why I've been put through this torture—and my son has a right to know." She wheeled around in a circle. "I don't understand why . . . things happen . . . the way they do!" She was getting all breathy. "Is it me? Is it something about *me*?"

Everybody was sitting around, looking uneasy because she had such a frantic way about her. Nobody spoke. She paused a moment and then shouted, "Will somebody answer me? Tell me! I want an explanation!"

Merwin had been sitting there not offering a comment of any sort, which was unusual for him, but then he spoke up. "Rita, I'm saying *nothing* and very little of that!" Sally chuckled. "And I'll tell you why. Frankly, I've had a bellyful, and you're being a bloody bore. Now let's get on with a drink and some important talk—like Jayne Mansfield, or whatever happened to hula hoops."

I was waiting for her to explode, but instead she cocked her head and looked around at each individual quickly. Then she laughed a short staccato laugh and said, "You're right. Oh, Merwin, you're so right! I've subjected all of my friends to months of . . . And now I'm being a bore! I apologize." They started telling her to forget it, but she held up her hands. "No . . . First I . . . I don't know what I'd have done without you. I love you all . . . and I'll prove it by making the next round of drinks!"

The scene was over so fast you could hardly believe it. In a second she was going around collecting empty glasses and everybody was making small talk.

My mother turned around, saw me still standing there, and said, "Oh, Josh—Josh, you look so tired. Go up and get a good night's sleep. And forgive your mother for making a fool of herself."

It took about ten minutes to say good night to everybody, what with accepting more congratulations; and when I was finally walking up the stairs I wished I had an escalator. My legs felt like petrified wood. I was pooped.

After I got in bed and turned the lights out, I heard somebody walking up the stairs. My mother came into my room and sat down on the bed next to me. She put her arms around me, held me very close for a long while, and then said, "He loved us, Josh! We're sure of that now, aren't we?" She started to sob very softly, but she made a great effort to snap herself out of it. "I'm sorry, baby, I'm afraid your mother needs a good cold shower." She patted me on the cheek. "You get a good sleep. And you don't have to go to school tomorrow. Stay in bed as late as you want and catch up." She kissed me good night and whispered, "I'm going to make something out of my life—for you. I don't know what I'd do without you." Then she left.

The way she said, "He loved us, Josh," made me feel terribly sad. I felt like crying my eyes out, but I was too tired to do anything but sleep.

Chapter 31

BEING a real ham, I was dying to go to school the next day, but I didn't realize until I was all dressed and downstairs that it was Saturday. Cecelia was the only one up that morning, and she and I had a great time at breakfast reading about my adventures in the paper. Merwin came down about ten, and the phones were ringing steadily from then on. All kinds of excitement was breaking loose. Jay called up about noon to say the TV series was going to start shooting at the end of the following week. They'd pushed the date up to get in on all the publicity. They wanted my mother for a meeting in town at three in the afternoon to start talking about schedules and wardrobe.

My mother seemed knocked out when she came downstairs, but by the time she left the house she looked terrific. Actresses really have a way of pulling themselves together. They're like chameleons. They can change from one moment to the next so you'd hardly recognize them. She was dressed fit to kill and seemed to be in pretty good spirits.

I thought it might be a peaceful day; but the phone never stopped ringing, and all kinds of reporters, men and women, came in and out all afternoon. It was like one continuous press conference. They were sorry to miss my mother on one hand, but you could also tell they were delighted to get me alone, figuring they could pump me for the lowdown on everything from soup to nuts without supervision. They did get way off the track, too. One guy even wanted to know if my mother slept in the raw.

Before my mother got home Lee called up with word that the handwriting experts had verified that the notes had been written by Ben. His wife had been notified, all charges were dropped, and there was only clear sailing ahead.

Or so we all thought!

There must have been about a dozen people for dinner that night again. It was kind of a double celebration. The end of the Ben thing and the beginning of a new career for my mother. She was very excited about the series. They were going to start shooting the following Thursday. They planned to film five segments in three weeks. This was an awful work load, but it had to be done because the director of the series, not thinking they were going to begin that soon, had sold a script of his own to "Playhouse 90" which he was also going to direct. This meant he'd have to take about three weeks off, so they had to get that many episodes ahead. Everyone agreed it was a good thing for my mother to have all this activity to take her mind away from Ben and the notes and the emotional reaction that would undoubtedly set in.

She was being a real sport that night. You knew she must have tons of thoughts way down deep inside her that were killing her about Ben, but she put on a very breezy, let's-get-to-it attitude and was a perfect hostess. Nobody got too drunk that night; everyone acted very well. Merwin was being pretty hilarious about his trip to New York. He hates to fly, and hardly ever does unless he's forced to.

"If I hadn't felt I had to be back to save Rita from the gas chamber, I'd have gone any other way from Greyhound bus to sedan chair. Flying absolutely petrifies me because, you see, it's so completely unnatural. I'm sure it scares hell out of everyone, only nobody admits it. And I don't mean just the passengers; I'm talking about the crew as well. Now here's my theory, and I'm convinced it's true. You know how, once the plane has taken off by some miraculous fluke, every so often the pilot or co-pilot strides back through the cabin, shaking hands and grinning toothsomely at the trapped occupants? Did you ever notice that these pilots, to the man, are well-built, rugged, handsome, happy, confident, reassuring individuals?"

"God, yes!" Stella said. "They're divine in their tailored uniforms with the gold stripes and those cocky little caps." She went on growling and licking her chops over them.

"Exactly my point!" Merwin cried. "They aren't pilots *at all*! The men that walk up and down charming the pants off everyone are *actors*! They're hired by the airline and kept forward in the cockpit or whatever the place is called. They work on a schedule . . . like models at a fashion show. Every hour or so one of them cleans his teeth with dental floss, puts his cap on at a rakish angle, and strolls back through the plane, chucking the kiddies under the chin, flirting with the women, and talking man-talk with the men. He fills everyone with a sense of false confidence, goes forward, reads the *Hollywood Reporter*, and has a cup of coffee until it's time for another appearance."

"Don't tell me the plane flies by itself!" Ef said.

"Oh, no!" Merwin said. "They do have pilots but nobody sees them. They wouldn't dare let them come out. The real pilots are nervous, frightened, sweaty little men with bad complexions, ill-fitting uniforms, and Gargantuan cases of dandruff and halitosis from being perpetually terrified. They have little high-pitched voices, and I suspect they wear parachutes. They're strapped into their seats screaming and bickering at one another, 'Watch out for that peak! . . . No, not that knob, silly—that one jettisons the left engine. . . . No, not down there—that's a night baseball game! *That's* the airport, those lights over there—I think!'"

The idea about the actors slays me!

Merwin was pretty much "on" all evening. Mainly, I guess because in spite of my mother's exterior he knew she was carrying around a lot of things inside her that didn't show. So he was taking the full weight of being entertaining on his shoulders.

Even though the next day was Sunday my mother went into town to read over the scripts they were to start filming and to attend pre-production conferences. Merwin was anxious to get back to his screenplay, so he holed up in his room as much as possible. It was pretty hard to concentrate, though, because our house was still the center of an awful lot of activity. The phone kept on ringing, various people dropped by, sometimes strangers would just pull up in the driveway, kind of circle the center flower bed slowly, and then drive out. Curiosity seekers.

Sid Traylor rode his bike over around four in the afternoon, and we horsed around with Monkey-Face and the dogs for a while. He wanted to hear a firsthand account of my hitchhiking and all that. He also told me about a whorehouse he'd found out about in Redondo Beach. We made these elaborate, detailed plans to attend, knowing damn well we'd both chicken out.

My mother got home around four o'clock and asked Sid if he wanted to stay and have dinner with us. He practically fell over himself getting to the phone to tell his folks he wouldn't be home until later on. She really dazzles Sid. I remember after the first time he met her he said, "If my mother looked like that I'd have her riding around in parades all the time!"

The phone kept on ringing; various people called saying they were thinking of driving down, but my mother put on this chilly manner when she spoke to them. She said no, this was family night, that we were all exhausted and were going to lie around and relax.

Merwin barbecued some steaks on the patio and we sat outside and had a great dinner. While we were eating dessert my mother put down her plate, sighed, and stretched her arms way out. "Oh, this is nice," she said.

"Unusual is a more appropriate word," Merwin replied. "It hasn't been this quiet around here in months. I may just fall to pieces."

My mother looked at me. "From now on we're going to get back to a normal routine. You start in with school regularly, beginning tomorrow, Josh. I know it might seem like a letdown, but we can't go on the way we have."

After dinner Merwin went back upstairs to write some more, my mother went up to her bedroom to read over the scripts she'd picked up that day, and Sid and I stayed in the living room watching television and talking.

We got into a big discussion trying to figure out which kids at school had "done it." Sid always had sex on his mind in one form or another. He's not obnoxious about it, though, like some guys—just intensely interested. Like he might make a life study of it. We must have picked out fifteen girls we were pretty sure of. The only thing was, when we started counting the guys, we could only come up with about three. Even they were suspect. Oh, a lot of guys went around bragging, but you could tell it was so much hot air.

"How come?" Sid asked. "If there are fifteen girls, there ought to be that many guys. Girls can't do it alone, you know."

"They probably do it with guys that go to other schools," I said. "Or else they go around with older men. Girls are funny that way."

"It's not fair," Sid said. He started in brooding about it, especially since he'd read an article recently where it said that the male was at the height of his potency between the ages of fourteen and twenty. "I feel like I'm wasting valuable time," he said. "Besides, masturbating's a drag!"

I tried to cheer him up by telling him about this friend of my mother's in New York. He's one of those vegetarian nuts, but there must be something to it because he's seventy-eight now and he's got a little girl three years old.

"Yeah, but I hate vegetables," Sid said. "Also, no matter how much we rationalize, the fact is we ought to get started as soon as we can."

I agreed with him. I'm always thinking somebody's going to drop the goddam hydrogen bomb before I get a chance to do it.

I tell you I really hate the bastards that invented nuclear weapons. To my way of thinking, they're the real villains. All this talk about how scientists invent things for useful purposes and the betterment of mankind is a bunch of crap. Scientists are supposedly bright, yet anyone with a brain the size of a pea knows that there hasn't been one miserable invention yet that hasn't been used in warfare. So how the hell can they go ahead figuring these rotten things up when they must know they're going to be used against their very own children?

I expanded on all this to Sid, and he got doubly worried. Before he left that night we practically made a blood pact to go to that whorehouse in Redondo Beach during the summer.

The next day was my first appearance at school since the notes had been found, and a VIP should only get such a greeting when he's sent on all these foreign missions. I was mobbed at every turn by kids and teachers alike. I couldn't get over the fuss everyone made. You'd have thought I'd *written* the notes instead of just finding them. I never had so much attention showered on me. I enjoyed it. Yet on my way home from school I got this guilty feeling about capitalizing on Ben's death. I made a vow to simmer down.

It was almost five o'clock when I walked into the living room. I could tell by Merwin's expression something was wrong.

"Mrs. Nichols died early this afternoon. She took an overdose of sleeping pills," he told me. "Your mother's not feeling too well. She probably won't be coming down for dinner. I've got to go into town, so you'll have to eat alone. I'm sorry, sweetie."

I didn't see my mother at all that evening. I had dinner in the kitchen with Cecelia, who was as depressed as I was. It's strange how sad the death of Ben's wife was to us when we didn't really know her. Not only that, but look at all the trouble she'd caused us. Actually, we had every reason to hate her, but we didn't. You just couldn't. I kept remembering her that night in the driveway.

The evening papers played it up big. Most of them featured a picture of her holding the two notes. There she was, gazing down at a note her husband wrote telling my mother he loved her. Those notes must have been the deciding factors. She was his wife, but he didn't leave her so much as a word. The realization that if he couldn't get a divorce—in other words, if he had to go on living with her—he'd rather be dead must have been overwhelmingly painful.

God, when you started thinking of the effects of Ben's death, the lives it had screwed up . . . and now another funeral.

The notes had been given back to us by this time. I guess my mother had hers up in her room. I put mine in my wallet; it's still right here with me. I took it out that evening and read it over and over again. I couldn't help getting a spooky feeling knowing Ben had held this same piece of paper and stared at it, figuring out what-all to say, only a short time before he killed himself. And his wife had held it, probably reading it again and again like I was doing. It made me touch the paper and turn it over and over, almost as if I'd get some other message from it.

That night I kept hoping my mother would come downstairs or else call for me to come up to her bedroom, because I wanted her to talk to me, to reassure me. I don't know what I wanted to be reassured about, specifically. Maybe that it wasn't the end of the world, that we'd go on. Mainly, that this mess was all over with and things would take a turn for the better. That's what I'm always hoping. But sometimes I get very tired.

Several times during the evening I walked up and down the stairs, really kind of stomping so she'd hear me and maybe call me in. Once I walked past her bedroom door down to the window at the far end of the hall. When I got there I opened and shut it several times like I was a big window repairman or something. There wasn't a sound from her room. Walking back the other way, I paused at her door, but I couldn't hear a thing.

I cried myself to sleep. I cried for Ben and his wife and my mother, and, most of all, for what might have been. I cried myself dry as a well. And I remember saying to myself just before I went off to sleep: "This is the end, now, of all that!"

Chapter 32

MRS. Nichols's death seemed to give everyone back their values and a sense of perspective. The publicity died down slowly but surely; curiosity seekers dropped by the wayside. Our lives got back to normalcy—not that we'd ever been there in the first place—relative normalcy, I suppose you'd call it.

My mother was working night and day to film the first five segments of the series. And I mean working! She stopped drinking, except for maybe a cocktail before dinner. She was up at six every weekday morning, and rarely got home before seven-thirty or eight. Then on Saturday and Sunday she'd be studying the scripts for the following week.

Merwin was buckling down to finish his screenplay, which was way overdue because of all the time he'd given us. For almost a week he was at it from six in the morning until late in the afternoon. Then he decided he'd better move back into town because he was having meetings at the studio every morning about revisions. Besides, he'd only come down to be with us in our "time of need," as they say.

As for me, the school year was coming to an end, which meant all kinds of exams and other activities for me to get involved with. I've always gotten good grades, not because I'm so smart, but because I have practically a photographic memory; I remember almost everything I read. It's almost like cheating. The only subjects I have trouble with are things like geometry and chemistry, where you have to figure out original problems. I dislike all mathematics intensely anyhow—except for counting up money.

We hired Cecelia on a regular basis because now we had money coming in, but it was lonesome not having Merwin there. I missed him. We got a letter from the Culps, saying they'd be back from Europe the first part of July. So my mother contacted several estate agents, and told them to be on the lookout for a house for us above the Strip in Hollywood. I was looking forward to getting away from Paraiso Beach and starting a whole new life for myself.

I don't mean to give the impression that just because we were each busily engaged in our own projects everything was a gay old time, because it wasn't. Very few people came to the house, mainly because my mother didn't have any extra time. And there was a basic soberness together with an unmistakable sadness hanging over us. It became part of our lives. I guess it was the swinging of the pendulum from hating Ben to the point of realizing you couldn't hate him; you could only feel sorry for him, miss him, and wonder why it couldn't have worked out as perfectly as we thought it would. My mother never spoke about him to me again. So naturally I never mentioned him either.

For a while our lives fell into a steady routine, which was unusual for us. We both got up at the same time in the morning and had breakfast together. Then we each went our separate ways. At night when she'd come home I'd mix her a cocktail and take it up to her room while she was getting all her make-up off and into a dressing gown. Usually, after dinner, she'd have me cue her for an hour or so. We'd go up to her bedroom and go over her lines for the next day. I'd leave the room after a while and work on my homework. Later on she'd call me back in. By this time she'd have gotten ready for bed and taken her pill; I'd sit on the foot of the bed and cue her some more until the pill started taking effect. When she started getting drowsy, I'd turn the lights off, kiss her good night, and tiptoe out. This was usually not later than ten-thirty or eleven. Then I'd go downstairs, turn the television set on, and finish my homework.

But toward the end of the second week of shooting I noticed she was getting extremely tired and edgy. She began yelling at Cecelia regularly, and she'd kind of take swipes at me over minor things, like wearing the same blue jeans three days in a row, or not cutting my fingernails, or leaning on the dinner table with my elbows. And you couldn't get her to answer the phone no matter who was on it. Toward the end of that week she even had me make excuses when Merwin called up a couple of times.

By the beginning of the third week she was more touchy than I'd ever seen her. When I'd be cueing her and correct her for transposing words or changing a line around, she'd snap at me and tell me to stop her only when she really loused the script up but not for minor things.

On Thursday of that week, when I came home from school, her car was parked in the driveway along with Jay's. When I went into the house Cecelia said she'd come home around one o'clock and gone straight up to her bedroom, leaving instructions that she wasn't to be disturbed no matter who called. Cecelia said *everyone* had been calling, and a short while ago Jay had arrived and was upstairs with her now. She said she heard my mother shouting a lot after he went up, but that she quieted down a few minutes later. Also Sally Knapp had phoned and was on her way over.

Something was up, and I was positive it wasn't an occasion for throwing hats in the air. I sat in the living room with an awful sinking feeling in the pit of my stomach, trying to figure out what could possibly have gone wrong. I'd been there about fifteen minutes when I heard a car turn in the driveway. I walked down the hall and opened the front door as Sally jumped out of her Thunderbird.

"Hello, Butch—where's Rita?" She looked distracted, to say the least.

"Upstairs with Jay. I haven't seen her yet. What's wrong?"

"Nothing serious. A little flare-up on the set with Thor Tanner, the director. They were supposed to wind up tomorrow, but they're going to run over a couple of days into next week—so it's panic time. Tanner, who's got a reputation for being an A-1 bastard, said something snide to your mother this morning and she upped and walked."

"They won't fire her, will they?" That was my first thought.

"No, baby, of course not. They've been working like

dogs under constant pressure. It's a wonder they haven't been at each other's throats before this." She went right upstairs to talk to my mother and Jay.

I put Penny and Lord Nelson on their leashes and we went for a long hike down Calle Vista, the opposite direction from the highway. Before I realized it I had tears in my eyes. Goddam it, another rotten crisis! Why the hell couldn't my mother control herself? Actually, I was annoyed at her. More than annoyed—I was angry. You see, by this time I wanted our lives to be simplified as much as possible. It looked like that would never be. I remembered my mother asking, "Is it me? Is it something about me?" And I wondered if it *was* something about *us*? Was there a whammy on us, an evil sign, or what? I guess I must have dragged the dogs for a couple of miles along Calle Vista, wracking my brain for some kind of answer.

I didn't get back to the house until about five-thirty, by which time one of the producers of the television show was there. They were all in the living room engaged in a powwow, but they stopped talking when I walked in. My mother gave me a very curt greeting, so I volunteered that I had a lot of homework to do and went upstairs to my room.

I hated that evening. I stayed in my bedroom waiting for my mother to come in and explain things to me. After a while I heard an awful lot of activity up and down the stairs and back and forth from my mother's bedroom. Finally, there was a knock on my door and Sally came in.

"Josh, your mother's driving into town with me tonight. She wanted me to tell you she'll see you tomorrow evening, and Cecelia will have dinner ready for you in a little while. Also you're not to worry. She's going to work tomorrow, and the producers are doing everything they can to get the whole bit straightened out. Okay?"

"If you say so," I said in the flat reading of all time. Sally looked at me for a moment. I thought she was going to say something more reassuring, but she only flipped "Chin up!" at me and left.

I walked to the window and watched Sally get into the front seat of her car with my mother. It looked like a funeral procession. She pulled away; the producer and Jay followed in their cars. I was really sore at my mother then. She hadn't even bothered to talk to me. I stood there staring out the window in a daze until I began cursing. I cursed my mother, Ben, God—everyone I could get my hands on.

Dinner didn't hold much interest for me; I picked my way through it. All the time I was trying to figure out something to do that would displease my mother. Not that I'd ever want her to find out about it—but something I could do that, if she *did* know about, would upset her. Right after dinner it hit me: the whorehouse in Redondo Beach. Without thinking twice I called up Sid.

"Hello, Sid—Josh. Listen, you want to go to that whorehouse tonight?"

"What!" he said, like he'd never even entertained the idea before.

"You heard me! I'm going. Want to come along?"

"On a school night?"

"Don't give me any lame excuses like that!" I told him.

"But we said we'd go this *summer*."

"So it's June now—that's almost summer. Besides, we didn't sign a contract or anything."

"Josh, my folks are home," he said in a lowered voice.

"What's that got to do with it? We're not going to bring the whores to your house. We're going over there."

"Yes, I know, but . . ."

I was getting mad at Sid, too. "Okay—skip it," I said. "Have you got the address?"

"You're not kidding?" he asked.

"Nope. If you know the address tell me."

"It's 128 Linda Street." He started getting all excited. "Listen, Josh, if you're really going you've got to promise to tell me everything that—"

"It must be miserable to have to get your kicks vicariously!" I said and hung up.

My mother had made an ironclad rule that I couldn't drive until I was sixteen, but Ben had taught me how on the q.t. I was practically sixteen at that point anyhow—and even if I hadn't been, I still would have taken the car. I raced upstairs, put on a new pair of gray flannels, a white shirt and tie, my best sport jacket, and headed out the door.

My mother always keeps an extra set of keys in an old work glove under the front seat of her car, so I piled in and took off, rather jerkily, because it had been quite a while since I'd been behind the wheel.

I felt like a big shot going down Sepulveda headed for Redondo, which is only a few miles from Paraiso Beach. Then a thought hit me: it would be just my luck to get myself killed in an automobile accident on my way to experience one of life's greatest thrills for the first time.

Finally, I came to Linda Street. I drove until I came to 128. It was an old, unpainted, funny-looking, three-story wood house. It looked like it belonged back East instead of out in California. Right next to it was a squat pink stucco building with a big neon sign that read "Church of the Sanctified Spirit." It's miserable to see a church all lit up with neon lights. Honestly, out here in California if somebody loses their job or has a free afternoon off, they open up a church. I think lots of them are fronts for bingo games and things like that.

I parked under a tree on the opposite side from 128. After I'd sat there staring across at the house for a while, I got to thinking either I had the wrong address or else somebody gave Sid a bum steer, because it looked like a plain ordinary house. The lights, sort of yellowish ones, were on in most of the windows, but all of the shades were drawn. I won't kid you; the minute I parked I knew that even if it did turn out to be the right address I wouldn't go in. Then I started laughing at myself for getting all dressed up in my new outfit to go to a whorehouse. I mean it isn't the type place where you make an impression sitting around in your best clothes.

After about ten minutes the door opened and a great big slob of a guy lumbered out. I couldn't see anything but a huge potted plant in the hallway because he shut the door quickly and walked off down the street. He was the kind of guy you'd expect to patronize a place like that, though. A few minutes later a car pulled up and a Mexican girl, very pretty but kind of cheap-looking, got out and went into the house. The car left. A little while later the door opened and a colored guy, in work clothes, came out. This must be the place, I thought.

I started giving myself a pep talk about getting up nerve to go over. I thought it'd be nice if I could pay them and then just sit around and watch! I mean only for the first time, so I'd get the hang of things and used to the atmosphere and all that—like a beginner's course. I wished a young guy around my age would either go in or come out. That would give me a little more courage.

I must have been sitting there like a dope for about a half hour when a car cruised by on the other side of the street, went very slowly down to the end of the block, and parked. I could see a little fellow get out and walk back along the sidewalk, kind of furtive-looking. As he passed under a street light I thought I recognized him. When he got about a house away from the establishment I was sure of who it was. The little coroner!

He stopped right in front of 128, took his pocket handkerchief out, and dabbed at his forehead. Then he reached in his pocket, took out a comb, and gave his fringe a working over. It killed me because that's all he had on the sides of his head and very little of that. Just as he was finishing he glanced over across the street toward me. At first he only saw the car and his eyes went right on by it; but then he did a take, looked back, and I guess he could tell there was somebody sitting in it—although it was so dark underneath the tree he never could have recognized me. That was enough, though. He shot his comb back into his pocket and walked very quickly down the block in the direction he'd been going, away from where he was parked. The poor little guy had been scared off.

I felt like a rat, so I quick switched the ignition on and pulled away, figuring that if he saw me leave he might change his mind and stay. I tore to the corner, turned up the first side street, and started heading back home in a roundabout way. I couldn't tell whether the little coroner stayed or not. It was hard imagining him going to a whorehouse, but I guess even coroners have to get their share.

There was a drive-in right on the corner when I finally

turned onto Sepulveda, and because I'd just picked at my dinner and was feeling a little empty I pulled in and ordered a hot fudge sundae. Setting out to go to a whorehouse and ending up with a hot fudge sundae. Talk about sublimation!

Chapter 33

THE only thing I could think about, that next day, was my mother. I kept hoping everyone had kissed and made up. But when I got home after school she and Jay were in the living room.

She'd showed up that morning but Tanner hadn't. The producers were unable to locate him, and word circulated around that he'd gone up to Lake Arrowhead for a long weekend before his "Playhouse 90" stint began. They'd made arrangements to get a temporary director in for the following week but he wasn't available until Monday. This meant they'd have four days' work to catch up with. They were already behind two, and then a third, because of my mother, and now another representing the day Tanner didn't show.

There was a nasty item in one of the columns that afternoon quoting Tanner as saying he didn't mind her blowing her lines all the time, but when she walked off the set—that was unforgivable. It also mentioned the fact that Tanner owned a piece of the series, so if anyone was replaced as a result of this fracas it probably wouldn't be him. The situation was growing more ticklish every minute.

Merwin got wind of the trouble and showed up that evening, but it was no use. Even he couldn't jolly my mother out of her rotten mood. I left them alone—after a dinner you would have mistaken for the Last Supper any day—thinking he could probably give her one of his pep talks. But about forty-five minutes later he shouted good night up to me and left. I came downstairs, but as soon as I walked into the living room she turned on the television set.

I kept wanting to ask her if she'd like to go over her lines for the following week, or talk, or *something*, but she just sat there staring at the screen. I knew she wasn't concentrating on the program—I could tell she was absorbed in her own problems, and I'd better not disturb her. About a half hour later she excused herself and said she was going to bed.

My mother and I really never got together over the weekend. I kept waiting for her to make an opening remark so we could have a discussion that would get rid of some of the tension, but she either kept to herself up in her room, or when she was around me she'd be so preoccupied with small details that a chance to speak up never presented itself. It was like she had blinders on.

Sally showed up Sunday afternoon to say the producers had arranged for her to have a little cottage on the lot during the next week so she wouldn't have the long drive into town and back every evening. This made her even more upset; she didn't want to accept it. You see, she didn't like the idea of getting a reputation for being high-strung and difficult to work with. Sally pointed out that lots of people working on series had an arrangement like that, and finally persuaded her to take advantage of it. They drove into town about nine o'clock that night.

My mother called up every evening. She kept saying work was coming along fine and they'd undoubtedly finish up Thursday afternoon. She said the new director was nice to work with, and talk like that, but she sounded tense as a steel spring. Her tone alone kept me from asking any leading questions about her over-all status with the series and her relations with Tanner, the regular director.

The school year wound up in a blast of ceremonies, awards, the school play, and finally, graduation on Tuesday evening. I was now a junior, but I was too concerned about my mother to devote much attention to whether I felt like one.

When she arrived home on Thursday she was bushed, but relieved that at last they were through this first batch of work. She and I ate alone that night. The only thing she wanted to talk about was the end of the school year and what-all I'd been doing during the week. Diversionary tactics, as usual. The only thing *I* wanted to talk about was her chance of continuing in the series; but I knew how tired she was, and I was positive that if I even began sneaking up on the subject there'd be a fracas. So I kept mum. We finished eating about nine-thirty. She went right up to bed.

I was feeling restless as hell because dinner had been so uncomfortable. After all we'd been through together, I kind of felt that we were getting to be strangers again. It's hard to explain—but our whole relationship was taking on a formal tone, the way it had been before we met Ben. When we were in the middle of all that trouble she'd been very close to me and as affectionate as you'd want. Or, if she was displeased, you sure found out about it in a hurry. But whatever the emotions, they were direct. Now we were lapsing back into the distant, almost remote pattern that had been established years before.

That night I realized how lonely my mother was. She'd been working feverishly in the midst of all sorts of people for weeks, and when she got home I was always there; Cecelia, too. Still I'd never seen her so lonely.

Later on while I was watching an old movie on TV it suddenly hit me that one of the reasons my mother was acting strange was that she must feel embarrassed in front of me for having caused trouble with the director. She'd said, up in my bedroom that night, that she was going to make something out of her life for me. Now I'll bet she felt like she was letting me down. Sure, that was it! No wonder she didn't want to talk about it until it was all straightened out.

I felt much better after thinking about it—rationalizing, I guess you'd call it. I made up my mind that if all went well with the series and we got moved into our own home things would gradually level off and eventually we'd be very happy and think back on all of this and laugh.

Along about eleven forty-five the phone rang. It was Jay asking to speak to my mother. He didn't sound any too happy. I thought right away he'd got word that she was out of the series. I asked him if I should wake her up.

"Use your own judgment, Josh. It's a pain in the ass. The last few batches of film they used today were defective, so they gotta do retakes."

"I better wake her," I told him.

"No. . . . Wait a minute. Is she sleeping soundly or did she just turn in?"

"She went to bed early, Jay."

"What the hell then . . . leave her be! But make sure she's up . . . say, by eight . . . and gets to the studio by ten."

I assured him I'd get her up on time and explain the situation to her, and we hung up.

When I finally went upstairs I thought I heard her calling to me. As I got to her door I heard her yell, "Oh, my God!" I opened it quickly and she was having a terrific nightmare. She was really thrashing from side to side in the bed. Then she said, "No, I don't believe it!"

I said "Mom—Mom . . ." several times because I figured it might be good to wake her up out of it, but she was so involved in whatever she was dreaming it didn't faze her in the least. I stood there quite a while.

She kept on mumbling things and finally she sat straight up in bed, took a deep breath, and said, "Oh, my God!" again as she was exhaling. Then she lay back down very slowly, rested her head on the pillow, and didn't utter another sound.

When she seemed to be sleeping soundly I went into my room, set the alarm for seven-thirty, and read myself to sleep for an hour or so.

When I went in to wake her up about eight the next morning and told her the news she hardly let me finish. She got right on the phone to Jay.

"Jay, what's going on? This tale about defective film! For God's sake, you're my agent—you don't have to give me stories like that!" She went on and on and finally called him a liar. During this she looked up at me very sharply as if to say, "Well, what the hell are you standing there for?" I went out into the hall and closed the door, but I stayed and listened. She must have kept him on the phone for almost a half hour trying to get him to admit that the retakes were caused by her. She finally hung up on him. I was down the stairs within two seconds of the time she got off the phone. I was worried that maybe she wouldn't show up for the retakes. That would really cinch the works. But then I could hear her banging and slamming things around upstairs. I figured she was in the process of getting ready to go to the studio.

The decision to take the dogs for a walk out in the back yard wasn't too hard to come by. I asked Cecelia to tell my mother where I'd be if she wanted me and took off. Penny tore down through the trees toward the barbecue pit the minute I opened the kitchen door and Lord Nelson wasn't far behind.

I made up my mind, for some strange reason, to go down too and look around. I'd never been there alone since I found Ben—only with the police, reporters, photographers, and once when I'd taken Sid down there to show him where it happened.

The hammock was long gone but you could still see the yellowish-brown marks on the lawn where the metal ends had killed off the grass. I stood there for quite a while staring at the spot where it had been.

There was nothing to be afraid of down there any more. The only mystery left was the mystery of the moment it happened. I've never stopped wondering exactly why, how, and when Ben actually decided to go through with it. Did he wander around down there, holding the gun, looking at it, and then decide not to do it only to change his mind later on? Or did he walk down very quickly and on a split-second impulse put the gun to his head and pull the trigger?

After I'd been down there for about three quarters of an hour I heard my mother's car pull out of the driveway. I was relieved that she'd actually gone in to work. I rounded up the dogs and went back to the house, where I found Cecelia in tears. My mother had given her a bad time. "Miss Rita just ain't the same lady like she used to be," she sobbed.

"What happened?" I asked her.

"You know how she don't ever eat breakfast when she's workin'? Juice and coffee and that's it. This mornin' she wants scrambled eggs, and it just so happen I use up all the eggs last night makin' that angel-food cake. When I told her she near snap my head off. I explain the egg man don't come around till about ten, and she says, 'That's gonna do me a helluva lot of good now, isn't it?' I start to apologize, but she storm right out of the kitchen, sayin' the place was run better when I was just workin' part-time than now, when I'm workin' for you folks full-time. You know that ain't true. I do the best I can—always."

She was genuinely upset. I tried to explain to her what a tough time my mother had been going through. I said maybe she'd gotten to the point where her troubles were ... like retroactive.

Chapter 34

SID Traylor called that afternoon around two and said he had something to show me, so could he come by on his bike. When he got to the house he was very secretive and asked where we could go to be alone.

"We are alone," I told him. "Cecelia's the only one here, and she's out in the kitchen."

"No, I mean really alone."

"Well, we can go up to my room," I told him.

The minute we got in the door he flicked the lock, sneaked over to the window, and peeked out like he was being followed.

"What the hell's the matter? You rob a bank or something?"

He unzipped his suède jacket and took out three books a little larger in area than paper backs but a lot thinner.

"I was going through my dad's trunk out in the garage and I found these."

"What are they?" I asked him.

"Pornographic books from France." He put them down on the bed.

That's what they were all right. There were three of them. *La Belle et La Bête*, which was all about a man and a woman, naturally. Then there was one, with three guys, entitled *Lucky Pierre*. The third one featured two girls called *La Vie en Pension à l'École*, translated *Life at Boarding School*.

They each had sort of a cruddy story, in French, but their main appeal was the fact they had all these blotchy pictures of everybody doing everything to everybody in every which way. We looked at the pictures, and I said, "The people that put these out must be queer as coots."

You see, here's the funny part about those books. The three guys were fairly attractive. I mean they looked clean and their bodies were in good shape. Then the two girls in the one about the boarding school were actually beautiful. They were very young and had great bodies. But the man and woman in the only book that was anywhere normal—they were really dogs.

The woman had this enormous ass that looked like the full moon, craters and all. Or an elephant's ass, like the oldest one in the whole circus. She had thin, stringy hair, snaggled teeth that looked like they were made out of Roquefort cheese, and breasts that swung down around her waist. The kind my uncle Al calls "hound's ears." She wore long stockings that were rolled down to a point right above her knees, and there were great hunks of flesh hanging over them. She had on enormous evening slippers that were so pointed she could have stabbed the guy with them.

The guy looked like he'd been in Dachau for about ten years. His chest was absolutely concave. His ribs stuck out so much it looked like he'd swallowed a couple of xylophones. His face could have been put together out of oatmeal, and he had no chin at all. I could go on about how unattractive he was, but you wouldn't believe it. He had on a funny little bowler-type hat, long black socks with garters, and he never seemed able to rise to the occasion—if you know what I mean. That book should have been called *La Bête et La Bête*.

They were the only people that didn't seem interested in what was going on, too. They were definitely playing to the camera. The woman was always showing as many of her decayed teeth as possible in her own special, cute, gruesome smile. And somebody must have told the guy he had great comic possibilities because he was mugging it up like crazy. In every picture he was kind of looking out at the reader, winking, as if to say, "Boy, am I a card?" But how can you laugh at somebody who's obviously in the last extremities?

On the other hand, the people in the other books were completely involved in what they were doing, which was just about everything. They got so involved, in fact, that a couple of times you had to turn the pictures upside down and sideways to figure out just what the hell was going on.

By the time we'd pawed over the pictures I'd "had" the

books, but Sid was really mesmerized. He begged me to translate the stories that went with them.

You see, I speak French fairly well from having had this French nurse for a couple of years when I was very young, and I've always kept up with it. I read it much better than I can speak or write it, however.

I began with the one about the two girls. It was really pretty crude, and I had some trouble with a few idiomatic sex terms that I'd never learned from my French nurse and certainly not in textbooks. After a while I got the hang of them. Actually, if you used your imagination you could figure them out.

About halfway through the book we heard a car pull up in the driveway. Sid jumped up from the bed, tore to the window, and peeked out between the curtains.

"Oh, my God, it's your mother!" he said, like we'd been caught burying a corpse.

"So what?" I asked. "She's not going to know what we've been doing."

"Quick, give me the books!" He was snatching them up, putting his jacket on, and stuffing them down the front. "I gotta get these back in my dad's trunk before he comes home from work."

"Why? Does he go out in the garage and read them every evening before dinner?" I asked him. I unlocked the door, and just as we started going out into the hall one of the books slipped out of his jacket and fell to the floor. "Oh, my God!" he said, as he swooped down on it.

"Will you simmer down!" I told him. "You're acting like a madman."

As we were walking down the stairs my mother and Jay practically flew in the front door. She greeted Sid very warmly and threw her arms around me and gave me a big hug. She was all smiles. I introduced Sid to Jay, but he wouldn't look either her or Jay in the eye. His face was red and all he'd do would be mumble and stare at the floor.

"Don't you feel well, Sid?" my mother asked him.

He mumbled something about a stomach-ache, tore out, hopped on his bike, and away he went.

My mother was tired but elated, if you can imagine that

combination; and Jay was practically beside himself, he was so happy. He'd driven her home because her car had conked out about a half mile from the studio and was in the garage being fixed.

When she started mixing a couple of drinks, I asked why everybody was feeling so well, because it was a drastic change from the way things had been the last week in general, and that morning in particular.

Well, first of all, she'd found out the retakes were actually caused by defective film, and weren't her fault. But that was the least of the good news. It seems that during their lunch break they'd seen the first episode of the series all put together—along with the producers and one of the sponsors—and everybody was delighted with the show and especially with my mother's work. They practically told her she was definitely in, and there was nothing to worry about, that they were sure she and Thor Tanner would get along in the future. The producers said Tanner was always finding fault with *everyone*, but if the results were good he didn't give a damn what kind of hell he went through.

She was really sauntering around the living room like a little girl. I hadn't seen her so "up"—I guess you'd call it—since before Ben died. She never sat down once; she just kept walking back and forth. One of Jay's girl singers was opening at the Crescendo that night, so he invited us to go in town with him; but she declined, saying, "Oh, Jay, I'd love to but I'm really bushed. I'm running on nervous energy. I'm positive when it's used up I'll fall apart in a heap."

After he left she looked at me, sighed, and said, "I woke up this morning feeling like I'd fought the Battle of Waterloo. I think I'd better lie down for a while and unwind. Will you ask Cecelia to hold off fixing dinner until I wake up?" She put down her drink, came over to me, and gave me a tremendous hug. "Oh, Josh—looks like this whole thing's straightened out! Isn't that marvelous?" I agreed that it was, and she practically trotted upstairs. I was beaming.

When she takes a nap it usually turns into about a two-hour deal at least. That's the funny thing about people who have insomnia at night. They can sleep like Rip Van

Winkle as long as it's not the regular time everybody is supposed to be sleeping. My mother can take a nap on a picket fence; but put her in a comfortable bed, without pills, any time after eleven P.M., and she's staring at the ceiling.

This evening, though, she'd only been upstairs about twenty minutes when the phone rang. I picked it up quickly so it wouldn't disturb her. It was Midge. She'd just got through saying hello when my mother got on the phone from her bedroom. We had a three-way conversation. Midge wanted to know if the date still stood for the next day to go look at houses. My mother said yes, she'd talked to the real estate women, who'd lined up about six places to show us. Midge agreed to pick us up about ten in the morning.

After Midge hung up, my mother said, "How's about going out to dinner, Josh? I just don't feel like sitting around this house tonight."

"Okay," I said. "What about your nap?"

"I think all I needed was to stretch out and relax. Where'll we go?"

"I don't care."

"Maybe Paganelli's . . . or any place you like, Josh. You pick."

"Yes, let's go to Paganelli's," I said.

"Oh, dear! What about Cecelia?"

"She's planning steaks anyhow. That's simple to cancel."

"All right, will you tell her—No, I'd better talk to her myself. Meet you at the bottom of the stairs in a jiffy." She hung up and before I could think about it I heard her coming down.

"Come on, slowpoke!" she called out. I met her in the hall. She grabbed my hand and ran ahead of me through the dining room and into the kitchen, pulling me behind her.

"Cecelia, would you forgive us if we deserted you tonight and went out for dinner? I feel like a date with my handsome son."

Cecelia laughed and said sure.

My mother went to her and threw her arms around her. "I've been a beast lately, Cecelia. Will you forgive me?"

Cecelia got all embarrassed and, of course, denied she'd given her a rough time.

"Don't give me any of that stuff. I know when I've been a wretch."

As we started to leave the kitchen she turned around and said, "Why don't you take the weekend off, Cecelia? We're going into town tomorrow anyhow. Unless you haven't anything to do?"

Cecelia started in cackling. "Oh, I can always cook up somethin' to do, Miss Rita. Don't you worry about that."

On our way upstairs my mother said, "You're my date tonight, so put on a tie and a jacket. Who knows—we might go on to the Cat later!"

"Great," I said. "The Cat" was really the Persian Kitten, a club overlooking the ocean, about eight miles south of us, where they had a show.

We went to our rooms to get cleaned up and dressed. It took me only about ten minutes. When I finished I went downstairs and waited for my mother in the living room. She came down about fifteen minutes later looking as beautiful as any woman has a right to. There was a glow about her. She took my arm and we walked out the front door. About two seconds later we were standing in the driveway laughing our heads off. We had no way to get any place. We'd both completely forgotten that her car was being fixed in the garage up in Hollywood.

"Let's have a foot race," I said. "Last one there has to pay for dinner."

"Only if you put on high heels," she said. "Otherwise I get a handicap."

Just then we heard the kitchen door slam and Cecelia came around the far side of the house. She was all gussied up, too.

"How about giving a couple of stranded pedestrians a lift?" my mother called out to her.

"Sure enough," she said. "Hop in."

We laughed and scratched until we pulled up in front of Paganelli's. We both hugged Cecelia good-by, thanked her, and told her we'd see her Monday. I said, "Don't do anything I wouldn't do—or if you do, be careful!" That threw her into hysterics. She finally pulled herself together and drove off with us waving after her.

Then my mother turned to look at me. She stopped, squeezed my hand, and said, "You're growing up to be a pretty good-looking fellow. I'd better keep an eye on Stella from now on!" We both laughed. In that one moment I felt closer to her and more secure *with* her than I'd ever felt, I think.

When we walked in the door who was sitting at the bar having drinks but Roy Clymer and Jeanette! We all whooped, hollered, and hugged one another. The Paganellis joined in, and before you knew it Mama Paganelli was in tears, as usual. We stayed at the bar for a while, and everybody was arguing about who was going to pay for the drinks. Finally, the Paganellis said they were on the house, and we all decided to have dinner together.

It was a strange evening. It was ... like on different plateaus. At first there was the excitement of being someplace and with people that you hadn't spent much time with in a long time. Everybody was joking and laughing and kidding. That part was at the bar.

Then we got to our table and ordered dinner, and all during the meal everyone was filling everyone else in with what had been happening. My mother told all about her TV show and the wild time she'd been through. Roy gave us the details of a couple of cases he'd been on and also explained that his position as head of the Paraiso Beach Police was solid now. Jeanette was enlarging her beauty parlor but, best of all, she'd just found out about a week before that she was going to have a baby. My mother ordered another round of drinks on that one. We were delighted. If you ever saw two people that would make great parents it would be Roy and Jeanette. And they'd been trying for years. I threw in a lot about school and got a few laughs with stories about the senior play and graduation. That part of the evening was fun. Eating up a storm and talking, talking, talking.

But after the dishes were cleared away and coffee and dessert were brought, we all ran out of conversation. I guess we were talked out. There was a silence of a couple of minutes while everyone was sugar-and-creaming their coffee, after which Roy reached across the table and patted my mother's hand.

"How've you been otherwise, Rita?" he asked in this extremely gentle voice.

She glanced up at him quickly, like you look around when somebody taps you on the shoulder. Her eyes got very wide. Then she looked down at the table and up again. Her mouth kind of tugged over to one side, almost a smile.

"Oh . . . all right, Roy. All right, I guess. Life goes on." Then she did smile, a great big smile, and tossed her head back. "How about an after-dinner drink, Jeanette? A toast to the baby. I'm putting in my application right now for the position of Godmother."

Everybody tried to go on laughing and talking after that, but it wasn't the same. Everyone was aware that something was missing. Not something—someone.

Then Papa Paganelli, who'd been out in the kitchen all evening, came over to our table. We all exchanged warm greetings, and he stood there grinning at us, nodding his head up and down. "Just like old times," he said.

We all agreed, "Yes, just like old times!" And the moment you said it, you knew you were saying just the opposite: "It can never be like old times again. Not here. And maybe not any place, because Ben is gone. He's dead. We've all been through his death together and by associating with one another we'll never forget it!"

From then on the party was on the skids. After a while my mother sighed and said, "Well, we'd better be getting home. We've got a big day ahead of us, haven't we, Josh?"

She argued with Roy about the check for a while, but he'd already spoken to the Paganellis and made them promise he could pay. When Roy heard her ask me to call a cab, he wouldn't hear of it. He said he and Jeanette were leaving anyhow and insisted on driving us home. It only took about ten minutes. When we got out of the car we all promised not to let so much time elapse again without seeing one another.

As they were driving away my mother turned to me and said, "Gosh, I didn't realize how tired I was. I guess it's catching up with me. I'm dead."

The dogs were all over us when we opened the front door. "Darling, would you mind letting them out for a minute? I think I'll go right on up to bed." She kissed me on the cheek, said, "See you in the morning," and went upstairs.

Even though the end of the evening hadn't been too upbeat, I was in a pretty good mood when I turned in that night. After all, I understood the reasons. My mother had been working like a demon. She'd been all keyed up, and now that these first shows were finished there was bound to be a letdown. Then again, being in a place and with people you associated most with Ben for the first time in ages was bound to be depressing. But our relationship—my mother's and mine—seemed to be on a good basis. That was the most important thing. I was looking forward to finding a house of our own the next day. I slept like a top.

Chapter 35

AT about eight o'clock the next morning I was awakened by all kinds of little noises. The john flushing, faucets running, and footsteps going back and forth. I knew Cecelia wasn't home, so I figured my mother must be up. That was one for the books—for her to beat me in the morning. Especially on her first day off in a long time. For some nutty reason I was feeling extremely warm and secure. I kind of squealed to myself a few times and dozed off for almost another hour.

When I woke up again I could still hear all this activity going on. I could make out the sounds of drawers opening and closing and closet doors and footsteps. By the time I got out of bed and went to her door I heard water running in her bathroom. I decided not to knock because she was probably ready for a tub.

I put on my blue jeans and went downstairs to let the dogs out. It was a beautiful day. I felt like a million. It's usually hazy or foggy on summer mornings down by the beach until about ten o'clock, when it burns off, but that day it was clear and the sun was shining brilliantly. After the dogs and I got back from a short romp, I uncovered Monkey-Face's cage and gave him an orange and some fresh water. He wanted to get out and play, but once you let him loose he expected to stay for a couple of hours, and, knowing we were going into town, I decided not to raise his hopes. I left him inside. I threw some sunflower seeds at Chauncey, who was rocking back and forth on his perch screaming, "Are you a Communist?"

When I got through with the pets I went upstairs. As I hit the top landing I heard my mother humming "Candy," the tune Ben and she had picked as "their song." I couldn't have been more surprised because the last time I'd heard it was when Ben had sung it with this uke he used to play.

She was humming it kind of jauntily, though. I walked right up to her door. I could hear the water sloshing around in the tub. She was still taking a bath.

Suddenly I felt way up on top of the world. I was overcome by an elated feeling that we were over the bumps now and the road was straightening out for us.

I decided to surprise my mother and fix her a breakfast tray. I tore down to the kitchen and started squeezing fresh orange juice and making real coffee. When she wasn't working she'd eat a little breakfast, so I began soft-boiling a couple of eggs. The reason she wouldn't have more than juice and coffee when she was working was because when she'd get to the studio there was always so much fiddling around before she'd actually get in front of the cameras that she'd have a bite to eat and more coffee just to fill in the time. She does have a slight weight problem if she doesn't watch herself, so she didn't want to eat too much at home before she went to work.

While the eggs were boiling I could hear footsteps going back and forth across the floor above me. They were moving very quickly. If I hadn't known she didn't have to go to work that day I certainly would have thought she was getting all dressed and ready to go to the studio.

There were some flowers on the window sill in the kitchen, and when I was fixing the tray I took a big yellow one with a black center, put it in a tiny vase, and placed it next to the napkin.

By the time I'd got the coffee, orange juice, and two pieces of Rye-Krisp on the tray and was cracking the eggs open it became very quiet upstairs. I couldn't hear her moving around at all. For a second I got panicky and thought maybe she'd left the bedroom and was on her way downstairs. I raced in through the dining room, thinking I'd probably meet her coming down the stairs, but she was nowhere in sight.

I was glad, because when I was very little she used to love to have her breakfast in her bedroom on a tray. Sometimes in bed; or if she was already up she'd have it on this antique desk she'd bought in France, one of her prize possessions.

Back in the kitchen I decided I'd better hurry. I finished fixing the eggs and gave the tray the once-over. It looked like a professional job, if I do say so myself. Penny and Lord Nelson were at my heels as I carried it upstairs. I walked down the hall to my mother's bedroom and stood in front of her door, deciding what kind of scene to play. The sun was pouring in from the big window at the end of the hall and the birds were twittering away like crazy. There weren't any sounds coming from my mother's room, though. I couldn't knock too well because I had my hands full with the tray, so I tapped on the bottom of the door with my foot.

"Darling?" I heard my mother call out. "Where have you been? I've been waiting for hours!"

I wondered how she knew I was preparing a tray for her. I dropped my voice as low as I could, put on a thick English accent, and made it very formal. I can do it pretty well because Merwin and I are always speaking with English accents—and Ben used to do it, too.

"Your breakfast tray, Madam!"

"Oh, darling, stop teasing. Come in—I've been primping for ages! Even washed my hair."

I thought maybe *she* was playing some kind of a scene, too, because her voice sounded very chipper and flirty and gay. So I went on with it.

"Is Madam quite decent?" I asked.

"Oh, you're a devil! An absolute devil!" I heard her say, and she kind of giggled. Something struck me funny. Then I remembered she always used to say that to Ben whenever he'd tease her or play a joke on her. It definitely threw me to hear her use that term. I didn't say anything for a moment. I just stood there. I don't think I was upset or anything—maybe a little confused.

Suddenly I didn't feel like going on with the scene. I don't know why, at that point, but I didn't. Finally I said in my own voice, "May I come in?"

There was a definite pause. Then I heard her ask, "Who is it?" in what seemed to me to be a perplexed tone.

Something told me to say "Mother?"—but I didn't say it loudly. And at the exact moment I said, "Mother?" kind of

277

tentatively, I thought I heard her call out "Ben?"—in the same way.

I almost dropped the tray. Right away I thought No, she didn't say Ben. She couldn't have. Maybe I was hearing things because we'd both spoken at the same time. But as I was thinking that, she spoke up again, only louder this time.

"Ben, is that you?" The sentence rang through the air and hung there for what seemed like minutes.

She must be kidding, I thought. But it was a funny way to kid, and she never did joke about things like that. It was torture standing out in the hall trying to figure out what was going on, so I started to juggle the tray in order to open the door when Penny, who had been dying to get in, jumped up against it with all his weight. The door clicked and swung open.

I would have walked right in but her bedroom was almost pitch-black. Because of the bright sunlight coming in from the window at the end of the hallway the difference between the light and dark was too great. I couldn't see for a second or two until my eyes became accustomed to the change. After a moment I could tell the Venetian blinds in her room must have been completely shut because all the drapes were closed and there was no light coming in through them at all. A little figurine lamp on a small table way over next to the wall by her bathroom door was turned on, but there was only a tiny yellow bulb in it, like a nightlight; and not only was it quite a ways from the bed, but it was also kind of behind a lacquered Oriental screen that jutted out from the wall. My mother had the master bedroom, and it was the size of an average living room. But this morning it seemed absolutely cavernous as I stood there straining my eyes to see in.

After a while I could make out my mother sitting up in the middle of this huge bed at the far end of the room, facing the door. I could make out her form but not her face or expression. I couldn't help wondering why, after having been up for an hour or so, she was back in bed. I'd expected her to be all dressed by this time.

"Who is it?" she asked, in a very annoyed voice.

"It's me. I brought you a—" I didn't get to finish.

"Josh!" she snapped.

"I brought you a breakfast tray."

"What?" she asked, reaching over toward the little lamp on the table next to her bed.

The bed and the whole left side of the room lit up. There she was, sitting up in bed with three pillows piled up behind her back. She kind of cocked her head, first one way and then the next, as she looked over at me. She had on this very fancy, powder blue, silk-and-lace bedjacket that Ben had given her as one of her Christmas presents. It had a soft gray fur collar around the neck. It was really for show. I'd never seen her wear it before, only when she tried it on after she opened the package. It was the kind of a thing she'd wear if she got the flu while staying at the Plaza Hotel in New York and had to give out an interview to a columnist in her bedroom. Her hair was all combed down and fell over her shoulders, and she had it tied with a blue hair ribbon. She never wore hair ribbons—at least I'd hardly ever seen her with one on.

She leaned forward a little to get past the light and see me better. She had this awful frown on her face.

I'd taken a couple of steps into the room, but then I'd gone no further because I got the feeling I was ... well, unwelcome. I just stood there, holding the tray, looking at her. She just sat there scowling at me.

Penny had been standing next to me after he jumped up against the door, but by this time Lord Nelson, who had been looking out the window at the end of the hall, came tearing down past me into the room. Penny joined in and the two of them raced over to the bed. Penny jumped right up on it, almost in my mother's lap, and Lord Nelson was hopping up and down at the side waiting to be picked up. He couldn't make it by himself because it was an extra large bed and very high.

"Get away! Get out of here. Get *down*!" My mother really hollered at Penny. Then she gave him a swat, a hard one, on the tail. He let out a yip, more from surprise than anything else, and jumped to the floor. Lord Nelson stopped bouncing up and down and crawled under the bed, his tail between his legs.

With the dog situation settled, she started straightening out the covers around her, patting them and smoothing them with her hands. I heard her whisper, "Damn it!" but it was almost to herself, like she'd forgotten I was even there. She became preoccupied with the part of the sheet that folded back over the blanket. She tugged at it so that it folded over and made an even border. Finally, she took the thin quilt that was on top and kind of fluffed it up in the air and settled it back down, pressing it flat with both hands.

Then she looked up and saw me. "Oh . . . yes . . ." she said, as if she were trying to get back to the point of a story she'd been telling. "Now . . . what is the meaning of this, Josh?"

I honest to God didn't know what to say, because I didn't know what was happening. So I repeated, "I brought you a breakfast tray, Mom."

"I know that! I know that! I don't mean—" She was so exasperated she cut herself off and took a deep breath. "What are you *doing* here?" she asked, like she thought I was supposed to be in Africa or somewhere. Her frown had changed to a quizzical look.

"What do you mean?" I asked.

She almost laughed as she said, "Now don't fool around with me, Josh. What are you doing here?" She said it as if she were saying, "All right, we've had our little joke—now let's get down to facts."

I thought to say, "I live here, dummy," or something like that, but I definitely had the feeling she *wasn't* kidding.

"Well . . . I . . ."

She made a tight fist and pounded on the bed covers next to her legs in little short punches, one punch for each word. "*Will you answer my question?*"

I didn't know what to say because all of a sudden I wasn't sure where "here" was. It somehow didn't seem to be there in the house, if you know what I mean. It was like we were two foreigners trying to carry on a conversation but not speaking the same language. We weren't connecting.

Then, quick as a flash, she changed her tone. "Oh . . . oh

280

. . . I see!" she said. "Ben put you up to this, didn't he?"
She almost had a sense of humor about it. "Well, you tell
him to get in here pronto."

I kept on standing there because I didn't know which
way to turn. I'd never felt so confused in all my life. I
looked around the room and got a wild desire to run over,
pull the drapes back, and open all the blinds so the sun
would come pouring in. Even with the light on it was dark
and close and musty in there. Actually, an awful unhealthy
feeling was taking hold of me. I was getting scared. I was
suddenly aware of the weight of the tray, and I began to
shake slightly. I heard the sound of the coffee cup rattle on
the saucer. I felt trapped.

"Well, don't stand there like a little idiot," my mother
said. "Tell Ben I want to see him."

"Mother . . . I . . ."

She became furious again. "Well, what is the *matter* with
you, Josh?" She practically ground her teeth when she
spoke.

I had to speak up, so I said, "Ben's not here!" I don't
know why, but that's all I could bring myself to say.
Somehow, I couldn't say "Ben's dead."

She put her right hand up to her forehead and shielded
her eyes for a split second. She shook her head ever so
slightly. "No . . . wait a minute," she said. She dropped her
hand, looked at me, and then put it back up to her head.
"What do you mean—Ben's not here?" Then she let out a
short, staccato little laugh and put her hand down again.
"Listen, *dear*"—she said the "dear" very sarcastically—
"Listen, *dear,* I've had just about enough of . . . whatever
this is you're pulling. I don't think it's funny one single bit.
And furthermore, I'm losing patience with the two of you."

The *two* of us! It struck me that either I was dead along
with Ben, we were all dead, or else the whole thing had
been a joke on me and Ben was hiding in the bathroom or
behind the drapes some place in that room. I felt like I'd
been turned to stone and would be standing there, frozen,
until somebody came and carted me away. I couldn't move
and I couldn't speak.

She kept switching back to things she'd already asked

me. "In the first place—answer me, how did you get here?"

"Mother . . . where? I don't . . . I'm all mixed—"

"Stop hedging! You know damn good and well what I mean!" Then she kind of exploded. "Ah-ha! Oh . . . oh, yes . . . don't think I don't know what's going on! You and your—I'm onto you, all right, young man. You don't fool me for a minute, not a minute! I'm aware of your—*big crush*—like a silly little schoolgirl! But, for God's sake, not on our honeymoon! Josh, really!"

I don't suppose I have to tell you what happened inside my stomach when she said that. It's a feeling I don't ever want to experience again.

Next, she clapped her hands together twice very briskly like people do in movies at servants. She spoke in a very sharp patronizing voice like she was dismissing the entire incident. "All right, that's enough, young man! Get Ben! Take the dogs out with you and get Ben! Come on, quickly now—no fooling around! How they ever got here I don't know. The whole thing's a very flat joke. Well, joke's over!"

"Mother, Ben's gone . . . He . . ." I couldn't finish.

"Will you stop saying that!" she screamed at me. "God-dam you! Stop it!" She started bouncing up and down in the bed like she was having a tantrum. "I won't have you talking back to me!" She looked around quickly, and then picked up a little silver cigarette box she kept on the table next to the bed. "Won't have it!" she screamed, and hurled it across the room at me. It hit the wall a good couple of yards from me, but it jolted me so that I started to back up and sloshed coffee and orange juice all over the tray.

"Get out of here—you little monster!" she hollered at me. "Get out!"

She started thrashing around, getting out from under the covers, and coming toward me. I turned and started to run out the door. When I got into the hallway I dropped the tray on the floor—the whole thing—right in the middle of the hall.

I began running toward the end of the hall and the head of the stairs. When you got to them you had to turn and face back toward the way you had come as you went down

282

them. I noticed Penny go running by me on down to the ground floor, but I didn't see Lord Nelson at all.

My mother tore out of the bedroom, across to the bannister, and leaned over the railing. The sunlight coming in the hall window blinded her for a moment and she threw her hands up to her face. She had on a sheer blue nightgown, and I could see right through it because of all the light. My stomach turned upside down; it was indecent. I was only about five steps down the stairs, not quite under her, so I stopped and looked toward the wall at my left, away from her.

"What a terrible trick to play on your mother!" she yelled down at me.

I turned toward her to say something, to try to explain, but I realized there could be no explaining.

Suddenly she stopped focusing on me and looked around her to the end of the hall, the window, back toward her bedroom, then down at me, and straight up at the ceiling. It was like she was having a fit of some kind; she kept snapping her head around in quick jerky little movements. I could tell she was straining to comprehend, to take in every inch of her surroundings. At first she looked bewildered. Then I could see surprise followed by shock register on her face as she realized she was there, in the house at Paraiso Beach.

I was still standing a few steps down from the landing. I wanted to run to the bottom of the stair and out, but I had the feeling she might try to follow me and fall or hurt herself in some way. The next thing I knew she grabbed ahold of the bannister with both hands and started rocking back and forth with the full weight of her body. It was like she was trying to tear the entire railing loose. She was holding on so hard I could see the white from around her knuckles spread through her hands until they were deadly pale.

Within moments her face began twisting itself all up until she had an agonized look like . . . well, like someone was operating on her without an anesthetic. The veins in her neck stood out until I thought they'd burst, and when it seemed like she was going to explode she got an even wilder look on her face, her eyes bulged out from their

283

sockets, and she let out a bloodcurdling scream—"Oh, God! Oh, my God!" She shouted so loud it bounced off the walls and richocheted down the hall. I thought she must have torn her vocal cords loose. She was leaning over the railing when she screamed it. Then she threw her head way back and said it again, only this time it was nearer a moan, like when she'd had the nightmare the evening before. She let go of the bannister, her hands flew up to her face for a second only, then she grabbed her hair with both hands and started pulling like she was trying to tear it out by the roots.

One last cry—"Ben!"—so loud and yet so constricted in her throat that if I hadn't been familiar with his name I wouldn't have known what she said. After this, she went completely to pieces, clutching at herself, moaning, shaking.

Just then Lord Nelson ran out from her bedroom and began growling and barking at her, darting toward her and retreating back again in little quick movements. She didn't even notice him.

"Nelson, come here! Come here!" I shouted, but he went right on, trying to nip at her ankles. "Mom, stop it . . . Mom, don't . . . Please!" I called out to her. I was just about to go to her—I think I had in my mind to throw my arms around her and hold her until this fit or whatever had passed—when she lifted her nightgown way up around her face. For a second I thought she was going to pull it over her head, but in one violent movement she ripped it all the way off.

I don't know what happened next because it was impossible for me to watch any more. I think she fell down to the floor but I'm not sure. I could hear her sobbing convulsively and I could hear Lord Nelson's insistent yapping, but I was on my way out.

She wasn't my mother any more. She wasn't even a human being. She was like some wild animal that had been struck down by a car out on the highway and was just spinning around by itself.

It was probably cowardly of me, but I flew down the stairs, out the front door—and away. I ran along the driveway to Calle Vista and up to the corner of the highway. I was hysterical myself by this time. I was crying so hard I was choking. I thought my heart would burst. I leaned up against a telephone pole to steady myself because my knees were turning to jelly. I don't know how long I cried before I knew I was going to be sick; it must have been quite a while. I did get sick finally, but I hadn't had anything to eat so there wasn't much to be sick about. I was mainly doing an awful lot of gagging and choking.

The next thing I heard was a horn honking. A car stopped and Midge was holding on to me. I don't recall what I told her about my mother, but I do remember refusing to go back to the house with her. She sat me down on some grass next to the telephone pole and told me to wait there until she came back.

It seems like I sat there in a daze forever. Cars loaded with people heading for the beach droned along in a steady procession. A pack of kids, weaving in and out among one another on their bicycles, straggled by. A stray collie ambling along the side of the highway about fifteen yards from me paused, and looked toward me with those sad eyes, trying to make up his mind whether or not to pay a visit. He walked slowly over to me and pushed against the calf of my leg with his nose. I wasn't crying any more; I was just sitting there with the sun boring a hole right down through my brain, stunned. He kept nudging my leg for a while like he was suggesting I get up and come along with him. When I didn't move he walked around me and stood by my shoulder, looking right into my eyes. He alone seemed to understand. I was just about to reach out, throw my arms around his neck and hang onto him, probably forever, when screeching brakes along the highway startled him and he dashed away through the weeds.

And birds! They were all over the place. I remember birds that morning. Birds when I took the dogs out, birds outside the hall window when I was standing there by the bedroom door with the tray, and now more birds. Every goddam bird in Southern California was down around our place that morning.

All this activity buzzing and humming by while two hundred yards away the end of the world was taking place.

And here's the odd part: these normal, routine, everyday

things were the dream world, the fuzzy, the intangible; and my mother's predicament was clear, sharp—the reality. Why didn't the rotten world stop, I thought! It should stop for a moment of silence for my mother.

At one point I saw Roy Clymer drive past in his police car with another man in civilian clothes in the front seat. I guess it was the doctor. A few minutes later Midge came back and helped me into her car. I don't remember anything about what she said because I was trying not to be sick again.

Then we stopped in the middle of the town of Paraiso Beach. Jeanette got in the car with us and held me very tightly until we arrived at her apartment. When we got out of the car I started getting hysterical again and crying and all.

They both hugged me and talked to me and made me lie down in the bedroom. I kept asking if my mother was going to die and they said no, no—of course not! Finally a doctor came and gave me a shot.

It was dark when I woke up. I was alone in a strange bedroom. I started screaming for my mother. I remember somebody coming in very quickly, and I must have tried to fight with them because then it seems like a lot of people were holding me down. The lights had been turned on but I wouldn't open my eyes because I had a feeling my mother was gone—and yet I didn't want to know for sure she wasn't with me. I must have had another shot or something because I went off to sleep again.

I vaguely remember traveling in a car and being carried some place and put to bed again. I recall letting it happen, whatever was happening to me. I just gave in.

When I woke up next it was still dark, but there was a lamp on. I saw Midge sitting in a chair reading. I was in the guest room in the main ranch building up at Andy and Midge's—the one my mother always slept in.

That was last June, over two months ago. I've hardly left the ranch all summer long. But tomorrow it's "Elliston time" again with my aunt and uncle. I'm kind of looking forward to the change. I don't think I like California too much. At least not for a while. And now that they're taking my mother back East to Menninger's I'll be fairly close to her. I'll go to visit her the minute they give me the signal.

I can't seem to shake that last picture of her out of my mind. Isn't it miserable that the first time you see a woman naked it's your mother and she's going crazy!

But you know, of all the thoughts I have about her the saddest come in the evening. I'll be reading or something—and suddenly I can't help wondering if she's lying there, all mixed up the way she must be, with that lousy insomnia.

Honest to God, now that I've told you practically everything I'd better quit talking about her or I'll get myself in a bind. I'm trying like hell not to dwell on the depressing things. I really am. The way I look at it—if we've gotten through this much without being demolished, we're not going to give up now.

That's what I've been doing this summer: trying not to get all screwed up *myself*. Of course, the first couple of weeks were rotten. I was in a tailspin like you couldn't imagine. But then I just took hold of myself. One of us has to "press on"—as Merwin says. And I made up my mind it's going to be me. But it sure took some concentrated thinking. Thinking and trying to figure out. I bet if I stopped thinking for a solid year I'd still be ahead.

I think mostly about my mother. She's going to get well; I know it. Not only because the doctors tell me so, but because my mother's a remarkable person. When you look back—she's always sort of just breezed along with things crashing and breaking all around her. Even on top of her. But she never once got bitter or gave up or stopped hoping. She's really been indestructible. All these catastrophes—and she kept singing above them. She's had to because they were all bombs anyhow. But finally she found something real—and I know what she and Ben had *was* real—but it didn't last. It ended. When you lose something so right, something that could be perfect for the rest of your life, that's when it really hits you. You've just got to take a breather.

I think about Ben, too. But it doesn't bother me. It even helps in a way. Because no matter what Ben did—he helped me become a person! And that's about the greatest

287

gift anybody could give you. At least I know I'm going to grow up now. To tell you the truth, I had my doubts there for a while. I thought I'd always be some kind of a retarded Peter Pan.

When I get up in that plane tomorrow I bet I'll have one helluva session with myself, like I usually do. I'll sort everything out in my mind and really make some concrete decisions about what-all to do with my life from here on out.

There's one thing I've already decided. Like Ben said— I'll keep looking for the Pony. Not that I actually believe I'll find it. But because when you really figure it out—that's the only way to go on living. The absolute only way!

I'll tell you one last thing, though. I have a sneaker I *will* find it!